Having Viking ancestors himself, **Giles Kristian** believes that the story of Raven has always been in his blood – waiting, like the Norsemen, for the right time to burst upon the world.

Inspired by both his family history and his story-telling heroes, Bernard Cornwell and Conn Iggulden, Giles began writing a thrilling tale of an English boy's coming of age amongst a band of marauding warriors from across the grey sea. This novel, *Raven: Blood Eye*, was published to great acclaim, including a wonderful accolade from Bernard Cornwell.

Giles currently lives in Leicestershire where he writes full-time, though he enjoys nothing better than working in his family cottage that overlooks the mist-shrouded Norwegian fjords.

To find out more about Giles and his writing, visit his website: www.gileskristian.com

www.randomhouse.co.uk

*Also by Giles Kristian*

RAVEN: SONS OF THUNDER

# RAVEN
## BLOOD EYE

Giles Kristian

**CORGI BOOKS**

TRANSWORLD PUBLISHERS
61–63 Uxbridge Road, London W5 5SA
A Random House Group Company
www.randomhouse.co.uk

**RAVEN: BLOOD EYE**
**A CORGI BOOK: 9780552157896**

First published in Great Britain
in 2009 by Bantam Press
an imprint of Transworld Publishers
Corgi edition published 2010

A CIP catalogue record for this book
is available from the British Library.

Addresses for Random House Group Ltd companies outside the UK
can be found at: www.randomhouse.co.uk
The Random House Group Ltd Reg. No. 954009

Penguin Random House is committed to a sustainable future for
our business, our readers and our planet. This book is made from
Forest Stewardship Council® certified paper.

Typeset in 11½/14½pt Sabon by
Kestrel Data, Exeter, Devon.
Printed and bound in Great Britain by Clays Ltd, St Ives plc

*Raven* is for Sally, with whom
I have crossed oceans

# TO MY FELLOWSHIP

Writing is sometimes called the 'lonely art'. It is. And it isn't. As important as the characters in the story itself are a host of real-life protagonists who jump aboard along the way. These folk are a rare and precious commodity to a writer for the simple reason that they *understand*. They get what we're up to day after day, month after month, year after year. Some of them *got Raven* so well that they even took it into their own lives and jobs, ballyhooing the story more eloquently than I ever could. These are the people to whom I owe so much, and it is my great pleasure to acknowledge them here.

My parents never made me conform. They know what I love and what drives me, and they have helped me in more ways than any one person can deserve. Pop, you are a jarl and a legend. Mum, you are the shore. I am proud of you both. Sally, I love you. Much love to my sword-brother James who shared his pay packet with me and has always supported my endeavours; to my beautiful sister, Jackie, who has always told me to 'never quit!'; and to Marky Mark who scraps like an old lady on Age of Empires (and still wins!). Thank you to Edie Campbell for being my second set of eyes, and to Roy and Eddie for loving historical fiction and encouraging me. Nikki Furrer championed *Raven* before anyone in the business, and in taking it on, my agent Dan Lazar of Writers House was my wave-maker. My gratitude to Peter Hobbs for 'putting a word in' and to Victoria Hobbs for steering my longship into friendly waters. Immeasurable thanks to Sara Fisher and Bill Hamilton of AM Heath who, one morning, gave me the best news I have ever received and made me dance around the bedroom like a drunken Viking on ice skates. To Tom, who convinces me that real jobs should be avoided and who always wants to celebrate, bottoms up! Thanks to the Milners for your love and support and to Stephen for giving me a desk to write at. To my pals in Manhattan, London and the Woodman Stroke Pub, we've not even started yet. Thanks to all at Transworld for your mead-hall welcome. Your office is my Valhöll! Finally, thanks to my editor Katie Espiner who made it her business to make writing my business. Katie, you released *Raven* into blue skies and for that you have my sword.

# AUTHOR'S NOTE

Although *Raven* features a group of fictional characters, the story's historical context is consistent with contemporary sources and the conjecture of many of today's medieval scholars. Of course, in the tradition of the sagas, *Raven* does not escape the odd embellishment or hyperbole. The *Anglo-Saxon Chronicle* is one of the most important documents to survive from the Middle Ages. Originally compiled on the orders of King Alfred the Great in approximately AD 890, it was subsequently maintained and added to by generations of anonymous scribes until the middle of the twelfth century.

The entry for AD 793 reads:

This year came dreadful fore-warnings over the land of the Northumbrians, terrifying the people most woefully: these were immense sheets of light rushing through the air, and whirlwinds, and fiery dragons flying across the firmament. These tremendous tokens were soon followed by a great famine: and not long after, on the sixth day before the ides of January in the same year, the harrowing inroads of heathen men made lamentable havoc in the church of God in Holy-island, by rapine and slaughter.

In AD 793 a flotilla of sleek longships sailed out of a storm and on to the windswept beach at the Holy Island of Lindisfarne, off England's north-east coast. The marauders who leapt from these grim-prowed craft sacked the monastery there, slaughtering its monks in what was seen as a strike against civilization itself. This event marks the dawn of the Viking age, an era in which adventurous, ambitious heathens surged from their Scandinavian homelands to raid and trade along the coasts of Europe. Fellowships of warriors, bound by honour and wanderlust, would reach as far as Newfoundland and Baghdad, the sword-song of their battles ringing out in Africa and the Arctic. They were nobles and outcasts, pirates, pioneers and great seafarers. They were the Norsemen.

# THE TRACKS OF THE WOLFPACK

**KEY**

- 🛶 Long house
- ⚔ Site of battle
- ○ Settlement
- 🌳 Forest

```
0        MILES        100
0        KM          100
```

FORTRIU

NORTHUMBRIA

NORTH SEA

IRISH SEA

MERCIA

EAST ANGLIA

Caer Dyffryn

OFFA'S WALL

Severn

King Coenwulf's Hall

POWYS

Wye

WESSEX

Ealdred's Hall

KENT

DUMNONIA

Wareham

Selsey

Abbotsend

ENGLISH CHANNEL

# LIST OF CHARACTERS

## WESSEXMEN

**Egbert,** king of Wessex
**Edgar,** a reeve
**Ealhstan,** a carpenter
**Wulfweard,** a priest
**Alwunn**
**Eadwig**
**Griffin,** a warrior
**Burghild,** his wife
**Siward,** a blacksmith
**Oeric,** a butcher
**Bertwald**
**Eosterwine,** a butcher
**Ealdred,** an ealdorman
**Mauger,** a warrior
**Father Egfrith,** a monk
**Cynethryth**
**Weohstan**
**Burgred**
**Penda**
**Eafa,** a fletcher

Egric
Alric
Oswyn
Coenred
Saba, a miller
Eni
Huda
Ceolmund
Godgifu, a cook
Hunwald
Cearl
Hereric
Wybert
Hrothgar

## MERCIANS

Coenwulf, king of Mercia
Cynegils
Aelfwald (Grey Beard)

## NORTHUMBRIANS

Eardwulf, king of Northumbria

## NORSEMEN

Osric (Raven)
Sigurd the Lucky, a jarl
Olaf (Uncle), shipmaster of *Serpent*
Asgot, a godi
Glum, shipmaster of *Fjord-Elk*
Svein the Red
White-haired Eric, son of Olaf
Black Floki

Scar-faced Sigtrygg
Njal
Oleg
Eyjolf
Bjarni, brother of Bjorn
Bjorn, brother of Bjarni
Kalf
Bram the Bear
Arnkel
Knut, steersman of *Serpent*
Tall Ivar
Osten
Gap-toothed Ingolf
Halfdan
Thorolf
Kon
Thormod
Gunnlaug
Thorkel
Northri
Gunnar
Thobergur
Eysteinn
Ulf
Ugly Einar
Halldor, cousin of Floki
Arnvid
Aslak
Thorgils, cousin of Glum
Thorleik, cousin of Glum
Orm
Hakon

# GODS

Óðin, the All-Father. God of warriors and war, wisdom and poetry
Frigg, wife of Óðin
Thór, slayer of giants and god of thunder. Son of Óðin
Baldr, the beautiful. Son of Óðin
Týr, Lord of Battle
Loki, the Mischiefmonger. Father of Lies
Rán, Mother of the Waves
Njörd, Lord of the Sea and god of wind and flame
Frey, god of fertility, marriage and growing things
Freyja, goddess of love and sex
Hel, goddess of the underworld
Völund, god of the forge and of experience

Midgard, the place where men live. The world
Asgard, home of the gods
Valhöll, Óðin's hall of the slain
Yggdrasil, the World-Tree. A holy place for the gods
Bifröst, the Rainbow-Bridge connecting the worlds of gods and men
Ragnarök, Doom of the Gods
Valkyries, Choosers of the Slain
Norns, the three weavers who determine the fates of men
Fenrir, the Mighty Wolf
Jörmungand, the Midgard-Serpent
Hugin (Thought), one of the two ravens belonging to Óðin
Munin (Memory), one of the two ravens belonging to Óðin
Mjöllnir, the magic hammer of Thór

16

My mother once told me
She'd buy me a longship,
A handsome-oared vessel
To go sailing with Vikings:
To stand at the sternpost
And steer a fine warship
Then head back for harbour
And hew down some foemen.

*Egil's Saga*

THE HEARTH IS SPEWING MORE SMOKE THAN FLAME, seething angrily and causing some of the men to cough as they hunker down amongst the reindeer furs. The hall's stout door creaks open, making a flame leap and tempting the acrid smoke to draw. Shadows edge around the room like Valkyries, the demons of the dead, hiding in corners waiting for titbits, hungry for human flesh. Perhaps they have caught a whisper of death in the fire's crack and spit. Certainly they have waited a long time for me.

Even in Valhöll a hush has fallen like a mantle of new snow, as Óðin, Thór and Týr lay down their swords, put aside their preparations for Ragnarök, the final battle. Am I too arrogant? More than likely. And yet, I do believe that even the gods themselves desire to hear the one with the red eye tell his tale. After all, they have played their part in it. And this is why they laugh, for men are not alone in seeking eternal fame: the gods crave glory too.

As though summoned to vanquish the shadows, the hearth bursts into flame. Men's faces come alive in the orange glow. They are ready. Eager. And so I take a deep, bitter breath. And begin.

# PROLOGUE

## England, AD 802

I DO NOT KNOW WHERE I WAS BORN. WHEN I WAS YOUNG, I would sometimes dream of great rock walls rising so high from the sea that the sun's warmth never hit the cold, black water. Though perhaps those dreams were crafted from the tales I heard men tell, the men from the northlands where the winter days die before they begin and the summer sun never sets.

I know nothing of my childhood, of my parents, or if I had brothers and sisters. I do not even know my birth name. And yet, perhaps it says much about my life that my earliest memories are stained red. They are written in the blood that marks my left eye, for which men have always feared me.

I was perhaps fifteen years old and thought myself a man when the heathens came. My village was known as Abbotsend and it was a dreary place. Supposedly it was named after the holy father who climbed into the branches of a tall oak and there remained in penance

21

for three years without food or water, preserved only by his own piety and the will of the Lord. Only when climbing down did the man fall and die from his injuries. And so it was that where he died became the place of the abbot's end. Whether the story is true or not I cannot say, but I suppose it is as good an explanation for the name as any and more interesting than most. Abbotsend lay on a windswept spit of land jutting boldly into the sea a day's ride south-west of Wareham in the kingdom of Wessex. Though no king would ever have reason to visit Abbotsend. It was a settlement like any other, home to simple folk who expected nothing more from life than food and shelter and the rearing of children. A good Christian might say that such a humble place was ever likely to be blessed and by that blessing suffer, as its namesake had suffered and as all martyrs do. But a pagan would spit at such words, claiming the inconsequence of the place was reason enough that it be culled like a sick animal. For the village of Abbotsend no longer exists and I am to blame for its end.

I worked for old Ealhstan the carpenter, felling ash and alderwood for the cups and platters he turned on his lathe.

'I know, old man. All men must eat and drink,' I would say wearily, interpreting Ealhstan's gesture of banging two plates together and nodding to some passing man or woman, 'and so shall we if we keep making the things others need.' And Ealhstan would grunt and nod because he was mute.

And so I spent most days alone in the wooded valley

east of the village, cutting and shaping timber with Ealhstan's axe. I had a roof over my head and food in my belly and I stayed away from those who would rather I had never come to that place, those who feared me for my blood-red eye and because I could not tell them whence I came.

The carpenter alone did not hate or fear me. He was hard-working and old and could not speak, and he would not indulge in such emotions. He had taken me in and I repaid his kindness with blisters and sweat and that was that. But the others were not like Ealhstan. Wulfweard the priest would make the sign of the cross when he saw me, and the women would tell their daughters to stay away from me. Even the boys kept their distance for the most part, though sometimes they would hide amongst the trees and jump out to beat me with sticks, but only when there were three or four of them and all full of mead. Even then the beatings lacked the fury to break bones, for everyone respected old Ealhstan's skill. They needed his cups and platters and barrels and wheels and so they usually left me alone.

There was a girl. Alwunn. She was red-cheeked and plump and we had lain together after the Easter feast when the only living things not drunk on mead were the dogs. The mead had made me brave and I had found Alwunn drawing water from the well and without a word I took her hand and led her to a patch of tall, damp rye grass. She seemed willing enough, enthusiastic even, when it came to it. But in truth it was a graceless fumble and afterwards Alwunn was ashamed. Or perhaps she was afraid of what her kin would do if they found out about us. Either way, after that clumsy night she avoided me.

For two years I lived with Ealhstan, learning his craft so I could take his place at the lathe when he was gone. I would wake before sunrise and take a rod and line down to the rocks to catch mackerel for our breakfast. Then I would scour the woods for the best trees from which Ealhstan would make whatever people needed: tables, benches, cartwheels, bows, arrows and sword scabbards. From him I learned the magic of different trees, like the way the yew's heartwood gives the war bow its strength whilst the sapwood makes it flexible, until in the end I knew from sight and touch alone whether or not a tree would suit a certain purpose. I would spend hours with the oaks especially, though I did not know why they fascinated me, only that they had some power over my imagination. In their presence, strange half-thoughts would weave a tapestry in my mind, its threads worn, the colour a dull faded brown. I would sometimes find myself mouthing sounds to which I could put no meaning and then in frustration I would name the trees and plants aloud to steer my mind from the fog. Still, I would come back to the oaks. I was drawn from tree to tree searching for great curving limbs in which the grain would run so strong that the wood could not be broken. But the old carpenter had no use for enormous oak timbers and chided me for wasting my time.

We had neither horse nor cart. Once, when I moaned about the work, Ealhstan leant back as though he had a huge belly and staggered around the workshop leading an invisible horse and cart. Then he pointed at me and waggled his finger.

'You're not Reeve Edgar and you can't afford a horse to share the work,' I said, guessing his meaning, and he nodded with a grimace, grabbed the scruff of my neck and pointed to the door. 'But you could if you didn't have to feed me?' I hazarded, rubbing my neck. The old man's affirming grunt was warning enough and I stopped my moaning.

And so my back and arms grew strong and the boys who had beaten me took to beating Eadwig the cripple who had been wont to gather the hazel branches they used on me. Though I was strong I was always pleased after a hard day to sit and pedal the pole lathe, which turned the timber this way and that as the old man teased form and shine from rough wood. At night, after a meal of cheese and bread, pottage and meat, we would go to the old hall and listen to merchants swapping news, or men reciting the old tales of great battles and deeds. My favourite story was of the warrior Beowulf who slew the monster Grendal, and I would sit spellbound as smoke from the hearth filled the woody space with a sweet, resinous aroma and tired men drank mead or ale until they fell asleep amongst the rushes, to stagger home at cock's crow.

This was my life. And it was a simple one. But it would not last.

# CHAPTER ONE

IT WAS APRIL. THE LEAN DAYS OF FASTING AND THE LONG
months of winter had been forgotten with the full
bellies of the Easter feast. The people were busy with
the outdoor tasks that the icy winds had kept them
from: straightening loose thatch, replacing rotten
fences, replenishing wood stores and stirring new
life into the rich soil of the plough fields. Wild garlic
smothered the earth in the shady woods like a white
pelt, its scent whipped up by the breeze, and blue spring
squill sat like a low mist upon the grassy slopes and
headlands, stirred by the salty sea air.

Usually, I was woken by Ealhstan's mutterings and
one of his bony fingers digging my ribs, but on this day
I rose before the old man, hoping to be away catching a fish for our breakfast before having to suffer his
ill temper. I even imagined he might be pleased with
me for being at the task before the sun reddened the
eastern horizon, though it was more likely he would
begrudge my being awake before him. Fishing rod in
hand and wrapped in a threadbare cloak, I stepped out

27

into the predawn stillness and shivered with a yawn that brought water to my eyes.

'The old goat got you working by the light of the stars now, has he?' came a low voice and I turned to make out Griffin the warrior leading his great grey hunting dog by a rope which was knotted so that the animal choked itself as it fought him. 'Keep still, boy!' Griffin growled, yanking the rope viciously. The beast was coughing and I thought Griffin might break its neck if it did not stop pulling.

'You know Ealhstan,' I said, holding back my hair and leaning over the rain barrel. 'He can't take a piss before he's had his breakfast.' I thrust my face into the dark, cold water and held it there, then came up and shook my head, wiping my eyes on the back of my arm.

Griffin looked down at the dog, which was beaten at last and stood with its head slumped low between its shoulders, looking up at its master pathetically. 'Found the dumb bastard sniffing around Siward's place just now. He ran off yesterday. First time I've laid eyes on him since.'

'Siward's got a bitch on heat,' I said, tying back my hair.

'So the wife tells me,' Griffin said, a smile touching his mouth. 'Can't blame him, I suppose. We all want a bit of what's good for us, hey, boy?' he added, rubbing the dog's head roughly. I liked Griffin. He was a hard man, but had no hatred in him like the others. Or perhaps it was fear he lacked.

'Some things in life are certain, Griffin,' I said,

returning his smile. 'Dogs will chase bitches, and Ealhstan will eat mackerel every morning till his old teeth fall out.'

'Well, you'd better dip that line, lad,' he warned, nodding southwards towards the sea. 'Even Arsebiter here has less bite than old Ealhstan. I wouldn't get on the wrong side of that tongueless bastard for every mackerel the Lord Jesus and His disciples pulled out of the Red Sea.'

I looked back to the house. 'Ealhstan doesn't have a right side,' I said in a low voice. Griffin grinned, bending to rub Arsebiter's muzzle. 'I'll bring you a codfish one of these days, Griffin. Long as your arm,' I said, shivering again, and then we parted ways, he towards his house and me towards the low sound of the sea.

A pinkish glow lay across the eastern horizon, but the sun was still concealed and it was dark as I climbed the hill that shielded Abbotsend from the worst of the weather blowing in from the grey sea. But I had walked the path many times and had no need of a flame. Besides, the old crumbling watchtower stood visible at the hilltop as a black shape against a dark purple sky. Folk said it was built by the Romans, that long-disappeared race. I did not know if that was true, but I whispered thanks to them anyway, for with the tower in sight I could not lose my way.

My mind wandered, though, as I considered taking a skiff beyond the sea-battered rocks next morning to try to catch something other than mackerel. You could pull in a great codfish if you could get your hook to the seabed. Suddenly, a metallic 'tock' stopped me

29

dead and something whipped my eyes, for an instant blinding me. I dropped to one knee, feeling the hairs spring up on the back of my neck. A guttural croak broke the stillness and I saw a black shape swoop up, then plunge, settling on the tower's crumbling crown. It croaked again and even in the weak dawn light its wings glinted with a purple sheen as its stout beak stabbed at its feathers. I had seen similar birds many times – clouds of crows that swept down to the fields to dig for seeds or worms – but this was a huge raven and the sight of it was enough to freeze my blood.

'Away with you, bird,' I said, picking up a small piece of red brick and throwing it at the creature. I missed, but it was enough to send the raven flapping noisily into the sky, a black smear against the lightening heavens. 'So you're scared of birds now, Osric?' I muttered, shaking my head as I crested the hill and made my way through stalks of pink thrift and cushioning sea campion down to the shore. A damp mist had been thrown up to blanket the dunes and shingle and a flock of screeching gulls passed overhead, tumbling down into the murk, leaving behind them a wake of noise. I jumped across three rock pools full of green weed, the small bladders floating at the surface, then on to my fishing rock where I knocked a limpet into the sea with the butt of my rod before unwinding the line.

After the time it takes to put a keen edge on a knife nothing had taken the hook, and I thought about trying another spot where I had once pulled in a rough-skinned fish as long as my leg with wicked, sharp teeth. It was then that I caught a strange sound between the rhythmic breathing of the surf. I wedged the rod in a crevice, the line still in the sea, and scrambled higher up the rocks above the shingle. But I saw nothing other than the sea-stirred vapour, which seemed alive like some strange beast writhing before me, concealing and revealing the ocean time and again. I heard only the shrieks of white gulls and the breaking waves, and was about to jump down when I heard the strange sound again.

This time I froze like an icicle. My muscles gripped my bones rigid. The breath caught fast in my chest and cold fear crept up my spine, prickling my scalp. The thin hollow note of a horn sounded again, and then came the rhythmic slap of oars. As if conjured from the spirit world, a dragon emerged, a wooden beast with a belly of clinkered strakes, which flowed up into its slender neck. The monster's head was set with faded red eyes, and I wanted to run but I was stuck to the rock like the limpets, fixed by the stare of a great bearded warrior who stood with one arm round the monster's neck. His beard parted, revealing a malicious smile, then the boat's keel scraped up the shingle with a noise like thunder and men were jumping from the ship, sliding on the wet rocks and falling and splashing into the surf. Guttural voices echoed off the rocks behind me and my bowels melted. Another dragon ship must have beached further down the shore beyond Hermit's Rock. Men with swords and axes and round painted shields stepped from the mist, their war gear clinking noisily to shatter the unnatural stillness. They gathered round me like wolves, pointing east and west, their hard voices rousing shrieks from gulls overhead. I mumbled a prayer to Christ and His saints that my death would be quick, as the warrior from the ship's prow stepped up and grabbed my throat. He shoved me at another heathen who gripped my shoulder with a powerful hand. This one wore a green cloak fastened with a silver brooch in the shape of a wolf's head. I saw the iron rings of a mail shirt, a brynja, beneath the cloak and I retched.

Now, after all these years, I might essay a few untruths. I doubt any still live who could prove my words false. I could say that I stuck out my chest and took a grip of my fear. That I did not piss myself. But who would believe me? These outlanders leaping from their dragons were armed and fierce. They were warriors and grown men. And I was just a boy. A strange and frightening magic fell across me then. The outlanders' sharp language began to change, seemed to melt, the percussive clipped grunts becoming a stream of sounds that were somehow familiar. I swallowed some of the fear, my tongue beginning to move over these noises like water over pebbles, awakening to them, and I heard myself repeating them until they became no longer just noises, but words. And I understood them.

'But look at his eye, Uncle!' the man with the wolf brooch said. 'He is marked. Óðin god of war has given him a clot of blood for an eye. On my oath, I feel the All-Father breathing down my neck.'

'I agree with Sigurd,' another said, his eyes slits of suspicion. 'The way he appeared in the mist was not natural. You all saw it. The vapour became flesh! Any normal man would have run from her.' He pointed to the ship with its carved dragon's head. 'But this one stood here as if he was . . . as if he was waiting for us. I want no part in his death, Sigurd,' he finished, shaking his head.

I prayed they would not see the fishing rod in the crack in the rock and I hoped the mackerel were still asleep, for mackerel fight like devils and if one took my hook the line would jump and the heathens would see me for what I was.

'I can help you,' I spluttered, buoyed suddenly by the hope that the outlanders were lost, blown off course on the way to who knew where?

'You speak Norse, boy?' Wolf Brooch asked, his strong, weathered face open now. The others were spreading out cautiously and peering northwards through the mist. 'I am Sigurd son of Harald. We are traders,' he said, staring at me as though wondering what I was. 'We have furs and amber and bone. The bellies of our ships are full of good things the English will like. We will trade with them' – he grinned – 'if they have anything we want.' I did not believe they were traders, for they wore ring-mail and leather and carried the tools of death. But I was young and afraid and did not want to die. 'Take us to the nearest village,' Sigurd demanded, his eyes so piercing it took all my nerve to look into them, and, just as no mackerel had swallowed my hook, I knew this man would not swallow my lie.

'Hurry, boy, we have much to give the English,' a giant red-haired heathen with rings on his arms said, grinning and clutching the sword's hilt at his waist.

So, with a sickness in my stomach and a spinning head, I led these Norsemen towards my home. And in my heart I knew I should have let them kill me.

I stumbled across the rocks and shingle, trying to keep my footing as the Norsemen pushed me on. I guessed there were about fifty of them, though half stayed with the ships as the rest of us climbed the grassy dunes where red-beaked oystercatchers trilled noisily, fleeing their scrapes among the tufts as we approached. The Norsemen gripped spears, axes and shields as though off to battle, none speaking now as the dunes gave way to solid ground and we climbed the scree-covered path leading to the summit of the hill overlooking my village. I let my mind tell me they would have found the place without my help. Abbotsend was just the other side of the swell and if they had taken to the high ground they would not have missed it. But the truth was I was leading them, as Griffin's dog might lead him to a badger's sett, and if there was blood it would be on my hands, for I had lacked the courage to die.

The Norsemen stopped on the ridge by the old crumbling watchtower, taking in the small settlement: a loose clutter of sixteen thatched dwellings, a mill, a hall and a small stone church. That was Abbotsend, but it must have been enough, for some of them grinned. The grip on my tunic was released and I seized my chance. I hared down the hill, throwing my arms out for balance and yelling to wake the dead. Folk looked up, then scattered, their panicked cries carrying up the hillside. Even back then we had heard of the heathens' savagery and thirst for plunder, and now the Norsemen were running too, to reach the village before its people could hide their possessions or find their courage.

I tripped sprawling into the mud between the houses where some of the men of Abbotsend were already forming a thin shieldwall. Others grimly hefted axes and forks, anything sharp enough to kill a man. I got to my feet as Siward the blacksmith lumbered from his forge, a bundle of swords in his heavily muscled arms, some without grips and pommels, others still black, yet to be polished and honed. He was handing them to any man prepared to stand and face what was coming. I ran to him.

'Out of the way, boy!' Griffin growled, grabbing Siward's arm before the blacksmith could give me a blade. I tried to take the blade anyway, but Griffin growled again and Siward turned his back on me and took his place beside the warrior. 'Hold the line! Straighten up, lads!' Griffin yelled to the eight men now standing with him. Griffin was the most experienced fighter of our village, but he had had no time to fetch his mail shirt or his shield and so stood armed only with his great sword. Arsebiter was beside him, his yellow teeth bared in a rolling snarl.

Ealhstan appeared at my shoulder, his eyes twitching madly.

'They said they were traders,' I said. By now, the Norsemen had formed their own shieldwall facing Griffin's, but theirs was longer and two men deep.

You brought them here? Ealhstan's eyes asked. The old man crossed himself and I saw he was trembling.

They don't look like traders, boy! his face said. By Christ, they don't!

'They would have killed me,' I said, knowing they were the words of a coward. Ealhstan hissed and pointed towards the eastern woods but I ignored him and he hit me with a bony fist, again pointing to the trees. But I had brought the heathens over the hill, and if I ran it would make me less than cuckoo spit.

'What do you want here?' Griffin demanded. There was no fear in his voice. His chest swelled beneath his tunic and his eyes narrowed as he assessed the men facing him. 'Go now and leave us in peace. Whoever you are, we have no quarrel with you. Go before blood is spilled.' Arsebiter's hackles bunched as he echoed his master's warning with three coarse barks.

Sigurd, his sword still in its scabbard, glanced at the beast, then stepped forward. 'We are traders,' he said in English, his accent thick. 'We have brought furs and much deer antler. And walrus ivory, if you have the silver for it.' The Norsemen behind him bristled with violence, like hunting dogs themselves straining at the leash. No, not dogs but wolves. Some began thumping their sword pommels against the backs of their shields in a threatening rhythm. Sigurd raised his voice. 'Will you trade?' he asked.

'You don't look like traders to me,' Griffin answered, spitting on the earth between them. 'Traders have no need of war shields and helmets.' Griffin's men murmured in agreement, taking heart from their leader's defiance. More village men had gathered now, having seen their families safe, and some of them had shields. These pushed into Griffin's line, whilst others stood behind armed with hunting spears and long knives.

Sigurd shrugged his broad shoulders and grimaced. 'Sometimes we are traders,' he said, 'sometimes not.'

'Where are you from?' Griffin asked. 'We don't get many outlanders here.' I saw him glance away and realized he was buying time for the village women who were dragging their children towards the eastern woods, though a slamming door said at least one had chosen to stay.

'We are from Hardanger Fjord. Far to the north,' Sigurd said, 'and as I told you, we are sometimes traders.' The word *sometimes* cast the shadow of warning.

'Do not threaten us, heathen!' boomed Wulfweard the priest, marching from his church holding a wooden cross before him. He was a huge man, a warrior once some said, and he set himself before the Norsemen like a squared stone from his church. He eyed Sigurd fiercely. 'The Lord knows the blackness of your hearts and He will not let you bring blood to this peaceful place.' He raised the wooden cross as though the very sight of it would turn the Norsemen to dust, and in that moment I believed in the power of the Christian god. The priest turned to me, plain hatred twisting his face. 'You are one of Satan's minions, boy,' he said calmly. 'We've always known it here. And now you have brought the wolf into the fold.'

Ealhstan grunted and dismissed Wulfweard's words with the flick of an arm.

'He's right, Wulfweard,' Griffin said. 'They'd have come anyway and you know it. The lad never rowed 'em here!'

Sigurd glanced at me as he drew his sword with a rasp, and Wulfweard looked at the weapon scornfully. 'You pagans are the last of the Devil's slaves and soon you will be dust like all non-believers before you.' He grinned then, his trembling red face full of the power of his words. 'The armies of Christ are washing your filth from the world.'

Some of the Norsemen shouted for Sigurd to kill Wulfweard then, as though they feared his strange words were the weaving of some spell. But to show he had no fear of words, Sigurd turned his back on the priest, lifted his great sword and thrust it into the earth before his men. Seeing this, the Norsemen took their own swords and spears and plunged them down with grunts of effort, sinking the blades into the soil where they quivered like crops in the breeze. Sigurd turned back to Wulfweard and threw his round shield at the priest, who jumped back. It struck his shin and must have hurt, though he showed no sign of it.

'We have come to trade,' Sigurd announced to the English shieldwall. 'I swear on my father's sword,' he said, placing a palm on the earth-sheathed weapon's silver pommel, 'I mean you no harm.' He glowered at Wulfweard. 'Does your god forbid you from owning fine furs? He is a strange god who would have you freeze when the first snows cover this village.'

'We would rather our blood froze in our veins than trade with Satan's underlings,' Wulfweard spat, but

Griffin stepped from his line and thrust his own sword into the earth beside Sigurd's.

'Wulfweard speaks for himself,' he said, never taking his eyes from Sigurd, 'and that is his right. But the red deer are thin on the ground this year because our king covets the silver they fetch and his men hunt them greedily. A good fur can keep a man alive. We have families.' He flicked his head towards the men behind him. 'We will trade, Sigurd.' And with that he stepped up and gripped Sigurd's arm and the two men smiled because instead of blood there would be trade. I exhaled and slapped Ealhstan's back as the folk of Abbotsend welcomed the outlanders with gestures and handshaking, and the relief of those who have avoided death by a hair's breadth.

Wulfweard strode off back to his church muttering damnation and Griffin watched him go, shaking his head. 'He's the custodian of our souls, Sigurd,' he said, 'but a man must look to his life, too. We're not dead yet. And whether you and yours pray to a dog's balls or a twisted old tree means nothing to me if we can take from each other,' he held up his hands, 'peacefully and in good faith, the things that make life better.'

Sigurd nodded. 'Ah, my own godi chews my ears often enough, Englishman,' he said, batting a hand towards Wulfweard's back. 'Let them have their sour apples. They trade in misery. We'll have our silver and furs.'

'Agreed,' Griffin said, then he frowned. 'We will have to send word to our reeve, of course. He'd spit teeth if he found out you'd landed here and not paid him his taxes.' Sigurd's own brow furrowed and he scratched his beard. 'Don't worry, Norseman,' Griffin said, putting a hand on the man's shoulder. 'If we're quick we can make our trade and you can leave before Edgar gets his fat arse down here.' He shrugged. 'We are not going to stop you sailing off, that's for sure.'

Sigurd turned. His men were pulling their weapons from the ground and cleaning their blades. 'We will keep our weapons sheathed,' he assured Griffin who, along with some of the other Englishmen, seemed suddenly anxious.

'Your word is good enough for me, Sigurd,' Griffin said with a solemn nod. 'Now I will speak to my people.' Sigurd gripped Griffin's arm in a final gesture of trust before Griffin turned and began to receive the questions of the other influential men of the village.

Sigurd turned to me. 'What is your name, red-eye?' he asked in Norse.

'Osric, lord,' I said, 'and this is Ealhstan my master,' I added, nodding at the old man and marvelling at how I had found the words in the heathen's language.

'You serve that tongueless old goat?' Sigurd asked. He grinned. 'Ah, I understand. You don't like being told what to do.'

'I assure you, my master has other ways of getting what he wants,' I said with a smile as Ealhstan prodded my shoulder irritably and waggled his hand like a fish. I shook my head and the old man grimaced crabbily before shuffling off. He would have to forgo his mackerel now and he was not happy about it.

'How did you learn our tongue?' Sigurd asked.

'I did not know I could speak it, lord,' I said, 'until today.'

'That priest of the White Christ does not like you, Osric,' he said, rubbing a thumb along his sword's blade to clean the mud from it.

'Most of the people here fear me,' I said with a shrug.

Sigurd pursed his thick lips and nodded. I had never seen anyone like him. He looked like the kind of man who would fight a bear with his own hands. And win.

'We are the first among our people to take our dragons across the ill-tempered sea,' he said, 'but even we are not without fear. Do you know what I fear, lad?' I shook my head. Surely nothing, I thought. 'I fear a dry throat. Fetch us something to drink. Mead greases the barter.' He smiled at the giant Norseman with the red hair and beard, who grinned back, and I turned to go and fetch mead from Ealhstan's house. 'Don't put a curse on the damn stuff, Satan's minion!' Sigurd called after me, mimicking Wulfweard. 'I'm thirsty!'

The Norsemen fetched goods from their ships while the local children and even some of the men buzzed around them, marvelling at their sleek dragon-prowed vessels, the likes of which they had never seen. The children helped carry the heathens' goods back to the village where noisy clusters of women waited, eager to see what these strangers had to sell. The outlanders' deer furs were thick and full and their whetstones were fine-grained, though Siward the blacksmith insisted they were not as good as English stones. They threw down leather skins and covered them with amber, much of which had been fashioned into beads, and leather jacks full of honey. There was dried fish, reindeer bone, and walrus ivory which proved very popular with the village men, for they bought every piece on show. Having obtained it cheaply they would later pay Ealhstan to carve the ivory into smooth or patterned hilts for knives and swords, or amulets for their wives. The last women and children abandoned their hiding places in the eastern woods and came to join the throng and barter with the Norsemen. They brought their scales to weigh coin and beads and gestured fervently, trying to make themselves understood, though Sigurd was needed to resolve several confusions and did so willingly, a smile etched in his strong face.

'Osric speaks their tongue,' Griffin announced above the bustle, winking at me, and soon the folk of Abbotsend forgot that I was Satan's minion in their rush to employ me as a translator to grease their trade. But I was pleased to do it and I wondered if these same folk who had shunned me would treat me well when the Norsemen left, because I had helped them. At first finding the words was like rooting for berries after the birds have been, but the more I listened the more I understood. I was too immersed in men's negotiations to wonder what strange magic was at work.

Old Ealhstan made a sound in his throat and nodded, fingering an oval brooch of bronze which a Norseman had thrust into his hands. At the heathen's feet dozens of the things sat on a smooth hide, glinting in the late afternoon light. Most of the trading was finished, but the village was still buzzing as folk compared their new goods and boasted about how cheaply they came by them.

'I don't think he sold many of these, Ealhstan,' I said, seeing how keen the Norseman was to sell a woman's brooch to a mute old man. Ealhstan made the sign of the cross, curled his dry old lips and pointed off in the direction of the church.

'The women feared they'd get too much earache from Wulfweard for wearing them?' I asked as he handed me the brooch. 'God-fearing women sporting pagan brooches.' I tried to imagine it. 'Wulfweard wouldn't like that. Wouldn't like it one bit.'

To the heathen's disappointment I placed the brooch back on the hide with the others. All were longer than a finger and some had projecting bosses of amber or glass shining amongst intricate, swirling patterns engraved in the metal. 'Where is Wulfweard, anyway? I haven't seen the red-faced bag of wind since this morning.'

Ealhstan shrugged his bony shoulders and wagged a finger at me. 'I know, I know, Wulfweard's a man of God,' I said. 'I should show more respect. Even though he wouldn't piss on me if I were burning.' A child squealed and we both spun to the sound. 'They're just playing,' I said, laughing as the giant flame-haired Norseman growled like a bear to scare the three children who were clambering over him, one on his back and the others on either arm.

'Come here, Wini,' one of the boys' mothers called nervously and in no time all three children were shepherded away, leaving the Norseman beaming from his great shaggy beard.

'They don't seem like devils, Ealhstan,' I said. Ealhstan's white eyebrows arched. You didn't think that this morning, those hairy caterpillars said. They're bloody-minded heathens and you'd do well to stay away from them.

But I did not want to stay away.

Griffin had waited until the sun was in the west before sending a man out to tell Edgar the local reeve that strangers had moored, meaning taxes were owed, and Sigurd had agreed to spend the night ashore sharing mead with the men of Abbotsend. In any case, his ships were beached and he could not sail until the next high tide, so would risk the reeve's taxes for a night on dry land. Word spread that the men were to gather in the old hall when it got dark and I watched the heathens pack their remaining goods in chests and skins. It seemed they were even more eager to begin drinking mead than they had been to sell their wares.

'You'd better join us, Osric,' Griffin called from behind two thick, folded reindeer skins in his arms. Arsebiter was at his master's heel. 'We'll need you to make sense of the heathens' babble. How is it you understand them, lad?'

'I don't know, Griffin,' I said. 'I've no way of explaining it.'

He shrugged. 'Well, I'll see you later.' He grinned and jangled an amber necklace that was looped over his wrist. 'When Burghild sees this she'll not mind me spending all night drinking with those devils!

Least, that's the idea.' The dog looked up at Griffin doubtfully.

'Maybe you should have bought her a brooch, too,' I said, stifling a smile, 'and some of that reindeer antler. Maybe one of those silver pins.'

Griffin peered round the skins at the amber necklace, then back to me, a dark frown gathering on his face. Then he turned and went on his way, with Arsebiter following him.

# CHAPTER TWO

MEN CRAMMED INTO THE OLD HALL LIKE TROUT IN A withy trap. It was loud and it stank, but heathen and Christian were getting along better than anyone could have hoped. Even Wulfweard was there, though I did not see him talking to any of the Norsemen. He sat on a footstool drinking mead and fingering the wooden cross he wore round his neck as though the thing would keep him safe from the evil he saw all around him. He looked up at the roof suspiciously, seemingly fearful that the men's carousing would shake the old beams from their joints to fall and crush us.

The hall had belonged to Lord Swefred, but he had been in the ground six years and had no sons. Now, shadow-shrouded cheese presses, butter churns and empty barrels cluttered one end, while the rest of the space was used for meetings, trade and private disputes. Any and all used the place and so none saw why they should pay for its upkeep. Weeds were bursting through the packed earth floor. There were no hangings to keep out the cold and the wattle was damp and rotting.

But this night the place was alive. I thought of the story of Beowulf, when the Geats gathered in the great feasting hall on mead benches studded with precious metals, amongst tapestries worked in gold which glittered on the walls as the glorious warriors rejoiced in the feast. Perhaps this hall had been glorious once, and now these proud heathen warriors from across the grey sea reminded the old, soot-stained beams what they once were.

The Abbotsend men had not wanted their women around Norsemen full of mead, so their sons passed through the hall with bulging skins, filling cups and handing out cuts of meat from two pigs roasting over the hearth. Sigurd had bought the pigs from Oeric the butcher and I watched hungrily as fat hissed in the flames and the delicious smell smothered the stink of wood rot, damp earth and men's sweat. Men who could not make themselves understood shouted, thinking this would help, and others laughed. The noise continued well into the night as I made myself useful, turning strange words into sense for drunken men. Later, furs and cushions and straw were fetched and men settled down to sleep. Because the hall belonged to no man, the heathens had seen no reason not to bring their weapons inside. They sat and lay around the hall's edge, each man's round painted shield, spear and sword leaning against the wall behind him.

'I've never seen so much mail,' Griffin slurred in a low voice. It was late and despite having beds to go to the Abbotsend men were settling in for the night. Some were already snoring. Griffin and I were slumped at the north end below the hall's only window, a narrow slit with vellum stretched across it. Most of the candles had guttered out, leaving only the stone hearth in the centre of the hall to cast its glow across the shrouded, sleeping figures. 'I've fought for King Egbert, and Beorhtric before him, more times than I care to remember, lad. I tell you, I've never seen better armed men.' He pulled a louse from his beard and examined it. 'We'll all be better off when they clear out.' His gaze returned to Jarl Sigurd, who was talking quietly with an older Norseman with a round face and a bushy beard.

'But the trade went well,' I said, watching Griffin absently crush the louse with a thumbnail.

His eyebrows arched. 'Aye, it went well,' he admitted. Then he shook his head, his eyes rolling. 'Burghild wants two of those big brooches, the bronze ones with the amber inset.'

'But the necklace?' I asked, remembering how proud he had been of his purchase earlier that day.

'She says it's no good having the necklace without the brooches to go with it,' Griffin grumbled. Then he caught my eye and we both laughed, waking a dark-haired heathen who managed a curse before closing his eyes again. I must have slept for a time myself then, for I was woken by the clunk of the latch and a creak of the hall door's iron hinges. The murmur of those still awake mixed with men's snores and I watched as old Ealhstan shuffled in, unnoticed by all but a few until the door's hinges gave one last creaking complaint. Ealhstan grimaced. Griffin jerked awake, spilling mead from the cup still in his hand.

'Nearly dropped off, lad. Where's he been?' he asked, nodding towards Ealhstan. 'Carving crosses for the pagans?' Then his eyes closed again and his head fell with a bang against the wall. Carefully, I took the cup from Griffin's hand and placed it on the ground out of harm's way as Ealhstan picked his way through the crowd over snoring, farting men.

'I'll go for the rod at dawn, old man,' I whispered, thinking Ealhstan had come to make sure I would be awake in time to catch his breakfast. But he batted the words away, frowning, and knelt with a wince. When he was happy that Griffin was asleep and that no one else was watching he stared at me, his thin face in shadow, his wispy white hair glowing in the firelight. 'What's going on?' I asked, and he put a bony finger to my lips. Then he took my hand and pressed something into it. I looked down to see a sprig of fern in my palm. I shrugged, divining no meaning from it. Ealhstan motioned that I should smell the leaves, so I rubbed the sprig between my fingers and sniffed. It smelled rank, like rotten parsnips, and I knew it was not fern, but hemlock. I have seen pigs and sheep die from eating hemlock; first they become excited, then their breathing slows and their legs and ears grow cold to the touch. They die swollen and stinking.

I dropped the leaves, spat on my fingers and rubbed my hands on my tunic. Ealhstan puffed up his cheeks and made the sign of the cross.

'Wulfweard?' I whispered.

He nodded, spotted Griffin's mead cup and picked it up, then pretended to sprinkle something into it. His eyes were slits below thick white brows. He turned and looked at Sigurd who was leaning against the west wall beside his great round shield, iron helmet and wicked, heavy spear.

I tugged Ealhstan's shoulder. 'Wulfweard means to poison Jarl Sigurd?' I hissed. 'You saw him gather hemlock?'

The carpenter spun back round, glancing at nearby heathens to make sure none had heard or understood. Then he glared at me and I nodded slowly, acknowledging the reproof. 'He's mad,' I muttered.

Ealhstan grimaced as though he agreed with me. Then he gestured to the hall's door and stood, motioning that I should follow him. Making sure not to wake the sleeping men around me, I got to my feet and followed Ealhstan silently out of the hall, casually loosening my belt as though I intended to relieve myself outside.

The night was dark and moonless. Two dogs were fighting over a fleshy bone. Someone's goose had escaped its pen and now sat on Siward the blacksmith's thatch, spreading its wings and honking proudly. Other than that, the village was asleep. I thought I could hear the surf breaking on the southern shore beyond the black hills. Then Ealhstan reached into the pouch at his waist and held something towards me without taking his eyes from mine. That's when I saw Alwunn, the girl I had lain with at the Easter feast. She stood in the eaves' shadow, wringing her plump hands and staring at Ealhstan. From the state of her knotted blond hair, I guessed the old man must have dragged her from her bed, and I felt a twinge in my stomach at seeing her.

'What's going on, Ealhstan?' I asked, looking at the small, bone-handled knife he had given me. A leather thong ran through a hole in the hilt. Ealhstan beckoned Alwunn irritably and she stepped from the shadows, giving a thin smile with her fat lips. She cleared her throat and glanced at Ealhstan once more for approval. He nodded and gave a grunt.

'Hello, Osric,' Alwunn said in a small voice. Her eyes widened and she touched her hair, suddenly embarrassed. She licked a hand and pressed it against an unruly hank, without success.

'What are you doing here, Alwunn?' I asked, aware of warmth kindling in my loins. 'Are you in your nightclothes?' She shifted awkwardly and I frowned at Ealhstan, who twirled his hand impatiently.

'The knife, Osric,' Alwunn said, nodding at the thing in my hand. 'It's important.'

'Doesn't look important,' I replied, running a thumb across the dull blade. 'You would struggle to skin a hare with this.' Ealhstan snatched the knife from me and held the hilt up close to my face. I took it back and examined the hilt. Two serpents writhed in the white bone, each beast appearing to swallow its own curling tail. 'It's skilled work,' I admitted. 'And pagan.' Ealhstan grunted. I shrugged. 'I don't understand. Why are you showing this to me?'

'I was there when they found you, Osric,' Alwunn said almost guiltily.

'So?' I said. I knew the story. I had been found

amongst the old people's burial mounds south-east of Abbotsend. No one knew where I had come from and I had been unconscious. When I woke, my mind was empty as a mead barrel at a wedding feast.

'Your head was bleeding and they thought you must be dead,' Alwunn continued, 'but when they rolled you over, your eyes were open. When Wulfweard saw . . .' she hesitated and pointed at my blood-eye, 'he cursed and said you had been touched by Satan.' She made the sign of the cross then, scared by her own words.

'I was lucky old Ealhstan needed an extra pair of hands more than he needed Wulfweard's fart-stinking sermons,' I said, smiling at the old carpenter, who grunted again. Alwunn looked horrified at what I had said and took a moment to check that we were still alone. The two dogs, perhaps seeing a hare, suddenly ran off into the night, barking wildly.

Alwunn winced. 'Ealhstan found that knife round your neck,' she said. 'He took it before Wulfweard or the others saw it.' She looked at Ealhstan. 'He feared what they would do. It is pagan, Osric,' she said, emphasizing the word, 'and what with your eye . . .' She shrugged and looked embarrassed again, as though she was ashamed of how the folk of Abbotsend treated me, but at the same time understood their reasons.

'As I said, the old man needed an apprentice,' I said, studying the knife intently now.

'Are you sure you don't remember anything about how you got here?' Alwunn asked, fighting with her unruly hair again.

I shook my head. 'I woke up in Ealhstan's house,

Alwunn. There's nothing before that.' I held up the knife. 'You've always known about this?' She nodded. 'Does anyone else know?'

'Why, Osric? Do you think they could treat you any worse?' she asked with a wry smile. I frowned at her. 'No one else knows,' she said. She looked at Ealhstan. 'I should go. If Mother knew I was out here . . .'

Ealhstan nodded and touched her shoulder in thanks. Alwunn shot me a parting look and ran off into the night, lifting the hem of her nightdress off the muddy earth.

'Why are you telling me now, old man?' I asked, tying the knife to my belt. Alwunn was right. What could they do to me now? For two years they had hated me but let me alone because I was Ealhstan's apprentice. I would not hide behind the old man any more.

Ealhstan stared at the knife on my belt but did not move to take it back. He gave a slight shake of his head and made the sign of the cross over his chest.

'I don't know what this all means, Ealhstan,' I said, putting an arm on his shoulder, 'but thank you.' The goose honked loudly and I turned to see a dark figure striding towards us.

'Is that one of Bertwald's birds?' Wulfweard asked, making the sign of the cross when he noticed me. He wore his priest's armour: the white woollen tunic reaching to his ankles and the strip of green silk which went round his neck and fell to his shins. 'I've told him he needs to put another foot on his pen. Given a bit of a fright and a little gust of wind, a goose can take to the sky for two hundred paces. I've seen it!' We looked at the goose and it flapped its wings angrily. 'Is that devil Jarl Sigurd still in there dreaming up more ways to offend our Lord and Father?' he asked Ealhstan, turning his back on me.

The carpenter nodded.

'About earlier, Ealhstan, by Cearl's place,' Wulfweard said. 'As luck would have it – though we must surely believe good luck to be nothing less than God's rewarding the righteous . . .' He pointed a fat finger, and I did not need to see his face to know the arrogant smile on it. 'Well, Ealhstan, I came across a clump of burdock hiding amongst the nettles and docks. I expect you're familiar with burdock's . . . loosening properties,' he rubbed his lower belly, 'and the relief the juice of its leaves gives to flea bites, snake bites and such like. But did you know that the oil from its roots, when rubbed into the scalp, is most soothing – not to mention restorative to hair?' Ealhstan grunted and Wulfweard squeezed his shoulder. 'Peace be upon you, friend.' Then the priest turned to me, his grimace animal-like in the darkness. 'Out of my way, boy. I go to witness the Lord God's work.' With that he pushed open the old hall's door, shot Ealhstan a wicked grin and went inside.

Ealhstan made to walk away, beckoning for me to follow, but I stood where I was beneath the rotting thatch. The carpenter made a low guttural sound in his throat and waved his arm bad-temperedly.

'You're going to let him poison the jarl?' I asked, horrified. 'He was lying about the burdock.' I sniffed the lingering musty scent of hemlock on my fingers as

Ealhstan gestured again for me to come away. 'I'm not going,' I said. 'We can't let it happen. Wulfweard is mad! His head is full of spiders, Ealhstan.' Though the old man frowned, I did not wait to see what he would do, but followed the priest into the hall.

Inside, someone had thrown more logs on to the hearth. They were spitting and cracking and the flames were jumping again, gilding the spicy smoke that billowed across sleeping men and around smooth roof posts. Wulfweard was standing above Jarl Sigurd, a cup in his hands, and some of the others were stirring as though expecting trouble. Wulfweard turned to the sound of the door. He saw me and curled his lip before turning back to the Norseman. I moved into a space by the hearth, feeling the heat on my face as Ealhstan entered the hall and crouched beside Siward the blacksmith.

'Your people are stumbling in the darkness, Jarl Sigurd,' Wulfweard said, his voice like the rasp of a sword from its sheath, 'but is it not the shepherd's task to save his flock from the wolf?'

'Fuck off, priest,' Sigurd mumbled, scratching his golden beard. 'I did not cross Njörd's sea to listen to you. Your words fall from your mouth like droppings from a goat's arse.' Some of the Norsemen laughed hard enough to wake others still sleeping.

'Go back to your White Christ house and sleep on your knees,' said the warrior beside Sigurd.

For a few heartbeats Wulfweard just stared at Sigurd. By the firelight I saw that the priest was trembling with rage and his free hand was a tight fist.

'I have come here in peace, heathen,' Wulfweard rumbled, 'and I was hoping you might accept Christ's blessing. You will be gone tomorrow.'

'The White Christ is here?' Sigurd asked, grinning and looking around the hall.

'Our Lord is everywhere,' Wulfweard replied, shooting a warning glance at the Englishmen in the hall. 'I would bless you in Christ's name, Sigurd, and in the morning I would baptize you and cleanse you of the evil filth that suffocates your people.'

I wondered then if Wulfweard had had a change of heart, or if Ealhstan had been mistaken about the hemlock. Perhaps the priest *had* been picking burdock for his moulting hair.

'Away with your spells, priest!' Sigurd said, flicking a hand at Wulfweard as an old Norseman with bones plaited in his lank grey hair stood and walked over to the jarl, 'or I will have my own godi turn your guts to worms.' The heathen wizard grinned maliciously, but some of the other Norsemen put their hands on their spears and sword grips. I touched the pagan knife at my waist, letting my thumb follow the forms of the writhing beasts in its bone hilt. The Norsemen had similar hilts sticking from sheaths at their own waists. I looked at these strangers, trying to see myself in them. They were mostly yellow-haired with fair beards, though one had hair as black as my own.

'I see you are not yet ready to receive Christ's forgiveness,' Wulfweard said, forcing a smile. 'Well, I have tried,' he exclaimed, holding his arms wide, 'and perhaps I have struck the first blow in the battle for your blighted souls.' He turned away from Sigurd, stopped, then turned back to face the Norseman, extending the hand clasping the mead cup. 'Will you at least drink with me, Jarl Sigurd? To show all gathered here that there is peace between us?'

Sigurd pursed his lips, then shrugged his powerful shoulders. 'I'll drink with you, priest,' he said, accepting the cup, 'if you will then leave me in peace.' Wulfweard dipped his head and took a step back. Sigurd raised the cup to his lips.

'No, lord!' I called, stepping forward over a Norseman. 'Don't drink it!' From the corner of my eye I saw men clambering to their feet.

Wulfweard turned and hissed at me, his big face so full of hatred that it looked fit to burst. 'Go back to Hell, Satan's slave!' he shouted, his voice filling the old hall.

'Hold your tongue, priest,' Sigurd said, shrugging off a fur and getting to his feet wearily. The men in the hall were separating into knots of Norse or English and more than one of the heathens picked up their great war spears. 'Speak, red-eye,' Sigurd commanded, beckoning me forward with an arm glittering with gold warrior rings.

The weight of men's stares pressed down on me, crushing my throat and squeezing my belly. Suddenly the only sound was the flapping of the hearth flames and my own heartbeat filling my head. I cleared my throat and pushed through the throng until I stood before Sigurd and Wulfweard. 'The mead is poisoned, lord,' I said in Norse.

Sigurd frowned, thrusting the cup to arm's length.

And Wulfweard must have known I had warned the Norseman, for he made the sign of the cross. 'Lies!' he yelled. 'Whatever he's spewing! Lies from Satan's own pus-filled mouth! Lies!' He stepped towards me and I thought he would strike me down.

'Then drink some yourself, priest,' Sigurd growled in English, offering the cup to Wulfweard. 'We will share the mead, but you drink first.'

Wulfweard closed his eyes and turned his face to the old roof, gripping the wooden cross that hung over his chest. He was muttering something, prayers, I think, under his breath.

'Drink!' Sigurd commanded and that one word was so heavy with threat that I could not imagine how any man could disobey it.

'The mead is mixed with hemlock,' I said, glancing at Ealhstan who gave an almost imperceptible shake of his head. 'You would have drunk the mead and you would have slept, lord.' I took a deep breath. 'By noon you would be unable to stand, your legs would be cold to the touch and you would piss yourself.' I did not know if this last part was true, but I thought it would sting a proud man like Sigurd. I was deep in the mire now and saw no point in trying to drag myself clear.

'It would kill me?' Sigurd asked, his eyes boring into mine, as a spoon auger bores into timber.

'I think so, lord,' I said, 'yes. You would die and tomorrow Father Wulfweard would claim it to be the work of God.'

'And the bloated pig would shout that the Christians'

god was more powerful than Óðin All-Father!' Sigurd roared, his hand falling to his sword's pommel. Then Wulfweard spat at me, reached into the long sleeve of his tunic and leapt at Sigurd. I saw the knife in the priest's hand, but Sigurd saw it too and jumped back with astonishing speed, drawing his sword at the same time.

'Father!' Wulfweard screamed as Sigurd stepped up and swung his sword into the man's head. The priest's legs buckled and he fell convulsing on the ground, clutching at his wooden cross as his grey brains spilled wetly from his skull.

The men of Abbotsend cursed and spat, looking to Griffin for leadership. And by the hearth light they must have seen doubt in the warrior's eyes.

'He was a servant of God!' Griffin yelled. Men were pouring out of the hall. 'A priest, Sigurd!' Griffin shouted, staring at the jarl as the Norsemen armed themselves and the Abbotsend men hurried into the night. Ealhstan was kneeling by Wulfweard and I grabbed the old man's shoulder and pulled him away, hardly believing what was happening, then pushed through to the door and out into the fresh air. Into the chaos. The Norsemen were forming a shieldwall, each man's shield overlapping that of the warrior to his right, and the speed and efficiency of their movements was frightening. But the village men were also forming a dense line in the shadows, gripping spears and swords, and more men were coming from their houses with shields and helmets.

'Get away, Ealhstan,' I said, as the world was suddenly

touched by dawn's red hue, 'it can't be stopped now. Come!' But Ealhstan shook his head and pulled away from me. When I grabbed for him again he slapped my hand and croaked what I took for a curse. Then the shieldwalls crashed together and the first grunts and screams battered the still air. I let go of the old man and saw Griffin thrust his sword into a Norseman's neck. *What have I done?* my mind screamed. I had spoken against the priest and now men I knew were dying and their blood would be on my hands. I ran to fetch Ealhstan's hunting bow, praying I would sink an arrow into a heathen's black heart before the end. I threw open Ealhstan's door and in the darkness smashed into his table, my chest thumping wildly as I felt myself running back towards the sound of fighting, clutching the bow, the string, and a sheath of arrows. Some of our men lay broken in the mud, their slick guts steaming in the weak dawn light, but some fought on, groaning as they were forced back over dead friends. Sigurd himself cut Griffin down. I saw a spray of bright blood slap Griffin's hair and I was terrified to see how easily these Norsemen in their brynjas slaughtered men without mail.

Ealhstan was pointing at Griffin and grunting, clawing at my shoulder as I fumbled to string the bow. 'I know, old man,' I hissed, sick because Griffin had been a friend to me. I nocked an arrow, drew back the string, held my breath, then exhaled slowly. 'Heathen bastard,' I spat, then loosed. A Norseman jerked violently, the arrow embedded in his shoulder. I scrabbled to put another shaft to the string and saw

Siward the blacksmith stagger backwards, clutching a spear in his gut and screaming. I loosed the arrow, but it flew wide and when I drew again the cord snapped, whipping my forearm. The Norseman I had hit strode towards me, careless of the blood slicking the mail at his shoulder. I stepped forward and swung the bow at his face, but he caught the stave and ripped it from me, then slammed a fist into my face. From the stinking mud I watched him drop Ealhstan and kick the old man once.

Then it was over. Only one of the Norsemen had been killed, but all sixteen who had faced them lay in their own blood and the heathens made short work of any still living. Except for Griffin. They dragged him through the gore to the man with the piercing eyes and the wolf's head brooch. To Sigurd.

'Before you die, you will see your village swallowed by flames,' the jarl growled, pointing to the houses whose hearth smoke still leaked through the thatch as though it was just another day, 'and in the afterlife you will know that you brought death to your people.'

'The Devil piss in your skull,' Griffin managed. Skin and hair flopped horribly from the side of his head and I saw the broken bone beneath. Blood ran down his face like threads of a web, dripping from his short beard. But his body would not die. 'You . . . will beg . . . Christ's forgiveness at the coming of judgement,' he threatened in a dry voice. 'I swear it.' Brave Griffin smiled as he said the words.

Sigurd laughed. 'Your god is weak. A woman's god. They say he favours cowards and whores.' The other heathens scoffed and shook their heads as they wiped their gore-covered blades on dead men. 'You are not weak, Englishman,' Sigurd went on. 'You killed a great warrior today.' He glanced at the dead Norseman, who had been stripped of his mail so that he looked no fiercer than any young man of Abbotsend, but for the many scars carved into his white skin. Sigurd frowned. 'Why do you follow this White Christ, Englishman?' he asked. Griffin's eyelids grew heavy and I hoped he would pass out. The Norseman shrugged. 'I give you to Óðin so that in death you will see a true god. A god who can make his enemies run from a battle back to their women in shame.' He then commanded his men to search the houses for booty, making sure to look in the hearth ash and in cooking vessels, even the thatch itself, for hidden treasures. The heathens did this quickly, fearing the arrival of the local levy, and began carrying bags of coin, tools, cloth, weapons and cured legs of lamb and pork over the hill to their ships. There were some screams, but not many. Most of the women had escaped into the woods and would not yet know their men lay butchered. I had seen Alwunn's father killed, but I knew she and her mother would have had the sense to get away. Poor Alwunn. But I had never loved her, and I am sure she did not love me.

I knelt by Ealhstan, waiting for the heathens to notice us, for then they would kill us along with Griffin. I dragged my arm across my lip and looked at the bright blood, realizing that I no longer trembled. The carnage I had witnessed had somehow cured me of fear. I gritted my teeth. Griffin must despise me for what I had done, but he would not see me cower at the end.

The Norsemen gathered seasoned timbers and built a pyre on which they laid the warrior whom Griffin had killed. One man took a spear and scratched a circle in the earth and dragged Griffin into it by his bloody hair. By now he was barely alive. The first thatch roofs broke into patches of flame and the dead Norseman's pyre began to crackle as the old grey-bearded warrior with bones plaited in his hair invoked their gods in a dry, low voice. A raven cried in the old ash tree, its head jerking hungrily as it watched the work of men, and I knew it was the same bird I had seen the previous daybreak by the watchtower above the beach. It opened its heavy beak and fluffed its throat feathers so that they stuck out like spikes. I looked back to Griffin and my stomach squeezed warm vomit into my throat.

Ealhstan groaned, trying to stand, but I pulled him down. 'Keep still, old man,' I hissed. Half of his face had swollen into a livid purple bruise. He sniffed the air. 'It's burning,' I confirmed, my eyes too full of Griffin's mutilation to be drawn to the flames now crackling angrily. 'They're doing something to Griffin. It's the Devil's work, Ealhstan.'

Griffin moaned pitifully, his ebbing life revived by horrible pain. Ealhstan grabbed for my arm, then flapped his arms, his rheumy eyes wild. 'The Eagle,' I breathed and those wide eyes said, *Don't watch, you fool! Christ save us, don't watch.*

But I did watch. I watched as the old godi used his hand axe to hack into Griffin's back. Again and again he smashed the ribs away from the spine and my world was filled with a proud man's screams. The two Norsemen holding Griffin down were spattered with his blood as he writhed in agony. Then the heathen godi hooked clear the last of the ribs, exposing the meat within, and his hands plunged into the gore and pulled out Griffin's lungs, laying one on each side of his ruined back like glistening red wings.

'They've opened his back,' I said to the old man, who had turned away. Then I lurched forward and retched, but my stomach was empty and there was just dry pain. 'The Blood Eagle,' I murmured, horrified to see in the flesh what I had only heard men talk of in whispers. Ealhstan crossed himself and began to make a low moan in his throat, as Griffin's screams became horrible, liquid gurgles lost amongst the crackle of burning wood and thatch and the roar of flame.

The godi stood and raised his arms to the sky.

'Óðin All-Father!' he called, shaking his head so that the bones in his hair rattled. 'Receive this warrior slain by your wolves! Let him sit at your mead bench so the White Christ cannot take him for a slave! Óðin Far-Wanderer! This eagle is a gift from Jarl Sigurd who rides the waves and seeks glory in your name.'

Sigurd stared at me then, at my blood-eye, and gripped the small wooden amulet on the thong round his neck. It was a man's face, but one eye was missing.

'Kill the old man,' he commanded with a flick of his hand, 'but not the boy. Bring him to *Serpent*.'

'He is a carpenter, lord!' I shouted in the heathen language. 'Do not kill him!' The bearded Norseman

64

I had first seen at the prow of the dragon ship shoved me aside and raised his sword to strike Ealhstan. 'He is skilled! Look, lord!' I said, drawing my eating knife from my belt and offering it up to Sigurd. The warrior above me snatched the knife away and glanced at it carelessly before flinging it at Sigurd's feet. Then he turned back to Ealhstan and grimaced.

'Wait, Olaf!' Sigurd said, examining the knife. Like the pagan blade Ealhstan had returned to me the previous night this one was short and simple, but its hilt was carved into the shape of a porpoise. I had never seen such a creature, but as a boy Ealhstan had found one washed up on the shingle and he had made the hilt from memory.

'It is bone from the red deer, lord,' I said, hoping that Sigurd's thumb stroking the white hilt was a sign he appreciated the workmanship. In truth, I had seen Ealhstan make much finer hilts for those who paid for them. Still, the knife was a gift and I cherished it. Only now did I realize that Ealhstan had given it to me to replace the heathen one he had found round my neck. Perhaps it had been his way of helping me begin a new life with him.

'It is skilled work,' Sigurd admitted, scratching his beard. The man named Olaf, whom the Norsemen called Uncle, opened his mouth to protest, but Sigurd stopped him with a raised hand. 'There is an empty bench at the oars now, Olaf,' he said, glancing at the warrior whose pale corpse was blistering wickedly as the searching flames licked it. The fire was eating through the seasoned timber and the man's hair crackled and burned brightly, giving off a foul-smelling smoke. 'Bring them both,' Sigurd said, turning his back on me.

And so we were dragged towards the sea and the waiting dragon ships which sat low in the water, heavy with the booty taken from the people of Abbotsend. The Norsemen took their places and began in unison to pull on the oars, dragging the sea past the slender hulls until a steady rhythm was set. And I looked towards the shore and breathed the yellow smoke of a burning village.

# CHAPTER THREE

I WAS MISERABLE. NUMB. EALHSTAN AND I SAT HUDDLED AT the stern by the Norseman at the tiller who grinned wolfishly whenever I caught his eye, as though he was amused that I had betrayed my people. And even though the folk of Abbotsend had hated me, and though it had never felt like my home, I believed I might have damned my own soul to drift for ever with the black smoke from burned homes. Ealhstan would not look at me and this made my chest ache. He had stood by me against Wulfweard, but now he blamed me, I was sure of it, and so I let the dark mood spread like a stain between us as I looked up at the sky, noting how much more infinite it appeared from the sea. Having burned away the morning's mist, the sun sat above us like the lord and judge of men and it seemed impossible that in the time it had taken to ascend its throne, a village had been wiped from the earth.

As I breathed in the heady mix of dried fish, pine and tar, the heathens laughed and joked and rowed as though nothing unusual had happened. Each man sat facing us on a chest containing his belongings, and whilst some stared at me as though wondering what I was, others would not meet my eye. *You are alive because they fear you, Osric,* I said to myself. *Men fear your Devil's eye, and these are men, aren't they?* So I closed my good eye, leaving the blood-filled one staring out at the Norsemen until some of them looked away. I tried to make them believe I could see into their thoughts and I think some of them feared that I could.

The dragon skimmed through the waves, her ropes and planks creaking rhythmically, and something grew in my stomach, writhing, encouraged by the sea's pitch and roll. Before long, I vomited bitter, green liquid and feared my stomach was tearing apart. My misery deepened still further with the cramps and dizziness.

At least we never sailed out of sight of land and this alone was the slender rein on my despair. We would aim out to sea to avoid sandbanks and rocks, but always headed inland again.

'We are sailing west, Ealhstan,' I said at the end of the day with the warmth of the falling sun on my face, 'which means they're not going home yet. These men come from the sea road far to the north.'

Ealhstan mumbled something in his throat that sounded like bastards and plunder and stinking, heathen pigs. And like him I knew there would be more death.

Later, as the Norsemen shared out their spoils, I caught sight of the treasures they kept amidships beneath oiled skins. Much of it was that which they had sold at Abbotsend but taken back after the fight:

cream-coloured ivory and reindeer antler, brown furs and chests brimming with brooches, yellow amber, whetstones and silver coin. I saw the necklace Griffin had bought for his wife, too.

'They're rich men, Ealhstan, these heathens,' I said, desperate for the old man to look me in the eye. I was beginning to wonder if his empty, withdrawn stare was due in part to the beating he had taken, and, though it shames me to say it, I hoped it was, because it tore my heart to think he hated me for what I had done. The swelling across his face was yellowing now. 'The ivory alone must be worth a fortune.'

He flicked a wrist and grunted.

'You think they pillaged every last trinket, don't you?' I said. 'From other villages long since burned to black ash.'

Without looking at me, Ealhstan made a fist and stared out to sea, shaking his head. And I knew what he was thinking. Men like these would sail off the lip of the world for a fistful of silver.

'How's your head, old man?' I asked. One of his watery eyes was squeezed almost shut by the swelling. He waved the question away as though to say he'd had worse. 'Old men bruise like apples,' I said as he prodded the swelling gingerly. 'I know, Ealhstan – if you were younger you would have cleaved one or two of these whoresons in two.' I gave him a wry smile. 'Split them like oak.'

He batted the words away with a grimace and I looked out across the waves but saw only the faces of butchered men. I rubbed my chin, touching my swollen lip. It still throbbed with each heartbeat. 'The bow let us down,' I said. 'The string was rotten.'

Ealhstan turned and our eyes locked. Got the luck of the damned, you and me both, they said, and now we're sitting here chewing our own vomit. Then he gave a gap-toothed grin and I glanced at the Norseman who had a piece of one of my arrow shafts still jutting from his shoulder. He rowed as though it was not there, but now and then I caught him grimace with pain. *They might be bastard heathens,* I thought, *but they are proud.*

It was early evening when a warning voice called clear and strong from the other ship. It is strange how sound carries across water and a man an arrow-shot away sounds as though he's nearby. Sigurd picked his way to the prow where his shipmaster Olaf stood shielding his eyes against the sun, looking landward. At the top of a great cliff a knot of riders peered out to sea, their spears pointing to the sky. Edgar the reeve must have learned of Abbotsend's fate and sent men to track the heathens along the coast, which they could do well enough on horseback along well-used paths whilst we must make do with a mere breath of a breeze. Sure enough, when we rounded a great chalk bluff, the scouts appeared on the west side and Sigurd cursed. It meant that he would be unable to seek a sheltered bay for the night, let alone more plunder.

Ealhstan sneered at the Norsemen as though he considered them swine with no stomach for a fair fight. Mark me and mark me well, his raised finger said, these shit-filled heathens blow more hot air than a

70

happy cow. He turned his head towards the steersman and tried to spit but there was just a dry popping sound and the Norseman hawked and spat a thick wad over the top strake in response. Ealhstan mumbled another insult, then hunkered down, wrapping his brown cloak around him and rubbing his empty belly.

'I'm hungry, too,' I moaned, scratching my ribs. 'Puked my innards out this morning. Feels like mice gnawing my guts now.' But instead of sympathy I saw blame in the old man's eyes; blame for bringing him a horde of blood-loving heathens instead of a basket full of mackerel. God help your wandering soul, was what his eyes said, and I wished the man still had his tongue so that I did not have to choose the words myself.

As a young man Ealhstan had agreed to be an oath helper to a man accused of theft. The accuser was rich and so one night three men tore out Ealhstan's tongue. Without a man to speak up for him, the accused was found guilty and died in thrall to the rich man. And so Ealhstan was mute, and now his rheumy eyes and my own guilt spoke for him.

Now he closed those eyes and shook his head, murmuring to himself, and when I looked at the stick-thin carpenter with his swollen face and his wispy white hair floating on the breeze I felt ashamed for being afraid when a mute old man could be so defiant.

With the arrival of a stiff northerly wind, Sigurd gave the order to raise the great woollen sail, allowing his men to stow their oars and rest. As the faded red sheet bulged, the Norsemen loosened their shoulders and necks and stretched their aching arms. Some of them took dice from their chests, or wooden figures half carved. Others sharpened blades or curled up to sleep. Two handed out dried salted fish and chunks of cheese, and a few cursed, boasting that they would rather make landfall and light a fire and eat fresh meat, even if it meant fighting the English.

As the sun fell to the sea, I sat at the stern, hugging my knees. The seasickness had weakened me, my stomach was empty and I wondered if the heathens would at last come for us, their blades eager to finish what they had begun at Abbotsend. I ran a calloused hand along one of the vessel's oak ribs, my fingers following the grain of the wood to the point where the rib met a hull strake as though the two smooth timbers were one. 'It's beautiful work, Ealhstan, you can't deny it,' I said. He huffed, then frowned and nodded reluctantly. 'Men used to call them surf dragons, least that's what Griffin told me once.' He nodded again. 'Surf dragons,' I whispered under my breath. I had asked Griffin about the name and he had laughed and said that we like to frighten ourselves half the time. He had shaken his head. Good oak is all they are, he had said. Good oak and pine worked by men who know the adze as they know the sea.

'Did you ever see one, Ealhstan?' I asked. He shook his head and raised his eyebrows as though he had never thought to find himself riding the grey sea in one either. Some came across the sea when Griffin was a boy. They say those were the first. At least that was when the priests began telling their stories and filling men's hearts with fear and their heads with nightmares. The Devil's ministers had come to defile God's houses and shit on saints' relics. That's what they told us. So men had sharpened their swords and made limewood shields, but the heathens never came. Not to Abbotsend. 'They're here now, old man,' I said, watching the Norsemen and wondering if Christ was planning some terrible vengeance on them for the death of His children at Abbotsend.

A wave broke over the top strake, drenching us. Ealhstan coughed and I wiped my eyes and ran my fingers along the smooth oak planks again. Griffin had been wrong. This surf dragon was more than oak and pine, much more. It rode the sea as though the waves were its subjects. And it was beautiful. My mind carried me back to the days I had spent with the oaks in the forest, always searching for the longest, curving limbs even though we had no use for them. How many such branches had been hewn and shaped to make Jarl Sigurd's ships? How many men had laboured, felling trees, splitting timber, drilling holes and tarring joints? I noticed a drip of tar that had set just below a dark knot in the strake at my shoulder. It looked like a tear beneath an eye and I picked it off with a nail, bringing it to my nose. It smelled sweet.

'Come here, boy,' Sigurd called. He stood on the mast support, one arm round the thick pole as the wind that rounded the sail blew his yellow hair across his face. I did not move. If old Ealhstan was not afraid, I would not be afraid either. 'The fishes must eat too,' Sigurd said, his voice edged with threat. 'But they would find you a sorry meal, I think. Come here, Red Eye.'

I got to my feet and stumbled into a Norseman who cursed and shoved me away as though he'd been burned. My legs had not yet learned the rhythm of the sea. I tried to bend them with the ship's roll. 'Do you know who this is?' Sigurd asked, tugging the small carving of a one-eyed man which hung at his throat.

'It is Óðin, the chief of your gods, lord,' I replied, remembering how Sigurd's godi had drawn Griffin's lungs out of his back. 'The Blood Eagle was done for him. A heathen sacrifice.'

'How do you know of Óðin All-Father?' he asked, his eyes narrowed. 'Your people worship the White Christ. The Christians shout that our gods are dead. Yet we kill the English and take their silver. We go where we please and your Christ does nothing to stop us. How can our gods be dead?' He clenched a fist. 'We are the spearhead of our people. We are the first. Do you think we could cross the angry northern sea if our gods were dead and could not watch over us?'

I shrugged. 'Wulfweard our priest says those who worship false gods are the Devil's turds.' But Wulfweard *was* dead, killed by the man standing before me. 'That is what he used to say,' I said.

'That fat man with the cross who tried to poison me? That red-faced pig's bladder?' I nodded. 'Did you like him?' Sigurd asked, as though he'd tasted something foul.

'No, lord,' I replied. 'He was a toad's arsehole.'

Sigurd nodded. 'It was a good thing to kill the priest. He talked too much.' He smiled. 'I have not known many Christians, but all of them were in love with their own voices. The toad's arsehole said you are from Satan. Satan is your devious god? Like our Loki? Loki weaves more schemes than a hall full of women.'

'Satan is not a god. There is only one God,' I said.

Sigurd laughed loudly. 'Fish puke!' he exclaimed. 'There are many gods, boy!' He waved at the sky. 'How could one god keep watch over so many men? There would be chaos! One god?' The other Norsemen laughed too, shaking their heads so that their plaits bounced as they played their games or worked on their carvings.

'Are you from this Satan? Have you seen him?' Sigurd asked. A wave broke over the bow, drenching a Norseman to the amusement of the others. The man cursed. 'Asgot my godi says I should kill you. I doubt he knows why, but that one's knife is seldom far from his hand.' I glanced at the old grey-beard, the speaker for the gods, who sat cross-legged away from the others. The bones tied in his plaits rattled as he cast a handful of stones on to a wooden board. 'But we are not foxes, hey? We don't kill for the simple pleasure in it.'

'I am not from Satan, lord,' I said. 'I have never butchered a man. I have never opened his back and hacked at the bones whilst he lived. Even the fox is not so cruel.'

Sigurd smiled, twisting his yellow beard between finger and thumb.

'I don't think you are from Satan,' he said eventually. 'You are from Óðin All-Father. Even Asgot says this is possible. Your eye is made from blood.' He pointed to the empty eye socket on the small carving at his neck.

'See here. Óðin traded an eye for a drink from Mirmir's Well of Wisdom. Do you understand me, boy? Even the gods do not know everything. Some, like the Far-Wanderer, crave wisdom.' I nodded, my stomach churning now that I stood, and I hoped the bile would not rise as vomit again. 'But Óðin is the Lord of War, too,' Sigurd went on, 'he is Lord of the Slain.' I touched my blood-eye as I looked up at this warrior who seemed to believe I was something other than what I was. 'What is your name, English boy?' he asked.

'Osric, lord,' I said, noticing crimson spots on his brown, weather-beaten face. Griffin's blood.

'There is war in you, Osric,' the Norseman said, absently scratching his beard and bending a knee in time with the ship's roll. 'For this reason I have let you live.' Sigurd's free hand fell to rest on his sword's hilt. 'There is war in you,' he repeated. 'And death too.' Then he turned and jumped up to the raised stern to signal to the other ship, ordering his men to look out for a safe place to moor overnight, for the danger of striking rocks was greater now in the failing light. The men on the cliff tops might know we headed west, but it would take them longer to cover the difficult ground than for us to sail round peninsulas, so Sigurd could risk mooring. Besides, those levy men would have to be fools to pick a fight with these Norsemen. And they were not fools. They were mostly farmers, craftsmen and traders. They were husbands and fathers. I had seen the Norsemen's slaughter. The memory of it flashed in my mind like fish scales beneath the waves.

'Hey, Uncle, it seems Njörd is watching over us

76

again!' Sigurd called, his teeth glinting like fangs in the weak yellow light cast by the cow's horn lantern he had lit so that his other ship would not lose us in the dark.

'That is why I would sail to Asgard itself with you, Sigurd the Lucky!' Olaf shouted from the sternpost, a great smile swelling his cheeks. He leant to pick up a coiled rope, one end of which he passed through a smooth rock before making a thick knot. 'I've sailed with many men, some fine, some fools, but you, Sigurd, you have the gods' favour.' They were happy because the wind that had filled the sail earlier had now died away, giving Olaf no problems in sinking the weight to test the depth of a small, rock-strewn cove. More important, there was little danger of being blown towards the rocks. Sigurd himself had spotted the bay and though it did not penetrate far inland, it would protect both vessels from the open sea.

'The Englishmen can bring their spears and their bows and we can be gone before they sink an arrow within a hundred strokes,' Sigurd announced happily to his men. He called to the captain of the other ship that we would be staying for the night, then slapped a bear of a man on the back, sharing some joke about the English with him.

'You hear that, lad?' Olaf asked me as he lowered the ship's iron anchor into the calm water, steadily feeding the rope through his hands. 'We can snatch this up and put out to sea in the time it takes to piss,' he said with a smile. Olaf was the oldest man aboard, except for the godi and Ealhstan, and he clearly loved being at sea. 'So you can tell the old man not to waste his time praying to that White Christ of yours.' He made the sign of the cross mockingly. 'You're on Sigurd's ship now, lad, and Sigurd is as lucky as a cock in a henhouse.'

'He's a cruel bastard to take an old man from his home,' I muttered in the Norseman's language, but Ealhstan gnashed his teeth and pointed to my mouth, suddenly snatching at something invisible, and I realized the gesture's meaning. He would rather rip out my tongue, making me mute like him, than listen to me using the heathens' words. To Ealhstan it was another betrayal and it burned my heart to see the disappointment in his eyes.

'Is he always so cheerful?' Olaf asked, nodding at the old man with a grin that revealed several dark teeth. 'Thór knows I have never met a happy Christian, apart from a man I met in Ireland once,' he said, his bushy eyebrows arched, 'and I doubt he was still laughing when he sobered up. Not with that headache. Drank like a fish, that one.'

Next day, Sigurd the Lucky put me to the oar. A Norseman had been killed at Abbotsend and I took his place. There might have been enough of a breeze to push us along, but I think Sigurd wanted to keep his men strong and hungry, the way a hunter starves his dog to make it more eager for the prey. Whatever the reason, it was relentless work pulling the blade through the water in time with the others and soon my arms and shoulders burned and my heart felt as though it would burst. Sweat coursed down my face and I could only brush at it with a shoulder. My eyes stung and my tunic was soaked. After a long time, the screaming pain dulled to an ache and the sweat dried up, and I found a strange peace in the monotonous rhythm. I lost myself in the motion of the stroke. Eventually I faltered and then they made old Ealhstan grip the stave too, and blisters swelled and burst on his skilled hands.

'A man does not need a tongue to row, hey, English-man?' one of the Norsemen said in broken English, leaning back with the stroke. Ealhstan did not even grunt a riposte, his lungs having no breath to waste as we pulled on the oar, struggling to match the Norse-men's backbreaking rhythm.

Over the next few days we hugged the coast, gaining shelter at night and making slow progress by day. *Serpent* and *Fjord-Elk* followed the shore like predators on the prowl and though it seemed to me that their crews kept one eye on the look-out for an easy target, I also felt that they were simply happy to be on the move. The Norsemen still feared making landfall in case the English had gathered a great number of spearmen, and Sigurd was content to wait until there was no longer sign of those who tracked us from the cliff tops and the shore. There was little wind, but Sigurd was in no rush and he harnessed what breeze there was, letting it push us westward. Eventually, we stopped seeing spearmen against the skyline and riders on the shingle, and yet I would still devour the coastline with my eyes for any sign of an English levy, and I would imagine these proud heathens dying beneath English blades. Sometimes, I thought I saw men peering out to sea, but they turned out to be rocks or trees and once even a sheep. In those days I learned that your eyes will fashion form from hope, the way old Ealhstan made something beautiful from rough wood.

One grey morning, a steady drizzle fell unfelt on to my sweat-drenched clothes as I peered up at the grassy bluff, lost in the rhythm of the stroke. My palms had hardened like seasoned beech and the blisters had become knot-like calluses. I started when Ealhstan grabbed my ankle. He was exhausted and leaning against the chest on which I sat rowing with all my strength so that he might rest. He pointed landward, put two fingers to his eyes and shook his head.

'You think I'm a fool, don't you, old man? Looking for something that's not there,' I said. He nodded, then resumed picking his teeth after a small breakfast of hard bread and dried codfish. At least the Norsemen were feeding us. Without food we could not row. 'The women must have told Reeve Edgar we were taken,' I said weakly, 'when they saw we were not among the dead.'

He cupped a pair of imaginary breasts and made a wailing sound in his throat.

'You're right,' I said. 'They'll be mourning their dead men, not worrying about the two of us.'

He frowned then and pointed at my oar, gesticulating for me to keep up with the heathens. I leant back, pulling hard on the stave, suddenly aware that I had come close to snaring the oars. You didn't have to watch the others to know if you were losing time, for you would hear the solitary blade hit the water behind the rest. 'If you stopped distracting me, old man . . .' I huffed, gulping air as I leant forward to pull again.

He shrugged his slight shoulders and pointed to my blood-eye. Then he walked two fingers through the air and pretended to spit. Folk will happily walk in the mire to avoid me, was what he meant. Then he scratched his bristly chin and pulled a sour face as if to say, And as for me . . . He clenched his swollen fists, popping several knuckles, then made the sign for cups and platters. 'So what if folk know your hands are not what they once were?' I said. 'You're an old man. They won't expect you to work their wood for ever.' But this brought a bitter smile to Ealhstan's lips, for I had struck the nail clean. He was an old man and I was an outsider. Why would anyone come for us, even if they knew where to find us? He pointed to my blood-eye and nodded towards the heathen in front of us, and I knew what his words would have been if his mouth still held a tongue: Keep fixing these bastards with that unnatural eye of yours, lad. Put some fear in their heathen bellies.

'Sigurd believes I'm from Óðin All-Father, their chief god,' I said, matching the Norsemen's stroke again. 'He says that Óðin put me in his way for a purpose hidden like a knife in a sheath.'

Ealhstan grunted, rapped his knuckles against his head and sprinkled something invisible across the deck, his way of saying I had wood dust for brains. Then he pointed at Jarl Sigurd, made the same gesture and touched the ship's top strake and banged his fists together. 'You think Sigurd is a fool and I am a fool to listen to him,' I said, 'and you think we might as well jump overboard, for a fool is likely to run his ship

81

aground before long.' I shook my head, and the old man grimaced, turning to look out across the sea once more.

But Sigurd did not wreck *Serpent*, and neither did his shipmaster Glum wreck *Fjord-Elk*, the other ship. When there was good wind, their great square sails pushed us westward, and when there was none, the Norsemen rowed as though they had been born at the oar. At night they fished and played games, sang, drank ale and arm-wrestled. A huge red-haired man called Svein sat for the most part looking miserable because no one would challenge him. But what I noticed most about the Norsemen was how much they laughed. They laughed at the smallest things, such as when Olaf complained about toothache or when his white-haired son Eric muttered a girl's name in his sleep. I noticed too that they were younger than I had first thought. Their faces were weather-beaten and their beards unkempt, but in their blue eyes I saw men in their prime, and this new familiarity made it harder to recall the savagery that I knew bristled within them, beneath the wind-burned, salty skin. Now of course I know that it is the young who are capable of the most terrible cruelty. A young man will kill without a second thought, then rejoice in the slaughter. But time will often smother the flames of his heart and the older man is more likely to sheathe his blade, seeing in his opponent his own son or his daughter's husband. These Norse were young men and laughter or no they were dangerous. They were killers.

'If we're lucky it will pass to the east before it breaks,'

Eric said. The youngest Norseman's face was turned up to the blackening sky so that his white hair fell straight, and from where I sat at my oar port he looked afraid.

'Not this time, son,' Olaf said flatly. 'I doubt even Sigurd can make Njörd smile today.' Olaf turned to me. 'Njörd governs the flights of the winds,' he called, sweeping an arm westward. 'He controls sea and flame . . .' he grinned sourly, 'and he is in a foul mood today.' Every man aboard was staring up at the evil-looking black cloud sitting so low in the sky that I could have shot an arrow into its belly to release the deluge. Round its edge was a halo of brilliant silver light, but we were far from its edge. An angry wind began to slap the woollen sail and rattle the shields that the Norsemen had mounted on *Serpent*'s sides that morning to warn off another dragon ship headed east on the horizon.

'We're in the storm's maw, Ealhstan,' I said, touching *Serpent*'s top strake and wondering how she would fare in the chaos of a violent storm. The old man was gripping one of the sheet blocks, his knuckles bone white. 'And we'll soon be in its belly,' I said. I had never been at sea in a storm and I was terrified.

'Next time, we'll sacrifice a younger bull before we leave the fjord, Asgot,' Sigurd shouted to his godi. He stood at the ship's prow, one hand gripping the neck of the dragon staring dully out to sea with its red eyes. He grimaced. 'That sack of shit Haeston sold me was a threadbare old beast.'

'Only a fool would insult a god like Njörd with a poor beast,' Asgot replied accusingly. 'Anger one of the kinder, less powerful lords of Asgard if you must.

83

Baldr perhaps. Freyja even, if you don't mind your cock shrivelling and dropping off,' he said, clutching his groin and shaking his head so that the bones in his hair rattled. 'But never Njörd, Sigurd. Never the Lord of the Sea.'

Sigurd bent his legs as *Serpent* rose and dipped. 'I swear old Njörd's appetite grows, godi,' he said, watching the heavens. 'Furl the sail, Uncle! Let's wet the oars and take her out there.' He nodded southward. Since the previous night, the coastline had promised only jagged rocks and sheer cliffs, and if the wind turned to come up from the south both ships would be tossed against them and broken. And so we gripped the oars and bent our backs, heading out to sea against a swell that kept dropping away so suddenly that my oar bit only the white hair that was spreading across the waves.

Night was falling and Sigurd had to make a decision that would seal our fates. We had to get away from the rocky coast, but row too far and we could lose our way, for the cloud would veil the stars and we would sail blind.

The reefing ropes whipped left and right as though the wind came from all sides at once. My oar's blade struck the white crest of a wave as I glanced over my shoulder at the distant cliffs, before *Serpent*'s bow rocked into the sky. She gave a great creaking sigh that seemed to say, Don't look back, Osric, there's just us now. No land, no safety, just wood and nails and flesh.

'Any further and we'll lose sight of land!' Olaf shouted above the swirling wind that whistled through the oar ports. 'There's no way of knowing which way the storm is heading, Sigurd! We'll have to ride Rán's daughters!' Rán's daughters were the waves, and as *Serpent*'s prow struck, they leapt across her top strakes to slap our faces and sting our eyes.

Sigurd frowned, salt water dripping from his hair and beard. The wrong decision could see his men drowned. But if they were afraid, they showed little sign of it. Some invoked their chosen gods. Black Floki challenged Njörd Lord of the Sea to do his worst, but the men around him cursed and told him to shut his big mouth. We rowed hard, as though muscle and sinew could challenge the might of wind and wave. But water was pouring in at the oar ports and the oars themselves were in danger of snapping under the swell's pressure. Rain and seawater drenched us, my face stung from the salt and I found it impossible to row in time with the others.

A great crack of thunder filled the world. 'Enough, lads! Get the oars in!' Sigurd called. 'Eric, tell Glum we're going to ride this one out,' he shouted, pointing to the oil lamp in its hollow horn sheath. Eric nodded, wiping rain from his brow as he took up the lamp and stumbled over to *Serpent*'s seaward side, grabbing hold of the sheet to steady himself. We stowed the oars, plugged our ports with leather bungs and prepared for Njörd's fury. Suddenly I was jealous of Eric, who had been given a task that would steer his thoughts from fear. 'Take in the shields!' Sigurd shouted, and I stood just as *Serpent*'s dragonhead prow lurched skywards. I stumbled into a chest and was flung back, striking my head on an oak rib.

Beside me Ealhstan made a long guttural sound as

another peal of thunder split the night. He clung to *Serpent*'s top strake, already looking like a drowned man. Something hit me in the chest as I lay in a sloshing pool of seawater. It was a length of tar-stinking rope.

'Tie the old man down or his bones will be washed overboard!' Svein the Red shouted as he staggered, unrolling the spare sail to help cover the small open hold at the base of the mast. 'And have a word with Óðin All-Father!' the red-bearded giant added with no hint of a smile. 'I don't swim well.'

The wind whipped the white hair from the waves and the ship creaked and moaned at the sea. I stumbled to Ealhstan, whose legs were trembling with the effort of fighting the ship's roll, and put my arm round him. 'Come, old man, you're not getting off this surf dragon without me,' I muttered in his ear, and he nodded and together we blundered to the mast. I sat him on the keelson, blinking through the stinging spray, and threw the rope around him and the mast. When I had made the knot, the old man put a hand to my cheek. 'We'll get through this,' I shouted and gripped his thin wrist. Bile had risen hot in my chest and my head swam with sickness.

Sigurd had unfurled the great square sail and he and Olaf and three others fought with bowline and forestay and backstay, moving in harmony with the ship so that it seemed they might remain standing even if *Serpent* capsized. They were trying to harness the wind rather than oppose it, but they were losing. I wiped my eyes against the driving rain, struggling to see *Fjord-Elk*. She was sometimes thirty feet above us, then thirty

86

below, her crew like wooden figures carved into the ship's deck. She looked like a god's toy.

'No, Uncle!' Sigurd roared into the wind. 'We can't win this one! Get her sail down before we're tipped out like bad mead.'

'Aye, she'll tear to shreds!' Olaf agreed as he fought with the sail. And so, with the sail down and no oars in the water, we were helpless.

'Sigurd's given *Serpent* to the fate maidens!' a man named Aslak called over his shoulder, clinging to a sheet block. 'The Norns will craft our future now.' Each man gripped his chest of belongings and the ship's top strake, waiting to see what future, if any, the Norns of fate had woven for him. Each man except Sigurd. He stumbled across *Serpent*'s deck, dipping his hand into a sodden leather bag and giving each man a coin, which they tucked deep inside their clothing with a nod of thanks. He passed by Ealhstan and came to me and I looked up at him as the wind howled and the thunder roared in my ears.

'I give them gold in case tonight we sleep in Rán's kingdom at the bottom of the sea!' he shouted with a grimace that could have been a smile. 'She will only receive those with gold and it seems she is casting her nets today. Rán is a greedy bitch, hey, Asgot!' he called to the old godi, who shouted something back and threw his hands heavenward, causing Sigurd to grin mischievously. Sigurd suddenly gripped the top strake as *Serpent* rode up a great wave, its dragonhead nodding to the gods before plunging down towards cruel Rán's kingdom and her hall lit by dead men's gold. 'Here, boy.' He removed the amulet of one-eyed Óðin from round his neck and passed the leather thong over my head. 'Now remind the All-Father who you are!' he shouted. 'Tell him to spare us so that we might do great things in his name!' His blue eyes and the white foaming crests of Rán's nine daughters were the only colours in a dark, threatening world. 'If Óðin listens, I will free you!' he shouted. 'If not, I'll give you to Njörd!'

I was drenched and trembling and I did not move. I touched the carving round my neck and wondered if Christ or His angels could see me wearing the heathen figure. Christ sees all, Wulfweard had said.

'I can't do it, lord!' I exclaimed, swallowing the vomit in my throat and grabbing *Serpent*'s top strake with both hands. I spat the foul taste into the sea. 'Óðin will not listen to me!' I barked. On steady legs, Sigurd drew his long knife and held it up for all his men to see. I stared at the blade, knowing it was about to cut my throat, but still my limbs would not obey me. His blue eyes bored into me and then he turned, took Ealhstan's head in one great hand and held the knife beneath the old man's chin. 'Leave him!' I yelled and grabbed Sigurd's wrist and instead of knocking me back down he stared at me. 'You won't harm him!' I said, clutching the wrist as though to let go was to die.

Sigurd blinked slowly and gave a slight nod and I took this to mean he would not kill Ealhstan and so I let go of his arm and stepped back, somehow keeping my footing as a great wave washed over me, burning my eyes with its cargo of salt and making me retch.

When he had lowered the knife I turned and picked my way to *Serpent*'s dragonhead prow, where I stood with one arm round the beast. Then I called to the sky.

'Óðin All-Father! Lord of the North! Save us from this storm! Remember me, Óðin! Remember me!' I don't know where the words came from, but I hurled them into the teeth of the storm, into the wall of whipping wind that swallowed them down. It ate my words as though I was nothing, and yet my defiance drew hot blood through my veins and stilled my trembling. 'Save us, Óðin! Save us and we will honour you!' *Serpent* reached the summit of a giant wall of water and then fell so steeply that she almost flipped over. I still clutched the wooden carving of the All-Father, holding it aloft, and as the ship righted herself I was flung forward over the prow, but I grabbed the top strake, and hung chest deep in the freezing water until something grabbed my shoulder and hauled me up, flinging me into the ship as though I were a codfish.

'Ha! Rán's daughters spat you back out, boy!' Svein the Red roared, beaming from ear to ear. 'Englishmen must taste foul! Those bitches will usually take anyone they can get their claws into!' I crouched in the hollow of the ship's bow, terrified and appalled, because I believed the Lord Christ had tried to drown me for invoking a heathen god. I shivered. Then I vomited, spewing up warm seawater on to *Serpent*'s seasoned timber hull.

On hands and knees I crawled to the mast, to Ealhstan, afraid that if I stood Christ or Njörd or any other god might see me and fling me back into the cold sea. And there I sat as the old carpenter scoured me with eyes as cold as opals. Water dripped from his top lip and he spat it away in disgust.

'I had to do it,' I said. 'What choice did I have?' But Ealhstan shook his head and closed his eyes and though it could have been to rid them of stinging salt water, I believed it was so he did not have to see me; me who had prayed to a heathen god and suspended my soul above Hell's fire.

Then Olaf pulled a dry fur from the hold and gave it to me. 'Here, boy, you did well,' he said, frowning as though wondering what I was. Behind him I saw Sigurd. He had two hands on *Serpent*'s top strake, his face turned up to the night sky. And he was smiling.

The storm broke. The low black cloud which had been the belly of the beast split apart to reveal a forest of stars. The seas fell and the stinging rain died, and for a time I feared the elements were simply regrouping to return and finish us off. After all the noise it was eerily quiet aboard *Serpent*. The men's low voices and the rhythmic creak of seasoned oak replaced the fury of wind, rain and sea. I tied back my hair with a length of tarred twine and sat at my place on *Serpent*'s port side, gripping her top strake with white hands and looking out across the grey sea.

'Don't worry, little brother. He's had his fun with us,' Sigtrygg said, slapping my back as he bent to scoop up water with a thin-lipped pail. Pools sat in the hollows of the sail that covered the hold, and our feet sloshed through water so that half Sigurd's men were busy bailing. 'Old Njörd will leave us alone now.'

Sigtrygg was a fierce-looking warrior whose face was ruined by lumpy scars, though it was clear he had never been handsome.

'How do you know?' I asked him, daring to take one hand from the hull. I found the smell of wood and tar somehow comforting, now that *Serpent* had fought for us and won. She had ridden the storm and I felt grateful to her.

'You're never safe at sea, Englishman,' Njal called from the steerboard side. His grin parted his fair beard through which he was tugging a comb. 'But that is what makes it so much fun!' The grin became a scowl as the comb stuck in his salt-matted hair and refused to budge.

Sigtrygg flung another pailful over the side, the water reflecting the starlight before splashing into the sea. He bent again. 'Somewhere some other mean bastard who thought it would be fine to sacrifice a half-dead bull is having a bad night,' he said, straightening. 'So long as it's not us, I couldn't give a fart.'

'We'll give Njörd your breeding bull next time, Sigtrygg,' Sigurd said, holding out his hand to me and nodding towards the Óðin amulet at my neck. I gave it to him and he put it over his head before helping Olaf inspect the sail for damage. The wind had stretched it, but it would retake its shape overnight. 'Better still, he can have you,' the jarl added, thumping Sigtrygg's soaking back. 'Get the oars out, lads!' he called. 'We've had our fun tonight.' And where they might have moaned at having to row again, the Norsemen seemed relieved to be taking a grip on *Serpent* once more; oars and steerboard rather than wind and waves controlling where she would go.

It never gets completely dark at sea, because any small light from stars or moon, even if they are veiled, reflects from the water. But it would have been too dangerous to sail and so Sigurd decided to row back towards land and anchor in the shallows. At the first sign of exposed rocks, we could back oars far more quickly than adjust the sail. By the time the heat from our bodies had warmed the water in our soaking clothes, we had found a bay sheltered from the west wind by a great peninsula, and Olaf had dropped the anchor to the sandy bottom. The crews of both longships settled down to sleep or played games by candlelight. Ealhstan and I sat together whilst white-haired Eric held Sigurd's lamp before his face and began to sing a song that Olaf told me was ancient when his grandfather was a boy.

'I can sing my own true story,
Tell of my travels, how I have suffered
Times of hardship in days of toil;
Bitter cares have I harboured,
And often learned how troubled a home
Is a ship in a storm, when I took my turn
At the gruelling night-watch
At the dragon's head as it beat past cliffs . . .'

The men were smiling and nodding in appreciation. They all knew the sea and knew that she would sometimes swallow even great men. But the sea was their domain too, and they loved her.

'Got a voice like honey, hasn't he?' a man named Oleg said without taking his eyes from Eric. 'Hard to believe, if you've ever heard his old man sing,' he added, nodding towards Olaf who glowed with pride.

'He sings well for a heathen,' I dared, but Oleg simply nodded. It was a fragile, beautiful sound and I thought Rán's daughters, those foam-headed waves, would take Eric if they could, to sing in their mother's hall for all eternity.

> 'Often were my feet
> Fettered by frost in frozen bonds,
> Tortured by cold, while searing anguish
> Clutched at my heart, and longing rent
> My sea-weary mind . . .'

Now Sigurd himself held up a hand and Eric smiled, inviting his jarl to take up the song, which he did in a voice neither sweet nor lovely, but gruff and full and true.

> 'Yet now once more
> 'My heart's blood stirs me to try again
> The towering seas, the salt-waves' play;
> My heart's desires always urge me
> To go on the journey, to visit the lands
> Of foreign men far over the sea . . .'

And then, with the sound of singing washing over me, I slept.

# CHAPTER FOUR

WE BENT OUR BACKS TO THE OAR. I WAS GETTING USED to the rowing now and preferred to do it alone, but I knew it took Ealhstan's mind off the seasickness, so I let him sit beside me against the top strake, his arms moving with the oar though taking little of the strain. There was only the whisper of a breeze this morning, meaning that every pair of arms was needed to pull *Serpent* through the still seas. But there was some strange comfort in the smooth stave that had blistered my hands, in the rhythm of the stroke and the plunge of the blades into the grey sea. Before, I had felt like a prisoner, but now I understood *Serpent*'s beauty, saw the magic in the way she flexed through the waves and carried us away from harm.

'I don't understand, Ealhstan,' I said, breathing heavily, 'how it is that I speak their tongue.' He stared straight ahead as though he had not heard me. 'The knife you found on me. How did I get it?'

He shook his lank white hair and panted, but I knew he was only feigning exhaustion. And so I kept the questions to myself. My mind reached back into the darkness, searching for an answer, but finding nothing. My earliest real memory was of waking up in Ealhstan's house. I remembered feeling hollow. Empty. Exhausted. Satan's dark angel. That was what Father Wulfweard had called me. After that, everyone avoided me the way they avoid cow dung in the fields. Everyone except Ealhstan. And though at first I could not speak his language, I fetched his wood and caught his fish and worked hard so that he would not think I was a useless, lazy foxtail, which was what Griffin called the other boys in the village. But Abbotsend was gone now, and maybe my answer with it.

Back came the oar again and again. There were twenty-six blades, all of differing lengths depending on the curve of the ship, and they sliced into the water in perfect unison. Ealhstan was grunting with each stroke now. I told him to rest but he would not.

'Stop your barking, Englishman,' Black Floki bawled across from the steerboard side. Dark-haired, dark-eyed and mean-looking, it was easy to see where he got his name. 'Fucking mute! You sound like an old woman being ploughed by a horse.'

'Ah, leave the old fart alone, Floki,' said Oleg, who sat behind him. 'You're bitter as an old maid.' Oleg was a short, tough-looking Norseman whom I had rarely heard speak before. 'Hey, Osric, the girls back home whisper that Floki was born to a spiteful old she-wolf on the foulest night of the year.'

'And that night she had a great thorn in her arse which made her even meaner than normal,' a warrior named Eyjolf put in. The other men laughed. 'Floki is just jealous because no one talks to him. Isn't that true, Floki?'

Black Floki's brow furrowed, making him look even meaner. 'I have to share a boat with Englishmen and you wonder why I'm bitter,' he spat. 'And I'm hungry,' he murmured under his breath. Norsemen cannot get enough meat. They crave it constantly and see it as their jarl's duty to provide it. But we had long ago eaten the fresh joints taken from Abbotsend, and Sigurd was keeping the salted pork and mutton in reserve. For, as I had learned, many days can pass before it is safe to make landfall. There was a plentiful supply of cheese and the Norsemen never struggled to catch fish, but that was it, cheese and fish every day. Even Ealhstan was growing tired of mackerel and I had never thought to see that day. Griffin would not have believed it had he still lived.

Bjarni jerked a thumb at Ealhstan. 'I would swim back to his smouldering pigsty for a leg of lamb,' he said, closing his eyes as though he could taste it. 'Or a side of beef. No, boar, that's what I'm craving.' He stretched out a leg, kicking his brother's backside on the bench in front. Bjorn swore. 'And walrus,' Bjarni said, 'the way Mother cooks it with pepper and chives and garlic. Even an old horse would go down well, now that I think about it.' Kalf picked up an empty mussel shell from the deck and threw it at Bjarni. It bounced off his head, but he did not seem to notice. 'Horse can be good so long as you don't overcook it.'

'You're not helping, Bjarni, you sheep's dick!' Kalf

said. 'We're all hungry. Give your tongue a rest, man.'

'Back home my slaves eat more meat than us,' Bjarni grumbled, taking a whetstone and running it along his long knife.

'Osric, this is your land. Where can we get hold of a fat pig and a few chickens?' Olaf asked. He was checking *Serpent*'s caulking, making sure the ship's flexing was not pushing the tarred rope out from between the strakes. The morning had begun brightly, but now the sky had turned grey and threatened rain, and I watched Olaf, hoping there would not be another storm.

I shrugged. 'It is not my land, Olaf,' I said in Norse, glancing at Ealhstan. I was hungry too, but even if I had known where to find good meat, I would not have told him. I had already brought death to one village. And so Olaf continued to check the caulking, and the Norsemen bailed water, played tafl, complained about being hungry, worked on carvings, maintained their war gear, talked of home, and combed their hair.

The next day, there was enough wind to unfurl the great square sail so that we could rest and stretch our aching shoulders and backs.

'He's a curse on us,' Black Floki said, sliding a black seashell across the tafl-board. Svein the Red swore as another of his pieces was captured. There were only three white shells left on the board and now Svein's king was vulnerable. 'We should let Asgot do what he wants with him,' Floki muttered, sliding a piece so that another white shell was surrounded. He looked up, holding my eye for a moment before curling his lip

97

and looking down at the board. Beneath his great red beard, Svein's face was pink with rage.

'What's pecking at your liver now, Floki?' Olaf asked. 'And let Svein take one of your pieces, for the love of Týr! Have a heart, man.' But Floki made two further moves, surrounding Svein's king and winning the game. Svein swore and swept a hand across the board, scattering the shells across *Serpent*'s deck, then stood and made his way cursing to the bow where he stood looking out to sea. 'You're a mean bastard, Floki,' Olaf said, shaking his head.

Floki picked up a white shell and examined it. 'The boy has stolen Sigurd's luck,' he said, raising an eyebrow but not taking his eyes off the tafl piece. Some of the other men nodded or murmured their agreement.

'If not for Osric, we would be suffering Rán's cold embrace by now,' Bjarni countered, pointing at the waves. 'She wanted us down there and don't tell me you didn't feel the bitch's hunger.' He glanced at me, an anxious look in his eyes. 'Whatever the lad said, it reached Óðin's ear.'

'My brother is right for once, Floki,' Bjorn added, looking up from the spoon into whose handle he was carving a swirling pattern. 'Osric is favoured. Like Sigurd. And whilst he's with us, we're favoured too.' He resumed working on the spoon. 'That's what I believe.'

'That weird eye of his tells me everything I need to know,' Bram said in his gruff voice. Then he shrugged. 'Sigurd brought him aboard. It's up to him.' I looked at Sigurd who sat polishing his mail brynja with a lanolin-soaked cloth. Sea air is bad for mail and Sigurd rubbed meticulously at the rings round the neck that showed signs of rust. He said nothing, but he was listening.

Floki pulled the thongs from his plaits and shook out his hair, black as a crow's wing. 'Since laying eyes on him we've kindled a fire in this land, turned its people against us. Our brother Arnkel has been carried to Óðin's hall and we came within a strake's width of a grave below the waves to be gnawed by fish until the end of days,' he said through twisted lips. He held up a palm. 'I know he warned Jarl Sigurd of the White Christ priest's treachery, but old Asgot believes the boy is dangerous. Ask him, Bram.' It was a challenge. 'Let us hear what the godi says.'

All eyes turned to Asgot, who stood gripping *Serpent*'s top strake and staring out across the wind-stirred waves. He turned to face us, his watery grey eyes narrowed in thought. 'Yes, Floki, at first like you I thought the boy was a curse on us. But now . . .' He shrugged. 'Now I am not so sure. It is never an easy thing to know the mind of Óðin All-Father. Óðin the One-Eyed,' he added, staring at my blood-eye. 'The All-Father can grant a great warrior favour in battle,' he said slowly, nodding his grey head, 'but he will take that favour away just as easily.' He snatched something invisible from the air. 'You can ask Jarl Sigurd why Óðin does this . . . if you do not already know. Why he can let good, brave men die.'

Sigurd held his brynja outside the shadow of the great sail, examining the iron rings in the sunlight. 'Óðin needs great warriors,' he said, frowning at his own work. 'He must gather fallen heroes to his own hall in preparation for the last day, when he will have to fight the final battle against the giants and the armies of the dark lords.' He laid the mail across his knees and looked at his men. 'You all know this, have known it always,' he said, 'for we learn it from our fathers who learned it from theirs. Those in Valhöll even now prepare for Ragnarök, the last battle.' Asgot nodded and Sigurd shrugged his broad shoulders. 'But these are the end of days,' he said. 'Ragnarök draws closer and Óðin gathers his army as he must. The boy is not to blame. That is what my heart tells me. The All-Father has given Osric to us for some purpose. Even you, Floki, cannot be sure this is not so.' Black Floki gave a slight nod, as though half accepting his jarl's words, and Sigurd began to rub the cloth across the iron rings once more. 'We will know soon enough if the gods have deserted me,' he said, not looking up from his work.

When I looked at Sigurd with his bright blue eyes, long yellow hair and full beard, it seemed impossible that his gods could desert him before he had filled his cup with glory. He was a jarl, a leader of men and a fierce warrior. He was a Norseman with a thirst for fame. I knew then that I would follow him off the edge of the world.

For two days and nights we sailed out of sight of land, using stars, cloud patterns and the flights of birds, so that any Englishmen watching from the shore would not know in which direction we were going. Then, when Sigurd was sure it was safe, Knut set the rudder to steer *Serpent* back towards land, her sail harnessing the wind so that the red dragon's wing flapped eagerly.

'This is a king's life, hey, Osric!' Svein called. At last, he had forgotten about his defeat at the tafl-board. *Serpent*'s hull sliced through the waves and I had to turn my ear from the wind to hear him better. '. . . being carried by the wind like an eagle!' he called. 'A king's life!' A great smile split the giant's beard. 'At last Njörd has sent us a good wind, hey! I did not join this fellowship for the rowing!'

'You chose to join, Svein?' I asked with a smile. 'I don't remember having much of a choice.'

'Well, you row like a Norseman now, by Thór! You should thank Sigurd for making a man of you.'

'You don't know you've been born!' Olaf shouted. 'None of you idle halfwits does! When I was your age, Osric, we always rowed. Rowed till our hands bled and our backs cracked. My father would call us women for raising her sail at the first belch of wind.'

'That's because in your day they had no wool to make sails,' Bjarni teased. 'The gods hadn't made sheep yet!' This brought a deep chorus of laughter which fed on itself until not a man aboard had dry eyes.

Just being aboard *Serpent* stirred my blood; the way the overlapping hull strakes vibrated with every oar stroke. The thrum of the rigging in the wind. The way she flexed through the sea like some great swimming beast. The name *Serpent* suited her. I stood at the prow as she dipped and rose, catching the sea spray in my face and licking the salt from my lips, relieved I no longer suffered the sickness that twists the innards of those not used to the sea. I looked at these warriors, these hard men from the north, and felt awed by their self-belief. They were masters of the ocean and the elements, or at least aspired to mastery. It seemed that each man was cloaked in an invisible confidence, and yet perhaps there was no magic in it. They were the inheritors of a great legacy. They were the lords of the sea, the keepers of an ancient lore handed down by their fathers and their fathers before them.

I suspected even Ealhstan was beginning to bear up to our fate. In his long life he had never passed the standing stones of his village boundary, but now he turned his face to the wind, a smile playing at the corners of his thin lips, and I wondered where his mind took him. Was he at last unfettered? Was he the eagle Svein had talked of, soaring high above the world, far beyond the troubles of men, where age and words count as nothing against the spirit's freedom?

We were heading east again, pushed along the southern coast by fresh winds from the north-west, and sometimes I saw outcrops of sea-battered white rocks that reminded me of Abbotsend, my home of two years. And then I was struck by the fear that had hit me when these men, strangers then, had come ashore with fire in their eyes. But though I feared them, I could no longer hate them, even after the terror and the blood. Those things were harder to recall now that I was amongst them, now their laughter filled my ears.

Later, as if in reply to our grumbling bellies, Sigurd came amidships and stood hands on hips, a wide grin parting his yellow beard.

'I've noticed that some of you have begun to row like women!' he bellowed, stirring a smattering of curses from the men. 'And if Njörd thinks *Serpent* is weak he will try to take her again. That's the mean old bastard's way, hey, godi?' Asgot nodded solemnly. Some of the Norsemen touched amulets and sword grips for luck. 'So we must put some strength back in your arms.' Sigurd bent his shield-arm with its warrior rings so that the muscles bulged. 'Who's for a juicy side of beef?' The men whooped with excitement and I felt myself smile. But then my stomach sank as I remembered the dead of Abbotsend. 'Knut!' Sigurd called to the steersman. 'Aim for that beach with the whale carcass on it. We'll land there if Óðin wills it.' I looked landward and saw a grassy hill, which was cracked by a stream that emptied frothing into the sea. 'Bjorn, Bjarni, stow Jörmungand,' the jarl said. This is what they called the dragonhead prow with its faded red eyes, named after the serpent that Norsemen say encircles the world. Sigurd slapped Olaf's shoulder as Bjorn and Bjarni hefted the fearsome carving. 'We don't want to frighten the land spirits today, my friend,' he said before turning to bark more orders.

'We're going ashore, Ealhstan,' I said, 'for beef.' He was pale as death from all the rowing and I decided that he would have to endure the sickness for I would not let him row again. 'I suppose we'll eat that whale, too, if it's not rotten.'

Ealhstan frowned and I knew what he was thinking. If there were a village nearby, one big enough to give Sigurd a bloody nose, the grounded beast would have been stripped to its bones. 'It could have washed up this morning,' I said, but Ealhstan grunted miserably and I knew he was agitated because it seemed that Jarl Sigurd knew what he was doing after all. As we approached the beach I watched white gulls circle and dive to the carcass. Soon I would hear their screeches and smell the green slimy weed the sea spews on to the beach.

The men were prickling with excitement, checking their war gear, combing beards and replaiting salt-stiffened hair. Olaf came and stood above Ealhstan, scratching his cheek as he looked down at him. 'Sigurd says the old cunny must check the steerboard rib,' he said. 'I replaced the withy, but the rib cracked that night of the storm and we're tending landward. The thought of an Englishman touching *Serpent* turns my stomach, but what can I do? Arnkel our shipwright was killed at your pisspot village.'

I nodded and translated for Ealhstan and he choked, showing his palms. 'I know you're no shipwright, but you can do the job,' I said, putting a hand on his shoulder to calm him. As far as I knew, Ealhstan had never set foot on anything bigger than a fishing skiff. He shook his head vehemently. 'At least pretend you know what you're doing,' I hissed, feeling Jarl Sigurd's gaze on the back of my neck. I could hear the rasp of the whetstone as the Norseman sharpened his long sword.

'You are either useful to me, or you are not useful,' Sigurd said. 'Think about that, old man.'

'He'll fix it, lord,' I said, kicking Ealhstan, who

mumbled something that would have been damned heathens, had he a tongue.

The Norsemen put on helms and mail, whilst Olaf dropped the anchor. Knut released the leather straps that ran through slits in the hull, holding the steerboard in position, then lifted the rudder from the water so as not to damage it in the shallows, for it ran deeper than the keel.

We had to cover our mouths and noses even before jumping from *Serpent* into water up to our waists, for the whale was rotten and the stink was terrible. Flies blanketed the corpse and two ravens stood on it, watching us between pecking at a great yellow eye.

'It's high tide, Sigurd,' Olaf said as the men ran two thick ropes to a couple of boulders. 'We have two hours before we risk getting stuck high and dry like him,' he said, nodding at the dead whale.

'We'll have filled our bellies by then, Uncle,' Sigurd replied, using his green cloak to wipe the seawater from his sword. 'What do the bones say, godi?' The strange old man had already found a flat rock on which he had strewn a handful of bones that looked like those from a man's backbone.

'They speak of blood, Sigurd,' he said in barely more than a whisper, his grey, watery eyes flickering over his chieftain's face. For a heartbeat Sigurd's brow furrowed, but then a smile came to his salt-cracked lips.

'Blood from the meat staining our beards, old man, that's what you see,' he said, glancing at Olaf who held his eye briefly.

Then Olaf rubbed his ample belly. 'I don't know

about you whoresons, but I can almost taste it,' he called, and the other men grinned mischievously. Sigurd sent four men to keep watch along the high ridge. The others fished, played tafl, or trained with sword and spear whilst the rest of us prepared to set off in search of fresh meat.

Ealhstan called my name. It sounded like Ovrik when he said it, and when I turned he was staring at me and I thought he was about to curse me for leaving him alone with the heathens. But then he stepped up and hugged me and there was strength in his old arms. I gripped his frail body, my throat tightening.

'I'll be back, old man,' I said into his ear, smelling the oldness on him. 'Just fix their ship and stay out of their way. Don't be a stubborn old goat, you hear me?'

He mumbled his consent and I pulled free of his embrace, turning my back on him. And swords, spears and shields in their hands, Sigurd's wolves set off, forgetting about their godi's magic and his talk of blood.

Though it was April, the air still held a whisper of winter's bite, so I was grateful for the woollen cloak Sigurd had given me. It had belonged to Arnkel the shipwright and when the Norsemen opened their friend's journey chest to share out his belongings, no one had wanted it. The musty brown cloak had seen better days, but it was big and it kept me warm as I clenched a fist round its edges and set off behind the Wolfpack. I felt like a fish half out of water, for I was both Englishman and Norseman, and yet somehow neither. So I whispered one prayer to Christ and one to

Óðin that we might find food for ourselves and not feed the carrion birds with the flesh of the dead.

In front of me strode the brothers Bjarni and Bjorn, their grey helmets dull and menacing in the weak spring morning's light. Their shields were slung across their backs, and their short ringmail coats were visible at their tunics' hems and sleeves. I was gazing at the wicked-looking battleaxes in their hands when Bjarni mumbled something to his brother and handed him his axe. He turned to face me and I stopped dead. The others began to climb a steep hillock, using great tufts of grass to pull themselves up, whilst I stood swaying on legs that still thought they were at sea. Suddenly I wished I were back on *Serpent* with Ealhstan.

'I have something for you, Osric,' Bjarni said. It was Bjarni's shoulder into which I had sunk an arrow during the raid on Abbotsend. His jaw was clenched and his hands made great fists. I thought he would kill me and I took a step back, but he grabbed the cloak at my neck and yanked me towards him. 'You'll need both hands to climb, unless you plan to command Óðin to send his flying horse to carry your arse up there,' he said, gesturing with his chin to the hilltop. Then he thrust something through the edges of my cloak and shoved me so hard that I fell on my arse. I looked down to see an arrowhead with some of the shaft still attached sticking through the cloak, fastening it as securely as any brooch. The remaining wood was stained dark with Bjarni's blood. 'It's your arrow, boy. You keep it,' he said. Without a smile or further word he turned, grabbed fistfuls of grass and began to climb.

At the crest of the hill, we saw that the land spreading into the distance was not flat, but undulating and heavily wooded. The stream I had seen from the ship was wider here, but not by much. It was rugged and coursing and clear enough for me to see its brown stony bed.

'This stream will take us to our dinner,' Sigurd said as we knelt to drink the fresh water from gourds or cupped hands. And we knew he was right, for men will always make their homes near such streams. They are like the veins in our flesh and we cannot live without them.

'I want you to offer a sacrifice, Sigurd,' Asgot the godi said, wide-eyed. He looked agitated. 'I told you I saw blood.'

'You always see blood, Asgot,' Sigurd said, waving the words away, 'you were born with a ship's rivet in each eye.' He stooped to fill his leather water bottle. 'We are far from our gods, you old sea urchin. What would you have me sacrifice?'

The godi turned to fix me with his stare. 'Are you blind, Sigurd?' he asked, clutching his sword grip. 'You drink from the stream but you do not *see* the stream.'

'Be careful, godi,' Sigurd warned, standing and slapping down the wooden stopper. 'Your tongue writhes like a worm.'

'Speak plain, Asgot,' Olaf said. 'We don't have time for your riddles.'

Asgot sneered and turned back to Sigurd. 'The stream is alive,' he hissed. 'It sleeps now, but it lives.' The men stopped drinking and backed away from the water's edge, stepping lightly. 'The dragon sleeps, Sigurd. If you intend to follow his course, you must make an offering. If he wakes to find that you have not . . .' He broke off and began praying to Óðin in hushed tones whilst the others looked to their jarl with grim faces.

Sigurd stared into the stream for a long time and then raised his head, his eyes marking the water's course into the distance. The pebbly shallows twisted through the landscape and I thought I saw the bony spine of a serpent or dragon lying asleep and hidden, waiting for unsuspecting men to cause offence.

'Well?' Sigurd asked, looking at each of his men in turn. 'Any of you volunteer to put himself beneath Asgot's knife? Come now. One of you must have woken this morning hoping the godi would bleed you for an English river spirit?'

Bjarni moved back to the stream, dropped his breeches and pissed into the water. 'Let the bastard feed on this,' he said, and the men took courage from his daring, except Asgot who looked horrified.

'There's your sacrifice, Asgot,' Sigurd said, as scar-faced Sigtrygg moaned at Bjarni for pissing in the stream before he'd had a chance to fill his water bottle.

'Fill it upstream, you witless fool,' Bjarni said. Sigtrygg's coarse reply was stopped short by his jarl.

'Dragon or not, we go on,' Sigurd said, 'unless you want to explain to the others why they'll be eating cheese and spitting mackerel bones again tonight.'

'The boy will do, Sigurd!' Asgot pleaded, his eyes wild. 'Let me have the boy. That should be enough. As you say, we are far from home. We must appease the local spirits, or at least try to make our own gods hear us.'

The other Norsemen turned to continue. Sigurd gestured to them as an end to the matter. 'I promised the boy his life, Asgot,' he said. He grinned. 'You know the gods, old man – you likely knew them when they were just men like us. But I do not think that Óðin wants Osric's blood. I would feel it if he did.'

Asgot shook his head. 'You walk a dangerous path, my jarl,' he warned, the bones in his greasy hair rattling.

'I know no other, Asgot,' Sigurd replied, looking at me, 'and none of my line ever died a straw death.' I nodded thanks, wondering about the men of my line, whoever they were, and whether they had died grey-haired and feeble, or with a sword in their hands. Then on we went, keeping our distance from the stream, and the Norsemen held their sword scabbards and kit to keep them from rattling as we followed the sleeping dragon onwards, hoping not to wake it with our passing.

Ivar led us. He was a tall, thin man renowned for his eyesight and it was not long before he spotted a brown smear against the light grey sky beyond the mound before us. Sigurd raised a hand and we crouched among the thickets and bracken. The jarl crawled to Ivar, his sword and mail jangling. The dark leaves of an elm rustled in the breeze. I inhaled the scent of hornbeam catkins wafting across the lowlands.

After a brief conversation Sigurd stood. 'On your

feet, men. You wouldn't trust a snake sliding through the grass on its belly and neither will the English. Easy now.' We tramped up the hillock, through heather and gorse peppered with silver birch, always following the stream, which grew wider amongst a copse of budding beech and oak at the hill's plate. It was from this cover that we looked across at a clutter of thatched dwellings spilling off three rolling hills. The houses were well constructed, their roofs pointing to the sky like arrowheads running almost to the ground on either side. It was a busy place, maybe four times the size of Abbotsend, and this meant enough men to ruin Sigurd's day if things went wrong. It also meant there would be at least one butcher, and more likely several.

'I will take Floki, Osten, Ingolf, Olaf and Osric,' Sigurd said. 'No shields, helmets, mail or axes.' Some of the Norsemen began to complain at this. They prized their arms above all else, especially their mail, and hated being without them. But they knew they could not wear their brynjas and remain inconspicuous.

'Let me come, Sigurd,' Svein the Red pleaded, the ghost of disappointment in his huge, open face. 'I can carry twice what Floki can.'

'There's no better load a man can carry than common sense, Svein,' Olaf teased. Svein's huge shoulders slumped. 'Óðin's words, lad, not mine,' Olaf added defensively. 'You should be with the ships in case the English come,' he said. 'We'll need your axe if they do.' Svein stood a little taller then and Osten slapped the giant's shoulder in consolation.

111

Sigurd smiled. 'You would attract too much attention, Svein. The English have never seen muscles like yours. This land is so mild that weaklings thrive in it. Stay here, my friend,' he said, and Svein shot a proud grin at Black Floki, who rolled his eyes.

Sigurd turned to those he had chosen and I looked at the men who came forward. They were the ones of average looks and would have the best chance of blending in, except for Floki. To look at him was to see pure mischief. Sigurd put a hand on my shoulder. 'It would be better if you wore a patch, Osric,' he said.

I put a hand to my blood-eye. 'I'll keep it closed, lord,' I said.

Sigurd shook his head. 'Cover it.'

Olaf put his hands on his hips. 'And you, Sigurd?' he asked. 'What will you do to look like an Englishman?' Sigurd's brow furrowed. He looked every bit a warrior and a Norseman too. And he knew it.

'I'll go, Sigurd,' Glum said. *Fjord-Elk*'s shipmaster stepped forward, loosening his plaits, and then shook out his dark salt-encrusted hair. 'I could pass for an Englishman. I just need Svein to stamp on my face so it's not so pretty.'

'Ha! At home I have a pig who is prettier than you, Glum,' Black Floki scoffed.

'That is no way to speak about your wife, Floki,' Halfdan said with a grin.

Sigurd raised a hand. 'All right Glum, you go instead of me.' He pointed to me, adding, 'But the lad does the talking. The rest of you keep your filthy mouths shut. And no fighting.'

'Who, us?' Glum said, leaning back in feigned dismay.

Some of the men wanted to remain among the trees where they could see the village and thus come to our aid if things went badly, but the risk of their being seen was too great and so the six of us went on alone, having agreed to meet Sigurd and the rest back at the ships when we had bought the provisions we needed. A light rain began to fall, turning the sky's colour from unpolished iron to soot black, but we were glad of it because men are less vigilant when trying to keep dry. A low rumble rolled across the clouds and Glum shared a furtive grin with the others.

'Thór's with us, lads,' he growled, touching his sword's grip as we marched on. I looked down at my own clothing and realized I would have to hide the pagan knife Ealhstan had found round my neck, and so I took it off my belt and tied it round my neck once more, tucking it out of sight. Then I glanced at the others for anything that might give us away as outlanders. Our tunics and cloaks were indistinguishable from English ones, but the Norsemen's brooches, buckles and clasps were not. In bronze, silver or gold they took the forms of fluid curves and intertwined beasts, and were clearly pagan things.

'Your combs,' I said to Osten, Ingolf and Floki who all had them hung round their necks on leather thongs. 'Tuck them inside your tunics. The English don't usually wear them like that.' They also covered their sword's hilts with their cloaks and ruffled their hair, believing that if Englishmen did not wear hair combs,

113

they must care little about their appearance.

'It suits you, Osric,' Ingolf said, pointing to the strip of linen I had tied round my head to cover my blood-eye. 'It'll give you a better chance with the girls, mark my words.'

I narrowed my other eye. 'I can still see into your black heart, Ingolf,' I said. He gave a gap-toothed grin, but a moment later I saw him touch the silver amulet of Thór's hammer Mjöllnir at his neck and I smiled.

'There's our meat,' Glum said hungrily, pointing to an open-fronted house at the summit of the east hill. It sat beyond the wooden stake palisade that protected the heart of the settlement. We stood in a clearing littered with the stumps of felled trees from where I could see the white carcasses of animals hanging from beams. There were birds strung up by their legs, flapping their wings vainly. Through the rain the breeze brought with it the smell of the place and after being at sea it was strange now to breathe in the stink of cattle and human waste, wood smoke and food. Glum tapped me on the shoulder and handed me a leather scrip bulging with silver coin. 'We'll wait here, Osric,' he said. 'When you've bought the meat we'll come and get it. Remember, they must think you are a slave running errands for your master.'

'Then you and the others must hide, Glum. Back there among the trees,' I said. 'You look like a pack of slobbering wolves.' Glum nodded, gesturing for the men to take cover. Another peal of thunder rolled up from the south and I gripped my cloak tightly round my neck to stop the rain getting in. Then I made my way along a muddy track towards the butcher's, my mouth watering at the thought of its juicy treasure.

'That is much silver you have in your hand, Osric!' Black Floki called after me. 'The gods will curse you if you betray us. And I will find you!' I did not have to turn round to know that Floki was gripping his sword hilt, and that his teeth showed like fangs amongst his thick, dark hair.

*The silver in my hand is that which you took from the men you killed, Norseman,* I thought. *Did the gods curse you for taking it from those who earned it through toil? I doubt it. It is more likely that Njörd sent you a good tide, that Thór laid a thick fog across the sea to hide your approach, and that Óðin God of War guided your blade to strike down your enemies.*

I tramped along a worn path that weaved like a spider's web catching every dwelling, and threw a stick for a dog that had come to sniff at me. I passed houses with open doors and saw women working hand spindles and looms, making the most of the poor light to weave their cloth. Many of the menfolk would be up in the pastures herding sheep before bringing them back to the pens for washing and shearing, though I passed two stretching a deerskin over a frame, too busy to notice me as they began to scrape off the hair and fat. My ears filled with the ringing of the forge and there was comfort in the sound so that I believed no harm would befall me as long as the rhythm remained unbroken.

Then I found myself standing before two hanging pig carcasses, several chickens, three flapping skylarks, and a brace of dead hares, one with a bloodied eye like my own. A rich, herb-scented smoke drifted from the dark interior of the house and I peered inside to see more hanging shapes, joints of meat being smoked, and my mouth watered at the sweet smell. I took a long, delicious breath as a great mass stepped out of the darkness, grey smoke billowing in its wake.

'You have beef?' I asked, peering round a pig carcass to meet the eyes of this bear of a man. He was almost as big as Svein the Red.

'Who wants to know?' came the gruff reply. He lifted the pig off its hook and slammed it on to a wooden bench whose grain was stained with blood. Then he pulled a foreleg wide, picked up a hand axe and brought it down with a great thud, severing the leg easily.

'I am Osric,' I said, holding out the bulging leather scrip, 'and I have come for meat.'

# CHAPTER FIVE

THE BUTCHER'S NAME WAS EOSTERWINE AND I WAS RELIEVED
that he did not ask how I had come by so much coin.
I suppose he was like every other merchant; he could
smell money and would not jeopardize his coming by it
with unnecessary questions.

'You'll never have tasted better beef, lad!' the man
boasted, hands on hips whilst Floki and the others
shouldered the joints of meat and prepared to head
back to the ships.

'My master will be the judge of that,' I dared, 'but
thank you, Eosterwine. And may God be with you,' I
added loudly enough for two newly arrived horsemen
to hear. I paid them no heed, slinging the brace of hares
over my shoulder and heading off towards the hill.

'They're eyeballing us, Uncle,' Glum hissed under his
breath.

'Warriors by the looks of them,' Ingolf said.

'Just keep moving and stop looking at 'em,' Olaf
mumbled through a broad showy smile. 'The bastards'll
think you fancy them, Ingolf.' Then the riders set off

slowly down the hill, heading towards a point where their muddied path crossed ours.

'We're fucked now,' Black Floki said with a vicious grin. 'We'll have to cut them up.'

'Ignore them, Floki, and hold your tongue,' I said.

'It's up to you now, Osric,' Glum said, the glint of violence in his ocean-blue eyes.

Laden with joints of meat, the six of us shuffled along the slippery path, careful not to lose our footing. I noticed that the ringing of the forge had stopped and I swore under my breath.

'That's some feast you men are in for!' The tattooed rider's voice was deep and sure. He was heavily muscled and his arms were bare but for the many silver warrior rings adorning them. Guessing that the man had spoken about the meat, Glum nodded and slapped the carcass on his shoulder.

'No feast, I'm sad to say,' I replied with a tired smile. 'My master is going on pilgrimage across the sea and we are fetching supplies for the voyage. We'll salt this lot and then it will have to last for many weeks, may the Lord protect us and bless our humble ship.' I smiled. 'Eosterwine assures me we have never tasted better beef.'

The warrior raised his thick eyebrows. 'Eosterwine brags like a king with two cocks,' he growled, then glanced at his companion; he was an older man with a jewelled sword at his side.

'An accident?' this other asked, nodding at my covered eye.

I stopped now and faced the riders, letting the Norsemen trudge on down the track. 'Hammer scale from the forge, lord,' I said, touching the strip across my blood-eye. 'I was apprenticed to a blacksmith but,' I shrugged, 'had to seek a new path. Can't say I'll miss Eoferwic my old master. He was a bastard.'

'Well, your new lord must be a worthy Christian,' said the older man, his back straight, hands resting on the lip of his fine saddle. 'A pilgrimage is a worthy undertaking. If only we could all summon the endurance for such work and abandon our more mundane . . .' he smiled, 'earthly responsibilities.'

'If ever a man was assured a place at our Lord's right hand, it's my master. He will not rest until he finds what he seeks,' I said. The man's eyebrows arched. 'Worthiness, lord, that is what he seeks,' I added with a solemn nod.

'And his ship is moored by the white rocks?' Rain dripped from his long nose and wilting moustache.

'Yes, lord,' I said. I saw no sense in lying and further arousing their suspicions. 'We sail on the ebbtide. If the wind favours us.'

'You sail at night?' he asked, shooting a glance at the big man.

'Our shipmaster claims he knows the sea as well as a heathen,' I said proudly, making the sign of the cross, 'and Lord Ealhstan trusts the Almighty to guide us and keep us from harm.'

'Then tell your master we shall turn a blind eye to the tax he owes us for mooring on our shore. Seeing as he is a good pilgrim with God in his heart.'

'Thank you, lord. I will tell him and I am sure he

will pray for you at the Lord's shrine,' I said, giving a shallow bow, but as I leant forward the small bone-handled knife swung out on the leather thong. I casually tucked it away and set off again along the muddy track, expecting to hear the rasp of swords pulled from scabbards. Instead, I heard the click of a tongue and a horse's whinny and I exhaled gratefully, for I knew the Englishmen had turned their mounts.

'Will they be back?' Glum asked when I caught up with the others.

'I don't know. They might,' I said. 'If it was up to me, I'd lash *Serpent* to Svein's back and tell him that Freyja herself was waiting for him across the sea with her legs open.'

Olaf smiled. 'You did well, lad. Sigurd will be pleased.'

'Make him leave, Olaf,' I said, wondering if the riders had recognized the pagan knife with its bone handle of carved beasts. 'Please,' I added.

Olaf's eyebrows arched and I guessed his thoughts. Sigurd was not a man who could be made to do anything.

We approached Thorolf on watch on the bluff overlooking the small bay and he straightened as we neared, his eyes devouring the joints of meat on our shoulders. 'Save some for me!' he pleaded, as we began down the narrow, muddy track to the beach where the Norsemen had piled wood for cooking fires away from the rotting whale.

'Just keep your eyes open, Thorolf, or I'll have you on dried codfish till you sprout fins and drink seawater!'

Glum threatened. 'We are not in Harald's Fjord now. The folk round here won't give a fart that your father says you're a kind lad who loves his mother. They'll nail your hide to a church door and spit on it twice a day.'

When Ealhstan saw me he nodded sharply. Then I saw him make the sign of the cross over his chest and I knew he must have prayed for my safe return. We stowed the meat in the ships' small holds, though Sigurd ordered fires lit for two huge joints of dark red beef marbled with thin threads of fat. It was still raining, but the wood washed up on to the beach was white as bone and twice as dry and would burn well enough.

Then Olaf caught my eye, scratched his bushy beard and gave a slight nod, and I watched him approach Sigurd. I went closer.

'Let's be away, Sigurd,' he said through a relaxed smile. 'It'll be good to put some brine between us and these English.'

'The men are wet and hungry, Uncle,' Sigurd said, picking a flea from his yellow beard and crushing it between his thumbnails. 'We're not leaving until they have eaten a good meal. Besides, the wind is from the south. I won't make them row against it with their bellies empty.'

Olaf squeezed the rainwater from his long, greying hair. 'We take a risk if we stay,' he said.

'If we were men ruled by fear, we would never have put to sea, old friend,' Sigurd replied, sweeping back his yellow hair and tying it with a thong. 'We will leave with the moon if you are worried about the English. But let them eat before you make them row.' He grinned. 'Our fathers were not men of the plough, hey?' Olaf nodded, accepting his jarl's decision, but now Glum stepped up. He picked up some dried seaweed and dropped it to test the wind.

'The boy thinks the English might come, Sigurd,' he said, touching his sword's hilt for good luck and looking at me. I moved closer.

'They were suspicious, lord,' I said, glancing at Olaf. 'It was in their eyes.'

Sigurd's brow darkened. 'I will not run from them, Glum,' he said. 'Óðin does not favour cowards.' Glum's face flushed red against the darkening sky and he seemed about to speak, but instead turned his back on Sigurd and marched away. 'Take off the patch, Raven.' Sigurd was looking at me, his beard broken by a thin smile.

'Raven?' I said, relieved to be untying the sodden linen strip that covered my blood-eye.

He nodded. 'The All-Father has two ravens, Hugin and Munin. Mind and memory. At night, these great birds perch on his shoulders, but every morning they fly away to see what is happening in the world. They are Óðin's messengers and since you are from the All-Father, you remind me of them.' He pointed to Black Floki and the others. 'Besides, you can't expect them to call you by an English name. It sticks in their throats.'

'Raven,' I said under my breath, feeling the word on my tongue.

'Raven,' Sigurd affirmed. Then he nodded to Olaf who stepped up and handed me a sword in a leather-bound scabbard. I took it with trembling hands, suddenly as mute as old Ealhstan. Sigurd smiled and gripped my shoulder, then the two of them moved back to the fire, leaving me holding the weapon as though it were the greatest treasure in all the world.

Ealhstan was watching me and there was sadness in his face as undeniable as the deep creases betraying his years. But I did not care, for I had been given a sword. So it was that the name given to me two years before by the man who had found me died. And because I was dark-haired, unlike most of the Norsemen, and because Sigurd believed I was from Óðin All-Father, I became Raven.

I watched the meat turning above the embers of a spent fire, but my mind rested elsewhere and I realized that the warmth I felt came not from the fire, but from pride. These men, adventurers and warriors, had accepted me into their Fellowship and their jarl had named me. Raven. I liked the name. And feared it. For though the raven is Óðin's bird, it is also a creature of carrion, a scavenger of the battlefield. A thing of death.

The meat tasted as good as it looked, but the eating was over too soon. The rain had stopped and though our clothes were still damp, we were content. Our bellies were full and our blood was strengthened, and by the time the moon silvered the dark ridged sea we sat around rekindled fires, laughing and singing. As always, young Eric's voice was the sweet honey to the others' coarse oats, and sometimes they would stop singing so they could listen to his melody, which quivered gently and rolled like the waves. Glum seemed no longer angry with his jarl and the two men banged their ale horns together as they drank, spilling the liquid into their beards and down their tunics.

'Those filth-loving halfwits must have swallowed Raven's tale about us being pilgrims of the White Christ!' Ingolf said, his gap-toothed smile glinting in the firelight.

'Well, I am embarrassed about that,' Glum slurred. 'Fucking pilgrims? Were those whoresons blind? My father would fall off Óðin's mead bench to hear us mistaken for slaves of the White Christ.'

Sigurd grinned. 'Your father and mine likely shook Valhöll's timbers years ago, Glum, when they challenged the All-Father to a drinking contest and fell on their faces,' he said, crashing his cup against Glum's, and laughter rang out into the night.

But I could not forget about the man with the drooping moustache and his vicious-looking friend, so I decided to keep watch from the moonlit rise above the beach. 'If Bram is asleep,' Olaf called, snatching a burning stick from the fire and waving it at me, 'set light to the drunken swine's beard!' And I smiled and nodded, standing for a while to let my eyes adjust to the darkness. Then, with the sword at my waist, I began to climb.

Bram the Bear, who had taken over sentry duty from Thorolf, was as famous among the Norsemen for his love of strong mead as he was for his ability to put it away. But as I pulled myself over the last grassy lip, I saw I would not need to wake him. Bram was down on one knee behind his round shield.

'Get down, lad,' he growled, peering into the darkness. 'We've got guests.'

'How many?' I asked, glancing at the horn strung over Bram's back. The blood pumped deep inside my ears.

Bram shrugged his broad shoulders. He looked left and right, scanning the shimmering oaks and hornbeams that covered the hilly ground. 'Some of the bastards are close,' he murmured. 'I keep catching their stink on the wind.'

I looked back down to the beach where the fires danced and the Norsemen lay unaware of the danger. 'We run now,' I hissed, 'and warn the others.'

'Or we could give these bastards something to remember us by,' he offered with a grimace. 'Slow them down a bit.' He was looking straight ahead, but I knew he had one eye on Valhöll as he drew his sword with a low rasp. 'Let our lads hear the English squeal like pigs.'

I gripped his shoulder. 'No, Bram, we run,' I hissed.

He turned to me, his jaw clenched. 'All right, lad, we run. On three.' I nodded. 'One. Two. Three.' And I turned and scrambled back over the ridge, sliding on loose stones and jumping over rocks, my sword scabbard banging against my leg and my cloak trailing behind like a bird's broken wing. And I knew that Bram was not with me.

There was no need to shout, for the men on the beach heard the clack of rocks and stood, swords drawn and shields raised, as I fell over my feet where the rough ground suddenly evened out.

'Raven?' Sigurd stood tall, his empty drinking horn in one hand, his sword in the other, staring at the crest of the hill.

'They're here, lord!' I said, standing and fighting for breath.

'How many?' he asked, throwing down the drinking horn.

'Too many,' I said, gripping my sword's hilt. A long flat tone from a Norse war horn challenged the noisy surf. 'Bram,' I said, looking up at the moon-silvered ridge.

'Shieldwall!' Sigurd yelled. 'Shieldwall in front of the ships!' But his men were already moving, forming a wall of flesh and iron.

'Kill the flames!' Olaf ordered. 'Or do you want to show the English where to stick their damned arrows?' Sigurd, Bjarni and Bjorn left the line and kicked the burning branches of the fire, raising a shower of sparks that crackled into the night sky. But the embers still glowed, cloaking us in an orange hue that could prove lethal once the English brought their bows within range.

'If you want a job done properly,' Black Floki said, stepping forward, dropping his breeches and pulling up his mail brynja. The embers hissed angrily as Floki casually pissed on them, then vanished in a cloud of grey smoke. The others cheered his daring, for even now the hillside was alive with black shapes, and fire arrows were clacking into the pebbles around us.

126

'The whelps are trying to light us up,' Olaf said, but the stones were still wet from the earlier rain and most of the flaming arrows sputtered and died.

'We should be out there on the bloody waves!' Glum barked, tightening his helmet's leather strap beneath his bearded chin.

'When did you become an old woman, Glum?' Sigurd asked, pacing along the shieldwall like a hungry wolf. 'Easy, lads, keep those shields up.' A flaming arrow struck Bjarni's helmet. 'That's it, Eric, tuck that chin in unless you want a second mouth.'

'Sigurd! They're out there too!' Old Asgot pointed his spear out to sea where dozens of flames danced above the waves. Fishing skiffs crammed with men clutching firebrands bobbed dangerously close to the sterns of *Serpent* and *Fjord-Elk*.

'Whoresons are going to burn the ships!' *Serpent*'s steersman Knut shouted, stepping from the line, but the man beside him grabbed his arm and shook his head.

Ealhstan made a sound in his throat that could have been laughter and I turned to see him crouched behind the shieldwall, a strange smile on his lips as the English materialized from the darkness into a seething mass of shields and helmets and blades.

'You promised me a land of monks and farmers, Uncle,' Sigurd said under his breath. 'One warrior in every ten, you said. These spawn don't look like monks.'

Olaf shrugged. 'Things have changed since I last came, Sigurd,' he rumbled. 'It's been ten years.'

127

Sigurd spat. 'Knut, take ten men on to the ships. If they burn, we're finished.' Knut nodded and he and his party ran into the surf, hauling themselves up the bow ropes into the longships. 'Right, lads,' Sigurd bellowed, 'let's hear some noise!' The Norsemen began thumping their swords against their shields until the clamour filled the night. 'That's it! Wake the gods! Let your grandfathers in Valhöll hear your battle song! Make old Thór jealous!' Sigurd roared. 'Show him how we make thunder!'

The English were fifty paces away now, forming their own shieldwall. Some even banged swords and shields like us. In spite of the moonlight, I could not make out individual faces, but from the size of the heaving mass I knew we were in for a terrible fight.

'Why aren't they shooting?' I heard Bjarni ask above the din and I realized he was right and no more arrows were coming at us. I glanced behind me at *Serpent* and *Fjord-Elk* and saw Knut and his small knot of men lining the deck with raised shields. They had even set Jörmungand the Midgard-Serpent at the ship's prow, though it was too late to scare off the land spirits now. 'They've not gone for the ships yet,' I said hopefully. Just one hurled firebrand could ignite their pitch-soaked timbers and then *Serpent* and *Fjord-Elk* would spit fire into the night sky.

Sigurd's eyes were narrow slits and I knew he was trying to understand why the English were holding back when they could have driven us into the sea.

'That's enough, lads!' he called, hefting his great round shield into the air, but one Norseman was still thumping with his sword. Sigurd snarled at him and he went still.

'You bonehead, Kon,' Black Floki hissed.

Sigurd walked forward and the shieldwall closed behind him. 'Have you come to fight?' he called in English into the shadows beneath the rise. 'Or are you going to stand there like fucking trees?' His voice echoed off the rocks, mixing with the sound of the surf. There was no reply. 'Well, English? I have mead to drink!'

A shadowed figure moved towards him. 'I have come to talk with you, heathen,' this man said. He was tall and well armed and his moustache was long and smooth. 'After that, we can fight. If you want.'

'Talk is for women!' Sigurd barked.

'So is mourning, heathen,' the Englishman said, 'which is what your womenfolk will be doing if you are foolish enough to piss on this opportunity.' Sigurd held his tongue. 'Come, Norseman. I will meet you halfway.'

'Don't go, Sigurd,' Olaf warned, having understood the conversation, for it was Olaf who had taught Sigurd the language of the English. 'They'll kill you.' Sigurd seemed to weigh up his chances, then rolled his broad shoulders, spat and stepped forward.

'I'll go, lord,' I heard myself say. Sigurd turned to me as I stepped from the shieldwall, the gap sealing instantly. 'Let me talk to them. I know their words better than you and will sniff out a lie, lord.'

Sigurd nodded, waving his shield forward. 'Go, Raven. Fly in search of the truth,' he said. I sheathed my sword and then, still holding my round shield, walked towards the English.

Up close I recognized the man as the rider with the straight back who had spoken to us up at the village. To his left stood the other man, the heavily muscled warrior with the silver arm rings. 'You speak for your chief?' the Englishman asked.

'I listen for him,' I replied. 'He will speak for himself, once I have told him what you have to say.'

The man nodded, running a hand through his sand-coloured hair. 'I am Ealdred. This is my land. As outlanders . . .' he paused and glanced at my sword, 'as sword-bearing outlanders you are a threat to the people who look to me for protection.' He jerked his head to the west. 'We have enough trouble with the Welsh.' He tipped his head to one side. 'Are you a threat?' he asked.

'We are more of a threat than you know,' I dared, meeting his eyes. I gripped my sword's hilt to keep my hand from shaking.

Beneath his long moustache, the corners of Ealdred's mouth hinted at a smile. 'I could give one word and you would see your ships burn,' he said. 'But you know that, don't you?'

'And without them we would have no choice but to fight until we fell or walked on your corpse,' I said. 'Have you ever seen the kind of death fifty mailed Sword-Norse can sow?' I gestured to our shieldwall. 'They are the finest warriors alive.'

Ealdred frowned then. 'You talk much for a man who claims only to listen. And your English is good,

130

for a heathen.' He stroked his moustache. 'Perhaps I can convince you that I have come with half a mind on peace.' He turned. 'Mauger, release the bear.' With that the burly warrior stalked back into the shadows, returning a moment later pushing forward a man whose hands were bound behind his back.

'Bram!' By the flickering light of English torches, I saw that his face and beard were dark with blood and his eyes were swollen shut. And he was limping.

'Never was much good at running, lad. Legs like bloody tree trunks,' he growled, looking ashamed to be tied up. Mauger shoved him forward and I drew my sword and cut his bonds before sending him back to Sigurd.

'That animal killed two of my men,' Ealdred said, his eyebrows raised. 'But I spared his life as an act of good faith.' It must have been the truth, I thought. By rights, Ealdred should have avenged his men with Bram's blood. 'So, heathen,' Ealdred said in a low voice, 'are you ready to listen now?'

I sheathed my sword and glanced at the English shieldwall. It was longer than our own. Much longer and four men deep in places. I gave Ealdred a curt nod. 'I'm listening.'

'Well, Raven? Has the Englishman come to fight or not?' Sigurd's eyes glinted in the dark. His men stood shoulder to shoulder, their painted round shields raised and their axes and swords hungry for flesh.

'His name is Ealdred,' I said. 'He is an ealdorman and the king's cousin.'

131

Sigurd pursed his lips. 'Which king?' he asked.

'Egbert king of Wessex,' I said.

'A real king!' Sigurd chuckled. 'Should I kiss his hand now or after I cut it off?' This was loud and in English.

'Tell him we want to fight the king, not his dog!' Olaf shouted.

'Ealdred says that your fame grows like a storm, my jarl, and that you have stirred fear in men's hearts and forced prayers to the trembling lips of God's children.'

Sigurd smiled at this. 'Does the man want to fight me or fuck me?' he called.

'He wants to drink with you, lord,' I said. 'Ealdred wants you to go to his hall and share his mead and discuss terms of trade.'

Sigurd leant back and laughed from deep in his belly. 'The king's cousin wants to drink with me, hey? Freyja's tits, these English are a strange people! Drink?' He turned to his men and then back to me, fixing me with an icy stare. 'Tell Ealdred to go and play with his king's cock and leave me alone. He comes here and threatens my ships with fire, then expects me to go to his hall and drink his mead? I am no whore!' he yelled. 'Ha! I'd sooner sail into the sun!'

'Lord, he has many warriors,' I said quietly. 'And they'll burn the ships. How can we stop them? This Ealdred will send his men to die against you. I can see it in his face.' Sigurd glanced at his men once more, lingering awhile on Bram who gripped his axe tightly, his bloodied face swollen and snarling. With one word from Sigurd they would all fight to the death. But would that be enough to earn them their fame? How would they be remembered if none lived to speak of their courage by the hearths in the halls of the north? For their enemies would weave a different story once they lay dead and their souls feasted in Óðin's Corpse Hall.

Sigurd frowned. 'What does he want from me, Raven? My amber? My whetstones?' He shook his head suspiciously.

I shrugged. 'He would not tell me, though he gave me his word that if you agree to go to his hall, he will have his men throw their firebrands into the sea.'

'He gave his word to you, not to me.' Sigurd shook his head and pulled at his beard. 'These are strange days, Raven, when you ask me to believe the word of a Christ-follower. And stranger still that I listen.'

'What choice do we have?' I asked. 'Ealdred has maybe two hundred spears.'

Sigurd scoffed. 'Only some will be warriors. Most would rather be sharpening their ploughshares or sitting by their hearths.' But even so, two hundred was too many and Sigurd knew we could not fight and hope to win. 'Very well,' he said with a nod towards the English, 'tell this Ealdred I will drink his mead. But I swear this by Óðin – if I smell English treachery, I will cut off his head.'

When I approached Ealdred with Sigurd beside me, the ealdorman did as he had promised and the flames in the fishing boats were extinguished. Darkness enveloped the longships once more and I touched my bone-handled knife, relieved that they were safe again.

'I am Sigurd son of Harald. The Lucky, some call me.' Sigurd stood tall before the English lord and his grizzled bodyguards.

'It is a fitting name,' Ealdred acknowledged with a wry smile, 'and your men must be grateful that their lord is not the kind of man to throw their lives away. Not when there is nothing to be gained from it.' He raised a hand into the air and I turned to see the fishing skiffs full of men and fire being rowed away from Sigurd's longships.

Sigurd glanced at the warriors around Ealdred and seemed unimpressed. 'We will come to your hall, Ealdred, but if I see a slave of the White Christ, I will fill his belly with steel.'

'A priest tried to poison Jarl Sigurd,' I said to Ealdred.

The ealdorman seemed surprised, then frowned and tugged on his long moustache. 'A whisper of the Holy Spirit on the breeze can tempt a man to desperate acts, Jarl Sigurd,' he said, making the sign of the cross, 'but I can assure you I keep my priests on a very short leash.' He smiled. 'So, shall we go?'

Sigurd laughed loudly, causing Ealdred and his men to look to each other in bewilderment. 'I will come when I am ready, Englishman,' he said and with that turned his back on Ealdred and walked to his men. And I followed him.

The Norsemen took up what Olaf told me was called the swine array, a wedge-shaped arrow formation with their backs to the sea. And battle ready they waited, shields and spears raised in the sickly light which

134

bounced off the water below the eastern sky. I was not given a place in the swine array but was made to stand behind with Ealhstan, for I was not a warrior, and each man in the wall must trust the man beside him to keep his shield raised, overlapping his neighbour's, and his sword arm strong.

'I don't know what Sigurd is waiting for,' I said to Ealhstan. He turned to look out across the breaking surf, which threw up a chill that made me shiver. The skiffs that had threatened Sigurd's seasoned timbers had been rowed out of sight, whilst Ealdred's men on the beach had retreated so that they were once again dark, shifting shapes against the pale rock of the rise before us. 'Why doesn't he go to the ealdorman's hall?' I watched the jarl talk with Olaf, the two warriors' iron helmets dull above white skin and unseen eyes. 'This will be stinging Ealdred's pride.'

Ealhstan pointed to the slate-grey sea's horizon, rounded his gaunt cheeks and blew into my face, and I suddenly understood. The wind came from the south and it was possible that the tide followed it. Sigurd knew that even if he could fight the English off long enough to board *Serpent* and *Fjord-Elk*, it would be tough rowing to get clear of the fire boats, which were surely still nearby. We would also endure a rain of fire arrows from the shore before we could pull the tarred, seasoned hulls out of range. The risk was too great even for Sigurd, and though it may have looked like stubborn Norse pride the truth was the jarl was buying us time. So we waited, and the sun broke free in the east, filling the world with pure light and revealing the Norsemen's tired faces. And still they did not break formation. So neither did Ealdred's men, until later in the day the wind dropped enough for Sigurd to give a firm nod and turn to his men, his eyes fiercely shining from his drawn face. At least one of his ships had a chance of getting away if Ealdred turned his spears on us.

'Stay with the ships, Glum,' Sigurd said, gesturing for *Serpent*'s crew to ready themselves, which they did gladly, relieved to sling their shields across their backs and move their cramping limbs. Glum rearranged his men into a smaller but still deadly swine array and Sigurd nodded that I should go with him to Ealdred's hall. He told Bram to stay behind with Glum too, because he was battered and limping. But Bram refused with a rumble of profanities and hefted his shield and spear anyway.

'Stay here, Ealhstan. I have to go with Sigurd,' I said, gripping his stick-thin forearm. The carpenter nodded and clasped my arm, his watery eyes exploring my face with equal concern and frustration. 'Keep your hair on your head, old man. I'll be back to make sure they've not made a heathen of you,' I said, trying to smile, but I knew the truth was that Ealhstan was worried for me, not for himself, and I left to follow Bjorn and Bjarni before Ealhstan's fears could become my own.

We climbed the rise strewn with birch and bracken and spiky green gorse buzzing with bees, passed through stunted oaks, elm and ash, and reached the clearing of stumps where Olaf, Glum, Floki and the others had waited when I went to buy the meat. Then, followed at a distance by the English, we descended the slope along the muddy track, and I wished I had a spear like the other Norsemen who planted the butts into the slippery filth to help keep their feet.

'We'll be rich men this time tomorrow,' Bjorn said to his brother Bjarni as we descended into the valley, shaped like a shallow dish, where Ealdred's folk lived, some within the protection of a low wooden palisade. The Wolfpack eyed the place hungrily, grinning at the thought of what it might offer: food, silver and women, all fine things to a Norseman. The stream had vanished into the earth at several places where the ground rose, but always it reappeared, flowing from the heart of the village, just as Sigurd had predicted it would, where it turned an old mill wheel whose rhythmic clunking disturbed the peaceful afternoon. A fine drizzle fell as folk moved about, herding animals, carrying water and firewood, weaving wool and making linen cloth. Hammers rang in forges, potters worked clay, and craftsmen of all kinds handled stone, glass beads, bronze, silver and bone.

'Rich or dead, brother,' Bjarni replied, adjusting the round shield on his back. Timber houses pockmarked the landscape, the smoke from their hearths casting a pall over the village in the gathering twilight. The sweet woody air reminded me of Abbotsend.

'Looks like a good place to raise cubs,' Olaf said, nodding at the piles of timber and half-constructed houses at the edges of the settlement. 'Plenty to keep a man busy round here. And good land,' he added appreciatively.

'We're building another church. Of dressed stone,'

137

Ealdred said, swaying in the saddle and pointing to a knee-high ruin beyond his mead hall. 'Our Father's house should not be made of straw and pig shit, eh?' The stones in place looked like the ones from the old watchtower on the hill overlooking Abbotsend, but the ones piled beside it were crude, unfinished blocks. 'My mason tells me it will take two years to build and that means three or four, but those ancient foundations are strong. The old people knew how to build. Makes you wonder what happened to them, doesn't it? A people like that.' Sigurd glanced at Olaf who shrugged disinterestedly. 'Used to be a heathen temple, the monks tell me,' Ealdred said, rubbing his horse between the ears. He held up a finger. 'The Lord shall have dominion.' The Norsemen scowled, and Ealdred scratched his head irritably. 'Not that you people would be interested in such matters, living outside the good Lord's shadow as you do.'

'Our gods go wherever we go, Englishman,' Sigurd replied in good English. 'Here,' he touched the amulet of Óðin at his neck, 'and here,' he said, thumping his chest.

'I wouldn't be you come judgement day, that's all I'm saying,' Ealdred muttered as he dismounted smoothly and handed the reins to a slave. 'Wait here. I will announce your arrival.' He disappeared into the hall, an imposing cob-walled structure with a high-pitched roof of new thatch. Sigurd turned to his men and put two fingers to his eyes, a warning to stay vigilant. A group of boys with wooden swords stood a short way off, watching us excitedly, whilst the men and women went about their tasks, but more slowly now, moving carefully and deliberately. And there was fear in their eyes. *You are right to be afraid,* I thought. *I have seen these men slaughter such as you. I have seen them burn houses like yours. I have seen them make the Blood Eagle.*

I patted Ealdred's horse's flank and the beast skittered and whinnied, tossing its head and almost breaking free of the retainer's grip. 'Horses can smell the sea on a man, Raven,' Olaf said, looking at the animal with its rolling eyes and the poor groom who was cursing and fighting with the beast. 'They fear it as we fear Hel herself and her flea-bitten beast.' Half black and half flesh-coloured, grim Hel guards the underworld and those damned souls killed by sickness or old age. 'Keep your swords tucked up in their beds, lads,' Olaf warned, 'and lower your axe, Eyjolf, bloody thing's like a cunny-hungry cock!' The men's laughter broke the tension for a moment, then Sigurd pulled them taut again.

'Look like the wicked, blood-loving whoresons you are, lads,' he said, rinsing his hands in the rain barrel by the hall's entrance. 'If the Englishman betrays us, we fight our way to the sea.' The men nodded and the gang of boys began to fight each other, showing off their prowess to these strangers, these blue-eyed men from the north who carried great war axes, spears and round painted shields.

I was tempted to run then, to tell Ealdred about the raid on Abbotsend and escape. But I knew if I did the Norsemen would kill Ealhstan, and even if they did not, I could not leave him. And if I ran, where would I go? Ealdred's people were strangers to me. They would likely fear my blood-eye as Ealhstan's people had.

As ritual demanded, the Norsemen left their weapons outside the hall where, Ealdred assured Sigurd, his grooms and servants would take excellent care of them. 'I have heard the Norsemen's reputation for the love of their weapons,' the ealdorman said respectfully. 'You have my word they will be safe, but they must stay outside.'

Sigurd agreed, but insisted on leaving five men, including Svein the Red, outside the hall to guard their arms. Small knots of Englishmen were gathering, watching us and arranging cloaks, tunics and brooches, and I wondered if they would join us.

'You see our reputation is well deserved,' Sigurd said with a wry grin to one of Ealdred's retainers. 'We love our swords more than our women. You can trust a good sword, even a beautiful one,' he grinned, 'but a woman? Never.'

The man seemed unsure for a moment before giving a shallow bow. 'You are my lord's guest,' he said, 'it shall be as you say. I will have mead brought to those who remain out here.'

'Come inside, Sigurd.' Ealdred stood at his hall's threshold. 'The sea air makes a man thirsty, don't you think? I have just the remedy.' Bjarni farted loudly, then shoved me forward and I entered Ealdred's hall.

The interior was ill lit with foul-smelling, flickering candles. A draught blew the hearth smoke in all directions and some of us coughed, having just come from clean air. Smoke-blackened tapestries swung slightly in

140

the gusts, keeping out the worst of the wind gathering strength outside. Two huge hangings showing Christ's crucifixion curtained off the far end of the hall.

'See their skinny god?' Bjarni said, pointing at the tapestries. 'He looks like a sparrow strung up to smoke.' He shook his head. 'These Christians are strange.'

'Here is my prayer to the White Christ,' Osten said, then gave a loud belch. 'I hope their food is better than their choice of god,' he added, nudging Thormod who smacked his lips hungrily. Njal kicked Sigtrygg excitedly as a pretty slave girl fed more wood into the hearth above which a cauldron simmered, giving off steam which smelled of carrots and onions. The girl pretended not to notice us, but as she turned to the table to begin cutting strips of meat for the pot, I saw an impish smile touch her lips.

'Did you see that, Sigtrygg?' Njal said, puffing up his chest. 'She likes the look of old Njal.'

'I saw nothing,' Sigtrygg said with a shrug, 'but don't worry, my friend, I'll let you cling to your dreams seeing as they're all you have.' But Njal was too busy eyeing the girl to take offence.

'Sit down,' Ealdred said, gesturing to the long oak table and mead benches running almost the length of the hall. The Englishmen I had seen outside were entering now, their scabbards empty but their eyes full of mistrust. 'Tell me of your travels,' he went on cheerfully. 'We had a merchant from far-off Frankia here some months ago, but he spoke no English and I wouldn't have trusted a garlic-reeking word from his mouth anyhow. How long have you been at sea, Sigurd the Lucky?' A hint of mischief touched his face beneath the drooping moustache.

'I will tell you my story soon enough,' Sigurd replied, 'but not with a dry tongue. First we drink. Just one cup,' he said, holding up not one finger but three. 'To the coming trade!'

'Of course, of course! Ethelwold, bring our guests something to begin with!' Ealdred called. In no time our alderwood cups were full of sweet mead, every drop as good as promised, and soon the ealdorman's hall was filled with noise as Norse and English shared their love of strong drink. Ealdred himself sat at the head of the table between the grizzled warrior who had questioned me the previous day and another man whose face was so scarred that his mouth was frozen in a grimace.

I found myself swaying as I sat, but Gunnlaug assured me it was normal after being at sea. The Norseman leant against me, his great bulk almost knocking me off the bench whenever he moved. 'I never thought English mead would taste so good,' he said, raising his cup to Ealdred. His fair beard was dripping with the stuff, and he wiped it on the back of his arm before giving a great belch.

'Our monks make it,' Ealdred called from the end of the table. 'Fair Honey Drop, they call it, though there's nothing fair about the price. They've got barrels of the stuff hidden away at the old monastery. Clever bastards make more money than I do!' He grinned, tilted his cup at Sigurd and drank deeply.

Sigurd raised his cup, spilling mead across the table, then hesitated, perhaps remembering Wulfweard the priest who had tried to poison him with hemlock. 'To the monks!' he called, inviting his men to bang their cups together in a clattering chorus. 'Long may their god fill their barrels with Honey Drop. Hey, Uncle, Óðin himself would wet his beard with this stuff!' I heard Svein the Red's booming laughter beyond the door and remembered that those outside had been given mead too. Ealdred's servants moved around the table filling cups from bulging skins, though I noticed some, including Olaf and Black Floki, refused more, and I saw them share a look of understanding. They would not let their wits be addled.

'You men must be hungry,' Ealdred said to white-haired Eric and Thorkel beside him. The two Norse-men grinned like devils when Olaf translated and Eric replied in Norse that he was hungrier than Thór after a day's giant-killing. Ealdred did not understand the Norse, but smiled anyway and leant back, giving a command to the retainer who waited at his left shoulder. Then he turned back to us. 'Bring my salt-dried guests what they've been waiting for!' he called, slamming both hands on the table.

Ealdred's cook began to ladle the steaming stew into bowls which his slaves brought to the table and set before us, but after Wulfweard's planned treachery at Abbotsend the Norsemen were suspicious of the food and would not take their spoons near it until they saw Ealdred himself slurp some of the stuff, oblivious of their fears. Seeing this they dug in, sucking air through puckered lips to cool the stew before swallowing, and in no time at all spoons were scraping on bowls' bottoms and we were given second helpings. The stew was flavoured with cloves and rich in meat – pork, hare and a tougher flesh which might have been goat – and after the previous night's feast by the breaking surf my stomach was soon hot and full and my head was looking forward to finding a straw pillow.

I was so tired I might not have noticed the booted foot beneath the wind-stirred tapestry of the crucifixion that vanished a heartbeat later when the hanging settled again.

A stab of fear stopped my heart and I glanced at Sigurd who was laughing with Olaf, then I watched Ealdred take a small bite of a honey and almond cake as he talked quietly to the big warrior beside him, who I realized had barely wet his tongue with the mead by his right hand.

'Hey, Gunnlaug, is the White Christ snarling or smiling?' I asked, forcing a smile and nodding at the tapestry at the hall's far end.

'If that weakling can smile with his hands and feet nailed to a tree, then he's . . .' he unhinged his jaw and gave a low belch, 'more of a god than I realized,' he finished, downing more Fair Honey Drop and wiping his beard on the back of his hand.

'I'll take a closer look,' I said, pushing myself up from the mead bench and moving towards the linen hangings, stumbling as though drunk so as not to arouse Ealdred's suspicion. I stood looking into the Christ's dyed thread face, for a moment wondering if the dead eyes of that white god were truly judging me for my sins. Then I stretched out a hand and pulled the tapestry

144

aside. A fist hammered into my face and warriors burst forward, screaming death to heathens, and suddenly the room was all swords and spears and bared teeth.

'Óðin!' Sigurd roared and the Norsemen jumped from the long benches and hurled their cups and bowls at the English.

'No!' Ealdred cried as the Englishmen snatched up swords hidden amongst the floor rushes and cut down Sigtrygg and Njal. Some ran to block the main entrance, but Black Floki tripped one of them and was on him like a wolf, savaging the man with his bare hands.

'I'll rip out your heart!' Sigurd growled at Ealdred who stood behind the huge warrior with the silver rings on his arms. The big man scythed his sword through the air to keep the Norsemen back. Then the door flew off its hinges, battering Ealdred and his man to the floor as Svein the Red sprawled on to the rushes beside the Englishmen. Norsemen scrambled for their swords and axes as the English went at them in a fury, hacking and stabbing. In the crush I grabbed a sword.

'Here, Sigurd!' I called, and he took the blade and turned with a roar towards Ealdred's men, for I had seen that a Norseman has no fear of death if he holds a sword. A man's elbow struck my head and hot blood slapped my face, blinding me. I fell into a pile of guts that stank, and I slid in the gore, trying to stand as knees and boots battered me. Somehow, I wriggled clear to a dark corner of the hall where a dying man's shit had sprayed the rushes, adding to the stench of smoke and wood and blood and sweet mead. Bjarni and Bjorn were amongst the English, hacking and

145

stabbing with their eating knives, desperate to make room for sword work. Black Floki ducked under a wild sword swing and thrust a blade into a man's neck, and Olaf made such a blow with an axe that an Englishman was cut in half at the waist. With slick hands I clawed at the blood in my eyes, trembling against the wall. A moment before, we had been sitting at Ealdred's table, but now the benches were slippery with blood and the room was filled with madness. Men screamed and the dark hall stank of open bowels and death. Then, like a cauldron boiling over, the fighting climaxed and ragged panting order won out. Norse and English parted into bloody knots, the dead littering the rushes between.

'Throw down your weapons, heathens!' Ealdred snarled. 'There need be no more killing.' He had survived the clash and now stood at the centre of his line which swelled as more warriors entered the smoky hall through a door hidden by the Christ embroideries.

'There are more of the troll-fucking goat turds outside, Sigurd,' Olaf said, breathing heavily at the main entrance where there was no longer a door thanks to Svein the Red. He turned to Sigurd, his expression unimpressed. 'But my wife puts more fear in my belly than these English.'

'What were you doing out there Svein? Weaving a wimple for your mother?' Sigurd asked, glancing at the thick oak door amongst the floor rushes. His yellow beard was matted with blood, though not his own. 'No one comes in that way, you hear me?' Svein nodded grimly. 'Olaf, Oleg, you stand with Svein. If I see an Englishman at my back, you'll be swimming home to your wives.' The three Norsemen rolled their shoulders and stood at the hall's threshold, their weapons inviting the English to come and die.

Inside, Ealdred's men were forming a solid shieldwall the width of the hall and three deep, and not all were men of trades. Some were clearly warriors, well armed with fine swords and helmets and some even with mail, though most wore leather armour. They were killers and Sigurd knew it. He must have known too that the trap we had sprung had been carefully laid.

'Tonight we drink in Valhöll!' he called and his men repeated the word, 'Valhöll! Valhöll!' They thumped their swords against their shields in a death rhythm and I slid up against a smooth timber post until I stood on unsteady legs. Sigurd turned to me then and I felt ashamed to be hiding in a dark corner like a mill mouse.

'The boy is no part of this, Ealdred,' Sigurd said above the din. 'We killed his kin and took him.' I stepped out of the shadows and wiped my gore-slick hands on my breeches. I was shaking.

'He wears your false god round his neck.' Ealdred's mouth was twisted with disgust.

Sigurd's hand went to his own neck and found the Óðin amulet was gone, lost in the fight. But I had snatched it up and now it hung at my throat. His eyes flashed, touched by a wolfish grin.

'Boy, tell Óðin we honour him this day,' he said.

'I will tell him, Sigurd,' I said, taking a step towards him. Then the Norseman turned to face his enemy. And the clash of arms filled Ealdred's dark hall like the coming of judgement.

# CHAPTER SIX

OLEG STAGGERED BACK FROM THE DOORWAY CLUTCHING at an arrow in his face. Eyjolf lay in the blood that pumped from the sliced artery in his thigh, white as snow on the red rushes. Yet the English could not break Sigurd's shieldwall. They had lost plenty of their own to these Norsemen, these death dealers whose sword skill was a wonder to behold. I stood by Olaf now, ready with a sword and shield to take my place should he or Svein be cut down.

'We can't lose with the All-Father watching over us,' Olaf said, spitting at a tapestry by the open doorway. 'We've made enough noise for him to find us. Glad to have you with us, lad,' he added. I clutched the sword grip with white knuckles and gripped the shield's leather-bound handle so tightly that I could feel the veins in my forearm straining. For I had chosen to die with these men, these warriors who had burned my village and taken my freedom. There had been no thought, just the vain hope to survive and hurt this treacherous ealdorman, and now the Norsemen buoyed each other with dark jokes. They filled Ealdred's hall with the warrior's pride, and it was all I could do to catch my breath in that stinking place of death.

'Come, Ealdred!' Sigurd snarled, breathing heavily. 'We've iron for all of you!' He spat a wad of blood. I stole a look at the English shieldwall and saw in men's eyes the seeds of doubt. Uncertainty made their movements cautious. Their own dead lay before them, whilst unbloodied fighters at their rear shouted at them to advance. I sensed that the balance had shifted. Seeing no way out, those I stood with accepted death now, embraced it even. But the English had thought it would be easy slaughter and now caught the whiff of their own deaths in the thick air and were afraid. The shieldwalls clashed again.

This is the blood the old godi warned of, I thought, glancing at Asgot who stood in the second line, thrusting his spear into English faces. His own face was contorted with rage and bloodlust and he seemed like an old grey wolf, long past his prime but with teeth and claws still sharp. An arrow thudded into my shield. 'Find a helmet, Raven,' Svein said, smashing his sword on to the raised shield of a man trying to force a way into the hall. 'Here!' Svein tore the shield from the man's grasp, grabbed his neck and threw him into the wet rushes at my feet. 'But kill the pig first.' The dazed Englishman drew his knife and slashed it across my shin as I brought my sword down to cave in his face with a crack. The body shuddered and was still. For a moment I was still, too, unable to take my eyes off the man's broken face and the white bone shining wetly between the gash. A moment before, he had been a living, breathing man with fears and hopes. Now because of me he was nothing. 'Hey, wake up, lad!' Svein shouted. I bent to the corpse and cursed it for trying to kill me. Then I took its bloodied helmet with its sweat-soaked sheepskin lining and limped to the door, my leg stinging like hell, though it was not bleeding much yet. 'It fits you,' Svein said approvingly, shoving against the enemy. 'You have Sigurd's luck, lad!' But anyone would have thought Sigurd's luck had deserted him as the shieldwalls clashed and clanged and desperate men grunted and heaved.

'The door, Raven, bring it here!' Olaf shouted. 'Quickly!' Guessing his intentions I hefted the heavy door from the rushes and slid it lengthways across the gap he and Svein defended, as an arrow clattered off the doorframe. Then I took two benches and set them against the makeshift barrier to lend it some weight. At least it would protect the Norsemen's lower halves from the arrows that came at us from a night now alive with moving flames. Torches streaked about like flying demons and harsh voices filled the shadowy landscape.

'Looks like every whelp in this cursed land has come to watch us die,' Olaf said, as he and Svein peered over the rims of their arrow-filled shields. Dead men littered the earth before them and it seemed that, for now at least, the English had broken off their attack at the hall's entrance. Inside, men still strained, slashed and cut.

'Sigurd will get us out of this,' Svein said in his deep

voice, and I realized I was wrong to think the Norsemen accepted death. Clearly Svein did not.

'Right now I'd settle for a barrel of Ealdred's Honey Drop,' Olaf grumbled, screwing up his eyes to allow the sweat to run over them. 'My tongue's bigger than my cock! How's it looking, lad?' he asked, peering into the night beyond.

Sigurd stood like a rock at the centre of his shieldwall. I had seen Ealdred's bodyguard drag his lord, like a carcass, clear of the mêlée to the hall's dark rear. 'Sigurd's holding them,' I said, knuckling my eyes. 'They keep trying to get down the sides, but we're holding them.' Then, like the last great wave before the tide turns, the English shieldwall closed again, its warriors desperate to tear a way through. They knew that one hole in the Norsemen's line would make the whole thing cave in, but the Norsemen knew it too and none of them would let himself prove the weakest stone; not whilst blood still filled his veins, or whilst he stood in the sight of his friends. The English failed again and began to shuffle backwards, the men at the rear allowing this to happen for the first time. Sigurd did not miss his chance. Stepping over broken bodies he took his line forward, keeping pressure on English shields until Ealdred's were forced back to the Christ tapestries and out of the door behind. Out they poured like bad ale stuttering from a skin, and when the last two Englishmen were at the door, Sigurd raised his shield.

'Stand, lads! Hold it here!'

'Let's follow them, Sigurd,' Bram said. 'We've got them on the tide.'

Sigurd shook his head, sweat and blood flying from it. 'Out there they'd surround us, Bram. Their archers would tear us apart.'

'I'm not getting an arse full of arrows now,' Knut said with a grimace, 'not after all this.' Bram clenched his lumpy, swollen jaw and nodded, accepting the decision. Outside, the night teemed with vengeful, shouting men. Olaf was right and it sounded as though every Englishman from near and far had come to destroy us. There were women out there too.

'I'm not getting killed by a woman's arrow,' Svein said. 'The skalds won't say that of Svein the Red.'

'There's more chance of Asgot kneeling to the White Christ,' Bram said with a grin, slapping the giant's back and checking his own sword's edge.

'Bar it,' Sigurd commanded. Bjorn and Bjarni barred the rear door and leant benches against it, and though we could still hear shouts outside, it was eerily quiet in Ealdred's hall. Now we were alone with the dead.

'Asgot, see to the wounded. Eric, help him.'

'This is the blood-eye's doing,' Asgot croaked, pointing at me. 'He has curdled your luck, Sigurd, and turned it sour.'

Sigurd glanced at me, then pointed his spear at Asgot. 'You're still breathing aren't you, godi?' he said.

'The gods keep me alive because I honour them,' Asgot said. The inference that Sigurd did not honour the gods was clear and for a moment jarl and godi stared at each other and the stifling air itself seemed to shudder.

'You heard your jarl, lad,' Olaf cut through the heavy

152

air, nodding at his son. 'See to the wounded.' Then Olaf caught my eye and I nodded in thanks. He dipped his head before turning back to Eric who set about his task with a grim set face. Olaf's son no longer looked like a callow young man. He was an equal now. He had shared and shed blood with these men and they would never forget it. We laid out the dead, Sigtrygg, Njal, Oleg, Eyjolf, Gunnlaug, Northri and Thorkel, straightening their limbs and leaving them uncovered so that their white faces gleamed waxy in the flickering candlelight. Asgot performed a death rite over them whilst the others saw to their own wounds and weapons or kept watch at the door.

'Our friends drink in Valhöll this night,' Sigurd said. Though he held his back straight, his eyes betrayed his exhaustion. 'They sit at Óðin's table with their fathers.' He glowered at each man. 'None of us living can ask for more than this.' His men grunted in agreement and it seemed to me they were jealous of their friends lying cold and stiff in the bloodstained rushes of Ealdred's hall. For those men's souls would soon enter the hall of the slain. Óðin's hall.

'Break the table,' Olaf snapped, palming sweat from his face. 'We'll use some to bar this door and the rest for the hearth. We could be here all night and I don't want you ladies catching cold.' We piled the English in the corner where I had hidden earlier, and covered them with their own bloodied cloaks. There were ten in all, not counting the ones at Olaf's door who were being dragged away into the flame-filled night.

'So much for English hospitality,' Black Floki

said, taking off his helmet to reveal a tangle of dark, matted hair. He kicked an overturned bowl, leaving food scraps amongst the rushes, then looked towards the hearth cauldron. 'Is there any stew left, Bjarni? Nothing makes me so hungry as killing.' I did not understand how he could think of food in the midst of all that shit and death.

'You should have gutted that dog Ealdred the moment you laid eyes on him, Olaf,' Gunnar said, checking the edge of his sword for damage. He cursed at a deep nick near the silver and bone cross guard. It would take hours of work with the whetstone to repair. 'If we get out of this, I'll be back on the next tide to burn this shithole to the ground.'

Olaf suddenly blanched and grabbed Sigurd's shoulder. 'They could burn it, Sigurd! They could burn the hall and us with it.'

Sigurd shook his head. 'Ealdred won't do that. He's a slithering snake, but this is his mead hall, Olaf.' He grimaced. 'He'll pay in blood for it.'

But Olaf looked unconvinced.

'Would you burn your own hall?' Sigurd asked him.

Olaf considered it, then shook his head. 'No,' he said.

'Ealdred might be dead,' the bear-like Bram countered, the eyes in his battered face shining with violence. 'Young Eric caught him with the axe. Squealing like a sow he was.' Olaf gripped his son's shoulder proudly and white-haired Eric straightened at the touch, but admitted he had only struck a glancing blow, not a lethal one.

Sigurd shook his head. 'Whatever he's thinking, he'll have sons out there and each of them with one eye on such a hall as this. No, they won't burn it,' he said, turning to Asgot who was kneeling by the dead, finishing the death rites with a flourish of his bony arms. 'What say you, godi?'

Asgot looked up at the beamed roof with its blackened thatch. Then with a hand he brushed away the rushes before him, took a pouch from his belt and scattered the bones across the cracked earthen floor. His face was pinched and closed, but then his eyes widened, seeming unnaturally bright in the dark hall. 'They'll burn it, Sigurd,' he said.

There were eighteen of us now. Olaf told me to arm myself properly and so I knelt by Njal's stiffening body and was struggling with his sword belt when Asgot hissed at me.

'Careful, boy.' His ancient face was full of spite. 'The death maidens are here in this hall.' His yellowed eyes rolled up to the roof beams. 'They choose the slain for Óðin. Carry their souls to Valhöll.' He grinned. 'They can be wicked bitches.'

As I fumbled with Njal's mail shirt, trying to pull it over his white face, I hummed one of the heathens' songs so that the demons of carnage would know that I still lived and not take me by mistake. Then I squirmed into the brynja, smelling the grease on the iron rings, and was awed by the weight of the thing. It dragged my whole body down and I feared I would be unable to move. And yet I found I could move well enough and the brynja's weight was then a great

155

comfort because I knew such a thing could turn an arrow aside.

The hearth flames licked the splintered wood of the table before bursting into life to throw an orange glow into every corner of the hall, vanquishing all but the deepest shadows. Every face was distorted by the firelight so that it had a fierce, animal-like aspect that was terrifying. I touched the wooden amulet of Óðin at my neck, feeling sure that he ruled in that place of death, no matter that the hall's owner Ealdred was a Christian. But the All-Father was a cruel lord. His wanderlust and vainglory had brought the Norsemen to a place that promised nothing now but their deaths. 'The gods love chaos,' Black Floki said, smiling bitterly and gesturing at my amulet.

'I'll wager the English followed us along the coast, gathering men as they went,' Olaf said, removing his blood-smeared helmet and wiping it on one of Ealdred's tapestries.

'If Glum and the others were here things would be more fun,' Svein the Red commented, pulling an ivory comb through his thick red beard.

Sigurd looked at me, his lips pursed in thought. 'Perhaps I should not have killed your red-faced priest,' he said, his mouth twisting into a smile. 'He did talk too much, hey? Someone would have done it sooner or later!' The others laughed and the sound was thick and full. The English outside must have thought it a strange sound to come from their ealdorman's hall. Sigurd turned to Eric. 'Can you get out, Eric? Past those turds and back to the ships?'

156

Eric thought for a moment. 'If you think I can, lord,' he said. Sigurd glanced at Olaf, seeking his friend's permission, though he did not need it. Olaf nodded discreetly.

'Good lad,' Sigurd said. 'You must warn Glum and the others.'

'What if the English have attacked them already?' Bjarni said, shrugging his powerful shoulders, and I suddenly feared for old Ealhstan.

'There's every chance Glum is fucking some Valkyrie on his way to Óðin's hall by now,' Bjorn added.

'I don't think so, Bjorn,' Sigurd said, his jaw tight. 'The men we fought here were fresh and Ealdred is no king. He doesn't have the warriors to fight in two places at once.' But Sigurd could not know that. He flexed a hand. 'Glum is alive,' he said, cracking the knuckles, 'and he'll spit teeth if we keep all the fun to ourselves.' I whispered a prayer to Óðin that Sigurd was right and the old carpenter was still alive as well.

'I'm a fast runner, Bjarni,' Eric said, already tying back his white hair. 'If I get past them, they'll never catch me. Not in the dark. A man can outrun a horse on rough ground. I've seen it done.'

Floki swore dismissively. 'Over a short distance it's possible,' Bjorn agreed, giving Floki a cold look. Outside, a dog barked.

'And dogs?' Bjarni said, turning towards the sound.

Eric looked down to the rushes then. 'I hadn't thought of dogs,' he said quietly.

'We should be encouraging the boy, Bjarni!' Bjorn snapped. 'You're not afraid of dogs, are you, Eric?' he said gruffly. 'Not English dogs, anyway.' Eric shook his head, grinned and drew his long knife, whose blade glinted in the flame light.

'You can do it, Eric,' Bjarni said, touching Eric's white hair. 'You're fast, I'll give you that. Didn't you win the foot race on Egg Island one summer?'

Eric smiled. 'I was ten years old, Bjarni,' he said, but it was clear he was pleased that Bjarni remembered the small victory.

'We'll create a diversion,' Sigurd said above the dog's barking, 'give those turds out there a night to remember us by.' He showed his teeth. 'Which of you has a plan Loki would be proud of?' he asked. The only answer was the loud crack of an ember from the hearth. 'Come, ladies, don't all speak at once. A strong arm kills but a cunning mind'll keep you alive.'

'We tear into them,' Halfdan said, his two blond plaits shining in the orange light. 'We go at them from the main door, screaming like demons, and in the confusion Eric climbs through there.' He pointed to the hole in the high roof that drew the hearth smoke. 'Then he makes a run for it whilst we're killing Englishmen.'

'And their dogs,' Floki added with a grimace.

'We fight our way clear back to the ships,' Halfdan finished, folding his arms to show that there was no more. The men gave their opinions, some for the plan, others against it. 'What else is there?' Halfdan asked irritably, holding out his hands.

Sigurd gave a curt nod and raised his hand to silence the others. 'It's not much of a plan, Halfdan. More

Thór's than Loki's,' he said. Then he smiled, his teeth like fangs. 'But I like it.'

Before a fight a man's bladder fills up, so putting out the fire was easy enough, but the acrid smoke was slung thick beneath the thatch and this, coupled with the small candlelight, meant that Eric did well to clamber up two upended benches to the roof beam which was closest to the smoke hole. There he crouched between the beam and the thatch, ready to pull himself out on to the roof as soon as the fight began.

'Here, lad, blow it hard as the bloody north wind,' Olaf said, passing his war horn up to Eric. 'Get a fire going again, lads, before they get suspicious, but only a small one, mind. We don't want to roast the boy. It would be a hard thing to explain to his mother.'

'I need four of you to stay in here,' Sigurd said, the words hanging heavy in the smoky air. 'The doors must be guarded in case we need to get back inside.' He knew he was asking much, not because it would be a terrible thing to be left behind, but because there would be less glory for those who remained whilst the others attacked. None of the Norsemen volunteered, though a couple of them glanced at me and I knew they wanted me to be one of the ones who stayed. 'Knut, Thormod, Ivar, Asgot. You stay.' Each nodded glumly. 'Raven, if you get a chance, fly after Eric and get to the ships. You'll only get in our way out there.' His eyebrows arched. 'Glum must decide whether to come and fight or take the ships home.' He looked at Olaf, both men aware of the risks.

'A hard choice, hey, Sigurd?' Olaf said, the prospect

159

lying heavy across his brow. 'If he comes, *Serpent* and *Fjord-Elk* will be as vulnerable as two hares in a snake pit.'

'I'll tell him, lord,' I replied, gripping my sword tightly to stop the trembling that had begun in my legs and spread to my fingertips. I had bound the wound on my shin tightly and I looked down, grimacing the pain away and noting that blood had soaked through the linen. 'It won't slow me down,' I said in answer to Black Floki's questioning eyes, and I meant it, though I knew the brynja would.

'Are we ready?' Sigurd asked. The blood on their clothes had barely dried and these Sword-Norse were once again preparing to sow death amongst their enemies.

'Wait, Sigurd,' Black Floki said. He was fixing a plait which had worked itself loose, spilling dark hair across his face. 'I want to see these Englishmen as I'm killing them.' When it was done, Floki put on his helmet, thumping it down securely. 'Let's make Týr wish he was with us,' he growled, invoking the Norse battle god whose hand was bitten off by the fettered wolf Fenrir.

'For Týr!' Svein the Red roared.

'Týr!' Bram repeated, hefting his axe, and the others invoked other gods too, such as Óðin and Thór, and some men called on the souls of their fathers.

Sigurd revealed his wolfish grin. 'Let us repay English generosity,' he said, nodding to Ivar and Asgot who removed the makeshift barrier. With a roar like a bear, Sigurd, son of Harald the Hard, charged into the firelit night, and the women who had come to watch the heathens die screamed.

In a heartbeat the Norsemen were amongst the English, slashing and stabbing with a fury like the wild ocean. They made no shieldwall this time, as the English would have surrounded it easily, but instead picked out the best-armed warriors and fought them man to man, desperate to break their enemy's spirit. I stood at the door of Ealdred's hall, looking for my chance, but it was mayhem as the English, who were now defending their homes, fought with ferocity to match the heathens'. The noise of battle, of iron on wood, and confusion and slaughter ripped into the night. Men cursed and screamed.

'Fly, Raven!' Knut shouted, and so I threw down my shield and ran towards the great dark hill overlooking Ealdred's hall, towards the shingle path that glistened wetly in the moonlight. The rings of my brynja jangled as I ran and then I tripped over something in the long grass, biting my tongue savagely. My mouth filled with blood and I spat, then something bright caught my eye. A shock of white in the moonlight. Pale arrow fletchings fluttered above the corpse. Eric had removed his mail so he would run faster and he had almost made it clear. Óðin's maidens found you, Eric, I thought, wiping bloody spittle from my chin. Air slapped my face from an arrow whipping past and I ducked and ran up the path, screaming, 'Come and take me if you can! Come, bitches of the dead! Come, demons!' I should have put Njal's sword into Eric's hand to ensure his place in Óðin's great hall, but to stay was to die and so I

161

scrambled on, following the stream and hoping to wake the dragon who lived there, for it would add chaos to a night already drenched in it. And the gods love chaos.

But when I pushed through the long, sharp grass of the brow overlooking the beach, my guts twisted and pulled taut. It was raining fire on *Serpent* and *Fjord-Elk*, burning brands flying into their hulls from almost a dozen small craft bobbing on the flame-lit sea. And Glum's men were teeming across both longships, slinging pails of water everywhere, picking up the firebrands with their bare hands and throwing them into the sea. A knot of Norsemen stood in a shieldwall before the ships, waiting for an attack from the darkness whilst their comrades struggled to save their beloved dragons.

I looked for Ealhstan among the throng, but it was too dark and I was too far away. Even with the flying firebrands, it was impossible to make out individuals, and so I yelled down to the Norsemen that Sigurd was fighting for his life. But even if they heard, which was unlikely, they had their ships to look to, for without them they would be stranded and it would be a miracle if any Norsemen survived to see the next sunset. Then, in the breeze that bent the long grass towards me, bringing water to my eyes, I would have sworn I felt one of Óðin's handmaidens swooping past, brushing my face with her breath as she flew towards Ealdred's hall. I knew Norsemen were dying so I turned my back on the struggle below, thumped my helmet down securely and ran back along the stream's bank towards Jarl Sigurd, finding my way more easily now that my eyes were accustomed to the night. I would have run straight past Eric's corpse, but I saw the cream-coloured war horn at his waist and stopped to rip it free before continuing.

I passed between the low hills, seeing a dim pall of light in the sky from Ealdred's village, then crested the rise and stopped to catch my breath, looking down into the settlement as the cries of the dying carried up to me. Sigurd's men had fought their way to the south side of the village where they had made the swine array, their backs towards me, their shields overlapping as they fought off the English. But then I made out a band of Ealdred's men cutting round from the west of the settlement, using the houses for cover as they sought to surround the Norsemen. There was no time to descend the slope and warn them. In a few heartbeats Sigurd's men would get blades thrust into their backs. I gripped the war horn and leant back, filling my lungs with cool, predawn air, then blew hard enough to wake the gods. The note soared into the night like the promise of approaching dawn and it was deep and long and true, and then a great cheer came from the darkness below. And the Sword-Norse were not alone in thinking their brothers had come to add to the slaughter, for the English suddenly broke off their attack and retreated, keeping their shields towards their enemies. I bent low, hoping the English would not see me, for then they would know I was alone, and I ran to Sigurd's swine array. Before I got there Black Floki turned, flashing his teeth at me in the darkness.

'The English are coming round from the west,' I said,

pointing to where I had seen the war band trying to blindside the Norsemen.

'I've seen them,' Floki hissed, stepping aside to let me take my place between him and Bram.

'Glum's not coming, then,' Bram growled, glancing down at the war horn still in my hand.

'They're trying to burn the ships,' I said, and Bram grunted as though he had already accepted that this would be a fight to the end. Arrows were thudding into shields and striking helmets.

'I say we leave this turd of a village,' Svein the Red said, as though it were a simple matter of just walking away.

'Eric?' Olaf said, keeping his eyes fixed on the torch-lit English shieldwall which was growing in density a spear's throw away. I did not reply. 'Well, lad? Is he with Glum?'

'I'm sorry, Olaf,' I said, feeling the weight of other men's eyes on me. Sigurd turned and held my eye, as though trying to take from my mind the manner of Eric's death, but Olaf remained silent. Then the big man strode forward, abandoning the relative safety of the swine array, and marched towards the English line.

'Well, you sons of goats?' he roared. 'You snot-swilling, shit-eating pig bladders! Come and feel my sword in your puke-filled bellies! Come, English dog-faces, come and feel my spear in your stinking brains!'

Sigurd stepped forward. 'I have seen old ladies fight better than you dung heaps!' he yelled at the English, and as one the swine array marched forward beating

164

their swords against their shields, until they were level with Olaf and Jarl Sigurd and spitting distance from their enemy. I quickly tied the war horn to my belt and gripped my sword in both hands. The battle fever shook my limbs and soured my guts, and the English, who were not as well armed and who did not resemble gods of war as these Sword-Norse did, must have seen their deaths approaching with the orange glow in the east.

# CHAPTER SEVEN

THE CHRISTIAN HEAVEN AND HELL SHOULD HAVE BEEN glutted then, with English souls torn from pain-racked bodies, and Óðin's dark maidens should have been bent low with the weight of brave warriors, ascending to the great hall of the slain. But two high-pitched blasts from an English horn sent a shiver through Ealdred's shield-wall and as one man it stepped back, leaving the broken dead between.

'Cowards!' Olaf yelled, still in fury's grip, his beard soaked with white spittle and his eyes impossibly wide. 'Whore whelps and cowards! Fight me! Fight me!'

Then the English wall cracked in its middle, leaving a dark passage from which a figure emerged. It was Ealdred himself, his sword arm bound in bloodied linen, but otherwise firm and grim-faced.

'Enough!' he shouted, ignoring Olaf, his eyes instead boring into Sigurd's. 'Enough of this madness! We are not animals!' His huge bodyguard was beside him. The man looked ravenous for death, as though he sought to avenge the harm done to his lord and prove his own worth if any who saw Ealdred's blood were in doubt. 'Sigurd, it was not meant to come to this between us. Where is the honour in senseless death?'

'You have no honour, Englishman,' Sigurd countered, spitting on the ground. 'You have no understanding of the word.'

Ealdred's long moustache quivered then, but he gave a slight nod and showed Sigurd his palm. 'The men who attacked you in my hall will be punished,' he said. 'As you know, it is no easy thing to keep a rein on warriors.' He winced in pain. 'Their hearts are burning brands but their wits are slow. They will be punished.'

But Sigurd, who still gripped his gore-slick sword, pointed the blade at an English corpse. 'I have seen to that myself, dog!' he yelled, and again Ealdred seemed to shudder.

'They were gathered merely as a precaution, Sigurd,' he said, 'but hatred of your kind is planted in us at our mother's tit. Our churchmen nurture that hatred and it grows strong.' He looked skyward. 'For my own part I wonder at the inconsistency of a God of peace who commands us to kill other men, even unbelievers.' Then he stroked his fair moustache. 'We might wonder how much is God's will and how much is our own.'

But Sigurd had no patience for the ealdorman's musings. He raised his battered shield and stepped forward, and there was violence in the movement. Ealdred's bodyguard moved forward too, but his lord muttered something to him and reluctantly the man took a step back. The English waited, deaf to the insults Sigurd's men hurled at them, their shadowed faces anxious or fearful.

'Whether you believe it was not my intention to attack you means nothing to me, heathen,' Ealdred spat, abandoning diplomacy now, the shadows sharp on his lean face, 'but for your own sake and for the sake of those who call you lord, don't be a fool. I know the empty ambitions of your black hearts. The thirst for fame consumes your people, Sigurd, twisting their sight and leading them to folly, to death and destruction for the sake of stories.' The ealdorman smiled emptily, but his men remained tight-mouthed, expectant of battle. 'Make no mistake, Sigurd, you will all die here' – he threw out his uninjured arm – 'in this Christian land. And your deaths will have earned you nothing of the renown you crave.'

'We will take our fame to the Far-Wanderer's hall, where our fathers will know our faces and drink with us again,' Sigurd called. 'For Valhöll!' he roared in Norse, bringing a cheer from his men.

But Ealdred shook his head slowly, and in that small gesture there was enormous power, perhaps enough to make even Sigurd doubt his own words. I was afraid of Ealdred in that moment, because I knew he possessed a sharp mind, sharp enough to influence men, for how else had he got so many to break themselves against Sigurd's shieldwall, his skjaldborg?

'Sigurd, your men are loyal, I can see that. They are brave and they have a talent for death.' He grimaced. 'Our widows will attest to that.' He nodded at Olaf and Svein the Red. 'They will follow you to the grave and

I commend you for them. But you can give them more than six feet of English soil. Hear what I have to offer you.' He raised both arms then. 'If my words fall short, if my offer stinks like pig shit . . .' he shrugged, 'we will kill each other and join our fathers.'

'Fuck you!' Olaf yelled, and some of the other Norsemen echoed the sentiment.

But Sigurd was a jarl. And a jarl wants more for his men than a hole in the worm-riddled mud of his enemy's land.

'Speak, Englishman,' Sigurd commanded, as though Ealdred were his slave, and Ealdred, because he had the mind of a fox and because he knew the tides of fortune had shifted to his advantage, bowed his head obediently and took another step forward.

'You have come upon a rare opportunity, Sigurd. I expect you have stolen many passable trinkets from Christians who could not defend themselves, but they are nothing compared to what you stand to gain if you do the king's will.'

Sigurd pointed to the ealdorman. 'You Christians are fools,' he said. 'We have known this for countless years. You build your churches by the sea and fill them with gold and silver. Who guards them? Christ slaves! Men in skirts, feeble as old women. Your god makes you weak, Ealdred.' Sigurd gestured to his own warriors. 'We have no fear of him. We take what we want.'

Ealdred's mouth twisted beneath the moustache and his bodyguard dropped a hand to his sword's hilt. 'Easy, Mauger,' Ealdred muttered. 'I don't want you ruining Sigurd the Lucky's reputation.'

'I would like him to try,' Sigurd challenged, staring at Mauger. That would be some fight, I thought.

'Egfrith!' Ealdred called, keeping his eyes on Sigurd. There was no reply from the mass of English warriors, whose helmets were illuminated now by torch-bearers to their rear, though their faces remained shadow-shrouded. 'Now, now, Father, don't be shy. Come and blind Sigurd with your piety.'

A murmur rose from the English and out from the gloom shuffled a monk in a dark habit. He was a small man, especially amongst the ealdorman's household warriors, and his bald head reflected the moonlight as he broke free of the shielded throng. His hands clutched each other within the habit's long sleeves and his feet were bare. Tufts of hair sprouted above each ear and his nose was long and sharp between close-set eyes. The man looked like a weasel. He looked up at Sigurd, his eyes narrowed as though it pained him to open them, and he sniffed loudly.

'At least this creature does not hide behind rotten words, Ealdred,' Sigurd said, nodding at the monk. He sheathed his sword to show he was unafraid of the White Christ's magic. 'This Christ slave wears his fear like a cloak. Look at the hate in his little eyes.' Sigurd spat. 'They are like piss holes in the snow.'

'Father Egfrith is a man of God,' Ealdred said, 'and to him you are an abomination, a heathen like the Welsh who claw at us in the west. Those piss holes see you as no more than a wild animal.' He smiled. 'Though the thing about Egfrith is that he's sure to have a mind on showing you the error of your ways, eh, Father? Are

170

you tempted to take your crucifix and prise the Devil from Sigurd's black heart?'

'Evil is a tarnish of the soul, Lord Ealdred, and the soul once stained cannot be buffed to a shine like a shield boss,' Father Egfrith replied in a nasal voice. Then he frowned, as though his mind plucked at a distant memory. 'Well, sometimes there may be salvation,' he muttered, before staring once more at Sigurd. 'But this beast is beyond redemption.'

'Come now, Father, where is your resolve?' Ealdred asked. 'Even a bear can be taught to dance. We've all heard you say as much in your mind-numbing sermons.'

'Not all bears,' Sigurd interrupted with a grimace. 'You should listen to the little man, Ealdred. Some bears know only how to kill.'

Father Egfrith scuttled up to Sigurd, his narrow face pinched in anger. 'I may not have the limbs of an oak, heathen,' he began, his head level with Sigurd's chest, 'but I warn you that the Lord God lends me strength you couldn't possibly comprehend.' He held Sigurd's eye and I thought the Norseman would snap him in two. But Sigurd gave a deep laugh and gripped my shoulder, pulling me forward from the skjaldborg.

'Raven, now I am sure you are from the All-Father. You could not be from this land. I will not believe it!' Behind us, some of the Norsemen laughed at the monk squaring up to their jarl, but others stood grim-faced, expecting the slaughter to resume.

The monk leant forward, peering at me through the

171

gloom. 'Is your eye black?' he asked. His face was pale and his teeth were yellow as a rat's.

'Red, Father,' I said, touching my eye. 'It is a clot of blood.' I smiled at his obvious disgust.

'Heaven help us!' Egfrith said, signing a cross in the air. 'I hope you know what you're doing, Lord Ealdred,' he said, turning and hoisting a warning finger at the ealdorman. 'The Almighty sees all. You cannot tame this man. Satan will not abide shackles.'

The big warrior on Ealdred's left fidgeted as though bored by the whole thing. 'Get on with it, monk,' he snarled, 'or I'll martyr you and give your bones to the heathens for their broth.'

'Patience, Mauger,' Ealdred soothed, while Father Egfrith shivered and closed his eyes as though gathering his resolve. Some of the English began taunting the Norsemen, whilst others began to chant, 'Out! Out! Out!' But Ealdred raised a hand and the men held their tongues.

'Do it, monk,' Mauger growled. 'We don't have all night. The men want to know if there's killing to be done.'

Father Egfrith opened his eyes, cleared his throat with a cough, and leant forward so that I could smell the mead on his breath. 'There is a book,' he began in a voice that was half whisper, 'a very precious book.'

'A book!' Sigurd exclaimed.

'Shhh!' Egfrith held a finger up to Sigurd's lips and Sigurd leant back, bemused. The monk spun round. 'This is a mistake, Lord Ealdred. This man lives outside God's shadow. It's impossible. Heaven and all the saints preserve us!'

'Careful, monk!' Ealdred snapped. 'We made an agreement, remember?'

'But I did not know . . .' the monk began, but Ealdred silenced him with a look that promised pain.

'You can't turn tail now, Egfrith. Not if you value my cousin the king's favour,' Ealdred said, forcing a smile. 'How *is* the new dormitory coming along? I expect my cousin will soon pay you a visit to see for himself how God's servants are spending his money.' He turned to Mauger. 'It is so important to improve our monasteries, don't you think, Mauger?' The burly warrior simply grunted. 'Monasteries are the salt for the preservation of society,' Ealdred said to Sigurd as though the fact were as obvious as that of the sea's being wet. He shrugged. 'At least, that's what I have always thought. Do you agree, Mauger?'

The warrior spat. 'I know little of such things, lord,' he said, 'but I have heard it said these monasteries teem with men who find sport in each other's beds.'

Egfrith's narrow shoulders slumped in defeat. He nodded slowly and turned back to face Sigurd. 'This book is precious,' he said, his eyes glinting in the flame light, 'more beautiful than any book in this dark land. It is a thing of rare power, Sigurd.'

I saw Sigurd's eyes suddenly light up. 'It is a spell book?' he asked, his curiosity pricked awake.

Egfrith made the sign of the cross and Sigurd flinched slightly. 'It is a prayer book, heathen. And, as I said, it is powerful.' Egfrith seemed aroused by Sigurd's reaction.

173

'It is a book of the four gospels copied from the holy apostles' own works by our dear Saint Jerome.' Egfrith closed his eyes for a moment as though savouring his own words. 'Never has there been such an object in this land.'

'Let me see this book, monk,' Sigurd demanded, stretching out an arm as though he expected Father Egfrith to hand it over.

'I don't have it, you fool!' Egfrith snapped. 'Saint Peter's beard, if only I did. But—'

'But we know who does,' Ealdred interrupted, taking a step towards us. Mauger came with him. The ealdorman inclined his head to one side. 'Unfortunately, the bastard Irish, who wouldn't know a holy treasure if the good Lord etched His own name on it and bathed it in divine fire, let it fall into the hands of that ignorant swine Coenwulf.'

'Coenwulf is king of Mercia, lord,' I said to Sigurd. Even in those days, the kingdoms of Wessex and Mercia were old enemies, and although Wessex's last king, Beorhtric, had made King Offa of Mercia an ally, the new king Egbert sought to forge Wessex as an independent kingdom.

'Now the fog begins to thin,' Sigurd said with a wolfish grin. 'Power tastes sweet, hey? In my homeland anyone who owns a longship believes he should be a king.'

'And you, Sigurd son of Harald? Do you believe you are a king?' Ealdred asked. The bones of his cheeks cast sharp shadows above the drooping moustache. 'You have brought two longships to our shores.' He

174

raised a hand. 'They are safe, on my word. I ordered them spared in the hope that we might come to some arrangement.'

Sigurd grimaced at the allusion to the threat to *Serpent* and *Fjord-Elk*, then shook his head. 'A man does not decide if he is a king. The men around him do that.' He removed his helmet and ran a hand through his long hair. 'But a man should consider well what he reaches for. Where I come from, kings don't live long. I have killed one myself.'

'He must have died from the stink,' Egfrith mumbled, sniffing loudly. 'Fish guts, if my poor nose is not mistaken.' I could see his nostrils twitching.

'King Coenwulf has the book. King Egbert wants the book. That's the bones of it,' Ealdred said. 'What is not so simple is how our good and pious king is to come by the thing. If it was up to Mauger here, we'd simply march into Coenwulf's fortress, snatch up the gospel book slaughtering any who got in our way, feast on the king's cattle, then march back to Wessex in time for breakfast.' He glanced at Mauger who simply shrugged his huge mailed shoulders. 'But life is never as simple as a warrior would have it,' he said, returning to Sigurd. 'The so-called peace between Coenwulf's kingdom and our own is as fragile as a bird's wing. Apply pressure in the wrong place and . . .' He raised his hands and snapped an imaginary bone. 'We do not want war, Sigurd. At least, not yet.' He stole a glance at Mauger, who gave the hint of a smile.

I looked at Jarl Sigurd, seeing his astonishment clearly beneath his great yellow beard. 'You want me to walk into this king Coenwulf's mead hall and take the book from him?' he asked.

'You are a thief,' Ealdred stated without judgement in his voice. 'You and your men would not be standing on English earth if you did not lust for plunder. Father Egfrith assures me that such is your people's nature from the moment you slip into the world until the day you are cast into Satan's pit.'

'Why don't you send your dog?' Sigurd gestured to Mauger who was stretching the muscles in his thick neck. 'Or any of those whelps,' he added, pointing at the anxious bearded faces in the darkness twenty paces behind the English lord.

Ealdred sighed. 'Because they are Christians, Sigurd,' he said in a voice too low for his men to hear, 'even Mauger here, though you might wonder, and Christians know the value of such a book. The spiritual value,' he added quickly, raising a finger. 'Finding such a holy treasure in his possession might tempt even an honest Christian to betray any oath he had previously sworn to me. I fear he would keep the gospel book pressed against his heart and vanish like morning mist to live out his life a hermit on some seagull-shit-covered spit of land in the grey sea.'

Father Egfrith nodded solemnly. 'For a believer, the book is more precious than life itself,' he said and it was clear he was describing himself.

'As I cannot trust a Christian to do it, I must look elsewhere,' Ealdred said, looking at Sigurd intently, as though he knew he was taking a great risk. 'You, Sigurd, you are a heathen. To you the book is nothing.

You can't understand its power. By Christ, I'll wager you can't even read.' Sigurd scratched his beard and Mauger grunted as though he believed reading to be a waste of time best left to weaklings. 'But I know you understand silver, Sigurd,' Ealdred said, 'you *read* that well enough. We shall pay you in silver for the book.' The ealdorman's lips spread in a thin line because he anticipated the Norseman's next words.

'How much silver, Englishman?' Sigurd asked.

'Enough to buy yourself a kingdom and the men to make you king of it,' Ealdred replied, his eyes like chips from a broken icicle.

'I will speak with my men,' Sigurd said, replacing his helmet. Behind him Olaf still bristled, his sword gripped tightly and his shield raised. 'Perhaps they would rather sail up your east coast and find more stone houses filled with gold and slithering worms like him,' Sigurd said, nodding at Egfrith.

Ealdred shook his head slowly. 'You are not leaving here in your boats, Sigurd. My king would take my head if I let you sail away to murder and plunder God's houses.'

Sigurd drew his sword, the rasp of steel splitting the night. I drew mine too and stepped back just as Mauger raised his own blade and put himself between his lord and Sigurd. Some of the English clamoured for blood and behind me the Norsemen began to thump their swords on the backs of their shields.

Sigurd's face twisted with indecision and Ealdred, who had not drawn his sword, held out his arms as though weighing two objects. 'Now, Sigurd, where

177

do we go from here? Fight and lose your ships and your lives, or become richer than you ever dreamed. I have heard it said that your race was spawned from a red-haired Irish bitch and a sharp-tusked boar, which accounts for your fast anger and slow minds,' he stepped boldly in front of Mauger, raising his wounded arm to hold the warrior back, 'but I don't believe any man would turn his back on what I offer.'

'Come, Norseman,' Mauger mouthed, beckoning Sigurd on with his free hand. Sigurd's lips pulled back and his men bawled that they would cut the English down. The rhythmic thump of swords on shields grew louder and I thought the night would drown itself in blood and that I would die. My arm fell to trembling again as the battle thrill gripped me.

But then Sigurd slowly sheathed his sword and the thumping and jeers subsided. He turned, fixing me with his fierce eyes.

'It is not our time, Raven,' he said. 'Only when we're worthy of remembrance will Óðin's dark maidens take us to Asgard.'

Then he turned his back on the English, showing no fear of them, and raised his hand into the dawn sky for all his shield-warriors to see. 'We are going to fill *Serpent*'s belly with English silver!' he roared, his breath misting in the cold air, and his men cheered.

Shadowed by the English, we returned to the beach to find that Glum and his men had saved the ships from the rain of fire. They were still arrayed in battle formation, weary and pale as the sun which had broken free of the eastern horizon. The English skiffs still bobbed on the waves, their men out of Glum's reach but close enough to the longships to threaten them again with fire born of the embers kept in earthen vessels aboard. But there had been no real fight, because the English had too few trained spearmen to close with the mailed Sword-Norse. Still, Glum and the others were clearly relieved to see us coming towards them with Sigurd and Olaf at our head. Ealdred's men gripped their spears and arrows and axes and swords ready, should we turn on them, and now, in the daylight, we could see that there were even more of them than it had seemed in the night. Not all were warriors; many were farmers and craftsmen bearing the tools of their trades as make-do weapons, but even a scythe wielded by a strong arm will kill a man well enough. Sigurd had already lost good men and had no wish to lose more.

Though we half expected the English to attack us at any moment, they did not, and so friends greeted each other wearily and recounted what had happened to them. The sun rose still higher, warming our stiff bodies. Ealdred gave us time and space to look to our dead. Apart from white-haired Eric, three more had been killed in the fight outside the hall, making eleven in all who would never again take their places at *Serpent*'s oars: Sigtrygg, Njal, Oleg, Eyjolf, Gunnlaug, Northri, Thorkel, Thobergur, Eysteinn, tall Ivar with the good eyesight, and Eric, son of Olaf. We wrapped them in their cloaks and carried them up a goat path to an outcrop that overlooked a sheltered cove. A rock was lashed to each corpse to take it down to the sea-bed, for there was no time to burn the bodies, and Sigurd

179

preferred them to rot in seawater than Christian soil.

'Njörd Lord of the Sea will take them,' he said, 'to sit in Valhöll with their ancestors.' The heathens were quiet now, absent the laughter that usually followed them like gulls after a fishing skiff. I have learned how the death of a friend can tear out your guts. I watched the Norsemen carry the bodies of those they had known since childhood, when they played in the same trees and listened at the mead hall door to their drunken fathers' tales of battles and sea monsters and girls in far-off lands. I watched Olaf bear his dead son in his arms the way he must have done when Eric was a babe. Before he was wrapped in his cloak, the young Norseman's face looked peaceful; white like his hair. His father's face, beneath the bushy beard, was drawn. And wet.

When it was done, Sigurd shouldered his great shield and gripped his ash spear. His men took this to mean they should prepare themselves, and soon we were ready to set off in search of the holy gospel book of Saint Jerome. Glum had suggested we sail up the east coast and head inland along the river Thames into Mercia, but Ealdred and his men had laughed scornfully.

'I will honour our agreement, Ealdred, on my father's sword you have my word,' Sigurd said, affronted by the derision.

'Your word means spit to me, heathen,' Ealdred said, 'but I know what your longships mean to you. You walk to Coenwulf's land, or they will be ash carried on the tide.'

Sigurd's face twisted, his thick beard trembling, and I

180

felt the rage come off him like heat from a hearthstone. For a moment I hoped he would kill Ealdred. He turned to his men, for a heartbeat holding the eye of Svein the Red and Black Floki and stony-faced Olaf, then he nodded.

'A jarl should be generous,' he said, addressing his Fellowship, 'and no jarl ever sailed with better men. It is right that your journey chests should bulge with a king's silver, and an English king's hoard is as good as any.' Then he turned back to Ealdred, resting his left hand on his sword's lobed pommel. 'A book for a treasure hoard?' He laughed, shaking his golden head. 'I will never understand Englishmen.'

And so, though in truth we had little choice, Jarl Sigurd somehow made it seem that we held the advantage and stood to gain much more than the English. There was no shame in the Norseman's face as he explained the plan to his men, filling their heads with visions of silver. Then we prepared to set off north on foot towards the kingdom of Mercia and the gospel book that would make us rich.

A score of English warriors clambered into the longships, torches burning in their hands, and Knut cursed them for fools for taking fire on to seasoned timbers caulked with tarred rope. *Serpent* was already scarred with burn marks. But there was nothing the Norsemen could do now except despise those who threatened *Serpent* and *Fjord-Elk*, and our mood darkened again as we made ready to leave. The main body of Ealdorman Ealdred's force had retreated up the steep hillside to the high ground to lessen the risk of a fight breaking out, for they feared us still, and their spear wall resembled a palisade, shield bosses and spear tips glinting in the afternoon light. I was watching them when I heard Black Floki curse.

'What in the name of Frigg's tits is the Christ slave doing?' he asked, nodding at Father Egfrith. The monk was hawking spit into his cupped hand and dipping a small knife into it.

'I think he's shaving his face,' Olaf said, staring in wonderment.

Floki touched his own beard, then his sword hilt for luck. 'And why would a man wear women's skirts?' he asked, his face a frown beneath the black beard. 'We are Sword-Norse, Uncle! And we're travelling with that?'

'He can wear a silk headscarf and a pair of tits so long as he makes us rich, lad,' Olaf said, slapping Floki's shoulder. 'You ever seen a Christ book?' Floki shook his head, still bemused. 'Well he has,' Olaf said, pointing at Egfrith, 'and that's why Ealdred is sending the little man with us.'

Bjorn thumped the earth with his spear's butt. 'Uncle, why don't we double back tonight when it's dark? We could slaughter these bastards and be on our way.'

Olaf shook his head. 'It's just as well you're not our jarl, Bjorn.'

Bjorn shrugged his shoulders and looked at Black Floki, who grimaced.

'They'll have men and bloody firebrands in the hulls till we're long gone, Bjorn,' he said unhappily. 'I'd rather fight every Englishman between here and the

182

northern sea than watch *Serpent* and *Fjord-Elk* burn to ash.'

'He's right, lad,' Olaf said softly, and Bjorn nodded, relenting. Olaf turned and continued barking commands at the Norsemen. It had been his and Glum's job to see that the longships were securely moored and their small holds watertight, and now he was allocating burdens of food and water for the journey. Olaf was an over-bearing presence as he checked the men had their whetstones and all their war gear and made sure they looked more like gods of war than mortal men, their mail polished to a sheen and their blades honed to a vicious edge.

'He has buried his sadness very deep,' Svein the Red said, nodding towards Olaf, who was now bawling at Kon for not combing the clotted blood from his beard. Svein hefted a sack of cured meat joints on to the back of a sturdy pony, one of three supplied by Ealdred. 'He buries it the way the yew tree digs its roots far into the earth.'

'You'd think Floki was the one who'd lost a son,' I said, hanging two dozen dried codfish, strung through the gills, across the pony's neck. The black-haired Norseman was still muttering to himself as he readied his brynja, straps and huge round shield. 'He's more miserable than a fasting monk on a feast day.' The slash in my shin was filling my leg with hot pain. I would soon need to bind it in fresh linen.

Svein laughed. 'Ah, there's more chance of those fish jumping into the sea and swimming back to Hardanger Fjord than getting a smile out of Floki!' he exclaimed, rubbing the small of his back and cringing. 'Thór's balls I'm stiff. This walk will do us good, I think.'

'Forget walking, Svein,' Bjarni said, slapping the hilt of the sword at his hip, 'we'll be dancing when the rest of Wessex realize we're Norsemen. How far do you suppose we'll get? You think we'll even smell Mercia?' I thought Bjarni was right. We would never pass for Wessexmen or Mercians. Our best hope was that no English fyrd would be gathered in enough strength to fight us. Olaf knew this too, I realized, which was why he wanted us to look vicious. His hope was that any who saw us would be held rigid by fear, or driven to flight.

We took every weapon from the longships so that each man carried a short or long axe, usually strapped to his back, a spear, a long knife and a sword. Several carried bows and all had steel helmets, leather gambesons beneath mail brynjas, great round shields, and sturdy leather boots. On Bjarni's shield a snarling green dragon writhed on a red background and his was not the only fierce painted beast amongst us. Sigurd said I had done well during the fight and he even thumped my back affectionately when recounting how I had blown the war horn to make Ealdred think Glum and the others were coming to sow their slaughter. As a reward he said I could keep Njal's arms. He also said I had proved worthy of the sword he had given me on the beach. None of the other men challenged the gift, and so I fingered the sword's leather-bound grip and smooth iron pommel, hardly able to believe I now owned such things.

'It's not a pretty sword like some, but it's the quality of the blade and the arm behind it that's important,' Sigurd said. He could see my pride in the arms and he nodded, satisfied with how I looked. 'A sword is like a woman, Raven. If you look after it, it will look after you. After a time, you don't even notice the way it looks, yet its worth remains.'

'Thank you, lord,' I said, sombrely, and Sigurd nodded. Then he was amongst his men, encouraging them and praising their bravery. I looked at Sigurd's Wolfpack and a shiver touched my spine. We may have been without our ships and in the land of our enemies, but we looked fearsome enough to freeze the blood. We were more than forty armed and mailed men. We were death walking.

Egfrith the monk shuffled over, rubbing his bald head and wincing. 'On this enterprise you will leave the talking to me,' he said, his eyes flickering and returning to my blood-eye as he spoke, 'for my inspiration in this task comes from a higher authority even than our king.' Svein the Red burped loudly and looked down at the monk with something like amusement, but Egfrith pointed a finger at the giant and I thought he was either braver than he looked, or a witless fool. 'And if you have any sense of honour in your twisted hearts,' he warned, 'you will keep your oath to Ealdorman Ealdred. No harm must come to any man, woman or child of Wessex.' Svein feigned terror, signed the cross mockingly and walked off laughing.

'Do you see that man, Father?' I asked, pointing to Asgot who sat away from the others, casting the rune

185

stones. 'I have seen him pull the lungs from a Wessex-man they defeated in battle. The man was still alive when they laid the lungs across his back.'

I don't think Egfrith believed me. 'What kind of beast would do such evil?' he asked, sniffing. 'Why would they do it?'

I shrugged. 'They did it because they respected the man's bravery. And they wished to honour Óðin.' I smiled. Egfrith had signed the cross in Asgot's direction. 'If I were you, Father,' I said, 'I would be more concerned that Ealdred keeps *his* word and hands back Sigurd's ships when we return. Wessex will know terror if he does not.'

Egfrith seemed to consider this for a moment. 'No pillaging,' he said, blinking his squinty eyes, 'and, Heaven forbid, no rape.'

'None would dare, Father. Not with you around,' I said and Egfrith frowned because he knew I was teasing him. Ulf walked past and barked in the monk's ear, and he jumped like a hooked fish. Ulf laughed and the monk flushed crimson with anger.

'Leave him be, Norseman!' someone shouted, and I turned to see Mauger at the foot of the track spilling down from the bluff.

'Mauger! You're back!' Egfrith exclaimed, throwing out his arms and shooting me a triumphant look. 'By Christ, Mauger, you've the manners of Saint Cuthbert himself, compared to these beasts,' he said.

'Come, Father,' the big warrior said, gripping Egfrith's bony shoulder, 'don't tell me this lot have you pissing your skirts already?'

186

'Of course not!' Egfrith said, puffing up his chest like a winter robin. 'I'm just surprised to see you, that's all. It is rare that Ealdred lets you off the leash. I thought he had left me alone with the heathens, a lamb amongst wolves,' he said, glancing anxiously at the bustle around him. 'And there's always the Welsh to think of.'

'The Welsh won't come near this lot, Father,' Mauger growled.

'I pray you're right, Mauger,' Egfrith said. Then he stood a little straighter. 'Of course, there is the divine righteousness of our search to buoy my spirit, to strengthen the will, so to speak, but quite apart from that I shall regard the whole thing as a penance, for even such as myself is not without sin. The soul must be cleansed at times.' He winced under Mauger's grip. 'That said, glad to have another Christian around.' His beady eyes seemed to be searching Mauger's, as though he hoped the big man would confirm his devotion to the faith.

'I'm no lamb, Father,' Mauger said, twisting a thick silver arm ring so that the most elaborate part was visible. Both his huge arms, criss-crossed with white scars among the tattoos, bulged beneath twelve such warrior rings. His pride in them was clear.

'You are coming with us?' Egfrith asked with sudden apprehension. Mauger nodded. 'Have you ever considered a penance, Mauger? A man like you, well . . . you must be stifled by your own sin.'

Mauger shrugged. 'Lord Ealdred's gone soft,' he muttered, 'and I'm coming with you, but you can keep your penance. I'm here to stop you bringing the Lord's wrath down on their heathen heads before they've done the job.'

'Of course,' the monk said with a sharp nod. 'It's just as well, Mauger, just as well. The Lord's justice blows like a purging gale and he with the power to summon it forth must possess wisdom in equal measure.'

'Balls,' Mauger said with a smile that revealed dark teeth. He gripped Egfrith's shoulder and looked at me. 'You and I both know I'm here to wipe your arse and make sure these devils don't cut your throat in the darkest hour of the night.' Egfrith blanched at the suggestion. 'Don't worry, monk,' Mauger said, winking at me as I held a skin into which Svein the Red poured water from a barrel. 'I won't let the barbarians lay a filthy hand on your curd-white arse.' Egfrith turned and shot Svein the Red a superior smile. Mauger looked a formidable warrior and Egfrith was clearly confident in the man's prowess. But Svein was being careful not to spill any liquid and did not look up from his task.

The sun had yet to ascend its throne when we took our last look at *Serpent* and *Fjord-Elk*, sitting majestically on the calm sea. It was ebbtide and the mooring ropes were so taut that a white gull sat on one of them pruning his feathers. As the small waves lapped the shore it seemed to me that those ships, those sleek proud dragons, longed to be cut free; as though they craved the open water away from this foreign shore and its men who threatened their timbers with fire.

'My father would piss on his pyre to see me turn my back on them,' Kon grumbled, slinging his round shield across his back as we climbed the rocky slope away from the beach.

'Aye, he would, Kon,' Olaf put in, 'but who has ever heard of your father, hey, lad? His name never carried to my ear. A man doesn't get remembered for taking the safest path. He just gets old.' Olaf grunted as he clambered up the steep trail, clutching tufts of coarse grass. I climbed in front of Ealhstan, helping him where I could. 'You've got to push yourself, Kon,' Olaf went on. 'Sigurd will make a man of you.'

'Or a corpse,' Bjorn added with a wicked grin.

There were forty-seven of us now, including Egfrith and Mauger, and we loped off like wolves on the trail of prey. Mail jingled, shields banged against axe staves and boots tramped. And poor old Ealhstan had to keep up. The Englishmen lining the ridge backed off a hundred paces so we could pass without risk of a hurled insult turning into a fight. But I could see them gripping their weapons and shields as tightly as their faces gripped their hatred of us as we struck north towards a wooded valley to the west of the nearest settlement. Mauger had assured Sigurd that the trees would hide us from view and with any luck none from the village would know we passed. He said Lord Ealdred would not tolerate the death of some brave fool whose kin would then ask why their ealdorman had allowed pagan outlanders to roam freely about the land.

'There weren't so many of them,' Svein said, spitting back towards the distant English warriors. 'We should have wet our blades.'

'There were more last night, you brainless ox,' Black

Floki replied, gripping his spear loosely. He was not a big man like many of the others, but he was hard and lean and there was an assurance in the way he moved that made him seem even more lethal. 'Ealdred and his household men hared off eastwards at dawn,' he said. 'Seems some English pissed their breeches at seeing a longship off the coast at a place called Selsey. Danes, I'd wager.' He pointed to Olaf who walked up ahead with Mauger and Father Egfrith. 'Old Uncle overheard Mauger telling the monk,' he said.

'I noticed you and Uncle were snuggling up to the Christians, Floki,' Svein countered, grinning broadly. 'Are you missing your woman, little man?'

'That bald Christ-loving bastard's prettier than you, you red-haired sack of shit,' Floki snarled. 'Besides, someone should keep an eye on them. I'd sooner trust a Dane. There's no honour in Christians.'

'The English think you *are* Danes,' I said. 'They think all heathens are Danes.' And it was true, for we had heard of Danes raiding the eastern coast, but never men from Norway.

'English bastards,' Floki spat.

The other men's faces were grim too, for they knew Floki was right to be wary, and they feared they might never see their longships again.

Sigurd was the only Norseman I did not see turn one last time towards the sound of the breaking sea now muffled by the grassy bluff. Straight-backed and head high he set the pace as though the future beckoned him on with its promise of glory, and we followed, braced by our jarl's resolve and our fine arms which rattled

190

rhythmically. Njal had been the same height as me, but I had to wear a fur jerkin beneath his knee-length brynja to fill it as Njal's thick muscle had done before. I was hot. The first summer insects buzzed madly, streaking by too fast for the eye to catch, and the sun was beginning to hint at the heat it would soon throw down on a land that had broken winter's shackles. I sweated like an ox in the yoke.

Egfrith seemed somehow taller now that he walked beside Mauger whose bare arms were covered in those dark tattoos of snarling faces and the silver warrior rings that winked in the sunlight. The monk even began to sing a psalm in a surprisingly strong voice, but Black Floki drew his long knife and threatened with gestures to cut out his tongue and eat it. When Egfrith grabbed at Mauger for protection, the English warrior shrugged him off, warning him that he would cut out the offending tongue himself if the monk did not shut up.

'You sing like a kicked bitch, Father,' he said, and Egfrith, who seemed deeply hurt by the insult, walked in sullen silence from then on, for which we were all grateful.

It was no easy thing to leave behind the vast, bracing freedom of the sea and all its promise. To these Norsemen, the sea was a rolling road to wherever they pleased. It was unbound and unfettered; endless. But now it was behind us, remaining in our memories only, as we moved inland. Nevertheless, I felt a strange sense of peace come over me when we got amongst the outer trees of the forest. The feeling grew stronger the deeper we went. Oak and elm, beech, hornbeam, thorn and ash denied light to the mossy, damp-smelling earth, and the twisting branches of ancient trees met above us as though exchanging news of the world beyond. The sights and smells and the harsh chattering of chaffinches took me back to the days I had spent alone in just such a forest, cutting timber for old Ealhstan until my back was filled with a warm ache and my hands were chafed raw. As I walked, my mind delved into the only memories I had, like roots thirsty for water, and though there was a strange comfort to be found in them, the memories were of being alone and the comfort was also an ache. For the past was dead to me now that I knew the thrill of the sea, the noise of battle and the fellowship of warriors.

'There are spirits here, Raven,' Bjarni said, his eyes rolling up to the leafy canopy. 'Can you feel them?' We entered a glade where the sun broke through, dappling the men with blades of golden light.

'Yes, I feel them, Bjarni,' I said. 'We all do.'

'They're watching us, brother, these spirits,' Bjorn said, running a hand over the dark moss creeping up an ancient tree stump. 'But they stay hidden. They are safe in the forest. Safe from the Christians who would banish them to some dark, foul, stinking place.' He gestured to Father Egfrith up ahead. 'Don't be fooled by his puny body.' He grimaced. 'His kind can kill spirits.'

'For once, the young speak wisely,' old Asgot put in, the words dry and brittle, the first he had spoken for hours. 'This land is sick with disease. The Christ followers have turned their backs on the old ways and the spirits hate them for it.' He swept an arm through the air. 'We must be careful,' he warned. 'The shades of this place must not mistake us for Christians.'

'How do we tell them what we are, old man?' Bjorn asked. 'Should we sing one of the old songs?'

'Not enough, Bjorn,' Asgot muttered. 'Not enough.'

'A sacrifice,' Black Floki said flatly, his top lip curled with ire. 'We should sacrifice the monk.' I looked back at old Asgot who now grinned like a child.

'No need to dull your blade, Floki,' I said, hoping my eyes did not betray the fear that twisted in my guts at the memory of Griffin's slaughter. 'The spirits are not blind, they are ancient and wise.'

'What do you know of shades, boy?' Asgot asked. The man hated me.

'I know there is more chance of Floki being mistaken for a March lamb than a Christian,' I said. Floki smiled at this and the others grunted their agreement. I hoped their thoughts of a blood offering had been borne away on the moss-scented breeze.

Deep in the forest we came across animal tracks, the muddy ground worn smooth by badgers, foxes, weasels and hares, though we never encountered the animals themselves. I hoped one of the Norsemen might take down a deer with his bow, but it was a foolish hope, for we were forty-seven men and must have sounded like thunder as we crashed through the ancient still-ness. The only creatures we saw were birds and insects, though there was always the chance that a boar might

193

charge from the undergrowth to smash someone's leg bones to splinters. I have known the beasts to be so intent on foraging that, when startled, they have fled from one hunter and impaled themselves on another man's spear.

We were still in the heart of the forest when the air turned cool and the gathering darkness made it dangerous to go on. Old Ealhstan was ashen-faced, tired and breathing hard. I saw him rubbing his hip, which often pained him, so I gave him a straight ash limb to lean on. But Sigurd would not risk one of his own men twisting an ankle on an exposed tree root or smashing his head on a low branch, and announced that we would spend the night on the mossy banks of a trickling stream. It was too early in the year for the biting flies that make brown clouds in such places, and so it was a good place to rest. And we were not alone in thinking it. Clearly, animals came here to drink from the stream, and deer gnawed the bark from nearby trunks so that they gleamed smoothly in the twilight. A huge fallen ash lay like a sleeping giant, slender saplings growing up around it, reaching for the light created by the old tree's demise. Ripped from the earth, the ash's enormous root balls were suspended some twenty feet up, resembling the giant's shaggy hair. The trunk would shelter us, whilst a large rock some ten paces away would provide cover for a fire and bounce its heat on to us as we slept.

The fire was crackling and popping angrily when Asgot began to cut a strip of bark as wide as his arm from the fallen ash. I watched the godi from a distance.

194

Ealhstan saw me watching and slapped my face to break the spell.

'I'm just curious, Ealhstan,' I said, rubbing my cheek, but the old carpenter made the sign of the cross and pointed to the Norse sword beside me and shook his head, the last of his wispy hair floating in the breeze. 'A man should know how to use a sword,' I said, 'it is how he protects what he loves.' I remembered plump, red-cheeked Alwunn from Abbotsend and wondered if I had loved her. I didn't think I had. Then I looked back to Asgot, but Ealhstan tugged my shoulder and pointed at my face. Then he looked up at the leafy boughs above us and pretended to spit. I knew he meant that by taking on the ways of the Norsemen I was spitting in Christ's face. 'I don't want to make cups, old man,' I said tersely, half regretting the words, though it was the truth. Ealhstan pointed at my hands and sneered as though to say I did not have the skill for carpentry anyway. Then he turned his back on me and lay down. We rested quietly until the silence grew too heavy, and I left the growing warmth of the fire to see what Asgot was doing.

'What will you do with it, Asgot?' I asked. He held the thick slice of bark close to his face, then sniffed it and rubbed a finger across its surface.

'Asgot?' I said, not liking being so close to the godi but eager to know what heathen magic he was making.

He did not take his eyes from the bark strip. 'This tree has lived for thousands of years, boy. Maybe since the dawn of the world, and it's not dead yet. Not fully dead, anyway. As it takes many men's lifetimes to grow, so it takes as many to die.' He held up the bark as though it was as precious as a bar of silver. 'This tree has seen many things. It has secrets, *Raven*,' he stressed the name scornfully, 'and it will whisper them to one who is willing to listen.'

He turned away, so I gripped his shoulder and he flinched at my touch. 'Will you show me, Asgot?' I asked, spellbound. I had heard of the rune lore, but who of us has seen it with his own eyes? Asgot's grey eyes narrowed with suspicion and he screwed up his face as though I stank. Then he stared at Sigurd who was laughing heartily because a flame had leapt up to singe Black Floki's beard. 'Sigurd likes you, Raven,' he muttered, 'and though he has his faults, arrogance and recklessness included, he is far-seeing. I will not deny it. And he respects the gods.' He frowned. 'Most of the time.' Then those eyes flashed and the godi's mouth twitched within his grey beard. 'Yes, I will show you,' he said. 'Soon enough.'

So we journeyed north day after day, rarely seeing a living soul as we pushed deeper into Wessex. A sense of unease had been swelling within the belly of the Fellowship and I grew to understand why. The Norsemen were venturing ever further into a land that was strange to them. It was a land of Christ worshippers, men who despised them. And they could no longer smell the sea.

'It bodes ill to be so far from our ships,' Ugly Einar said. He was a flat-nosed man with a ruined lip and whenever he looked at me I knew he saw me dying beneath his broad-hilted sword.

'And going further still,' Glum moaned, looking up to the leafy canopy and the blue sky beyond. 'Nothing good can come of it, Einar. Only a fool tempts the Norns. I swear I can hear their fingers weaving a dark, bloody pattern for us.'

I knew there were at least two or three men of *Fjord-Elk* who agreed with their shipmaster. Ugly Einar belched loudly. 'Raven and the tongueless old fool have brought us bad luck,' he said, thumbing at me over his shoulder.

'What are you scared of, Einar?' Bjarni challenged him. 'Look around you, man. This is good land and there's plenty of it. We'll send our sons here one day, hey, Bjorn!' He slapped his brother's shoulder. 'They'll turn the soil and grow fat on pork and mead.'

'Brother, they'll take pasture from the English and live like kings,' Bjorn replied, kicking the head off a tall white mushroom, 'and all because we took English silver and drenched the land with English blood.'

'You two are too dumb to know when your luck has drained away,' Einar countered miserably, tipping an imaginary cup upside down. 'Men will always fight for land like this, even after you take it from them. The English must have won it themselves once. Farmers don't own rich soil for long, not unless they are as handy with the sword as they are with the plough. Remember that, Bjorn. Your brats' swords will never be dry.'

'You're an ugly, whinging woman, Einar,' Bjarni said.

Einar grimaced, his strange lip white beneath his flat nose. 'Say what you like, but it'll be you next, lying stiff and bloodless like the others. Like young Eric with your arse full of arrows.' He glanced quickly at Olaf, then seemed encouraged that he had not heard. 'Thór's balls, Bjarni,' he blurted, 'the English runt put an arrow in you and you let him live!' I shrugged awkwardly at Bjarni, who raised his eyebrows as though he had surprised himself by sparing me. 'As for that dry-mouthed old bastard,' Einar continued, pointing at Ealhstan, 'he follows behind like a stray dog begging for scraps.'

'The lad's more of a Norseman than you, Einar,' Bjarni said, winking at me mischievously. Anger flared in Einar's face then.

'Einar's an ugly whoreson,' Glum added, 'but he's right. We should do what we are good at and leave the mercy to the White Christ followers. Did you know they are told to love their enemies?' He clutched his sword's hilt and I think he feared the words themselves. 'Mercy is the same as weakness.' He nodded. 'And Óðin All-Father despises weakness.'

'He despises cowards, too,' Svein the Red rumbled, 'and men who do not honour their jarl.' The inference was clear and Einar and Glum wisely held their tongues, for Svein would sooner fight ten warriors with his bare hands than betray his oath of loyalty. And his oath, like every man's in the Fellowship, belonged to Sigurd.

That night after making camp, I took the small knife which Ealhstan had found round my neck and turned

198

it over in my hands, as I often did, in the hope that the feel of it might kindle some spark in my mind to burst into memory. But the two swirling serpents carved in the white bone hilt were silent, their secrets safe as a dragon's hoard.

'Men are not supposed to think so much, Raven,' Bjorn said, beckoning me to my feet, an ash spear in each hand. I had barely stood when he threw me one of the spears and gave a great beaming smile. 'Let's make better use of our time.'

And so, that night, my lessons began. Bjarni and Bjorn taught me how to kill with sword and spear. The next night, they taught me the use of the round shield, and the night after that they showed me how the shield was not merely for defence but could be used in the attack, to smash a man's face to bloody pulp. They worked me hard, making me repeat every move, whilst introducing new techniques that tested me sorely.

For my part I found that the more cuts and bruises I got, the better I became at avoiding them next time. Techniques that had at first felt clumsy became instinctive. Moves began to flow one into another, my feet working in harmony with my upper body as they stirred the forest litter. I sought openings in the Norsemen's defences, desperate to land blows in vengeance for my pains.

At first we fought with our swords wrapped in cloth, but even then we risked breaking bones and the blades themselves, so Bjarni made Ealhstan fashion practice weapons of ash, and because they were light I borrowed several of Svein the Red's great silver arm rings to add weight to my thrusts and shield parries. I admit during these bouts I let my imagination roam freely and in those wanderings the warrior rings were my own. Eventually, when at last I had mastered the basics, the other Norsemen took an interest in the fights, and every night I would take on all comers and they would batter me. I never won in those early days.

# CHAPTER EIGHT

'YOU'RE GETTING HANDY WITH THE SWORD, RAVEN,' OLAF said, tearing off a chunk of stale bread before handing the loaf to Black Floki. My shoulders ached from the previous night's training, but I felt a strange joy in the discomfort, as though my muscles and limbs had earned the right to rest. The forest floor was damp with dew and the day promised to be warm and bright. 'Still clumsy with the spear though, but the spear is not as easy as it looks,' Olaf added. 'Oh, every man and his dog uses the spear, but few do it well.' The ghost of a smile touched his face. 'My Eric was a good lad with the spear. But not as good as you with the sword. Comes natural to you, eh?'

'Like falling asleep after a good ploughing,' Knut said distantly, his mind no doubt on some braided blonde beauty.

'I've not won a bout yet, Uncle,' I said, rolling my shoulders to rekindle the warm pain. But Olaf's thoughts were of Eric.

'He'd have taken you with the axe, I'd wager,' he

201

said. 'We spent months with the axe. It takes a rare skill and even then many years to master.'

'One of these days I'll give Bjarni some bruises to match these,' I said, rubbing my left arm, which had taken a hundred blows beneath the shield and was an angry purple. Olaf blinked slowly, then gave a shallow nod of thanks for my poor attempt to steer his mind from his son.

'I miss the lad,' Bjarni said, a sad smile hiding in his beard. 'When we return to Harald's fjord, I'll pay a good skald to sing of how he wet his axe in that worm Ealdred's blood.' The smile cracked several drying cuts and one of them spilled new blood into his beard.

'Eric was brave, Uncle,' I said, 'and his mother will be proud of the way he served Jarl Sigurd.'

'No, Raven, she won't,' he said, shaking his shaggy head. 'She cursed me for taking the lad away and she'll have my balls for getting him killed.' Now Olaf smiled but there was no warmth in it. 'I'll be lucky to eat another good meal as long as I live and breathe.'

'Quiet your bleating, Uncle,' Black Floki said. 'Your woman's no dried-up stick yet. You'll have another son, you old bastard.' I thought Olaf would burst with anger then, but he simply stared at the fire, which was pale in the dawn light, and half raised his eyebrows as though Floki was right. 'No woman stays angry for ever,' Floki added, plaiting his glossy black hair. He turned to me. 'They never forgive you, Raven, you'll learn that much, but they still like a good hump on a cold night just like the rest of us.' A murmur of agreement stirred the camp.

'Does Sigurd have a son?
golden-haired jarl who sat
priest and his bodyguard Ma

'He did once,' Olaf replied
broken by a horse's kick. Se
Sigurd's fury could have turn
shaking his head in rememb
died before he could talk.' I
man like Sigurd must have a st
things, but old Asgot reckone
the gods and I think Sigurd b
trying to win Óðin's favour ever sn
can bet your teeth on that. The All-Fathe
jarl like Sigurd.' His smile was warm this time. 'L
at him. He's not far off a god himself, and that's why
men follow him. Any of the lads you see here would
die in the shieldwall with Sigurd.' Olaf pursed his thick
lips. 'Even Floki would cross Bifröst, the shimmering
bridge, with Sigurd. Am I right, Floki?'

Black Floki thrust his knife into the tree stump he
was sitting on and looked up, his eyes dark as bottom-
less wells. 'I long to spend the afterlife in Valhöll as
much as any Norseman,' he said in a low voice, 'and
any Norseman who knows Sigurd Haraldson knows
there's a stout bench and a gilded cup waiting for him
at the high end of Óðin's hall.' He grimaced as he
pulled the knife free. 'I'll be at Sigurd's shoulder when
the death maidens come for him. That much I know.'

'That may be sooner than you think, cousin,'
Halldor said. Halldor was obsessive about sharpening
his weapons and always expected a fight. At first I

ether it was fear or bloodlust
, but now I know it was not fear.
e that English priest is taking us?' he
g the edge of his bone-handled knife.
it his measly throat and bury him here
thickets. Let his white arse wear a crown
in the afterlife. His god would like that, I

remind you of that when we're sharing out the
glish king's silver, Halldor,' Olaf said, standing and
walking off to take a piss. The others were readying
themselves for the day's journey. 'Then you'll be glad
you left his arse alone,' he called over his shoulder.

I had thought we were making fair progress, but later
that day Father Egfrith moaned that we were too slow
and would be lucky to reach King Coenwulf's stronghold before judgement day. 'We English have little to
fear from Norsemen if they all amble like old women
on their way to market,' he complained, shaking his
tonsured head and giving a loud sniff. He was still wary
of my blood-eye, but the fact that I spoke his language
compelled his tongue to wag in my direction, and
though I disliked the man I realized he was right about
our slow pace. The truth was that the Norsemen were
cautious creatures on land, as though they had stowed
their confidence aboard their longships, and though
Egfrith was a weak-looking man there seemed little
wrong with his thin white legs as he strode at the head
of the company, urging us to keep up.

'Norsemen prefer rowing to walking, Father,' I said

with a smile, enjoying the weight of the shield on my back.

'Then perhaps they should walk on their arms,' he retorted, pleased with his wit and glancing to the sky as if seeking his god's approval.

'Do you know what they love even more than rowing?' I asked, but he did not know, so I told him. 'Pulling out the innards of English monks,' I said, trying not to smile. 'I am sure you will find them . . . interesting companions.' I watched him from the corner of my eye, seeing his face drain of colour. Beside him, Mauger was grinning. I admit I enjoyed tormenting the monk, even though I knew there was no honour in it. I was like a child pulling the wings off flies or cutting worms in half. It was cruel, but it was fun.

'How did you come to be with the Norsemen, lad?' Mauger asked. The dying sun was glinting off the rings he wore on his thick, tattooed arms. Few of the men travelled in their mail now, though Halldor always did. Floki's cousin would have had mail instead of skin if he could.

'I chose to join them,' I lied. 'Life in my village was the life of a sheep.' I thought it was something Svein might say.

Mauger grinned. 'And I suppose the mute old man *chose* to join them too,' he said, and I supposed he knew the truth of it all.

I glanced back at the old carpenter and felt a pang of guilt for not walking with him at the rear of the column. But he was still angry with me, and for my part I had little to say to him. Besides, Sigurd had asked me to walk with him at the head, and I was proud to do it. 'Ealhstan was always kind to me,' I said.

'Raven has a Norseman's heart, Mauger,' Sigurd said, stepping up to cuff the back of my head.

'They say you heathens have black hearts,' Mauger said, 'but I don't believe it.' Beneath the thick beard his face was hard, like carved rock, and mostly without expression.

'And they do!' Egfrith exclaimed. 'A pagan's heart is black as pitch and empty, empty as a bishop's belly in the Lenten fast.'

'Horseshit, Father!' Mauger said. 'I have killed Danes before and their innards are red same as yours and mine.' He gave a wry grimace. 'Though their hearts were smaller,' he said, clenching a fist.

'Were they infants, Mauger? These Danes you killed?' Sigurd asked, winking at me. 'Sucking at their mothers' tits when you butchered them?' The Norsemen laughed and so did I, but Father Egfrith stiffened and looked at Mauger as though he expected a fight, and I shivered then, for I would not have wanted to fight Mauger. He would have killed me in the time it takes a heart, black or red, to beat. But the English warrior merely glowered and I was relieved, because hatred needs a drawn blade to kill.

That night a man named Arnvid made a stew of mutton, turnips, mushrooms and barley, and when it was ready I took a steaming bowlful to Ealhstan who was already asleep amongst the thick ribs of a beech trunk, a fur pulled up to his chin. I touched his bony shoulder and he opened one eye with a scowl, then murmured something unpleasant.

'You must keep your strength up, Ealhstan,' I said, putting the bowl in his lap so that he had to take it or let it spill. 'Though it might be worth getting the monk to bless it first,' I said, nodding at the stew. He brought the bowl to his face and sniffed. His nose crinkled disapprovingly. 'I don't think Arnvid is much of a cook.' I grinned and the old man grunted, then slurped at the stew, his eyes all the while boring into mine so that it was almost painful. Ealhstan had been like a father to me. He had shared his home and his livelihood with me and most of all he had accepted me when others had not. But that was before, and like dreams that fade on waking my memories of that time were dissipating, being replaced by a new and hard reality; a reality which my youth with its vigour and ambition craved more than anything. I was becoming a part of this heathen fellowship. I was drawing on the Norsemen's experiences, on their beliefs and their myths, like a tree that sinks deep roots in search of water. Yet each root I laid was like a nail of betrayal in the old carpenter's heart. I could see it in the way he looked at me and it made me feel ashamed.

'Eat up, old man,' I said, thumbing a drip of stew from the grey whiskers on his chin. Suddenly, he grabbed my hair above my left ear and gripped it tightly and I did not know if he wanted to hit me or hug me. Then he made a sound in his throat, nodded and stroked my hair roughly. 'I'll be back to make sure you've eaten it all,' I warned him, pointing at Arnvid's stew, then I stood, feeling the glow of the fire play across my face, and walked away from the old man, trying in vain to swallow the lump in my throat.

Later, a warrior called Aslak interrupted my sword training with Bjorn. Aslak was a lean man like Floki, his muscle taut and hard. I had seen him fight and his footwork was quick, his feints were flawless and he wasted little strength on poor thrusts. There was a cold assurance about the man. And now he wanted to fight me.

'Bjorn and Bjarni have taught you how our women-folk fight,' he said with a brown-toothed grin, 'but it's time you learned a man's work, Raven.'

Bjorn bowed in mock reverence and walked off to sit with his brother as Aslak took up the wooden sword and made some practice cuts through the air between us.

'I'd prefer to fight you when you're fully grown, Aslak,' I said, for even in that short time my shoulders had broadened, my arms had thickened and my arrogance had bloomed. My body had devoured the training and now it ached to be tested. Aslak smiled at the insult, then came at me like a streak of lightning from Thór's chariot. I threw up my left arm, catching the blow on my shield, and sprang back out of his reach. He came again with a flurry of strikes, some of which I blocked, though plenty caught my shoulders and one glanced my head.

'My helmet, Svein!' I called. Aslak wore his already. I caught the helmet, thumped it down and gave a low roar like the ones I had heard from Sigurd at Ealdred's hall. Then I attacked, smashing the wooden sword on to Aslak's shield and this time forcing him on to the back foot. He thrust his shield into my face and I felt my nose crack. Blood filled my mouth and tears blurred my eyes as I dropped my sword and grabbed for Aslak's shield, pushing it out wide and lurching forward, crashing into him so that he stumbled backwards, tripping over Svein's outstretched foot. I leapt on to him, hands clutching at his neck, and butted my helmet into his face. I was full of fury, but Aslak somehow wriggled free and slammed a fist into my eye. I tried to rise but the fists kept coming, smashing into my cheek and jaw. Then my world turned black as blindness.

When I woke, a fresh wave of pain broke over me and I vomited.

'It's just the blood you swallowed, Raven,' Svein said. 'Makes you puke. We put you on your side but you must have drunk enough of the stuff.'

Gingerly, I put a hand to my swollen jaw and broken nose. 'Do I still look pretty?' I asked, then spat. My nose felt three times its normal size and was stuffed with congealing blood.

'Your hair is the only pretty thing about you, Raven,' Svein said, laughing. 'At least you broke Aslak's nose too, and he's not happy about it.'

'That takes the edge off the pain,' I said, smiling. I could not breathe through my nose, but my head was full of the metallic stench of blood. 'He battered me, Svein.' The others were sitting around three crackling fires, talking in low voices and playing games.

'He battered you,' Svein confirmed with a nod, 'but you learned a good lesson.'

'Did I?' I said, wincing at a shooting pain in my head.

'Of course you did, lad. You can learn a hundred cuts and pretty dances, a hundred tricks, and it'll do you as much good as a spoon with a hole in it.' He frowned. 'Or a comb with no teeth,' he added, holding up his old antler comb. 'It's blind, bloody fury that puts men down. And you put him down, lad. You could have finished him. Maybe.' He shrugged his huge shoulders. 'Next time, you will.'

'Thank you, Svein,' I said, for without the Norseman's help I would not have put Aslak down. 'But I'll do it alone next time.'

He shrugged again. 'I've never liked the runt,' he said, beginning to pull the old comb through his thick red beard. 'He had his way with my sister when we were children. Denies it of course, but I'm not as dumb as they think I am.'

I grinned despite the pain and tried to imagine what Svein's sister looked like. In my mind she was not pretty. 'You're protective of her, hey, Svein?'

He nodded and tugged at a thick red knot of curled hair. 'But I don't need to be,' he said, wide-eyed. 'She's even bigger than me.'

A fresh May breeze blew through the camp, rustling the beech and oak and bringing the long hollow hoot of an owl. Someone moved away from the fire and the orange glow fell across the dried blood on my tunic.

'Where's Ealhstan?' I asked, spitting another wad

of bloody phlegm and sitting up to search the flame-lit, flickering faces. There was no sign of the old man amongst the shadows beneath the beech tree where he had been sleeping.

Svein scratched his groin. 'Having a shit, maybe.'

'I hope he's off somewhere making me a curved sword so I can fight Aslak from behind a tree,' I said. But something was gnawing at my guts and suddenly I feared for the old man. I stood up as a wave of nausea hit me, making me retch. But my stomach was empty and I just spat more blood. 'I'm going to look for him,' I said, dragging my forearm across my mouth.

I walked through the camp to men's jeers and the odd compliment, and passed Aslak who nodded grimly. His nose did not look broken, but Svein said it was, and I grinned at him before kneeling by Bram. 'Bram, have you seen Ealhstan?' He was drinking as usual, but even when drunk Bram did not miss much.

'Haven't seen him since before your dance with Aslak, Raven,' he replied, pursing his lips. 'Now you mention it, old Asgot's scuttled off somewhere, too.' He frowned and craned his neck, peering through the groups of hunkered men. 'Glum's gone, and Ugly Einar.'

'And Black Floki,' I added.

'No, lad, he's on watch out there,' he said, pointing northwards towards the higher ground where, before there were men, a great rock had burst through the mossy earth. It was a good natural vantage point and because of it Sigurd had been happy to set a smaller watch than usual.

211

'Want me to come with you?' Bram asked. I shook my head. 'Ah, I'm not tired anyway,' he said, hauling himself to his feet with a grunt. 'I enjoy our walks. Remember last time?'

'Last time the English cleaned their boots on your face, Bram,' I said.

He batted the words away. 'You should be a skald, lad, the way you decorate a story.' He stumbled. 'The ale was strong tonight,' he muttered, blinking the drink from his eyes. 'Well, come on, Raven, time to fly.' He flapped his arms. 'Let's find your old man before he stumbles into a boar pit. Here,' he said, handing me a spear and snatching up his own.

As we moved away from the camp, the men's voices became muffled and the smell of smoke gave way to the pungent aroma of tree bark and forest litter. The moon was full and huge, but black clouds skated across her to extinguish the silver shafts that pierced the canopy. We trod carefully, using our spears to push through the low branches, and made our way towards the higher ground where Black Floki stood watch.

Bram stopped and I heard leaves being ripped from a low plant. 'I'll wait down here, lad,' he said, pulling down his breeches and squatting. 'Give Floki a kick in the bollocks if he's snoring up there.' Then he gave a great fart.

Once amongst the rocks I could see better, for there were no trees to shut out the moonlight, and when I had climbed to the low summit I saw a figure sitting at the far edge.

'What do you want, Raven?' Floki said without turning round. 'Uncle sent you to check up on me, did he?'

'No,' I replied, angry with myself for letting Floki hear me approach, though I couldn't say how he had known it was me. 'I'm looking for Ealhstan,' I said casually. 'The old goat's wandered off.' I walked up to Floki and crouched beside him, following his line of sight into the dark forest. 'Have you seen him?'

Floki turned to me, his thin lips twisting into a half-smile. He was crouched in the shadow of a smooth boulder so that his lean face looked as black as his hair, but the moonlight slashed across my own face. After my fight with Aslak and with my blood-eye I must have been a terrible sight.

'A few of the lads clattered off through there some time ago,' he said, pointing into the thicket. 'Haven't been back this way, though. Well, don't you look pretty tonight.'

'Did you get a look at them?' I asked, my heart pounding in my chest. 'What were they doing?'

'Hunting?' he suggested, though I knew he did not believe that. He stared at me. Somewhere out there in the black forest a wolf howled, the sound cutting through the night. Floki spat and clutched the hilt of his sword with his left hand to ward off evil. 'Asgot was one of them, I'll tell you that much,' he said. 'You could hear the old bastard's coughing a mile off. Don't know who the others were.' I made to rise, but Floki grabbed my shoulder. 'You'd be better to leave things alone, Raven. Take this warning. There are those of us who believe you and the tongueless old man have brought us bad luck.'

I shrugged off his hand and stood. 'Maybe I have brought you bad luck,' I said, staring into his narrowed eyes and gripping my spear. 'Your own jarl said he saw death in me. What do you see? Do you see your own death, Floki?' I dared. 'Do you fear it?'

Floki grinned then. 'Go, Raven,' he said, nodding in the direction he had pointed before. 'Weave your own fate if you think you can. For some I think it is too late.'

At that I ran down into the woods, letting the branches claw my face and hands. The wolf howled again and I knew that the Norns, those maidens of men's fate, were weaving their dark patterns. And I knew I was too late to stop them.

A little deeper into the forest I heard a man's voice, but when I froze to listen there was nothing besides the sounds of the night. Whoever it was had heard my approach, but stealth meant nothing now and so I pushed on in the direction of the voice, stumbling over roots in my haste. The low sound of a single speaker was clear now, and there was something about it that stopped my heart. Then, sooner than I had expected, I was there, facing an ancient oak whose ridged trunk dominated the small clearing. Glum and Ugly Einar stared at me wide-eyed, as though they had been expecting the All-Father himself. Then they turned back towards the old oak and I saw Sigurd's godi, Asgot, standing in the shadows. I knew it was his voice I had followed. The old man's face was smeared

214

with something dark and the whites of his eyes shone strangely in the gloom.

'Where's Ealhstan, Glum?' I asked, pointing Bram's spear at him as my right hand gripped the sword's hilt at my waist.

Asgot continued his incantations and Glum, without turning to face me, pointed up towards the oak, to its twisting black branches and shady fluttering leaves. Keeping an eye on Glum, I drew nearer and rounded the broad trunk. And I found my friend. Ealhstan hung from the base of a thick branch, an arm tied to each dividing limb. His naked body burned silver in the moonlight.

'Ealhstan!' I cried. But the old carpenter was dead. Or at least he should have been, but his left leg twitched horribly. A black gash ran the length of his torso and the meat of his guts hung from the next branch like a heavy rope. I vomited bitter-tasting lumps.

'I'll kill you!' I roared at Glum. I launched the spear at him but it flew wide. I fumbled to draw my sword as Einar and Glum drew their own weapons and braced for my attack. Asgot shuffled deeper into the shadows.

'Come, Raven!' Glum shouted. 'I shall give Óðin your corpse too.' I stepped forward and swung my sword madly. It felt as light as a stick and it seemed that Glum and Einar were rooted to the ground, so slow were they. My sword struck Einar's, breaking it in two, and his white eyes stared as I stepped up and scythed my blade into his head, screaming like a wild animal and spitting vomit. As he collapsed I yanked the blade free, sending chunks of brain flying, then blocked

Glum's sword and slammed my foot into his groin. He staggered back and I stepped up, swinging my sword, which was hungry for more flesh and bone.

'Stop, Raven! No more!' Bram's voice rang out. 'Stop, lad, or I'll put you down!' Then I could not move at all. My rage burned but my body had turned to granite and I struggled until I realized that Bram's arms bound me as securely as the magic fetters bound the mighty wolf Fenrir, so that the more I struggled, the tighter the bonds became. 'Enough, lad! If you don't hold still, I'll knock you out!'

'It's over, Raven,' came a voice from behind a flaming torch. Sigurd's face flickered in the orange light.

'I'll kill him!' I roared.

'No, Raven. You will not. There has been enough death this night,' Sigurd said, watching two of his men drag Ugly Einar's corpse through the blue forest flowers that stirred like the sea as flame light and breeze played across them.

I was done now. Empty. Bram must have sensed it for he let go and stepped away. I stood on trembling legs and wiped the spittle from my lips. 'Let me cut him down, lord,' I pleaded, staring at Ealhstan hanging there. The old man's leg was still now. He was gone.

Sigurd frowned and shook his head. 'The body must remain where it is. The sacrifice has been made and it would dishonour the All-Father to take it back.'

'No, lord,' I spat angrily.

'It stays, Raven,' Sigurd said, his eyes cold as steel. Then he turned to Asgot, who had Ealhstan's blood smeared across his cheeks and in his grey beard.

216

'Finish the rites, godi,' he commanded. Asgot nodded obediently as Mauger stepped into the clearing, a spitting torch in his hand. Father Egfrith was with him and when the monk saw what had been done to Ealhstan he gave a low moan and fell to his knees, making the sign of the cross with one hand and holding his stomach with the other. Even Mauger spat in distaste and crossed himself.

'You are devils! You are the turds of Satan himself!' Egfrith shrieked, accusing the Norsemen gathered there. 'Satan's turds! Ministers of evil!' Even I could not tell much of what he ranted, for he seemed maddened by the scene, and perhaps the ale had made him brave. I was living my own nightmare. I thought the Norsemen would kill him just to shut him up, but instead they ignored the monk and gathered beneath Ealhstan's body, muttering prayers to their gods and clutching their pendants and their swords. They were awed by Glum's sacrifice to Óðin and now sought to play their part in it to be assured of the god's favour. Even Sigurd paid his respects to the ancient oak's grisly fruit, muttering words I could not hear, and when he had finished he turned to Glum who stood apart from the others, bent over with one foot on a fallen ash. He was picking bits of Einar's brains from his brynja and examining them.

'Come here, Glum,' Sigurd said, the three words heavy with violence. The jarl's golden hair hung loose, giving him a wild aspect amidst the moon-bathed clearing. A number of the Norsemen held torches now, orange light tempering white, and by the combined light

I saw defiance in the face of *Fjord-Elk*'s shipmaster. He strode across the clearing and squared up to Sigurd, clutching his silver Thór's hammer pendant over his broad chest. Aggression came off the man, and Svein the Red stepped up to his jarl, loosening his huge shoulders.

'Óðin All-Father demanded a blood sacrifice,' Glum said, insolence curling his lip to reveal his teeth like a vicious dog. He turned his head and spat. 'Asgot has warned you many times, but you have been deaf to it.'

Sigurd's glittering eyes betrayed no emotion as he fixed them on his friend's. 'You have always served me well, Glum,' he said simply, 'and for this I will not kill you. But now you have dishonoured me. The sacrifice was not for you to make.'

'I did it for the Fellowship.' Glum threw the words away, knowing they were useless now. Then he looked at me and spat again. 'You favour the red-eyed boy when you should slit his throat. He has turned the Norns against us. You cannot bring back your son from the dead, Sigurd.' Sigurd's hand went to his sword's grip and the muscle in his cheek bounced beneath the golden beard. Svein growled, stepping forward, but Sigurd raised a hand to stop him.

'If you ever say another word about my son I will kill you, Glum,' Sigurd said. Glum nodded submissively. 'Would your father have betrayed his jarl?' He needed no answer. 'It is not for you to decide Óðin's will. What do you know of the All-Father? You have always honoured Thór. Honest and brutish suits you, Glum, but Óðin is a jarl's god and you do not have the wits for him.' Glum hawked and spat at Sigurd's feet, but Sigurd ignored the insult. Instead he turned to Asgot. 'As for you, old man, if you were not in your winter years, I would leave you here in this land of Christ worshippers.' He glanced at Father Egfrith, who knelt quietly in prayer now, his eyes closed. 'I would leave you to their mercy. You would die here and I doubt Óðin's dark maidens would be able to find you. You would never see his great hall.'

Asgot screwed up his wizened face, terrified by Sigurd's words.

Sigurd nodded solemnly. 'But you served my father before me and he valued your wisdom, such as it is, so I will not take from you your place at *Serpent*'s oars.' Then he turned back to face Glum, and Bram stepped forward as though he knew what was to come. 'Hold out your arm,' Sigurd commanded in a low voice. All the Norsemen except those on watch were now gathered in the clearing, their fists clenched and their jaws set. Light and shadow played across their faces, and they looked somehow otherworldly. I knew the ancient shades of the forest were watching too.

Glum pulled the three warrior rings from his left arm and put them on his right, then thrust the left out, the muscle in his cheek contorting as he gritted his teeth against the coming pain. He opened and closed his hand over and over, perhaps hoping to remember the sensation, then looked at Bram. Without a word spoken, Bram seemed to understand, for he nodded and stepped forward to grip Glum's wrist. Then Sigurd, son of Harald the Hard, drew his great sword. A shard of moonlight cut across the blade, revealing the smoky, swirling pattern that gave the weapon both beauty and strength. It was a wicked, hungry thing and it lusted for blood.

Sigurd hesitated and for two heartbeats the great sword hung in the darkness. Then it came down in a flash of iron, into Glum's left arm, severing it at the elbow with a wet sound. Bram blinked as blood sprayed across his face and he stood holding the limb, glancing at the silver finger ring that Glum had forgotten to remove. Glum's legs nearly buckled, but somehow he summoned the strength to stand, though he shivered with the pain and his breath came in ragged gulps. But then Black Floki stepped forward and thrust his torch on to the gushing flesh to stop the blood, and Glum could not hold in a cry of pain which soaked the forest. I smelled the meat burning as Floki held the flame to the wound.

'I leave you with one hand to grip sword and tiller,' Sigurd began, looking down at the blackened stump, 'and you'll still get a shield on what's left of that one.' Bram tugged the ring from the dead finger and handed it to Glum who just stared at Sigurd, his face writhing with pain and hatred and disbelief.

Then Sigurd turned to me and I admit I shivered when I looked into those hard eyes. 'You have killed one of my men, Raven. One day, Einar's kin may come to claim the blood price. That is their right. I could do it myself.'

'Yes, lord,' I said, bowing my head.

220

'But you were avenging your own kin's murder and I would think less of you if you had not.' With that Sigurd turned and set off back towards the glow of the campfires.

Ugly Einar's friends took their long knives and began digging a pit for his body, for they knew they could not risk a Wessex fyrd seeing the light a pyre would cast into the night sky. After Ealdred's hall, the Norsemen harboured a newfound respect for English warriors and did not wish to fight again so soon. Some were hurt still, their cuts tended by Asgot and Olaf who had long experience of battle wounds and the herbs with which to treat them. Thorgils and Thorleik helped Glum back to the camp where they would fill him with ale for the pain. Svein the Red put an arm across my aching shoulders and gave a tired smile.

'Come, Raven,' he said quietly, 'we have entertained the gods enough for one night. It's time to sleep.'

'No, Svein,' I replied, pulling free of his arm and stepping up to press my palm against the oak's massive trunk. It felt hard and strong and enduring and I wondered what magic had been done there that bloody night. 'I'll sleep here,' I said. So I sat beneath the ruined body of a mute old man, and angry tears squeezed my throat because I should have protected him but I had not and now he was gone. If Svein saw my tears he said nothing about it and I did not care anyway. I was more disgusted with myself than any Norseman could have been, for I had repaid an old man's kindness with neglect and betrayal and I feared for what kind of man that made me.

Eventually, the sleep of the dead took me down into nothingness. And Svein stayed with me.

A dark mood lay heavy upon the Fellowship when we set off the next day. The Norsemen had hated burying Ugly Einar in the earth, for they believed it was not for a great warrior to rot amongst the worms. Raging flames would have borne Einar's soul to Valhöll as swiftly as an eagle soars into the clouds. Still, they knew Óðin's maidens would find their friend to fight for the gods in the last battle, for Einar had been a Sword-Norse and he had died with his sword in his hand.

According to Egfrith we were in Mercia now. A steady drizzle was falling, dripping from the trees to soak through our clothes. Ealhstan was gone and I was afraid. The old man had been the last thread tying me to the life I had known before the Norsemen came, his presence the whisper of conscience in a new world. Now the thread had been severed and there was no going back.

I clutched the Óðin amulet hanging at my neck and wondered what the All-Father made of the sacrifice he had been offered the previous night. Could a Christian, even one sacrificed by a godi, gain entry to Valhöll? Ealhstan had not been a warrior, but Sigurd told me Óðin was the lord of words and beauty and knowledge too, and so perhaps, I thought, he would have a use for the old man.

Then my hand fell to the lobed pommel of the sword at my waist, the weapon that had avenged Ealhstan with Ugly Einar's blood. The leather-bound grip was worn smooth, but silver wire spiralled round it to prevent the sword's slipping from a sweaty palm. It was simple and deadly and beautiful. It was mine.

The Norns of fate were weaving still. And I was a Norseman now.

# CHAPTER NINE

TWO DAYS LATER AT DAWN, FATHER EGFRITH WARNED Sigurd that we were close to King Coenwulf's stronghold. The monk seemed to have forgotten the horror of Ealhstan's sacrifice and clearly relished being out among the wonders of the Lord's creation, as he put it; so much so that in his excitement he forgot to loathe us. The little weasel face chattered constantly. 'Unlike some of my world-shy brothers I have travelled literally *and* spiritually, as I believe is one's duty . . .' he was saying, until Sigurd jabbed the butt of his spear into his shoulder, silencing him for a while.

Soon after, Olaf called a warning. 'Keep your eyes open, lads,' he said, putting on his helmet so that he was all grey steel and brown beard. 'There'll be fighting before long, less my bones are lying.' The Norsemen put on their own helmets, which they carried on spears over their shoulders, and tightened straps, boots and belts, for there was every chance that the Mercians had planned a welcome for us.

'Coenwulf's a scrapper, Sigurd,' Mauger said,

'and he'll have men riding his borders looking for Wessexmen who've strayed too far from their hearths. The truce prevents war, but it won't stop a man getting a length of spear in his belly if he's not careful. The cunnies won't be expecting Norsemen, mind. That'll piss on their holy fire. When they come across forty stinkin' heathens in coats of mail!' He smiled at the thought, a rare expression for him, and I wondered whether Mauger had ever been a child, or if he had been spawned a warrior with scars and beard and malice.

Ash and oak began to give way to fast-growing firs and birches, warning us that men managed this land. Having long since taken the best wood, the Mercians planted trees that did not take countless generations to grow. A little further and the forest would thin, becoming wild heathland and eventually yielding to rolling pasture and sheep meadows. We would not go unnoticed for long.

Some of the Norsemen still looked at me with distrust in their blue eyes, and I felt more than one curse prick my skin like an elf's arrow, muttered by men who blamed me for Glum's mutilation. They respected their jarl's right to administer it, but in their eyes Glum, Einar and Asgot had only been acting on their collective fears. They were in a strange land, governed by a strange god – who would not understand their wanting to feel the All-Father's presence? If this could be achieved through the death of an old man, and a Christian at that, then so be it. Still, I took some comfort from the fact that they did not seem to hold

Einar's death against me. Vengeance is a man's right and Norsemen understand this intimately. They would miss their ugly friend, but they were ambitious men who knew they followed a strong jarl towards riches and glory.

That day, I believed they would follow Sigurd anywhere, for we were now in the heart of Coenwulf's kingdom and a great distance from our ships. Though some whispered that we had strayed too far from our gods too, I don't think I was alone in thinking that wherever Sigurd the Lucky went, Óðin and Thór could not be far away.

Later that day we made camp in a vale between two scarp slopes, the eastern one covered with short oaks, birch and bracken, and the western one worn down to rock and clay, patched with tough grass. The flood plain narrowed at this point, the river that once must have coursed through the place reduced to a trickling brook thickly lined with mosses and ferns full of grass snakes.

There was a chill in the air, but there would be no fires this night, for Mauger and Father Egfrith agreed that we were less than a day's march from the king's fortress. The Wessex warrior advised using what remained of the forest as cover before crossing open pasture. There was already a chance that we had been seen and for this reason Olaf believed we should hit the fortress quickly, before the locals had a chance to ready themselves. But Sigurd agreed with Mauger that we should rest once more so as to be fresh for whatever lay in store.

'He's scheming, lad,' Bram said, gesturing to Sigurd. 'I've seen that face before. It's his Loki face. While we're sleeping, Sigurd will be scheming.' Sure enough, later that night, as most men lay asleep in their cloaks, Sigurd's plan was born, and it was Father Egfrith who prised it from him. The monk shivered, sniffed, and tugged Sigurd's sleeve as the jarl was drinking from his water skin.

'What will you do when we come to King Coenwulf's hall, Sigurd?' Egfrith asked, one eye on Black Floki who had scooped up grit from the stream bed and was rubbing it across the rings of the brynja on the rock beside him.

'We'll sing Coenwulf a lullaby, hey, Uncle!' Sigurd said. 'And he'll hand over the book with a smile and a plate of honeyed oat cakes, and two or three young women with soft thighs and hard tits.'

Olaf grinned, then scratched his thick beard and frowned. 'The little man has a point, Sigurd. There's going to be a river of blood before this thing is over.'

'Perhaps,' Sigurd replied, pursing his lips, 'but perhaps not. I have spoken with Mauger about these Mercians. It seems Coenwulf has his hands full dealing with King Eardwulf of Northumbria. This Eardwulf's people pick at his northern borders like crows on a gut string. Then there are the Welsh snapping at him from the west.' Sigurd leant forward, threw back his head and grabbed his long golden hair before tying it back. 'A man must command many spears to be a king of rich soil, like Coenwulf, hey, Mauger? It's easier to lay claim to the sea, I think.'

227

Mauger took an ale skin from his lips. 'They fight like dogs, Sigurd,' he confirmed, ale dripping from his beard as he raised the skin again.

Sigurd nodded and looked at Olaf as though assessing his friend's resolve, for Olaf had already seen his son killed and there was no denying the risk we were taking. 'Mauger and Raven will go to Coenwulf and tell him that Eardwulf's warriors have crossed into his lands from the north,' Sigurd said. 'Not just lone wolves, but a raiding party.'

'Raven, tell him that King Eardwulf himself is ploughing Mercian cunny,' Black Floki added with a smirk, still cleaning his mail.

'Oh yes, Sigurd!' Father Egfrith exclaimed. 'I shall write to the king confirming the raids. He's a Christian king after all and will believe the word of a servant of Christ.' He sniffed loudly and wiggled his fingers. 'Oh, I shall enjoy writing! There is none in Wessex with a finer hand, may the Lord strike me down and maggots spawn in my mouth if I lie.' He made the sign of the cross and raised his eyes to the sky, suddenly fearful, then grinned haughtily at Olaf as though Sigurd's plan was entirely his own. Mauger looked at Egfrith, his expression grim. 'Well, it's true, Mauger,' Egfrith said defensively, holding up his right hand to show off the ink-stained fingers. 'Who else round here knows his letters?' He made a strangled laughing sound. 'Not a stinking, foul-minded one of you, so help you God. But I do know mine.'

'Coenwulf will believe the word of a Christ monk?' Sigurd asked, shaking his head in wonder. Why any warrior would believe a man who wore no sword and prided himself on being able to scratch shapes into a dried calf's skin was beyond Sigurd.

'Oh yes, he'll believe me,' Egfrith confirmed with a wicked grin.

'And I was beginning to like this Coenwulf,' Sigurd said disappointedly, running a comb through his golden beard. 'Mauger tells me the man is never more cheerful than when sending his enemies screaming into the afterlife.' He turned to Olaf again. 'When the king takes his warriors north, we'll burn his hall and take the book . . . providing he doesn't take it with him. Who can say what a Christian is likely to do?' he asked, glancing at Father Egfrith.

Olaf smiled, taking a small whetstone from his scrip and spitting on it before running his knife across it. 'You should have told me you had the whole thing planned out,' he said, blowing across the blade. 'I like to know the details when it comes to arranging a fight.'

'The only thing you worry about is how you're going to fill your belly after a day's killing,' Sigurd replied, slapping Olaf's back. 'Now get some sleep, old friend. You too, Raven,' he added, fixing me with his fierce eyes. 'Tomorrow we wake the gods.'

The next morning, I set off with Mauger, leaving Sigurd and his Wolfpack to make their final preparations and pray to their gods of battle for a great victory or a good death. We would travel along the banks of the mighty river called the Severn, as this would enable us to cut round King Coenwulf's hall to approach from the north, making our story about Northumbrian raiders more believable.

I hoped that because we were just two men no one would confront us to ask our purpose, but I doubted we would go unnoticed, for we wore our battle gear and carried great round shields. Mauger had removed most of his silver warrior rings; such rewards would have marked him as a great fighter and the Mercians would wonder why they did not know him. Yet even without the rings the man looked ferocious.

We barely spoke at first, moving fast along the riverside where mosses, ferns and liverworts stirred with rats and voles. Damp-loving alder and willow lined the banks, providing perches for brightly coloured kingfishers. These birds streaked like arrows down to the ripples that betrayed fish breaking the surface to snatch at insects.

When Mauger did speak, it was usually a question about the Norsemen. 'Did it feel good the other night?' he asked, the sweat beading on his beard and the flushed face beneath. 'When you killed that ugly heathen bastard?'

'Yes, it felt good,' I said truthfully, 'and I would have killed Glum too if Jarl Sigurd hadn't stopped me.' Though I doubted I could have scratched Glum before he cut me down.

'You admire that whoreson, don't you, lad?' Mauger said, meaning Sigurd. 'That bastard took you from your home – no point denying that, lad – burned the place to the ground and split your old friend's belly before dragging his guts round a tree. And you'd still die for him. You're a bloody fool.'

'Sigurd didn't kill Ealhstan,' I said.

'Might as well have. They're all the same. Heathen bastards.'

I shook my head. 'You're wrong. Sigurd sees something I could never have dreamed of before. He weaves his own story and I will be a part of it.'

'You want some of these, lad?' he asked, touching a bracelet of twisted silver which circled the bulge in his upper arm. Pride lit his eyes.

I eyed the ring hungrily. 'I want what they want, Mauger, what Sigurd wants,' I said, as something rustled in a grass tussock and then plopped into the water. There was a bend in the river, slowing the current enough for frogs and grass snakes to set their traps. 'I will follow Sigurd and he will give me glory,' I said, embarrassed by the admission.

'Pah! Glory is never given, lad.' Mauger spat with a grimace. 'You have to take it at the end of a bloody sword, and you're as likely to be killed by another man chasing the same bastard dream. Staying alive is the only thing a warrior should set his heart on. He can expect or hope for no more.'

'But men remember us for the things we do, Mauger. The great things,' I said, wondering how many men he had killed. 'Olaf says the skalds in the halls of the northlands already sing songs of Sigurd. His name is known. Men fear him, and even the grey sea cannot confine his fame.' I lengthened my stride, forcing Mauger to do the same. 'Our names will resound in the drinking halls of kings. They will become ingrained like smoke in stout oak beams, felt by our sons and their sons after them.' I touched the amulet at my neck. 'But only if we are worthy. That is what Sigurd says. Only then will Óðin send his death maidens for us when our time comes.'

'You believe in their gods too?' Mauger asked gruffly.

'I have seen the Wolfpack fight, Mauger, as have you. I have seen them kill as though it were as easy as drawing breath. Their gods love battle and battle is the path to glory. They are my gods now. Maybe they have always been,' I dared, hoping the Christian god was not listening. I stepped up again, so that Mauger had no more breath to waste on talk. In those days I was arrogant and intoxicated by the Norsemen, and I believed the Norns of fate wove our futures. But I also believed we could guide their old hands, and for that I was a fool.

'That must be it,' I said later, pointing to the east where we could make out wisps of grey smoke rising to dirty the sky. A lone cloud suddenly snuffed out the watery sun above us, casting the yellow gorse and bristle grass into shadow and stilling the cry of a warbler nesting nearby. I took this as a good omen, meaning that the great warrior king of Mercia would be blind to our ruse. The shield slung over my back was starting to rub and I looked forward to taking it off.

'Aye, that's it all right,' Mauger confirmed, scratching his thick beard. 'We'll keep going until we reach that hill in the distance, then track east and come in

from the north. You remember the story?' He palmed
sweat from his brow.

I stared at the rising smoke, wondering what lay
in store for us at Coenwulf's hall, then touched the
pommel of my sword, the sword I had killed with.
'I remember,' I said. I felt for the amulet of Óðin at
my neck, tucking it deep inside my clothes, and then
checked the rest of my gear, my mail, sword scabbard
and helm, in case they bore any pagan designs I had
overlooked. A swineherd called a greeting. Mauger
raised a hand and we carried on, heads bowed, along
the drying mud track which led up to the walled
settlement. The smell of wood smoke and animals
filled my nose, which was still swollen from the fight
with Aslak, and I shuddered at the risk we were taking.
For the ruse had begun and we had grave news for
King Coenwulf.

'The ditch shouldn't be a problem for your friends
but the wall looks sturdy enough,' Mauger muttered.
'Arse and bollocks!' He had trodden in fresh cow shit.
'You'll not get in uninvited,' he said, wiping his boot
against a clump of grass beside the path.

'It'll burn,' I said, remembering Abbotsend in the
grip of yellow flames.

After the time it takes to fletch an arrow and before
I could think about changing my mind, we stood at the
threshold of King Coenwulf's fortress. Sweat chilled
the skin between my shoulder blades and Mauger
suddenly seemed a hostile presence beside me.

'We have important news for the king,' he said to the
older of two guards who stood either side of the open

gateway. They gripped long spears and wore leather armour, and they looked us up and down, seemingly unimpressed by our mail and arms.

'What news?' the guard asked, leaning the point of his spear towards Mauger. 'What business do you have with the king?' The younger man was staring at my blood-eye, so I turned to fix him with it and he looked away.

'What I have to say is for my king, Coenwulf the Strong,' Mauger blurted, 'not for some little prick who ought to know he's unworthy to hear words meant for the Lord of Mercia, hammer of the Welsh and future king of Wessex. May your rotten tongue fall out, you worthless arse leaf.'

The guard blanched and stiffened and for a moment I thought he would turn his spear on Mauger for which he would die, but he must have known this too, for he stretched his neck awkwardly and then turned to the younger man.

'Stay here, Cynegils. No one gets in, understand, lad? Not even the bishop of bloody Worcester with a box of forgiveness.' He looked us up and down once more and shrugged. 'Come on then,' he said. He turned, spear in hand, and marched into King Coenwulf's stronghold, and we followed him.

The place was full of noise. A watermill creaked and an iron corn-grinding wheel moaned. Chickens clucked about on ground churned to mud by countless feet. Pigs grunted and cattle lowed and goats munched on tufts of new grass. At least two forge hammers rang out, men and women called from house to house, horses

234

whinnied, children played, and infants cried. I felt as though I was drowning.

'Wait here,' the guard said, striding off towards two more warriors in leather armour, who guarded the door of Coenwulf's hall. One of them disappeared inside. An old grey hunting dog came to sniff at Mauger's boot, but he kicked the beast and it looked at me as though wondering how I could let such a thing happen, before padding back to flop down beside the hall's entrance. The guard reappeared.

'King Coenwulf, Lord of Mercia, hammer of the Welsh and warrior of the true faith, grants you an audience. You will remove all blades before entering the king's hall.' We left our swords and knives with the guards and entered the dark interior, coughing from the smoke slung among the thick old beams of Coenwulf's hall. At the far end sat the king himself on an ornately carved throne. Behind him were tapestries depicting a warrior with wings and a great flaming sword. The needlework was poor, but the image was striking none the less. Between us and the king a woman stood stirring a cauldron suspended above the central hearth, and two young girls sat in a corner sewing by sooty candlelight.

Coenwulf beckoned us forward. He was flanked by two huge warriors, both wearing mail and iron helmets and holding great ash spears.

Mauger cleared his throat. 'My lord king,' he began, 'it is a great honour . . .'

Coenwulf grimaced and batted the words away with ringed fingers. There was a brief silence as he shifted

235

in his throne, then he twirled a finger, summoning Mauger to continue.

'We have come from Eoferwic in the north of your kingdom, my lord,' Mauger said, ditching the formalities, 'and we bring word that King Eardwulf is burning your land. That whoreson has killed many good men and we only left the fight when all was lost.' The king was scowling now. 'My lord, it was no easy thing to leave, but we knew our duty was to inform you of Eardwulf's treachery,' Mauger pressed on. 'I only pray Christ forgives us for not giving our lives avenging the innocents.'

'Eardwulf has broken the treaty?' Coenwulf asked, leaning forward in his throne and staring at Mauger with dark, brooding eyes. He had a warrior's build and his face was scarred. One of the wall-mounted torches spluttered and went out, distracting the king for a moment. 'Why have not my spies informed me of this treachery?' he asked, dragging his teeth over his bottom lip. 'Unless the sly dog has dug them out and slit their throats.'

'So it is as I feared and we are the first to bring this news,' Mauger said, glancing at me, his expression all gloom. Then he shook his head slowly and I was impressed by the warrior's guile, for I had thought him a brute, no more than a grizzled fighter. I would remember he was more. 'I fear our kinsmen gave their lives and even now lie dead on the field.' Mauger made the sign of the cross and I stared at Coenwulf, not daring to look at Mauger for fear of pulling a thread from the weave of his lie.

The king sat back in silence, scratching his black beard.

'We of Eoferwic have kept our spears sharp, my king, ever watchful of our faithless northern neighbours,' Mauger said, 'but most of your people there are farmers, not warriors. We were ill prepared for an invasion.' Mauger's shoulders slumped and he suddenly seemed exhausted.

'An invasion of Mercia?' Coenwulf's eyes flamed for a heartbeat. 'You have proof of this?' he asked. A woman took the dead torch from the wall and held it in the hearth flames till it burst back to life.

'Proof, my lord? Only the blood on my sword, not yet dry,' Mauger answered grimly. Then he shrugged and stepped forward. 'Oh, and a letter, my king. The scratchings of some monk, though I'd wager the man hitched up his skirts and ran at the first sniff of trouble.'

'Hold your tongue, man!' King Coenwulf clamoured, his voice filling the dark hall. 'The word of a man of God will not be disparaged! Our faith is our greatest weapon against the heathens and devils who writhe in the darkness beyond our borders. You would do well to remember it. Bring me this letter!'

'My lord,' Mauger muttered, giving a shallow bow, and one of the king's guards stepped forward to take the offered parchment. I could not read, but Egfrith had assured us there was that about the dark flowing markings that was deliberately imperfect, which an astute man might take for terror, as though a trembling heart had steered the hand. To me it seemed incredible that those small twisting shapes invoked a voice from far away; a voice that implored Mercia's warrior of God to rescue his flock from the Northumbrians. As Coenwulf clutched Father Egfrith's parchment I saw that his hands were trembling. He called for someone to fetch his abbot, then roared at the slave girl as the torch went out again. White spittle had gathered at the corners of his lips and he closed his eyes, taking a deep breath as though trying to contain his rage. The abbot soon appeared. Red-faced and breathless, he hurried to where Coenwulf sat holding the parchment in the air, then took the thing and began to read, squinting in the darkness. After a few moments, the abbot leant and whispered in the king's ear. Coenwulf's eyes widened as though he no longer saw us standing before him, but saw instead King Eardwulf himself riding through Mercia, a flaming torch in one hand and a sword in the other. I clenched my jaw to keep from smiling, for King Coenwulf of Mercia had the fire of battle in his eyes.

The king's face was dark and grim-set when he rode out later that day at the head of his war band. His household men, those with warrior rings and the finest arms, rode behind him, whilst after them went the men of the levy wearing whatever leather or iron armour they owned, clutching spears or scythes or hunting bows. Coenwulf had expected us to ride north with him, but Mauger had grumbled that we were exhausted and begged that we be allowed to follow on once we had a meal in our bellies. The king had spat in disgust and waved us away coldly, and I'm sure Mauger's request confirmed his suspicion that we were cowards. I liked Coenwulf then, for he seemed like a man who would rather command a farmer with a pitchfork and a stout heart than a man in mail with no stomach for the fight. So we stood awhile by the great gate, watching the war band disappear as a veil of white cloud filled the sky and blurred the sun. Again I marvelled at the magic of the written word, which could stir a heart to action as surely as a battle cry. And a part of me feared this gospel book we had been sent to find, for it must surely be a powerful thing indeed.

Then we set off south to fetch Sigurd and his Norsemen, hoping the book that King Egbert of Wessex was so desperate to get his hands on was not on a horse walking north.

# CHAPTER TEN

'HOW MANY WARRIORS WENT WITH HIM, RAVEN?' SIGURD asked. His eyes shone as though he believed the Norns of fate were weaving the most wonderful pattern.

'No less than seventy,' I replied, 'and thirty of those were his own men. Real fighters, my lord. The rest were levy men. He left maybe twenty household men behind that I saw. There are others too, but they shouldn't give you much trouble.'

'We should send the monk in to steal the book,' Olaf said, staring at Father Egfrith in wonder, for we all knew it was the monk's letter rather than my and Mauger's presence which had convinced King Coenwulf to ride north. 'He knows what the thing looks like.' He shrugged. 'Damned if I've ever seen a book before. Heard about them, though.'

'No,' Mauger said, shaking his head, 'too risky.' He wore his warrior rings again and they obscured the fierce tattoos on his arms, clinking whenever he moved. 'If they catch wind that it's the book we're after, they'll bury the damned thing so deep we might as well stand around picking our arses till judgement day.' He thumbed at Father Egfrith. 'He might be a sly old stoat, but if he went alone he'd have to fool churchmen like the one who whispers in Coenwulf's ear, and some of them are sharp as a Frank's blade. They're cunning bastards, take it from me. You've never had to raise war silver from priests. Blood from a stone,' he said, spitting.

'Mauger is right,' Sigurd said. 'They must not know we want the book. But they're headless now, like a dandelion in a strong wind. Their king has gone.' He pursed his lips. 'When we attack, these Mercians will be trying to save their own sallow skins. We breach the walls, we go in hard, and we take the book.' He looked at Svein the Red, who wore a silver hammer at his throat. 'Thór would approve of such a plan, I think,' he said with a smile. Svein grinned. 'Are we all agreed?' the jarl asked, lingering a moment on Glum who nodded, his ruined arm bound in a leather sheath. Every man gave a grunt or a nod and the Wolfpack readied itself to fight.

'Did it escape your mind to tell me how stout the wall is, Raven?' Sigurd asked when I pointed to the distant settlement. It was dusk and the drizzle had become rain which dripped from the nasals of our helmets as we stood taking in King Coenwulf's lair.

'It's big, lord,' I admitted, 'and well made. But the ditch is shallow.'

'It won't burn easily in this rain, Sigurd,' Olaf said. 'Looks like we'll have to wait for an invitation.'

'Don't worry, old man,' Bjarni put in, 'the womenfolk

will pull us over the walls and into their beds now their men have gone.' He grinned wickedly. 'But it'll take three or four of them to help me up. My balls are heavy as a bag of silver.'

'English women would sooner straddle their swine than climb aboard you,' his brother Bjorn said, receiving a cuff around the head in return.

'Whatever we're going to do, we'd better do it fast,' Glum said, waving his short, sheathed arm. 'No time to starve them out. When Coenwulf realizes we've made a fool of him, he'll be shitting blind fury. The man's pride will bear him back here faster than Sleipnir.'

Asgot had told me of Sleipnir, the eight-legged grey horse of Óðin, faster than all other beasts. Glum was right, we did not have much time.

The Mercians could not see us yet, for we were still a distance off and our painted shields were slung across our backs. Furthermore, we stood in a hollow of open pasture amongst docks, nettles and cowslip stems cropped short by cattle. Father Egfrith started when a yellowhammer burst from a nearby patch of sedge, trilling madly as it took to the sky.

Sigurd watched the bird for a moment, then nodded. 'Asgot! Let them see us for what we are,' he commanded, and the old godi produced Sigurd's banner, a wolf's head on a red cloth, and tied it to the point of a long ash spear. Then Sigurd turned to Father Egfrith. 'Start praying to your god that the book is in there, Englishman,' he said through his teeth, 'for if I lose a man for nothing, I'll take your head.' The monk blanched and we set off up the far side of the hollow, our mail and arms jangling, leather belts and straps creaking, and our stride forewarning of death.

We crested the swell of land two bow shot lengths from the fortress. Some men who had been working in the fields saw us and fled back across the ditch and bank, leaving an earthen kiln belching yellow smoke, and by the time we stood before the stout wooden palisade a sparse forest of spears topped the defences. Sigurd wasted no time. He sent five Wolfpacks of five warriors round the edges of the fortress to cover any other gates, and, though we were too few to properly surround the place, it would take a brave man or a fool to risk hopping over the wall in a bid for freedom. Before long, the grey-bearded face of a warrior appeared above the main gate.

'Who are you?' the man demanded in a clear, strong voice. It was a voice that betrayed no panic, yet the spear blades atop the palisade swayed uneasily, suggesting that the men who gripped them did not share Grey Beard's mettle. 'What do you want here?' he called.

Sigurd paced forward purposefully, his mail polished to a shine and his golden hair plaited for battle. Týr himself could not have looked like a greater warrior.

'I am Sigurd, son of Harald the Hard,' he boomed. 'You will open this gate, or everyone within will die.'

'What do you want from us, Dane?' Grey Beard asked, casting his eye over the rest of us. Olaf cursed the man under his breath. The Mercian's gaze lingered on Father Egfrith who I saw now wore a rich scarlet cloak instead of his habit. A silver cross wet with rain hung at his neck, positioned to catch the eye and reflect what remained of

243

the pale sunlight. But beneath this new finery, the monk looked more frail than I had ever seen him.

'Open the gate, Mercian!' Sigurd demanded. 'Then I will tell you why we have come to Coenwulf's hall.'

'King Coenwulf is at table and will not welcome your presence here, Sigurd son of Harald,' Grey Beard said sharply. 'Leave now before someone informs him. You must know our king's reputation. He is a great and fearless warrior. A Christian warrior.' These last words were heavy with threat. 'King Coenwulf could deal with you as a man squashes a louse between finger and thumb. Go now! Go whilst you still can, and even then I would watch my back.'

'Your king is off waving his sword in the north, Grey Beard,' Sigurd yelled, pointing along the worn track, dotted with horse droppings, which Coenwulf had taken earlier that day. 'If you lie to me again I will cut out your tongue before I strangle you with your own innards.'

The guard turned and shouted a command and Mauger grabbed my shoulder.

'Tell them to raise their shields, Raven,' he hissed, just as the Mercian defenders appeared at the palisade with arrows on their bowstrings. But the Norsemen had already unslung their round shields and held them before their faces, and the arrows that came either stuck in the limewood or were deflected harmlessly away.

Behind his shield, Olaf nodded at his jarl, for the Mercians had just revealed their strength, at least in terms of bowmen. There were not enough to worry us.

Sigurd lowered his shield, which sprouted two white-fletched shafts.

'You have just called the birds of carrion to this place, Grey Beard,' he said, 'and they will come like a black cloud to block out the sun.' At that, Father Egfrith moaned and collapsed and Svein the Red dragged the monk unceremoniously back from the shieldwall at the gate.

When darkness fell, we lit torches and fires that hissed in the rain, a fragile ring of flame around Coenwulf's fortress. The Norsemen were well practised at constructing shelters from slender branches and the oiled leather cloaks they wore against sea spray and deluge, so we were comfortable enough. I took in the scene, the campfires of each band casting light on to the wooden walls, and it seemed to me as though a great host was laying siege to the place. But in truth we were not enough.

'What if Coenwulf comes back?' Bjarni asked. His face was etched in concentration as he closed a ring on his brynja that had broken at the join. We were sheltering from the rain, but we remained battle ready in case the Mercian defenders should come at us in the night.

'It will take him two days to reach his northern borders,' Father Egfrith said, rubbing his bald pate as he sat in his shelter on a bundle of hazel branches covered with long grass. 'Though God knows he'll make the return journey in half the time when he learns the truth.' His yellow teeth flashed in the flame light and I wondered if the monk should be taking such pleasure in the deception of other Christians.

'When he thinks there's a Wessexman, or, worse, some Welsh bastard, warming his throne, old Coenwulf will ride so fast his beard'll blow off,' Mauger added with a grimace.

Olaf joined us, a flaming, spitting torch in one hand, his shield in the other. Water dripped from helmet and shield. He had come from checking the Wolfpacks surrounding the fortress. 'There's only one other way out of the place and Aslak has it covered. Problem is, there's no easy way in. It's tight as a weasel's arsehole.' He looked to Sigurd, who had stood to receive his report. 'We'll have to burn it tomorrow, Sigurd,' he said, turning his face to the dark sky. 'If this rain ever stops.'

'No, Uncle,' Sigurd said, scratching his yellow beard. 'I have another idea.' He turned to me, his eyes glittering like fish scales in the firelight. 'Raven, you know of Óðin and of Thór, of Rán and of Týr Lord of Battle, but what do you know of Loki?'

'Only what I have heard from the others, my lord,' I said, 'that Loki is a cruel god and that any man who trusts him is a fool.'

'Ah, piss,' he said. 'Loki is famed for his wickedness and his wiles, yes, but all the gods have their pride, even Loki. Which of them would not be honoured by a warrior's seeking his help against these Christians, these followers of the White Christ who spread their twisted belief across the world as a farmer hurls swine shit across his field? Loki is, above all things, cunning. He has more stratagems than there are hairs in Bram's beard.' Bram grinned proudly. 'I have asked Loki the

246

cunning for his help . . .' Sigurd's full lips spread into a smile, 'and he has given it to me.'

I learned then of Sigurd's plan. Father Egfrith was not sick at all. He had faked his collapse in front of the Mercians earlier that day.

'And the scarlet cloak?' I asked the monk. He was hiding in his shelter so that none on the palisade would see him. He looked like a rat in a hole.

'If the Mercians are to believe I am a bishop snatched from my flock by heathens, I must at least dress like one,' he replied, flicking a spot of dirt from the shoulder of the fur-trimmed cloth. 'Who would not pity one of the Lord's messengers who found himself in the midst of barbarians?' He was clearly enjoying the prospect of the deception Sigurd had woven with Loki the mischievous.

The Mercians stayed behind their walls that night, perhaps hoping we would move on to easier pickings, or that their king would return to give battle in the shadow of his own hall. The next day, Egfrith died. Kalf and gap-toothed Ingolf found some chalk which they crushed and rubbed into the monk's skin to give him a deathly pallor, and then we wrapped him tightly in an old balding skin, and Sigurd put round his own shoulders the scarlet, fur-trimmed cloak and clutched the silver cross, wrapping its chain around his fist. Then, as the sun rose in the east, Sigurd, Olaf and Svein stood before the main gate like gods of war. After standing there in silent, sword-bearing judgement, Sigurd eventually called up to the defenders, who had not left their posts all night.

'Fetch the grey-beard I spoke with yesterday!' he commanded.

'I am here, Sigurd,' came the reply as the guard appeared spear in hand. 'What do you want from us? There is nothing for you here. My king will soon return and when he does you and your men will die where you stand.'

'Go on, old man,' Sigurd called, 'you shrivelled goat's prick!' He held up a hand and snapped his fingers together. 'Use your old tongue while you still have it!' This brought the hint of a smile from the warrior, who must have been one of King Coenwulf's household men and therefore an experienced fighter, for it is customary to hurl insults before a fight, and the Norsemen are good at it. 'Open the gates and let me in, you squirrel's turd,' Sigurd demanded. 'I will bring ten men with me, no more. You have my word.'

'The word of a heathen means nothing to me,' Grey Beard replied, spitting over the battlements. 'You are all the Devil's turds and you will be washed away by a holy rain, just like the bastard Welsh.'

Sigurd muttered to the others and as one they turned on their heels to walk away.

'Wait!' Grey Beard shouted. 'Where is the man who yesterday wore that red cloak? He is a man of the Holy Church if my eyes did not deceive me.'

'He was the bishop of Wilton,' Sigurd replied, holding out his fist and letting the silver cross fall until the chain pulled taut. 'And a more pathetic worm I have never come across. Here, take this if you believe it will do you any good. I will have it back soon enough.'

With that, he threw the cross into the sky and for a brief moment it reflected the rays of the new sun before disappearing over the wooden palisade.

'Did you murder the good bishop?' Grey Beard asked, his face betraying revulsion at the thought even as he sent a man after the small treasure.

'I would have,' Sigurd answered, 'if fear or some other feeble sickness had not done it for me. And may your White Christ use the man as a footstool in the afterlife,' he finished, before turning away once again.

For the rest of the day nothing happened and that night some of the men began to say that if the Mercians did not surrender soon, they would be in for a hard fight against a vengeful king. But Sigurd seemed not in the least worried. Sigurd had asked a favour of Loki, god of mischief, whom most men shun because they are afraid, and even the gods have their pride.

The next day, a man was heard calling from atop the main gate. After a long time, Sigurd went forward to hear what he had to say. It was Grey Beard and he looked tired and agitated.

'Let me see the bishop,' the Mercian said.

'Why?' Sigurd replied, holding out his hands. 'That toad is beginning to stink! I have told my men to cut off his limbs and hang them in the forest for the ravens.'

'Let me see him,' Grey Beard pleaded, to which Sigurd shrugged and called for Svein to bring Egfrith to the gate, wrapped in the old skin, his face pale in death. Svein dumped the body on the ground and I was amazed that Father Egfrith did not give a yelp.

'Here is your corpse, Mercian,' Sigurd spat. 'Your

god found no reason to keep this one alive, it seems.' Then Olaf covered his nose and mouth as though the body stank, and even Sigurd stepped away from it, grimacing.

'I will buy the bishop from you,' Grey Beard said, 'for thirty silver coins.'

'Pah!' Sigurd said, batting the words away with his hand. 'I will soon have all the silver I want. Enough to bury you in, Grey Beard.'

'Not if King Coenwulf returns whilst you stand there watching the grass grow tall,' Grey Beard said with a grim smile.

Sigurd tilted his head in the pretence of considering the offer.

'You can have the priest for all I care,' he said. 'It will save my men the unpleasant task of cutting him up. I don't think even the ravens would want him. His stink would make their beaks fall off.'

Grey Beard nodded. 'I will have a coffin lowered over the wall,' he said, 'and you will have your thirty silver coins.'

Before the pale sun had fully risen, Svein the Red and Bram the Bear hefted a heavy oak coffin to the place where our makeshift shelters most obscured the Mercians' view.

'Are you sure you want to do this, Raven?' Sigurd asked, putting a hand on my shoulder. 'If they discover you, they will kill you.'

I nodded. 'The only thing I fear is the Mercians putting me straight in the ground,' I said. Though I feared much more than that. I had lived amongst

Christians and my head had been soaked with their rantings about their god being the one true god, a god of inconceivable power. And here I was about to steal a treasure belonging to that god.

'No, no, they won't do that,' Egfrith said, wagging his finger. His skin was still covered with chalk, which made the whites of his eyes and his teeth look even more yellow. 'Why would they buy the body only to bury it?' he asked scornfully. He sniffed. 'After treating the corpse with spices, they will display it in their church crypt in the hope that pilgrims and good Christian folk will pay to come and behold the martyr.' He looked at Sigurd, his expression stern. 'For they will announce that the bishop was cruelly slain by the heathens.' Sigurd shook his head in disbelief, then shrugged as though it mattered nothing to him. 'Now, Raven,' Egfrith continued, 'if the book is there, it will be by the altar, or in some other place of prominence. You should expect someone to be guarding it, keeping a vigil. A child if you're lucky, or even a woman.'

'The gods will be watching you, lad,' Olaf said with a nod. His face looked kind in the morning light. 'Sigurd says your life thread and his are woven together. You'll be fine.'

'I hope so, Uncle,' I said, managing a smile. My palms were clammy and my bowels turned to liquid as they wrapped me with my sword in the leather cloak so that even my face was covered. I wore no mail or helmet. Stealth would be my only armour once inside the fortress.

'Orm has cut air holes in the sides,' Sigurd said.

'They're small. You can't see them when the lid's on.' He patted my chest. 'Remember to keep stiff.' He grinned. 'The bishop has been dead a good many hours.'

I made no sound, nor moved a muscle when Svein hoisted me on to his shoulder and carried me to the open ground before the main gate and the Mercians, whom I felt watching me even from inside the skin, and there the Norsemen laid me in the oak coffin and sealed the lid with pine tar. That was when I smelled the rotting hare Black Floki had placed in the coffin to add the stench of death to the ruse, and I cursed him for having thought of it.

I heard a clink which I took to be Grey Beard's purse of silver coins hitting the ground.

'Leave the bishop there and retreat one hundred paces,' Grey Beard called. The next thing I heard was the creaking of the heavy gates and the grunts of the Mercians as they hefted me into their fortress, cursing the heathens for their wickedness. Eventually, they set the coffin down and I guessed I must be in King Coenwulf's church, as the Mercians' voices echoed off stone walls. I stayed as still and as quiet as a dead bishop. I waited for an eternity in the stinking dark and prayed that my gods were watching and that the Christians' god was not.

After a long time, I began to feel things crawling on my skin and knew they must be maggots from the dead hare. Slowly and painfully, I repositioned my right arm and pulled the leather wrap below my eyes, then peered through a breathing hole. Sigurd was right; the hole was small and I could see nothing of the room beyond, but I guessed that night had fallen and that I had been in the coffin too long, constrained more by fear than the stifling casket. For all I knew, King Coenwulf might have been fighting Sigurd in the meadows beyond the palisade whilst I lay in that foul-smelling space. I could do nothing about the maggots and so closed my eyes, concentrating, stilling every sinew to help my ears decipher the world beyond. I heard nothing but the flickering of a torch and the scrabbling of mice on the rush-strewn floor. I was drenched with sweat, and the maggots crawled, and my body ached from keeping so still, and when I did try to move, my legs prickled horribly so that I had to clench my teeth to keep from cursing. Eventually and painfully, through small movements, my limbs came back to my body and I suddenly knew that I had to escape the coffin before it convinced me I was truly dead, before the maggots began to feed on living flesh. But even then it took an age to inhale the courage to break out, for I knew those breaths, however shallow and suffocating, might be my last.

Orm had spread only a thin layer of pine tar at the top end of the coffin's lid and several thumps, which I feared would alert a guard, proved enough to break the seal. My lungs drank the cool air as I prised off the lid and clambered out into the dark interior of Coenwulf's church. Then I whispered thanks to Loki that I was alone. And my heart froze. There, by the small stone altar, a warrior in a short brynja was sleeping, his ash spear across his lap and his head resting back against a priest's knee cushion. The man was snoring loudly and I was amazed I had not heard him before. Beside him, on the oak altar illuminated by a spitting tallow candle, lay the holy gospel book of Saint Jerome. And it was beautiful! Its cover was a plate of silver beaten to a knife blade's thickness and inlaid with a gold cross studded with dark red and green gems. I stared at it and I shivered, because I knew that by seeing it I was somehow inviting it to try its power over me. But it was not mine yet and I was not its.

The guard was snoring happily, but I could not risk his waking when I opened the church door. I put my sword to his throat and watched his Adam's apple rise and fall a hair's breadth from the blade's point. 'Óðin, guide my sword,' I whispered, though I could not miss. I gritted my teeth and thrust, but the blade stuck in the gristle of the man's gullet. His eyes opened in terror and I shoved the blade further until the point struck the stone wall behind. The man gurgled wetly, horribly, and dark blood drenched his mail. It pooled in his lap as he died, and I did not feel elation, but instead felt treacherous. Then I picked up the book, which was heavy because the back cover was also a silver plate. I placed it in a leather sack slung across my shoulders and walked to the church door, pulling it open a finger's width to peer out into the night. People with torches were moving about the place, the flames throwing strange shadows across the wooden buildings and palisade. The Mercians were finding it hard to sleep with a Norse war band prowling beyond their walls. Then my stomach lurched, because two figures broke free of an eave's dark shadow and were coming towards me, their hands clasped, arms swinging. I pushed the door shut, too hard, and stood behind it, gripping my sword and wishing I wore my mail. Five heartbeats later, a woman giggled. Then the door creaked open.

'Be still or die,' I hissed, teeth bared, sword raised.

The man stepped in front of the girl as I kicked the door shut. 'Don't hurt her,' he said, his voice edged with threat. He was young, but he wore mail and had a sword at his hip.

'Shut your mouth, Mercian,' I growled, stepping forward to pull his sword from its scabbard, whilst keeping my own pointed at his throat. 'Over there.' I pointed to the darkest corner of the church. 'On your knees.' The girl did as she was told, but the man hesitated, staring at me with dark, hate-filled eyes. 'Do it now, or I'll kill her,' I said. He fell to his knees as I pulled the skin from the coffin and cut it into strips to tie the man and woman together back to back. I gagged them too and the girl whimpered and grasped for the man's hands when she saw the ashen-faced guard whose ripped throat looked like a grim, black grimace hung with scraps of flesh.

'You'll live, if you keep still and quiet,' I said, sheathing my sword. 'I have what I came for.' The girl looked to the bare altar and I heard shouting outside. I drew my sword again and braced for the door to burst open and warriors pour in with sharp blades and fury. But they did not come and the shouting continued, so I went to the door and opened it slightly. And then I knew why the Mercians were shouting. Men ran in every direction as panic gripped the fortress. Sigurd was burning the gate.

255

Bright orange sparks swirled into the black sky and women's screams cut through the night. I took my chance and ran, not south towards the main gate, but west towards a smaller gate beyond which I knew Aslak, Osten, Halldor, Thormod and Gunnar stood guard. In the panic no one gave me a second glance. I passed men arming themselves and women running for safety with their children, until I arrived before the western gate, which was illuminated by a pair of great noxious flaming torches. Two guards prowled anxiously in the shifting shadows, as though they resented having to remain there whilst other men headed for the main gate to face the enemy. I strode towards them, head down, gripping my sword tightly, the blood pumping in my ears.

'What's happening down there?' the nearest man asked, rolling his shoulders restlessly. I answered by slashing my sword across his face. He dropped. The other raised his spear but I smacked it away with a wild swing, then rammed my sword into his open mouth. I yanked the blade free, ran to the gate and hefted the beam from its brackets, dropping it by the corpses.

'Aslak! Aslak! It's me, Raven!' I called as I pulled one of the thick doors open. I did not want a Norse spear in my chest. There they stood like hungry wolves, swords raised in the shadows.

'I thought they must have made a Christian of you, Raven,' Aslak snarled as he loped past, eyes and teeth gleaming. 'Let's see what we can find, lads!' he roared.

I stepped up and grabbed Aslak's cloak and he spun

on me. 'We can leave, Aslak,' I said, 'I have it! I have the book!'

'There's silver in there, Raven,' he snarled, nodding towards the shadow-shrouded dwellings. 'If we die in this land, we'll die rich.' With that he pulled free and the small band of mailed Norsemen ran into the madness to sow their slaughter.

'But I have it, Aslak!' I called after them, gripping the leather sack containing the holy book of Saint Jerome. But even if they heard, they did not care, because their bloodlust was up. For what was a book to men who could not read? To men who cared nothing for the gospels? What was a book compared with silver and furs and the warm flesh of a woman? I had opened the gate into King Coenwulf's lair. And the wolves had come to kill.

I suddenly thought of the young man and girl I had left bound in the church. In their fury the Norsemen would kill them where they knelt. I imagined cold steel sinking into the girl's pale flesh and the thought sickened me. I ran back into the mad thunderous night. Into the slaughter.

# CHAPTER ELEVEN

THE KILLING DID NOT LAST LONG. BY THE END, TWO NORSE-men's souls had been carried to Valhöll by the Valkyries, Óðin's death maidens. I saw the body of Grey Beard, the man who had spoken for the Mercians, but now his beard was black with drying blood and his eyes stared in lifeless shock. Sigurd had cut out his tongue just as he said he would.

Jarl Sigurd spared the women and children so that they would live to utter in fear the name of Sigurd the Lucky throughout Mercia, and King Coenwulf would know that Norsemen fought like demons. Raucous birdsong filled a new dawn as we marched back south-wards, the weak sunlight touching my left cheek. We had the book, for which we would be made rich beyond our dreams. And we had Weohstan and Cynethryth, the two who had discovered me in Coenwulf's church.

In that night's chaos, two Norsemen from *Fjord-Elk* had reached the church before me, and how their eyes must have lit up when they saw Cynethryth! But I had already killed three men that night and the bloodlust was upon me, and I had entered the church snarling at the Norsemen to seek their pleasure elsewhere. They had seemed ready to kill me, but Mauger burst in, his sword bloody, and the big Wessexman stood before the prisoners and persuaded the Norsemen that the couple would make valuable hostages. So, on Mauger's advice, Sigurd brought the Mercians along so that we might use them as currency should King Coenwulf catch up with us, which was more than likely, as we travelled on foot and he had horses.

I was walking beside Sigurd who was rolling his shoulder as though it pained him. He glanced at me. I looked away.

'What's on your mind, lad?' he asked. 'If there's a bad taste in your mouth it is better to spit it out.'

I hesitated. 'Are you injured, lord?' I asked. It was a poor attempt to deflect him.

He gave me a knowing look and I took a deep breath. 'Why did you attack the Mercians, lord? I had the gospel book. We could have been away without so much bloodshed.'

Sigurd seemed to consider this for a while, then he nodded, acknowledging that my question was a fair one deserving of an answer.

'These men risk their lives every time they unfurl the dragon's wing or dip their oars in the grey sea,' he said. 'Each day we spend in this land could be our last. Even a hunting dog must be let off the leash, Raven, to taste his freedom and be what he is.' He nodded towards the Norsemen in front. 'And these are wolves.' He smiled. 'A jarl should reward his men for standing in the shieldwall, don't you think? Silver. Women.' He shrugged. 'Whatever they hunger for.'

'I understand, lord,' I said. And for the first time I did understand. These men lived at the edge of life and they thrived in that place, like a wind-whipped pine on a desolate outcrop. Plunder was their reward. Enough had died for it. As for myself, I trained with these Norsemen. I ate and drank of their ambitions. Most of all, I had become a killer of men, like Black Floki and Bram and Svein, and yet I wondered if I would come to savour the killing as they seemed to.

'We don't have the men to row both *Serpent* and *Fjord-Elk* home,' Knut said, scratching at a patch of dried blood that filled the rings of his brynja. We had stopped to drink from a narrow brook. 'We'll need a good wind.'

'Raven, tell the Englishman that that bastard Ealdred better stick to his side of the bargain,' Bram added, belching loudly. 'If there's so much as a scratch on *Serpent* that wasn't there before . . .' He twisted an imaginary head off an imaginary body. We had drunk every drop of ale in King Coenwulf's hall before burning the place to the ground, and now our heads ached and our eyes were sore from the smoke.

'You'll get your ships, heathen,' Mauger said, after I had translated Bram's threat. 'Once Lord Ealdred has the book, you'll have your ships. The silver too.' The Englishman staggered off to piss.

Father Egfrith seemed impossibly happy. There was no sign of the scarlet cloak and he wore his simple habit again. He had been singing his psalms, but thankfully was now reduced to humming them because Black Floki had introduced him to the butt of his spear. In truth I preferred the monk when he was feigning death and, what was worse, he seemed grateful to me for my part in retrieving the holy book, which he now carried on his back. He seemed somehow taller, more vital, with the thing in his possession, and I know I was not alone in wondering what Christian magic lay beneath the bejewelled silver sheath, amongst the vellum and ink.

'Your jarl was wise to trust the holy gospels to my care,' Egfrith said proudly. Now that we had the book, Sigurd wanted nothing more to do with it. He would not even look at it. 'It could not be in safer hands,' the monk went on. 'Besides, simply being near the wonder's sacred leaves might cause a heathen horrendous pain.' I looked at the monk. 'Oh yes, Raven.' His eyes widened. 'It has the power to blister a heathen's skin and rot his bowels. That you bore it from Coenwulf's church without harm gives me reason to believe there is still hope for your soul. Slender hope, of course.' He stopped to consider me carefully. 'I think you will burn in hellfire for all eternity.' He scratched his head. 'But there may be some slender hope. Do butterflies not begin life as hairy worms?' He seemed pleased with the comparison.

'I care more for a dog's turd than your precious book, monk,' I replied, staring at him with my blood-eye. The little man recoiled, making the sign of the cross before my face, then shuffled off to annoy someone else. Though some of what he said knotted a worm of fear in my gut, the fear of an unseen power, I had chosen my god and he was not a god of the meek.

Sigurd made me responsible for the hostages and so I walked beside them, though I did not expect them to cause any trouble. Their hands were tied, they were surrounded by blood-stained heathens, and they looked terrified, but at least they still breathed, and this must have given them a glimmer of hope – enough perhaps to stop them from trying something desperate. Looking at them reminded me how wretched I had felt in their position. I thought of Ealhstan and the memory stirred a gloom in me, like an oar blade reaching beneath the sun-gilded surface of the sea. But the old man was gone now and it served no purpose to think of him, so I watched our prisoners, wondering what life we had torn them from.

I have never known my age, but I guessed that Weohstan was two or three years older than me. His mail was well crafted and his movements were assured. He wore his dark hair cropped short and he was handsome enough to make me conscious of my own broken nose and red eye. His shoulders were broad and his arms were thick, and his eyes were full of hatred. There was little doubt he was a warrior and even less doubt he would cut my throat given half a chance. Cynethryth was about my age, a girl just become a woman. Golden-haired and green-eyed Cynethryth. Bjarni said she was too thin and Bjorn mumbled that he had seen bigger tits on a dormouse. Perhaps her nose was strong for a woman and her eyes a little too far apart. But she was the most beautiful thing I had ever seen, and that day, as I walked beside her, I cursed under my breath because I had terrified her and now she must hate me. More than once she glanced at me, but always looked away the moment our eyes met, and I believed she saw me as an unfeeling, wild creature. It was nothing new. Sigurd believed my blood-eye marked me as a favourite of Óðin, and that had certainly saved my life. But to a good Christian girl I was a lost soul. I was something hateful that belonged to Satan.

That night, we rested just long enough to eat a meal of dried fish, cheese and some rich smoked meats meant for Coenwulf's table, for though we had gained the safety of thick forest, Mauger assured us that the Mercian king had not held his throne by keeping his sword sheathed. 'His dogs will be on our scent, Sigurd, don't you doubt it,' he had warned the jarl. 'We'll be looking over our shoulders till we make Wessex and even then it might not be ended. Not if Coenwulf believes King Egbert's behind all this.'

'If he finds us, he finds us,' Sigurd had replied loud enough for all to hear. 'We will see who is the hunter and who is the prey.'

There was no fire, no singing, and no fighting. Just forty-five men, a monk, and one young woman taking their food, resting their sore feet, and expecting at any moment Sigurd to give the word to set off once more. None complained that we would be marching through the night, for every step southwards took the Norsemen closer to their beloved longships. As they sat, their hands clenched and unclenched, hard, calloused palms eager to grip the oar again, even their soft beards

263

longed for the salt of the ocean to encrust them.

'I swear I'd sooner row to Asgard itself than walk another mile!' Svein the Red hollered, rubbing the life back into his tired feet.

'I'll remind you of that next time Sigurd gathers a crew to row him to the home of the gods, you red-bearded brute,' Olaf mumbled, happily munching on a honeyed oatcake. He had found a dozen or more freshly baked beside a Mercian hearth. He had also found the woman who made them.

'Toss me one of those and I'll tug the All-Father's beard when we get there,' Svein said, grinning. He caught an oatcake and spent the next while sniffing it and making a low rumbling sound, which I took to be contentment. Olaf grinned and shook his head. The deal was made and Svein seemed happy with the terms.

I wondered if our prisoners felt the same stunned sickness I had felt when I had left Abbotsend burning behind me – when I had seen through smoke-stung eyes people I had known lying torn and bloodless. I watched the prisoners and they watched us, their jaws clenched in hatred and their eyes sometimes fearful, other times fierce with hope of vengeance, as though they believed their god would strike us down with spears of lightning.

Father Egfrith was sitting with them, soothing Cynethryth with words I could not hear, when Weohstan caught my eye. 'Loosen Cynethryth's bonds, heathen,' he demanded suddenly. There was no fear in his voice. 'The rope is too tight. It's hurting her.'

I stood and went over to them. The skin of Cyne-thryth's wrists was raw and her hands were blue from lack of blood. I took my knife and cut the rope and when it was done she spat in my face. Weohstan grinned sourly as I wiped the spit with the back of my hand.

'She'll not make a good wife, Raven,' Bram warned. 'You'd do better to marry your own right hand, lad.'

Glum wiggled a finger on his remaining hand at me. 'That English bitch would cut off your worm while you slept and you'd wake up choking on it,' he said with a grimace.

I was glad Cynethryth did not understand the Norse-men, for I was still in spitting range. 'I'm sorry for what happened to your people,' I said to the girl, ignoring Weohstan. 'That old grey-beard could have saved his people. We only came for the book.'

'That old grey-beard was my friend,' Weohstan spat, 'and his name was Aelfwald. He would rather open his own gut with a dull blade than allow a heathen to get anywhere near the gospels of Saint Jerome.'

'And now he is dead and we have the book anyway,' I said, holding his dark eyes. 'Aelfwald was a fool.'

'Be careful, boy,' Weohstan hissed. 'This rope won't hold me for ever.'

'But it holds you now,' I said, handing a hunk of bread to Cynethryth, 'and so you need a woman to feed you.' His hatred was almost a living thing, writhing in the space between us.

'Raven, get them up,' Olaf called as a buzz spread through the camp, 'time to go.' I yanked Weohstan to

265

his feet and we set off in the darkness to put as much ground as possible between us and the king of Mercia.

The next days passed peacefully as we entered the heart of the old forest. Asgot pleaded with Sigurd to sacrifice the Mercians, but Sigurd wanted them alive as surety against an attack by Coenwulf, which grew less likely with every step southwards.

'You do not honour the gods as a jarl should,' Asgot complained. His hair rattled with new, small, white bones, and it sickened me to think they might have been Ealhstan's. 'It is your duty to make sacrifices, Sigurd! My hands were never clean of blood in your father's time.' He grinned wickedly. 'If it moved, Harald slit its throat and offered it up.'

'Aye, then it's a wonder you are still breathing, old man,' Sigurd answered. 'You buzz in my ear like a fly. One day I will tire of you.'

'No you won't,' Asgot said, scowling. 'Even with your arrogance you would not dare lay a hand on me.' But there was doubt in the old godi's eyes and I smiled to see it. For Asgot had hung Ealhstan's flesh in the sacrificial oak and it was only my loyalty to Sigurd that kept me from taking his head. No, that is not the whole truth. The truth is I feared Asgot. He was a bloodthirsty old hawk, and where to my mind Sigurd embodied the illustrious inhabitants of Asgard, Asgot the godi gave flesh to the gods' vicious sides. Their malevolence came off him like a foul stench.

Every night I listened to the Norsemen talk of their gods. They loved the old stories, the legends which each of them embroidered in the telling, and mostly they loved having fresh ears to try their tales on. They spoke of Thór's battles against the giants, of Loki's mischief-making and Óðin's wanderings amongst men, and the creation of the nine worlds, all of which are held together by the giant ash tree called Yggdrasil. For my part, I could not get enough and even though the stories were somehow familiar to me, like half-remembered dreams, I drank every uttered word like a man with an insatiable thirst.

The other thing I did every night was fight – against Bjorn and Bjarni mostly but sometimes the others too. Even Aslak, whose nose I had broken, taught me his favourite moves so that soon I could disarm a man of his shield using the one-handed axe. Weohstan always watched these bouts, I believed searching for my weaknesses so that he might kill me when the chance came.

I was aching and bruised one morning from fighting Bjarni when I walked at the head of the Wolfpack with Weohstan and Cynethryth. Black Floki had warned Sigurd that the girl would slow us down and I had thought he was probably right, seeing as Cynethryth was clearly a nobleman's daughter and would in her everyday life have had someone to walk for her. But as it turned out, the girl was strong and defiant and kept up easily. And of course she was not burdened with shield and mail and arms as we were. I had left her hands untied despite Bram's calling me a soft fool. But I knew Cynethryth would not run without Weohstan. She still clutched the blue flowers he had pulled from the dew-laced forest litter at daybreak, their weak stems now bound by a strip of birch bark, and I felt her beginning to take a grip on me too as we pushed further into pungent-smelling, thick forest little touched by sunlight or man.

'The Englishman, Raven,' Sigurd said, gesturing towards Weohstan, 'he would give his eyes to put a blade in your throat.' He grinned wickedly. 'But I think it would not be easy. You are a natural fighter. I think Bjarni Soulripper would agree.'

'Ah, I was being easy on the lad, Sigurd,' Bjarni said, winking at me.

'It's true, lord,' I said, embarrassed. 'He feigns tiredness. Drops his shield on purpose to encourage me.'

'Only so I can turn you when you come blundering on,' Bjarni said. 'Svein has more subtlety!'

I smiled at Bjarni, then turned to Sigurd. 'I am grateful, my jarl,' I said, gripping my sword's hilt, 'for everything.' I meant that I was grateful that these Norsemen taught me their skills, that they gave me their fine arms, that they had taken me into their Fellowship. But I did not know how to say it.

'I know, Raven,' Sigurd said, 'I know. And you will be a great warrior one day. When you were born, the Norns wove it into your life's thread, into your destiny. I am sure of it.' He stopped, gripped my shoulders and stared into my eyes as the others continued past us like a stream around a boulder. 'There is something I have been meaning to give you since that night at King Coenwulf's hall,' he said.

'I couldn't eat another oatcake, lord,' I grumbled, holding my belly.

He laughed. 'What kind of jarl would reward his warriors with oatcakes? Still, such a man would have Olaf's loyalty!' He grinned at Olaf who was passing, then pulled a thick silver ring from his right forearm and handed it to me. I took it, staring in awe at the treasure that was in the form of a two-headed serpent, the heads snarling at each other where the circle was broken. I put my right hand through, but the ring was too big for my forearm, so I pushed it up above the muscle at the top of my arm. After a while my face ached from smiling.

That night, we made camp by an old charcoal pit. The earth that had been dug away to reveal the fuel had been piled up to make a great wall round the hollow, but it had long since been overrun by birch and pine and thorn so that it would provide perfect cover for us and our fires, so long as we were careful not to set fire to the ground itself. Sigurd sent four men up on to the mound to begin their watch, though none of us expected King Coenwulf to find us now. Mauger had advised Sigurd to cut south-west away from the Mercian king's lands to disguise the fact that we had come originally from Wessex, and that morning we had crossed the Severn, killing a pock-faced ferryman to take his craft from shore to shore.

'If Coenwulf learns that King Egbert was behind the raid, the treaty between our kingdoms will not be worth spit. It'll drown in a tide of English blood,' Mauger said, shaking his head. 'Our little diversion should confuse those Mercian bastards for a while, they're witless whoresons most of them, but they won't believe you're Welsh. Not when they realize it was all about the book. Christ's balls, Sigurd, the Welsh are devils. Wild-eyed sons of bitches who make your men look like monks!'

But there had been no sign of a Mercian war band and so we settled down beside our fires to sing our songs and feast on what remained of the food we had taken from Coenwulf's fortress. The night was cooled by a fresh breeze from the east and I sat with my friends, Svein, Bjarni, Bjorn, Black Floki, Bram, Olaf, Hakon, and the rest, staring into the glowing embers of a dying fire. Three empty skins lay over a birch branch, the ale that had filled them now swelling our own bellies. Two more were still being passed around the camp, but most of the men lay asleep beneath cloaks and oiled hides.

'I remember my first warrior ring, Raven,' Olaf said with a hiccup. His eyes closed and he held his chest dramatically before releasing a great belch. Only Sigurd and Bram had more silver arm rings than Olaf. 'Got it for killing a boar with this,' he slurred, drawing his long, antler-handled knife. 'Just this. I was younger than you, Raven,' he said, nodding his heavy head. 'Much younger.'

Bram batted the air. 'Pah! Your brother had put two arrows in the beast before you got a sniff of it, Olaf. I remember,' he said, wagging an accusing finger.

'Which only made it angrier! Anyway, what do you know, Bram? You were likely full of ale in some whore's bed,' Olaf slurred, forgetting that Bram would have been just a boy then too. He belched again. 'Best damn boar I ever tasted,' he said, cuffing my head.

'One day I'll have as many rings as you, Olaf,' I said, fingering the solid silver serpent that was now a part of my body.

'Maybe you will, lad,' he replied, scratching his thick beard. He nodded at Sigurd who was snoring a short distance away. 'He's as generous a lord as ever took a dragon across the sea. Stay near him, Raven. You'll earn your rings.'

'That's if you don't mind stepping in another man's guts,' Bjarni put in with a smile. 'Sigurd has made us all rich men.'

'Aye, and we'll soon be rich dead men,' Glum muttered, gesturing with his short, leather-sheathed arm.

'Watch your tongue, Glum!' Svein the Red barked, 'or you'll be using your feet to pick your teeth!' Glum's kinsman Thorgils scrambled to his feet and drew his sword and Svein stood up, inviting the man on. Another of Glum's kinsmen, a big man named Thorleik, stood and lowered his friend's sword arm. Glum sat glowering at Svein.

'Enough, cousin,' Thorleik said, gesturing for Svein to back down too.

'Put your damn blades away before I rip the ale-soaked skin from your backs, you blood-loving sons of whores,' Olaf growled, sweeping an arm through the air. Those asleep, including Sigurd, were stirring now, and my own hand found my sword's grip, part of me hungering for the chaos that would come with swords and fury, because I hated Glum for what he had done to Ealhstan. But Olaf doused the sparks before they could

271

flame and the Norsemen settled down again, bristling but subdued by the ale in their bellies. Mauger was grinning, no doubt enjoying the prospect of heathens spilling each other's blood, whilst Weohstan also watched intently, though it was impossible to guess his thoughts. Cynethryth was asleep with her head on his shoulder, her blond hair covering half her face and falling across his chest. The sight of her quelled the bloodlust shivering through my body and, when Weohstan fell asleep, I watched the flame light play across her face.

Eventually, I slept. And my dreams were filled with death.

# CHAPTER TWELVE

THEY SAY THE DARKEST HOUR OF THE NIGHT COMES BEFORE the dawn. That is when Glum came for me. I woke with a blade at my throat and might have struggled but for the knife Thorgils held beneath Cynethryth's chin. Thorleik stood a little way off in the shadows guarding Weohstan and Father Egfrith, and before I could knuckle the sleep and ale from my eyes my hands were tied and I was stepping over snoring men, a blade pushing me on. I looked towards the mound, thinking the men up there must surely hear us moving through the trees. Then I shivered, remembering. Glum and his kinsmen had offered to take the dawn watch. The dogs had planned their treachery well.

'Make a sound and I'll leave your corpse for the wolves,' Glum hissed, ramming his sword's hilt between my shoulders. Then he spun me round and ripped the bone-handled knife from my belt, the knife that was my only link to my dark past, and threw it into the brambles on the forest floor. Weohstan, Cynethryth, and Father Egfrith were stumbling on ahead as Glum's men hurried to distance us from the Wolfpack. Branches and thorns attacked from the darkness, ripping our faces and hands, but Glum knew he had crossed a line from which there was no return. He had split the Fellowship and betrayed his jarl, and Sigurd would kill him if they met again. Sigurd had already taken Glum's arm. Now he would send the man's soul screaming to the afterlife.

'Shhh!' Thorgils hissed, pulling Weohstan down to the forest litter. The rest of us crouched. A horse whinnied and nickered softly. A gentle breeze rattled the leaves above us, carrying the chink of arms and the creak of leather. A heartbeat later, the sound of breaking twigs filled the dark, dank stillness as the forest was disturbed. But the riders were not coming towards us. They were heading west towards the Wolfpack. They were heading for the Norsemen who slept, trusting their sword-brothers to warn them of an enemy's approach. Only those Norse were no longer on the earth mound, looking out into the night. They were instead pushing southwards with their English prisoners and the book of Saint Jerome.

My brynja, helmet, sword and shield lay back where I had left them by the fire and I felt helpless in just a tunic, leather jerkin, cloak and trousers, but thankful at least that I had fallen asleep with my boots on. I felt for the All-Father amulet at my throat, seeking its comfort, then shivered again as the first sun rays idled through the forest canopy, gilding the leaves, then touching the damp earth and warming my cheek. I was waiting for the forest to burst, to ignite with the roar of battle as Sigurd's men woke with King Coenwulf's riders amongst them. But then I realized that we had come a long way already and if we heard anything, it would be no more than a distant moan. I offered a prayer to Óðin god of war and Týr who loves battle that my friends still lived, that Svein and Floki and Olaf and Sigurd even now stood over the English dead, drinking the last of Coenwulf's ale in victory.

'You are a worm, Glum,' I said, spitting at his feet. He turned and slammed his fist into my face. I grinned at him, blood spilling from my split lip. 'He doesn't know I'm going to take his other arm and stick it up his arse,' I said in English.

'Not if I get to him first,' Weohstan barked as Thorgils shoved him on, threatening in Norse to feed his tongue to the crows.

'Where are they taking us, Raven?' the monk whimpered in a small voice, but I did not know where, so said nothing, and the only answer the little man got was a dig in the back from Thorleik's spear butt.

It was a warm day now and the forest had thinned so that I could see the sun above the budding boughs, a pale gold disc in a white sky. Sweat ran from my forehead, stinging my cut lip, but Glum gave us no water and we could only watch enviously as the Norsemen gulped from a full skin. Cynethryth was as white as the sky. Her golden hair was lank and the hem of her skirt was tatty and full of thorns.

'Let the girl drink, Glum,' I said, 'or do you fear her as you fear me?' They were foolish words and I knew it. Even one-armed, Glum was a fierce warrior and of course he did not fear me.

'You are only alive because you speak their tongue,' he said, nodding at Weohstan, 'and you may be useful to me.' But perhaps a part of him was wary of my blood-eye and perhaps he still wondered at his jarl's interest in me, for he hesitated, then took the skin from Thorleik and held it to Cynethryth's lips, allowing her to drink. Weohstan must have guessed what I said because he nodded his thanks as the girl quenched her thirst.

'Now, ask the monk if we're nearing his land, Raven,' Glum said, taking the water from Cynethryth and shoving the stopper back in. 'Give me a reason to keep you alive.' The forest broke here, giving way to patches of rough grazing land watched over by copses of elm and ash, and I wondered if we had crossed back into Wessex.

'You'll give the book to Lord Ealdred in return for the silver he promised Sigurd,' I said to Glum. I knew that only the promise of great riches could have bought these men's betrayal, but I still wanted to hear it from Glum's own mouth.

'Sigurd owes me, boy,' he said, holding up his leather-bound stump. 'Bastard owes me.'

'Then where, Glum? You think Ealdred will let you stay in his land? Blood-letting heathens like you? So where will you go? You don't have the men to row *Fjord-Elk* back across the sea.'

'I'll buy men,' Glum said, sweeping the stub through the air, 'or pay for passage on another ship. I don't care which.'

276

'Sigurd will follow you to the world's edge,' I said, dragging my bound arms across my sweaty face. 'The gods favour him.' I looked at Thorleik and Thorgils, hoping at least to plant the seed of doubt in their minds. 'He will find you. All of you. You know it.'

'He'll find a hundred warriors eager to greet him,' Glum snarled, nodding at his kinsmen to bolster their resolve, 'a hundred Sword-Norse who call me jarl. I'll have the silver to buy them,' he grimaced, 'and they will find me a more generous lord than Sigurd the Lucky.' He spat the last words. 'Ha! He's probably dead any-way, belly-speared in his sleep by some Mercian whelp. Now ask the monk where we are.'

I glared at him. 'You believe Sigurd the kind of man to die in his sleep, Glum? You think that's what the Norns have woven for him?'

He hit me again and it hurt. Then he stretched his neck awkwardly. 'Ask the monk where we are, Raven,' he said, scratching at his beard, 'and perhaps I'll make you rich enough to lead your own war band.'

I turned to Egfrith who was watching us intently, his face pale with exertion and fear as he mumbled prayers to his god.

'Where are we, Father?' I asked, deciding to make myself more useful to Glum alive than dead. I nodded to the monk that he should answer truthfully for all our sakes.

He continued his murmuring for a moment, then sniffed loudly, dragging his sleeve beneath his long nose. 'Tomorrow we'll cross the Severn again,' he said, raising his bushy eyebrows, 'then it won't be long before we come across Lord Ealdred's scouts. Or rather they come across us. If the Welsh don't find us first.' He sniffed again.

I translated Egfrith's words and Glum nodded. 'Who are these Welsh?' he asked casually.

'They are heathens, Glum,' I said, and he nodded approvingly, 'but that won't stop them hurling their spears at us. They are raiders from the west. They steal cattle and they kill Englishmen.'

'I like the sound of these Welshmen,' Glum said, smiling at Thorleik. Then the Norseman stepped forward and cut through the rope binding the monk's hands.

'Thank the good Lord!' Egfrith exclaimed, rubbing his chafed wrists. Glum turned and looked into my eyes, then swung back round, slicing his sword into the monk's head. Egfrith's legs collapsed and he dropped like a stone. Cynethryth screamed and I saw that her face was spattered with his blood.

'This Christ slave's blood is shed in your honour, Óðin,' Glum said, closing his eyes and turning his face to the sky, the sword dripping. I recognized relief in his face because he no longer feared the spells Egfrith might have cast at him. Cynethryth was trembling. Weohstan grimaced and made the sign of the cross with his tied hands. 'Thorgils, get the book,' Glum commanded. He moved to wipe the gore-slick blade on Egfrith's habit, then thought better of it, sheathing the sword unclean. Then he pulled his sleek beard through his fist and examined his hand. The palm was red with Egfrith's blood and he seemed surprised. 'What are you waiting for, man?' he barked at Thorgils. 'The book! Don't piss yourself, the priest can't use his magic on you now.' He bent and wiped his bloodied hand on a dark crown of curled dock leaves.

But Thorgils still hesitated, his blue eyes shrouded beneath a heavy brow. 'Make the Englishman carry the book,' he said, looking up at Weohstan. 'Or her,' he said, turning to Cynethryth, suspicion narrowing his eyes.

'When did your balls fall off, Thorgils?' Glum asked, then he stepped forward and picked up the leather sack containing the book. He roughly slung the sack across Cynethryth's shoulder and smeared the remaining blood from his hand across the tunic over her breasts. 'If anything happens to it,' he said, drawing his knife and holding it to the girl's stomach, 'I'll slit you open like a fish.' I was proud of the girl then because although she could not understand him, I saw baleful hate in those green eyes, and I knew she would have plunged the knife into his heart if she could.

The flies were gathering on Egfrith's face as we set off again leaving him for the creatures of the forest, and I wondered what the Christian god would do to us for killing one of his servants. Then we turned to a sound that can chill a man to his bones. It is a forlorn sound, though I have come to love it. 'Aaarrck! Kaah! Kaah!' A great raven sidled and hopped on to the monk's face where it croaked again three times. The Norsemen grinned like wolves as Óðin's black corpse-reaper accepted their offering.

That night there was no moon. It was a night

279

belonging to the things of the forest, a night for spirits and things even more powerful, for men say that on such nights the gods themselves take human form and wander amongst us unrecognized. They say that Óðin All-Father sometimes roams the world seeking knowledge and observing the deeds of great warriors who might fight for him in the last battle at the end of days. Ragnarök.

We lit no fires and I was sorry, for a fire would have warned off the menace I felt stalking amid the black forest. Neither did we sing of riding crest-topped waves in sleek ships, or of hewing down our enemies in the shieldwall. Instead we sat in silence beneath the canopy of an ancient ash whose deeply ridged trunk crawled with sweet-smelling columbine. I took strength from the tree's eternalness, hoping the ash would inform the malevolent night spirits which amongst us were oath breakers and betrayers, and which had been betrayed.

Ealdorman Ealdred's men did not find us the next day and I wondered if Father Egfrith had lied about our being so close to Wessex. Perhaps the monk had hoped Glum would drop his guard, giving Sigurd and Mauger a chance to catch up with us. Or perhaps he had simply been mistaken. Either way, I realized we were now further west than we needed to be. When cutting through dense forest you will naturally take the easiest route and over a time this can make a great difference. We were way off course.

'You shouldn't have killed the little turd,' Thorgils moaned to Glum the next day when at last the

Norsemen let us drink our fill from a trickling brook. I had thought even my bones were dry as old sticks. 'The Christian was the only one who knew this land. We're lost, cousin.'

'And I'll leave you here alone if you question me again, you pig's prick,' Glum snapped, slurping water from his cupped hand as big Thorleik quietly filled the empty skin. Glum had made us travel through the night, but in the darkness we had lost our way.

That dawn as the sun rose, Glum realized we had been moving east most of the night. Later we entered a rock-strewn clearing, and as the sun slipped behind the rolling western hills Thorgils spotted an old shepherd's hut high up the bluff where elm, ash and oak gave way to gorse and heather.

Big Thorleik shook his head, making his blond plaits dance. 'We should stay down here amongst the trees, cousin. It's safer.' He pointed his spear towards the hut, which was about to fall into shadow as the sun fell in the west. 'We'll be seen from miles around if we move about up there.'

'Who's going to see us, cousin? The hares and the badgers?' Thorgils said, throwing an arm to encompass hills and woodland. 'Just for once I want to sleep under a roof.' He winced, clasping his hands behind his back in a great stretch. 'I ache all over.'

'Just now I'd take a good night's sleep over a good young cunny,' Glum mumbled, frowning. 'You saw that fat fucking raven the other day, Thorleik.' His eyebrows arched. 'Old Asgot would have said that was a good omen. I say it is a good omen.'

281

Thorgils nodded, putting a hand on Thorleik's shoulder. 'Óðin favours daring. He's with us, cousin. It pleases him that we'll soon return to our own land with English silver. And we will honour him, Thorleik.' He glanced at Glum who gripped his sword's hilt proudly. 'As Sigurd should have done.'

Thorleik dipped his head in acceptance, unslung his round shield and gripped it in readiness, and then we made our way up a shallow ravine untouched by the setting sun, towards the shelter. We had not bargained on the Welsh.

Thorleik had left the hut to take a piss, but now he burst back in and leant against the old door. 'There are men out there, Glum,' he hissed, 'or wolves.'

By the weak light of a grease lamp I saw fear flare in Glum's eyes and knew he thought Sigurd had found him. 'What did you see, cousin?' he growled, standing to fetch his round shield from where it leant against the cabin's wall. A thin breeze whistled through the gaps where the brittle daub had crumbled away, causing Cynethryth to shuffle closer to Weohstan.

'It's black as a Saracen's arsehole out there. I couldn't see past my own prick,' Thorleik said, thumping his helmet down. 'But they're there all right, and they know we're in here, whatever they are. Týr knows I near enough pissed on one of them.' He rolled his broad shoulders and grabbed his ash spear.

'I hate this land,' Glum muttered, snatching up his own spear, and in a few heartbeats the three Norsemen were armed and battle ready. They looked like grim gods of war, dealers of death in their mail and helmets, hefting their spears and round, scarred shields with their dented iron bosses.

'The Welsh have come for us. Give us weapons, Glum,' I said, pushing myself up against the wall and holding out my bound wrists. 'We'll fight with you.'

He stared at me with his dark eyes and I thought he was about to kill me. But then, because despite his treachery he was still a Sword-Norse, so he would not deny me a place in Valhöll at the mead bench of the slain, he cut my bonds and handed me the spear.

I glanced at the Englishman Weohstan. 'Only you, Raven,' Glum said, turning his back on me to face the door. I could have killed Glum then, run him through with his own spear. But I was a Norseman too. And my god was watching.

Glum kicked open the door. The four of us stepped out into the darkness. There was nothing. No sounds or shapes moving like spirits, only the rolling gorse reflecting what little light touched the world that night.

Thorgils let out a great laugh, turning to Thorleik. 'You were scared of your own prick, Thorleik, you big bastard!' he shouted. Then there was a thud and Thorgils grunted, staggering back with an arrow in his chest. Suddenly, the heather sprang up and came at us, shrieking, but the wet thud of Glum's sword striking meant our enemies were flesh and could be killed. Thorleik and Thorgils threw their spears, thrust with their shields and slashed with their long swords, grunting as they killed. I lunged with the spear, sinking it into a man's shoulder, the battle lust upon me. My

283

eyes adjusted to the gloom and I saw the fiends for what they were, sinewy men with muddied faces, crude blades and small black shields. Two jumped on to Thorleik, snarling like dogs and dragging him down with claws and iron. Glum roared as he hacked a man from the shoulder to the hip, but the sword stuck and two more mud-blackened warriors speared him and he screamed in pain. I turned and ran back inside the hut where Weohstan and Cynethryth stood in a dark corner waiting for the end, and I cut their bonds with the spear's blade.

'Run!' I told them, turning to face a black-shielded warrior who stood snarling in the doorway. I gave a great shout and rammed the spear through the shield into his chest, twisting it before yanking it free, then I was outside where arrows were thudding into Thorgils, bouncing off his helmet and shield as he roared and killed. Weohstan snatched up Glum's sword and swung it into a man's face before turning to deflect a spear thrust. Thorgils went down, crying out to Óðin with his last breath. Cynethryth screamed, the sound cutting the night like a knife; then, as if by some dark magic, the black-shields were gone and I fell to my knees, gulping air as Weohstan gave a great roar and cursed his god and Jesus and the saints. The black-shields were gone. But Cynethryth was gone too.

'Welsh bastards!' Weohstan spat on a dead man, yanking off Thorgils's belt and pulling the brynja from his battered body. Through a tear in the sky the stars cast a silvery hue across the scene, revealing nine dead Welshmen amongst the slashed bodies of Glum,

Thorgils and Thorleik. Silently, we took mail, helmets and weapons from the dead, including two Welsh throwing spears each, along with the heavier Norse ones. Then, in war gear slick with cooling blood, we faced each other and the clouds healed, concealing the stars and casting the land into darkness.

'Come, Norseman,' Weohstan spat, planting his feet apart and hefting a round war shield, 'let us finish it.'

'You want to die now,' I asked him, 'or after we get Cynethryth back from those Welsh whoresons?'

He was already striding towards me, but stopped then. 'You mean to go after her?' he asked, and even in the darkness I could see suspicion and hate in his eyes.

'I mean to go after the book, Weohstan,' I said, lowering my shield slowly, 'but two swords have more chance than one. Your death can wait until we both have what we want.'

Weohstan lifted two spears, then thrust their points into the earth with a grunt. He stepped forward and gripped my arm, his mouth a grimace and his eyes dark beneath the helmet's rim. He looked a different man now he was armed for battle, and I knew then that he was a killer like me.

We slung our shields across our backs and took up our spears. Weohstan offered up a prayer to the White Christ and so I muttered my own to Óðin whose name means frenzy. Then we ran west across the heather-cloaked hills and though there was no way of knowing where the Welsh war band had taken their prize, we were free and on the move. And we had thoughts of vengeance to push us on.

# CHAPTER THIRTEEN

WE SLEPT FOR A SHORT TIME AMONGST THE HEATHER AND woke when the first pink laced the eastern horizon. I felt empty, hungry and cold as I shook the morning dew from my gear, imagining the fear Cynethryth must be feeling. If she still lived.

'Look, Raven!' Weohstan called. I was taking a piss and I turned to see him pointing to the west where I made out the great earthen wall and palisade built by Offa, the last Mercian king, during his wars with the men of Powys and Dyfed. It was a huge bank and ditch and must have taken many years of labour. 'Not the wall, you blind bloody heathen, there, maybe a mile from the bank, do you see it?' I was shaking my head when I saw it, a grey smear against the brightening sky. 'The bastards are having their breakfast,' he added, the grimace twisting his handsome face.

I pulled up my breeches and touched the Óðin amulet at my throat.

'I could eat,' I said, slinging the shield across my back. We had no way of knowing how many men were down there, and the fact that they were not afraid to light a fire suggested they were confident enough. They would never expect two men to come after them and that was our advantage, for we were not just two men; we were warriors. And I had my god with me. And he was a god of war.

We took the low ground to prevent our silhouettes from standing out against the rising sun and soon found ourselves on the near side of the hill that hid the Welsh war band, and there we watched the smoke drift lazily eastwards on the breeze. It was warm. Sweat ran down our faces to drip from our beards as we crawled along the hill's summit to its far edge from where we saw the Welsh sitting round their fire. There were eight of them, their faces still covered in the mud that had made them invisible fiends the previous night. Cynethryth lay apart from the men, her legs and arms tied and her face turned away from us. Only the twitch of a leg told me that she was still alive.

'There are too many,' I whispered. 'We'll have to wait till dark. Surprise them.'

'No,' Weohstan said, gripping my wrist and nodding towards Offa's wall, 'by then they'll be across the ditch and we'll be up to our necks in Welsh bastards.' He stared into my eyes. 'We hit them now,' he said, his jaw clenched, and I knew he would go alone if he had to. 'Now,' he hissed, and I nodded because I knew he was right. If we were lucky, the Welsh would be stunned from losing so many men during the fight at the shepherd's hut, but soon they would turn to the English girl they had carried away and they would care nothing that she was young or that her face was bruised and dirty and her hair matted and tangled. Then Cynethryth would be better off to strike her head against a sharp rock. Sigurd and his Wolfpack were probably dead, making me the last of a broken fellowship. I had no home and nothing to lose. And the Welsh had Cynethryth.

I tightened the helmet strap beneath my chin and prayed that I would use well the skills I had learned. But mostly I prayed that the battle fury would take me and that that rage would make my enemies fear me. 'Kill well, Weohstan,' I said, grinning.

He nodded. 'Kill well, Raven,' he replied, his eyes full of violence. We got to our feet on the crest of the hill so that the sun hit our backs, casting long shadows down the slope before us. I turned my face to the sky and roared so that Óðin would hear me and guide my sword to help me kill.

The Welsh scrambled to their feet, grabbing their weapons and small shields as we ran down the slope yelling our battle cries. Weohstan sent a Welsh spear like a lightning bolt into a warrior's chest and to this day I have never seen such a throw, but I waited until I could not miss and sent my own light spear through a man's neck before he could raise his shield. Then I threw Glum's knife to land beside Cynethryth and rammed my shield into a Welshman's face, crushing it with the iron boss. I swung my spear in a wide arc, making two men jump back, and saw Weohstan plunge a Norse spear into a bare chest.

The bloodlust raged in me as I battered with my shield and jabbed with my spear, but something struck my helmet and a spear ripped into my back, scraping my shoulder blade. I yelled and spat in fury, twisting to swing the haft of my spear against an enemy's temple, dropping him. Blades battered me, some glancing off my brynja, others striking true. I heard Weohstan yelling madly too, then saw a Welsh war club strike his face. His legs buckled and Cynethryth screamed a wild cry like that of a hawk and plunged Glum's knife into the man standing over him. I threw my heavy spear and drew my sword as a warrior slammed his axe into my shield, then I swung the sword up into his chin, cleaving his face in two.

'Bastards! Whoresons and Devil's turds!' I screamed, wildly swinging my sword from side to side, spinning round seeking more enemies, hungry to send more wet crimson flying through the air. I struck flesh, stumbled, fell to one knee and clambered up again, then stamped on the body at my feet. Twice more I fell, before somewhere beneath the madness, amongst the bloodlust, I heard a shrill repeating sound that slowly took shape.

'Raven! It's over! It's over!'

I threw my shield into the gorse and turned to look at Cynethryth through eyes full of salty, stinging blood.

'Are you a death maiden?' I heard myself ask, trying to fight the shuddering gripping my body. My legs buckled, but I stood straight again. 'Am I to join Jarl Sigurd now?'

'Raven, it's me, Cynethryth,' she cried, tears streaming down her cheeks. 'Cynethryth.' Then she wrapped her arms around my waist and held me tight as though

289

she could take the shivering pain from my body into her own. I realized I was not dead and that she was no Valkyrie. She was Cynethryth. Beautiful Cynethryth. And somehow we had won.

'Oh, no! God help us!' Cynethryth said. She pushed me away suddenly and ran to where Weohstan had fallen and there she fell on her knees. I turned to the west where the bracken-covered hills rolled like the swollen grey sea before a storm, and I saw men coming towards us. Though they were still far off, I saw they carried black shields.

'Is he breathing?' I called, stumbling over dead Welshmen to stand above Cynethryth. There was a gash across Weohstan's temple where the club had struck, and his mail was torn and bloodied, though I could not tell if the blood was his own. 'Does he breathe, Cynethryth?' I asked again, glancing up to see the Welsh coming fast like war hounds, and just then I would have preferred it if they had been English warriors laden with brynjas, helmets and iron-rimmed shields. Because then we would have more time.

'Can you carry him, Raven?' Cynethryth asked, but her green eyes betrayed that she knew I could not, and she ran her fingers through Weohstan's brown hair, clutching him desperately.

I shook my head. 'I'm finished. I can't fight them,' I said, wondering if this was the end the Norns of fate had woven into my life's thread. I had fought well and there would be no shame in it. Then fear stabbed me, for what would the Welsh do to Cynethryth after they had torn the breath from my belly? She looked down at Weohstan and kissed his forehead, letting his blood lace her lips, and I did not interrupt her despair, but instead whispered to Óðin that I would make one more kill before the end. But then Cynethryth stood, hefting a Norse shield which she slung across my back. She took up the leather sack containing the gospel book of Saint Jerome and grabbed a stout spear.

'Here,' she hissed, closing my hand round the spear's haft and throwing my other arm about her shoulder. 'Lean on me, you bloody heathen beast.' My strength was gone. I was wounded, I did not know how badly, and it was all I could do to stay on my feet as we clambered up the east hill, leaving Weohstan, dead or alive, to the Welsh. 'Faster, Raven!' Cynethryth barked, dragging me on as I planted the butt of the spear with every other step, grimacing against the pain. 'Move, you filthy son of a goat!' She pulled me on, whipping me with insults, rousing the last embers of my heart into flames of defiance, for we both knew that if we did not make it to the trees before the Welsh crested the last hill, they would catch us.

'Leave me,' I growled, falling to my knees. Dizziness blurred my vision and darkness was creeping in from the corners of my eyes. 'Go!'

'No, Raven!' she howled. 'I'll stay here! I'll stay and watch them kill you and then they'll rape me to death!'

I cursed, summoned the last dregs of will and dug in with the spear, offering my hand to Cynethryth to haul me on. 'Stubborn bitch,' I said.

We made the tree line without turning to see if our

pursuers had crested the last hill, and scrambled into the forest like hunted wild animals.

'A little further, that's all.' Cynethryth drove me forward, picking me up when I fell, and when the forest became denser we crashed through the brittle lower branches of pines and birch, the sound of breaking wood and the blood gushing in my ears filling my dark world. Then I remember no more.

When I opened my eyes I thought I was blind. Slowly, they adjusted to the clinging darkness. The forest was oppressive and still, the screech of an owl or rustle of a badger the only signs of life around us. I was shivering. I tried to sit up, but a firm hand pushed me down.

'You're stronger than you look, Cynethryth,' I mumbled, then slipped into my own dark place once again.

'Drink, Raven,' a voice said some time later, and I felt the cold rim of a helmet against my lips. Water ran down my chin as I slurped. I had not realized how thirsty I was. 'I found a stream while you were sleeping.' Cynethryth's loose hair tickled my forehead.

'It's salty,' I said, licking my cracked lips and lying back again.

'I rinsed it out but the sweat's deep inside the leather,' she said quietly, carefully placing Glum's helmet in a cradle she had made from sticks. 'I hid your shield beneath some brambles.' Her voice sounded strange, as though the night ate her words as soon as they were spoken. The air smelled musty and damp and when I stretched out a leg, my foot hit solid wood. 'We're

292

inside an oak, Raven,' Cynethryth said in a low voice. 'It must be very old.' I shifted, but a burning pain in my back held me rigid. 'Keep still or you'll open the wound again. I stitched you with this.' She held up a fine bone needle.

I touched it with my finger and winced. 'Not very sharp, is it?' I said.

Cynethryth shrugged. 'I used a thorn to pierce the skin. It's just as well you were asleep. I thought you were dead.' In the darkness I saw her nose crinkle. 'You smell dead.'

'What did you use to close the wound?' I asked with a shudder.

Her lip curled as she lifted the ragged hem of her tunic from which she had pulled a thread to sew up the slash, and I caught a glimpse of her torn underclothes. 'It could have been prettier, but I left my best linen in Mercia.'

'I am sorry, Cynethryth,' I said, taking her hand and squeezing it. A wave of pain flooded my back. 'I'm sorry for what we did.'

She pulled her hand away. 'You are heathens. You do what you do. You are like beasts, wild creatures with no fear of the Lord's judgement.' She pointed a finger at me. 'But you should fear it, Raven.' I thought I saw the same hatred in her eyes that had been in Weohstan's.

'Then why did you save my life?' I asked. 'You could have run. Left me to those shit-faced whoresons.'

'I could have,' she said simply. Then she sat back against the trunk and looked out through a narrow slit at the black forest beyond. Somehow, she had hauled

293

my heavy, mailed, unconscious body through that opening. 'I am a woman,' she said, 'but that does not mean I do not know what honour is. You men wear your precious honour like an ermine cloak, but you do not own all of it.'

'But you hate me, Cynethryth.'

'You came for me,' she said. Then she shrugged and peered out through the split again. 'You came.'

'No.' I shook my head. 'Weohstan came for you. I came for the book.' Just then a loud crack echoed off the forest trees and we held our breath. For a long time we stayed silent in the damp darkness of the hollow oak, afraid that the Welsh were prowling the forest. Then we slept.

In the morning, Cynethryth smeared a fresh poultice of herbs, crushed leaves and clay across the cut in my back and we ate the hedge garlic, seeds, roots and the few berries she had gathered in my helmet before dawn.

'You will need some meat to build up your strength,' she said, screwing up her face as she chewed a bitter berry. 'A man can't live on these.'

'The ones picked from the south side of the bushes are the sweetest,' I said, pouring a fistful of greenish berries into my mouth. 'They get more sunlight.'

'I know that, lord,' she said mockingly, and I shrugged, chewing the gritty fruit. It was a bright morning and our hiding place inside the old oak did not seem so safe now that daylight poured in through the split.

'You haven't speared me a boar for breakfast?' I

asked with a weak smile, baiting the girl when I should have been thanking her. 'Thór's teeth, I shall never wed you, woman.' But Cynethryth had no smiles for me this morning.

'Do you think he is alive?' she asked. The gospels of Saint Jerome sat in her lap. I shifted back, afraid of the thing with its jewelled cover and hidden secrets. 'Speak truthfully, Raven. Whatever you believe.'

I tore my eyes from the holy book and looked into Cynethryth's. 'I believe he is dead, Cynethryth,' I said softly. 'After what we did to them . . .' I shook my head. 'Those bastards would have finished him.' In truth I thought there was another possibility and that was that the Welsh might have taken Weohstan for ransom or surety against Mercian raids. But they might just as easily torture him to death. Cynethryth did not need false hope and so I made her believe he was dead. Cynethryth's green eyes filled with tears, and when she closed them the tears spilled down her dirty face.

We stayed in the hollow old oak one more night, and that night Cynethryth found a dead raven by the tree. She took one of its wings and plaited it into my long hair so that the glossy feathers shone in the moon-light. 'Now you really are a Raven,' she had said, the ache of losing Weohstan dulling her eyes like a skin of ice. 'Now we can fly away. Far away.' I did not feel as though I would be able to walk properly, let alone soar like a bird, but I thanked her anyway.

'You sound like a pagan,' I had accused her, and she had made the sign of the cross then, but she left the raven's wing in my hair and I thought I would never

untie it and one day it would be no more than a stinking, rotten scrag.

We ventured out into the forest then, hoping the Welsh
war band had given up searching for us. They had
already taken much Mercian silver from Glum and
with any luck they would have slipped back into their
own lands beyond King Offa's wall. I was weak, but
Cynethryth said the wound in my back was healing
well given that I was trudging across difficult ground
instead of resting in straw. We were heading south.
After all that had happened, I still had the book and
I knew I must fulfil Jarl Sigurd's part of the bargain
by putting the treasure in Ealdorman Ealdred's hands,
for only then would *Serpent* and *Fjord-Elk* be returned
to us. Though what I would do with two longships, I
did not know. But for Sigurd's honour and perhaps my
own too, Ealdred would have the book. I would have
my freedom.

'Would Ealdred have paid Glum good silver for you
and Weohstan?' I asked as we walked through gorse
and bracken, a thin rain falling to wash the blood from
my mail. I knew that I risked her tears by mention-
ing Weohstan, but I needed to know something about
the ealdorman I would soon have to face again. I still
walked with the spear taking much of my weight so as
not to twist and risk tearing open what Cynethryth had
sewn.

She shrugged but said nothing, so I breathed in the
air which smelled of rain, and pushed deeper. 'Glum
thought if he gave you to Ealdred, the Mercians would

pay to get you back. I suppose he was right. I'd wager Ealdred would not turn his back on the chance of having something the Mercians want. There were whispers flying around the fires that you were King Coenwulf's daughter,' I said, watching her face for signs of the truth. 'You don't look like a princess to me.'

'And you have known many princesses, have you?' she said. I shrugged. Cynethryth pursed her lips and bent to snatch a slender hazel branch from the forest floor. 'Coenwulf might give a fur or two to have me back at his hall, Raven,' she said, 'if he still had a hall. But not for the reasons you think.'

'So you're not his daughter, but you are nobly born,' I said, 'that much I know.' She raised one eyebrow. 'I was teasing before,' I said. 'Your clothes, your bearing. Your father is a rich man, whoever he is. He must be known throughout Mercia.'

'Shhh, Raven.' She turned to face me, pressing a finger against my lips. 'I am no Mercian. Do I sound like one?' She shook her head. 'You are a strange heathen boy.'

I leant on my spear and held out a hand, inviting her to explain, and she shook her head as though wondering how I could be so stupid.

'I'm Ealdorman Ealdred's daughter.'

'His daughter?' The news struck me between the eyes. 'Then what were you doing in Coenwulf's fortress?'

A shadow of pain skated across her wet face. 'I was to marry King Coenwulf's kinsman,' she said, 'to help heal the wounds between Wessex and Mercia. I was

297

to be a peace-weaver, Raven. Father says the treaty is falling apart. My marriage was meant to bring the kingdoms together and put an end to the fighting.' She frowned. 'But I know my father and I know what I am worth to him.' She spat those last words as though they were poison. 'He would give me to Mercia to buy the time he needs to build his army for the day King Egbert marches against Coenwulf. Ealdred is land-greedy, Raven, and I am the price he would pay for war on his own terms.'

Peace-weavers. I had heard them called peace-cows also and powerful men have always used their daughters for such ends, but I had never considered that those daughters, women born to privilege, might not embrace their destinies. I thought of how I had helped the Norns pull free and sever the thread from my life that would have seen me take old Ealhstan's place at the pole lathe, amongst the sweet-smelling wood dust.

'Peace-weavers pay a heavy price too, Raven,' Cynethryth said. 'They trade themselves for trinkets and fine linen and they live in the cold, empty space between two families who can never bury their hatred. They have two lives and none at all.'

I understood Cynethryth then, for like a peace-weaver I was not whole. I was without a past and so neither English nor Norse. Cynethryth palmed the rain from her face and pushed her wet hair behind her ears. I could have looked at her for ever. 'I would have been married the day after Weohstan and I found you in Coenwulf's church,' she said, whipping the hazel branch through the air.

'So Weohstan is King Coenwulf's kinsman,' I said, thinking I understood.

'Almighty Christ and all his saints!' she exclaimed. 'A child's wooden sword is sharper than you, Raven.' She threw the hazel stick away. 'The man I was to marry was called Ordlaf. I suppose he might be dead. He rode off with the king because the Northumbrians were raiding the borderlands.' I said nothing. 'Anyway, I don't like him. He's a Christian,' she said, as though this made it better, 'but he's even more of a beast than you.'

'I don't believe it,' I said with a grin. 'Does he stink as bad as me?'

'No one could stink that bad,' she said, almost smiling, 'but you'd think he was a heathen. You would like him, I don't doubt. Maybe you should marry him if he is alive.' Her eyes shone with mischief then. 'And Mauger? Did you not notice that he was always close by me? From the moment you and your godless friends took us hostage?'

'I thought that ox wanted to have his pleasure with you,' I said, a flush of blood warming my cheeks. 'I don't trust him. He's a bastard.'

Cynethryth giggled. 'Old Mauger has known me my whole life,' she boasted. 'My father sent him with Jarl Sigurd to bring me back to Wessex. Perhaps he decided that it was too late to save the treaty. Too late even for a peace-weaver. He's no fool. He'd use me, but not for no gain. Not if he doubted the outcome. There are other kings with other cousins. There are other bargains, other trades to be made.' She began to walk on and I kept up with her.

'So your father sent Sigurd for the book and Mauger for you.'

'Yes,' Cynethryth said, 'but you did Mauger's job for him by keeping me in King Coenwulf's church. He just had to make sure your filthy heathens kept their hands off me.' She said it as though this task was easily within the Wessex warrior's capabilities and I wondered what he would have done if Svein or Bram or Black Floki had tried to have their fun with the girl.

'Well, he didn't do a very good job,' I said petulantly. 'Where was Mauger when Glum and his turds came for you in the middle of the night?' She frowned at that, which I took to mean she also wondered why Mauger had not woken to protect her.

'I can't believe he's gone,' she said then. 'It seems impossible. We were not close. Never.' She shook her head. 'My father says Mauger's a vicious man, that he loves his sword more than he loves any living soul. Can a man have such feelings for a piece of iron, Raven?' she asked, and my hand went instinctively to my sword's pommel, and that was enough of an answer because Cynethryth grimaced. 'Anyway, I expect he killed his share of Mercians that night in the charcoal pit. Father will miss him.' I remembered the sickness in my stomach at watching armed riders heading for Sigurd's camp. 'Mauger was the greatest warrior in all Wessex,' Cynethryth added almost proudly. My head was spinning as I tried to make sense of everything I had heard, though one piece still did not fit with the rest, like a knife rammed into the wrong sheath.

'Weohstan was your lover?' I asked accusingly.

300

'You were faithless, even on the night before you were supposed to be married to another? I saw you two holding hands outside the church.'

Now Cynethryth smiled bitterly and her eyes, the colour of ivy, filled with tears as she walked. 'He was my chaperon.' She cuffed an eye. 'Officially, anyway. In truth he was supposed to remain with King Coenwulf as surety against my father's attacking him.'

'So he was not your lover?' I said.

'Weohstan was my brother.'

# CHAPTER FOURTEEN

WHEN WE REACHED THE WESTERN BANK OF THE SEVERN river we found a boatman and his simple son and the man offered to row us across the narrowest part in his leaky old skiff. He was not so keen when I told him we had no money, nor did he believe Cynethryth was the daughter of Ealdorman Ealdred of Wessex, but he did believe my sword looked wickedly sharp when I showed it to him, and we were soon in Wessex.

We passed through a small village where Cynethryth was known to the folk who lived there and they gave us some bread and cheese and smoked ham. The women clucked around her, horrified by her ragged looks. But they were wary of me and I did not blame them, for I wore all my war gear and carried the painted round shield and had not yet cleaned the blood from them. I was used to people staring at me, for my blood-eye had always inspired fear, and I suppose I had come to relish their fear. I have heard men say that to have a man's respect is a far greater prize than to have him fear you. This is untrue. Fear is what freezes your enemy's heart and keeps his sword in its scabbard. Fear is what makes a man fight alongside you when he might otherwise fight against you. Respect is like a bejewelled mead cup, or the stone-encrusted cover of a prayer book. It is an unnecessary luxury, so I let them fear me.

We had not long left the village when riders approached us across a wide meadow of milkwort and marsh marigolds, their shields slung casually across their backs and their spears resting across their saddles. When they were a hundred paces off, one of the riders raised his hand and the band formed a crescent which could easily close to make a ring of death if the leader gave the word.

'Lady Cynethryth?' one of them exclaimed, reining in his stallion, which tossed its black head bad-temperedly. 'Is that you?' She had washed her face, but her long tunic was ragged, a Norseman had taken her fine brooch and a Welshman had taken her cloak. Though an old woman had combed the knots from her hair, it was still a filthy yellow rather than bright gold.

'Of course it's me, Burgred!' Cynethryth replied sternly, rubbing his mount's nose and calming the beast. 'Are you going to sit up there staring like a beady-eyed chicken? Give me your horse, man. My shoes are full of holes.'

'Of course, my lady,' Burgred said gruffly, seemingly irritated that his stallion was nuzzling Cynethryth's cupped hand. He gestured for one of the other men to give up his mount.

303

'And is my companion to walk, by Christ?' Cynethryth asked, pointing at me. 'He's weary from killing Welshmen.' The Wessexmen looked at me suspiciously, at my blood-eye and the raven's wing in my hair, then one of them grudgingly slipped from his mount and handed me the reins. So I rode back to the place where Norsemen had died, where I had fought with Sigurd's Wolfpack, and where our futures had been struck like silver coins: Ealdorman Ealdred's hall. And I rode with his daughter Cynethryth and the holy gospel book of Saint Jerome.

When Lord Ealdred saw me with Cynethryth his face darkened and his mouth twitched beneath his long sand-coloured moustache. He looked towards the fortress gate, no doubt wondering where the other Norsemen were, then threw his cloak over his shoulder and took Cynethryth in his arms, watching me suspiciously over her head.

Cynethryth tugged her father's moustache affection-ately, but Ealdred pulled away and eyed me for a while, and there was distrust in those eyes.

'Come, daughter,' he said, then nodded to me and turned towards his hall, leaving his slaves and retainers hurrying about the place, organizing an impromptu feast to celebrate Cynethryth's safe return.

After telling of what had befallen the Wolfpack, Cynethryth told her father about Weohstan, and tears fell amongst the rushes as she spoke. Ealdred's face seemed to melt like tallow, though his jaw remained clenched so that the muscle in his cheek twitched like

304

an insect trapped beneath the skin. He turned from Cynethryth and bellowed in fury, frightening the slaves, who cowered and hurried out of the hall to find other jobs to do.

'If not for Raven I would be dead too, Father,' Cynethryth said, taking Ealdred's hands in her own. Ealdred suddenly glared at me and his eyes were cold and hard like river stones.

'You fought alongside my son?' he asked, his hand pulling away from Cynethryth to rest on his sword's pommel.

'Yes, my lord,' I replied. 'Weohstan fought like Beowulf himself. Killed more of the whoresons than I did. We would both be dead if not for him.'

Ealdred's eyes flickered with pride, then he stood silently, staring at me as though he did not know whether to embrace me or cut my throat. Eventually, he nodded.

'I owe you a great debt, Norseman,' he said with a scowl, twisting his moustache round his finger. 'My daughter is very precious to me.' He turned and gave Cynethryth a smile that held both grief and love. 'Very precious,' he repeated. Then his face darkened again. 'But I had an agreement with your Jarl Sigurd and he has failed to honour it.' Slowly, as though he bore a great weight across his shoulders, he sat on one of the long mead benches beside the great hearth.

'No, lord,' I said, stepping forward to place the sack containing the holy book on the oak table. I glanced about the hall for signs of the bitter fight, but saw none other than the new door of pale oak which stood out against the dark stained wood of the rest of the hall. The White Christ hangings still swayed in the breeze and there might have been a dark bloodstain above the god's thorn-crowned head.

Ealdred's eyes flicked from me to Cynethryth, and then to the sack, which he stared at for some time. Eventually, his shaking hands touched the drawstring and his fingers began to work feverishly on the knot. 'It cannot be . . .' he mumbled, his long moustache quivering, 'it is not possible . . .' But it was possible, and Lord Ealdred of Wessex roared for someone to bring him a torch to illuminate one of the greatest treasures in Christendom. He held the book at arm's length as though fearful of it, then with a finger stroked the inlaid cross of fine gold within the book's silver cover, lingering on the precious red and green stones set in each corner. 'Beautiful,' he whispered, shaking his head in awe. 'So beautiful.'

Cynethryth stood behind her father, looking over his shoulder, and I dared step closer to the holy book, though I admit I was afraid of it. The cover alone would fetch a fortune, but that was not the source of its power. Just to witness its hold over Lord Ealdred was enough to remind me never to touch the thing again. I was no Christian. I told myself that whatever magic lay within its vellum leaves had no hold over me. And yet Father Egfrith, Ealdred, Weohstan, Cynethryth, King Coenwulf of Mercia, and even King Egbert of Wessex all coveted the book. I had learned always to be wary of that which inspires men. Even fools who pray to a god of peace will fight with their last breath for the mysteries scratched in ink on a dried calf's skin. They will kill with a war god's fury for words.

Ealdred turned the stiff pages, his eyes hungry for every swirling pattern, every elaborate knot of green, purple, blue, and gold adorning them. Some of the patterns formed writhing beasts like those carved on to the prows of Sigurd's longships, and I did not know if they had words inside them too, or whether it was only the small black shapes that spoke to those who knew their magic. 'Cynethryth, go and let the women tend to you,' Ealdred said, tearing his gaze from the book. 'Your mother would roll in her grave to see you in such a state.'

'Don't be silly, Father,' she replied, beginning to plait her dirty hair. 'I'll wash later. I want to stay with you and Raven. Besides, you always adored Mother's hair when it was wild and untamed.'

Ealdred did not take his eyes from the gospel book. 'You are not your mother, Cynethryth,' he said, dragging his lip over his bottom teeth and flicking his hand in a gesture for a retainer to escort the girl from the hall. Cynethryth stormed through the door and I watched her go.

'Do you read, Raven?' Ealdred asked when we were alone.

I shook my head. 'Never had reason to, lord. At least, not in the time I remember and I doubt I had reason before that.' He looked confused then. 'My mind is dark,' I said with a shrug. 'I have no memories of my life before two winters ago.'

He still looked confused, but waved it away. 'Of

course you don't read,' he said, returning to the intricate designs. 'There is no reason why you should.' He smiled, running a finger over the image of a woman holding a small man. At her shoulders were men with wings and long pointing fingers, but why they had not flown away I do not know, for the woman was ugly as a stoat. 'The wolf has no love for the shepherd's fire and so he will never know warmth,' Ealdred said.

'The wolf's teeth are sharp, my lord, and his eyes see well in the dark,' I said. 'He has no need for the shepherd or his fire. It would only make him soft.'

Ealdred carefully closed the book and looked up at me. 'I can use a wolf,' he said. 'It seems you have a talent for death, Raven.' His eyebrows arched as he tenderly placed the book back into the sack and stood. 'More important perhaps, you have a talent for staying alive. I thought Mauger had that talent, but it seems even he was mortal. I can give you a good life,' he said, 'if you give me your oath. Swear to be my man, you and your sword mine. I can be generous to those who serve me well.'

'I have a lord and I am bound to him,' I said, instinctively touching the silver ring on my arm.

'Sigurd is dead,' Ealdred countered, his lips parting to show his teeth. 'You owe him nothing now. Or do Norsemen serve ghosts?'

'We don't know that they are dead,' I said. 'Coenwulf's men might have ridden past Sigurd's camp. Even if they found them . . .' I shook my head, 'I do not believe they could have beaten the Wolfpack.' Of course it was possible. Sigurd's men had been asleep and their enemies no doubt outnumbered them greatly. But I had witnessed Ealdred's cunning that night on the beach before *Serpent* and *Fjord-Elk*. I did not trust him, and I wanted the ealdorman to believe that Sigurd would be back for his longships.

'Then where in God's name are they?' Ealdred asked, putting a hand on my shoulder. 'Do you think I can have a heathen war band wandering King Egbert's land? My people won't tolerate it, Raven!' He leant in close to me, so that I could smell the sweet mead on his breath. 'My God won't tolerate it,' he growled.

'What of the silver you owe Sigurd?' I asked. 'And his longships?'

Ealdred twisted his moustache round a ringed finger. 'You brought me the book, Raven. Not Sigurd. The silver is yours. The boats too.' He hesitated. 'If you want them.'

I nodded. 'There is something else, lord,' I said, and he frowned because he thought I would ask for more when he had already offered me enough. 'There is a chance that your son is alive. I said nothing before because I did not want to stir hope in Cynethryth, but Weohstan was breathing when the Welsh got to him.'

'Then they would have gutted him, you fool,' Ealdred said with a grimace, angry that I had steered his mind back to his son's fate. 'We show those bastards no mercy and they show none to us.'

'My lord, the Welsh lost many men. Too many. They paid a heavy price for one night's hunting.'

Ealdred raised an eyebrow. 'Even more reason

why they would want to spill his blood. Anyway, the whoresons breed like hares.'

'They would have seen that Weohstan was high born.' I smiled. 'Your son *is* a killer, but he looks like a nobleman.' The ealdorman was still frowning, but now he nodded slowly and I knew that his heart had grasped the slender thread of hope. 'The black-shields must have known he was worth more to them alive than dead.' Ealdred's eyes closed and he turned his face to the smoke-blackened beams above. 'Give me forty men,' I said flatly. 'Not levy men, but proper fighting men. I will cross King Offa's wall and find your son. If he is dead I will slaughter his killers and bring you his body so that you might bury him as you would, with honour.'

Ealdred might have laughed at my arrogance. He might have pointed at my one warrior ring and asked how a man with his first beard would lead Wessex-men, warriors who had fought many battles for their lord and king, against the Welsh. He might have asked if I was drunk, or shouted for his warriors to run me through for my vanity and for stirring false hope. But Ealdred did none of these things. He looked at me as a man looks at a wild animal that has no understanding of its own mortality. To Ealdred I was a strange, god-less creature with no fear of this life or the next, and I believe I intrigued him.

'Why would you do this?' he asked, staring at the raven's wing in my hair. 'You've already said you will not swear fealty to me.'

'My jarl is somewhere out there,' I said, picking

dried blood from the rings of my brynja's shoulder and crumbling it between thumb and forefinger. 'After I have found Weohstan, I will find Sigurd.' I smiled at Ealdred then. 'I will find him before your god does.' And although that is what I told Ealdred, there was another reason why I would wet my sword with Welsh blood. I would bring Weohstan back to Wessex for Cynethryth.

That night Ealdred gave his people a great feast to celebrate his daughter's return and because, he said, she had escaped the bed of a Mercian sheep-lover before blooding his linen. He did not mention the holy gospel book of Saint Jerome, but that did not surprise me. You did not shout about owning such a treasure unless you wanted jealous men to covet it for themselves.

New rushes were laid, fires were set, and come evening the ealdorman's mead hall thronged with his people. Warriors, craftsmen, traders and merchants paid their compliments to Ealdred's family, made friends with his friends and gorged on swan and beef, pork and trout, wine and good sweet mead. Ealdred even managed to look mournful as he read a passage from a simple leather-bound book in memory of Father Egfrith, 'so cruelly slain by the heathens'. Then he had other priests say prayers before we were made to listen to one of his young nephews play the reed pipe. Thór's balls the boy was bad. The sound reminded me of a newborn's squawking and even Ealdred seemed relieved when the boy's mother led him ashamedly from the hall.

I did not sit with Cynethryth, but was given a place amongst the men I would lead out next morning. Not the forty I had asked for, but thirty. Ealdred feared to strip his lands of so many warriors and was quick to point out that King Coenwulf had done just that, which was why the Wolfpack had been able to steal the gospels of Saint Jerome and burn down his hall. Neither were the thirty all proper fighting men. I learned that twenty of them were fyrdsmen, farmers and merchants fulfilling their obligation of sixty days' armed service to their lord. And that night there was no shortage of mead to make them brave, even though it was a false courage that they would piss away come morning. The other ten were warriors, grizzled veterans of many fights who wore their battle scars as proudly as they wore their warrior rings, and I was glad of them. They reminded me of Mauger and each was eager to earn more silver rings fighting the Welsh. I wondered which of them we had fought in this very hall weeks before.

Many times during the night I tried to catch Cynethryth's eye, but she sat amongst cousins and aunts and high-born friends who were making such a fuss over her that she was never likely to notice me. I thought our eyes met once, but she looked away so quickly that I wondered if I had imagined it, so I began babbling to the man beside me to take my mind off the girl. At the high point of the feast, when the clamour in Ealdred's hall sounded like the wild song of the shieldwall, I saw Cynethryth give an empty smile, whisper in her father's ear and then leave the bench.

'I need to piss,' I said, breaking free of the throng

to go out into the night. The new oak door creaked closed behind me, muffling the rowdy voices within as I drank in the cool night air, hoping to clear my head. If anything the fresh air along with the absence of others made me feel worse and for a moment I thought I would vomit. I had no idea where to look for Cynethryth and I doubted my tongue would speak any sense even if I found her, so I cursed and turned to go back in. Then I saw her by an ancient yew, the tree's dark branches silhouetted against a sentry fire before the fortress's main gate. Cynethryth leant against the gnarled trunk, staring into the flames.

'Cynethryth?' I spoke the name softly so as not to startle her, but she did not move and I thought she must not have heard. 'Cynethryth? Is everything all right?' She pressed the heels of her hands against her eyes, then turned to face me, and I saw she had been crying. 'What is it?' I asked. 'What's wrong?'

'How could anything be wrong?' she asked coldly, turning back into shadow. 'Everyone is happy. Is it not a feast to remember, Raven?' She gestured to the noisy mead hall. Cracks leaked a warm yellow glow out into the night and a wave of dizziness washed over me. I was about to confirm that I had never been to a greater feast, but then I thought better of it.

'I don't understand, Cynethryth,' I said, scratching the short beard on my cheeks.

'Why would you?' she snapped. 'You're a man.' She shook her head. 'My father is ealdorman and they all fall over themselves to please him while he drinks himself out of his mind.' I held in a belch, wondering how much mead I had poured down my throat. 'Ealdred will piss himself and take some girl to his bed and when the sun comes up he'll go hunting with the girl's father.' She stepped away from the yew tree and turned to look me in the eye. 'What about my brother? Damn Ealdred! What about his *son*?' she exclaimed. 'Weohstan is barely cold and they celebrate with goose and swan and God knows what else, but I know it should not be eaten tonight. Not tonight.'

'Ealdred is happy to have you safe home, Cynethryth,' I said. 'What father wouldn't be?'

'Oh, Raven, pull your head from the mud. He is happy to have the damned book. That's why he celebrates,' she said. 'Because of the book. Don't be fooled by his piety!' The word was heavy with disdain. 'Silver is my father's god. Can you imagine what the book is worth?' Just then the mead hall's door swung open, releasing curses, shouts and laughter into the night. A man staggered out and dropped to his knees to puke. I thought of the Norsemen we had laid out in the mud before throwing their corpses into the sucking surf.

'Your father is an important man, Cynethryth,' I said. 'Of course his heart aches to have lost his son. But a lord cannot show weakness. Not in front of his warriors.' I remembered the empty look in Olaf's eyes when his son Eric with the white hair was killed by bowmen three hundred paces from where I now stood. The Norseman had put the sadness away so as not to weaken the younger men's resolve. I reached out and took Cynethryth's hand. 'Ealdred will grieve in his own way,' I said quietly.

She pulled away. 'He would not be grieving at all if he had not sent you and your devils to King Coenwulf's hall. If you had not come. It is because of you that Weohstan is dead. Because of you, Raven!' I had no reply to that and so I watched a plume of black smoke rise into the star-filled sky. 'And I am not the fool you take me for. You and my father are the fools if you think I believe your lies.'

'I don't understand, Cynethryth,' I said.

'He told me that you are leaving tomorrow to find Jarl Sigurd.'

'And I am,' I said, frowning.

'It has nothing to do with Weohstan?' she asked, daring me to lie. There were many things I would have gladly done to Cynethryth then, beautiful Cynethryth with her golden hair and her green eyes and strong nose, but lying was not one of them, and so I looked away. 'I know you're going to cross King Offa's wall to look for my brother. Well, you're a fool. Weohstan is dead and you will soon be dead, too, and because you are a heathen you will go to Hell and you will be damned for all eternity.' And though Cynethryth probably believed this, there was a gleam of light in her eyes, like the last ember amongst the ashes, and that gleam was Weohstan. She would not say it, but she had not given up hope of seeing her brother alive and that was enough for me to walk into a hundred Welsh spears, spitting fire and fury as I trod.

Then Cynethryth ran off into the night, and I was left staring up at the stars, which would not seem to stay in their places.

                    *          *          *

At cock's crow I awoke amongst the reeds in Ealdred's
hall. The place stank of mead breath, sweat and stale
food, and I stepped over stirring bodies to collect
my war gear and move outside. It would be a warm
day. The scent of violet bellflowers, yellow birds-
foot, and magical red clover rose on a June breeze as
men and women began their day's work. Chickens
clucked and scratched in the dirt, dogs barked, cattle
lowed and the forge rang out. I stretched my aching
neck, drew some water from the well and tried to wipe
the sleep from my eyes.

A hand gripped my shoulder and I turned to greet
Penda, one of Ealdred's household warriors who had
been recalled from a scouting mission along the Wessex
coast. Penda looked like a man who would kill you
for the fun of it. You could almost smell the violence
coming off him. He wore no beard or moustache – a
great livid scar carved from his left cheek to beneath
his chin, on which no hair would grow. But the hair on
his head stuck out in all directions. During the feast the
man had made it clear that he disliked me, though he
had grudgingly admitted I could drink well for a pup.
He did not know that late in the night, when the timber
roof had begun to spin around my head, I had left the
table and puked my guts into a hawthorn bush.

'Feels like someone pissed in my ear while I was
asleep,' he grumbled, squinting in the daylight and
holding the back of his head. His arms were heavily
tattooed with swirling shapes and his taut muscles
showed beneath a simple mail brynja. It was too warm

now to wear a thick gambeson beneath the mail and so most men wore a thinner one of toughened leather.

'I feel as fresh as a corpse,' I replied with a grin.

Penda drew in a deep breath, his eyes following a young red-haired girl as she left the well with two heavy pails. 'It's a fine day for killing Welshmen, Raven,' he said, pursing his lips and whistling after the girl, whose tunic was thin enough to reveal the swell of her behind as she walked. 'It's always a fine day for killing Welshmen,' he repeated, never taking his eyes from her. Penda wore silver and gold warrior rings on both arms and a beautiful sword whose grip was adorned with silver wire and whose pommel was set with amber. He saw my eyes fix on the weapon. 'Here,' he said, drawing the sword and handing it to me. 'I'll let you touch it, but be careful. I don't want your mother taking a poker to my arse if you cut yourself.'

'It's beautiful,' I said, testing the sword's balance and slicing it through the air.

'Got it from a Welsh chief,' Penda said, 'after I cut the bastard into joints.'

'It's a Welsh blade?' I asked, making another cut through the air, which Penda frowned at because it was clumsy.

'Of course it's not a Welsh blade, whelp!' he said, bemused. 'Their swords are as likely to shatter as cut cleanly. Their smiths are idiots. Or else their iron's no good. That's why they're always raiding. Fucking thieving sods. The mad bastard who waved this at me must have taken it from a rich Mercian. Like to think it might have belonged to King Coenwulf himself. Can't be many with a blade like it.'

I shook my head. 'I've seen Coenwulf,' I said, 'and he's a big bastard. Wouldn't use a toothpick like this. But don't worry, Penda,' I teased, handing the sword back to him, 'if the Welsh put a spear in your belly, I'll look after it for you. I'll even clean the blood off it.'

He leant forward and waved a hand before my eyes. 'You still drunk, lad? A Welshman ending Penda the Fierce?' Then he spat a gob of phlegm that narrowly missed a beetle crawling past my foot. 'There's more chance of a Norseman becoming king of bloody Wessex,' he said.

'Could happen one day,' I said, imagining Sigurd sitting at the head of King Egbert's mead bench.

'You *are* still drunk,' he growled.

'Maybe,' I said, 'but drunk or not, we need to get going.' I nodded towards the hall. 'Go and shake the sleep from those sorry-looking whoresons in there.' I found a louse in my beard and squashed it with my thumbnail. 'I don't think they like me,' I said.

'I *know* they don't like you,' Penda laughed, 'but I'll screw a flea-bitten, saggy-titted Welsh whore before I'll do your dirty work, whelp.' And with that he set off after the red-haired girl. 'You're bloody well leading them into Wales,' he called, 'so you can start by leading them out of their beds.'

I took a spear that was leaning by the open door and used the blunt end to wake the drunken farmers, traders and craftsmen I would be taking to fight the black-shielded Welsh. And I wished I were leading Norsemen.

318

# CHAPTER FIFTEEN

THE PEOPLE OF EALDRED'S FORTRESS GATHERED TO WATCH us set out. Children fought with wooden swords, enacting the victories we would have over the Welsh, whilst their folks looked on with apprehension. The men of the fyrd made a brave show of it, proudly displaying whatever weapons and helmets they possessed, though only a couple of them owned any mail and the others were dressed in toughened leather. The real warriors made no fuss at all. To them it was just another raid.

'They don't look much, but they'll fight well enough,' Penda said as I cast my eye over the war band preparing to march out. 'Wessexmen know how to fight, Raven. It's in their blood. Even the merchants.' He grinned. 'Getting their guts cut out is bad for business. So they learn how to kill.'

They did not look like fighters to me. 'The Welsh will piss their breeches when they catch sight of us,' I murmured.

'They might when they notice that eye of yours,' Penda said. 'Even the Welsh believe in the Wicked One.'

'The Wicked One?' I said.

'Aye, old Belial.' I shrugged. 'Crooked Serpent. Abaddon,' Penda added. 'Satan, lad!' he shouted.

'Crooked Serpent?' I asked.

'Aye, that's one of his names, whelp. Thought you'd know that, you being a bloody godless heathen.' I thought of Jörmungand, the Midgard-Serpent who the Norse believe encircles the earth and after whom Sigurd had named his ship's dragon figurehead. 'You got a girl somewhere, lad?' Penda asked. 'Cos God help her if you do. The poor bitch must shiver at the thought of you planting another like you in her belly.'

Just then I spotted Cynethryth. She was standing beneath the old yew tree where she had left me just hours ago, before the sun had risen to cast the hard light of doubt on our undertaking. She wore a blue mantle that ended a finger's breadth above the ground, over a pale yellow smock whose sleeves were embroidered with fine blue thread. A narrow belt emphasized her slender waist and her golden hair hung loose and uncovered. Nor was she wearing a brooch befitting her rank. Instead, a simple silver chain hung across her chest, suspended from two small round mantle pins. Her skin was pale, her mouth was a tight line and her eyes were unreadable. And by Freyja she was beautiful.

Someone said my name and I turned to meet Ealdred who wore a dark green cloak edged with white ermine fur. Beneath it he wore a fine mail brynja, its rings polished to a lustre. But the brynja was not new. It had seen battle.

'My lord,' I greeted him, checking that my sword,

which had been Glum's, came cleanly from the scabbard. That morning one of Ealdred's smiths had sharpened the blade and his apprentice had dripped melted sheep's fat into the sheath's wool lining. I could still smell it.

'Find my son, Raven,' Ealdred said. He looked past me at the warriors assembling, his face expressionless behind the long moustache, though I thought I caught a hint of doubt in those hard eyes.

I nodded. 'I'll find him, lord. Then I'll be back for my jarl's silver.' Ealdred held my eye for a moment, then nodded, and I watched his back as he walked away towards his daughter.

'Don't even think about it, lad,' Penda said, following my eyes to Cynethryth. 'Ealdred would have someone like me cut your throat for even dreaming about her lily white arse.' But I watched Cynethryth anyway, until she flushed and tugged on her father's sleeve, drawing his attention elsewhere so he would not notice my staring. Then, as the sun rose higher in the east, casting its brilliance on to helmets and spear blades and shield bosses, I and thirty men of Wessex marched out of Ealdorman Ealdred's fortress.

After the first few miles, the levy men began a drinking song and I thought of the Norsemen who were always singing, yet by the time the sun began to slip from his throne the only sounds were of boots striking the earth, sword scabbards banging against shield rims, and iron and leather fittings jangling and creaking. I was sweating heavily in Glum's brynja and helmet, carrying his shield across my back and his sword at my waist, and I prayed to Týr Lord of Battle that I would not dishonour the fine arms as Glum had. That dog had betrayed his lord and his Fellowship and I imagined his one-armed soul wandering the afterlife, spurned even by his ancestors. Surely such as he would have no place in Valhöll at Óðin's mead bench. But if he was amongst the chosen, I wondered what would happen when the Valkyries bore Sigurd son of Harald to the All-Father's hall. For not even death can turn aside vengeance, and the ancient beams of Valhöll would shake then and their dust would fall like dry rain upon the living.

We crossed streams still swollen from the winter rains and marched through forests of oak, ash, and elm, even cutting through a great enclosure used by kings of Wessex for hunting red deer. We tramped through meadows where white lady's smock grew so thick it looked like a mantle of fresh snow, and crossed fields where knapweed and marsh bedstraw were losing their heads to grazing sheep. That night, we ate well and slept soundly and next morning we woke to another fine day full of the noise of marsh tits and song thrushes. Swallows twisted and turned effortlessly, plucking winged insects from the sky, whilst yellow wagtails as gold as dandelions ran nimbly between the feet of grazing cattle. Life was everywhere in a day that gave no whisper of the death to come.

The Wessexmen resented me. It was in their eyes and in the way they looked to Penda to lead them. But I had expected as much, for I was an outlander to them and had never stood beside them in the shieldwall.

Furthermore, I was a pagan and a Norseman, and Englishmen have always despised both.

By the third day, we had left King Egbert's kingdom and I found myself once again in Coenwulf's land, in Mercia. At dusk a man called Eafa made his feelings towards me plain.

'Hey, Egric, did you know that Norsemen screw their neighbours' pigs? Not their own, for that is considered uncivil, but they screw their neighbours' animals. Did you know that?'

'No, I did not,' Egric said, glancing at me. 'Why would they do that?'

'Because the pigs don't smell as bad as their women,' Eafa said.

It was not the first insult Eafa had aimed at me, but at last the man had found the courage to speak them loud and plain rather than letting them escape like farts. The other men laughed, their own way of slighting me.

'Are you going to let that prick make a fool of you?' Penda mumbled. Eafa was a fletcher by trade and a big man, but his bulk came from fat, not muscle.

'You think I should put my spear down his throat?' I asked, scanning the sun-touched hills for Mercians or Welsh raiders.

'I try not to think, lad,' Penda growled, 'but the men won't stand with you in the shieldwall if *they* think you're a coward.' I knew Penda included himself in this and for a moment I was tempted to open Eafa's belly to show Penda I was no coward. Instead I turned and Eafa's eyes widened as I rammed the butt of my spear into his gut, making him double over. Then I brought the haft down on his helmeted head and winced because I thought I might have killed him. But Eafa had a fat head, too, and he struggled to his hands and knees, shaking his head and moaning.

'We have too few men as it is, Penda,' I said loud enough for the others to hear. 'I'd be a fool to kill one of them, even a useless pig's bladder like Eafa. Better to let the Welsh do it.' Eafa was in no state to fight me and I don't know that he would have in any case, because I had embarrassed him once and once was enough for Eafa. Some of the men cursed me and others helped the fletcher to his feet, but none made a move against me, and I was relieved. I had taken a risk and it had paid off.

'I'd have hit him harder,' Penda said as we continued on our way. Later I wished I had hit him harder, because Eafa's mouth began flapping again so that after two days I admit I admired his imagination where Norsemen and animals were concerned.

And then we came to Offa's wall, which marked the western edge of Mercia. The ground before the barricade had been cleared of trees and bushes that might have provided cover for raiders, and a great ditch had been dug before the high earthen bank on which stood a palisade of sharpened oak stakes.

'Are we going to flap our arms and fly over it?' a man named Alric asked as we lay on our bellies on a hillcrest overlooking the barrier.

'Bloody right we are, Alric,' Penda said, 'should be easy seeing as we're all bloody angels!' He scratched the scar across his face. 'Or else, just for the fun of it, we could wait till dark and climb over the damn thing. You hear that, Eafa?' he said, looking at the fletcher. 'Think you can haul your fat arse over that little wall down there?' Eafa grimaced and Penda turned to me. 'Raven, you'll catch Eafa if he falls, there's a good lad.'

'Like a pig on a spit,' I said, holding Eafa's eye and tapping the haft of my spear. 'We're exposed up here,' I said, turning back to Penda. 'We'll take cover now and come back tonight.' The Wessexman nodded and we began to crawl back from the ridge. 'You still think we should cross here, Penda?' I asked as we gathered our shields and prepared to seek cover till nightfall. 'We could move north and cross the river in boats.' For a little further north the wall ended, replaced by the river Wye which formed a natural territory marker coursing eastward before snaking back into the Welsh lands. Only near a place called Magon does Offa's bank and palisade rise again, attesting to Mercian dominance. I had learned all this at Ealdred's feast before the mead had emptied my head of sense.

Penda shook his head. 'Here, we'll have to cross the wall *and* the river behind it.' He grinned at the Wessexmen. 'Making it the most difficult part.' They grumbled, though they saw the sense in it, for no Welshman would expect raiders to take the most difficult path. 'With any luck, the sheep-shaggers won't be watching this area too closely,' Penda said, and I was glad to have him with me.

That night we became shadows. We used ropes to

climb over the oak stakes, which was easy for most of us, and then found a shallow part of the river to cross, which was not easy. Ealdred had given us wine skins and we blew these up and used them to keep our heads, swords, and rolled up brynjas above the water as we crossed. I whispered my thanks to Loki the cunning that there were no Welshmen waiting to greet us as we clambered shivering in our undergarments from the Wye's muddy west bank. Then, throwing my wet hair back, I remembered the men who had attacked us at the shepherd's hut, and I scooped up a handful of mud and smeared it across my face. 'It will make us invisible, like spirits,' I said in answer to questioning looks. Some of the men muttered under their breath and others made the sign of the cross as though my words offended their god, but soon every man had covered his face and hands with thick mud so that by the stars' silvery half-light only the whites of our eyes gleamed to suggest we might be men, not demons.

We knew that if we followed the river we would come across villages and settlements, for folk will always live beside fresh water, but there was no way of knowing where Weohstan had been taken. One of Ealdred's household warriors, a solidly built man named Oswyn, seemed to know the land better than most.

'There's a settlement on the next bend in the river,' he said, his teeth bright against his blackened face. 'It used to be a big place, but we burned it three years ago.'

'I remember,' Eafa said with a grimace, examining the fletchings on one of his arrows. 'They'd taken some little 'uns from Hwicce, seven or eight of 'em, I think.

So we burned seven or eight of their villages.' He ran the feather flights across his tongue. 'Bastards rebuild 'em faster than we can raze 'em.'

'Then we hit them tonight,' Penda said, 'and if Weohstan is not there, we move on while it's still dark. Try the next place.'

'No, Penda,' I said, gripping Glum's thick ash spear. 'If we hit the place now, some will get away. Bound to. They'll run to their kinsmen and we'll have Welshmen all over us by sunrise.'

'Aye, we'll be haring back to Wessex,' Oswyn said, 'and we'll be damned lucky to get half the way before they do for us.' He spat at the thought.

'So what do you suggest, Norseman?' Penda challenged. All eyes fixed on me and I took a deep breath, accepting that the Norns might be weaving a pattern that would have me lead these men to their deaths.

'We take one man from this village Oswyn talks about and we make him tell us what he knows. Word will have spread if Ealdorman Ealdred's son is being held round here. They'll need to have something to show for losing so many warriors.' Penda nodded grudgingly and I pushed on. 'We find out where they're holding Weohstan and we get the bastard to take us there.' I said these words remembering my first meeting with Sigurd and Olaf, and the terror that had turned my bowels to liquid when they had made me take them to my village.

'You want to walk into a man's house and drag him from his bed,' Penda asked, 'hoping that neither his woman nor any other Welsh bastard notices us?' I grinned at Penda and in the darkness I saw his teeth flash like fangs.

Oswyn was right. The place was small. There were only nine or ten dwellings, though you could still see the blackened stumps of old timbers sticking up from the ground like burnt fingers, their charcoaled surfaces catching the starlight reflected off the river. Perhaps the timbers had been left as memorials to the dead, though it was more likely that the survivors had their own lives to look to. We crouched in the darkness like wild dogs choosing our prey.

'That house there,' I said, pointing to a crude dwelling built beside a tumbledown woodpile. 'The lazy bastard who lives there shouldn't give us much trouble.'

Oswyn shook his head. 'No, Raven, that's the place we want,' he said, nodding at another house, nearer the water.

'He's right,' Penda said. 'The noise of the river will cover us.' I nodded, acknowledging Oswyn's cunning with a smile. 'Any volunteers, ladies?' Penda asked in a low voice. White eyes stared back at him and I wondered what I looked like, for my blood-eye must have been invisible.

'I'll go,' I said, unslinging the shield from my back and taking off my sword and scabbard. I would have to move silently, like a Valkyrie across the field of the slain.

Penda nodded, removing his own gear. 'Two of us should be enough,' he said, giving his own shield to a warrior named Coenred. 'Be ready to move, lads, as soon as we have the scrawny devil by the scruff of his neck.' Then the two of us crept towards the house by the river and I wondered what we would find inside.

We were flat on our bellies by the time we reached a pigpen woven from hazel. The stink filled my head, making my eyes water, and some of the animals grunted softly, stirring in their sleep as we studied the round, thatched house. The door faced north. There had once been another house facing it, but no longer, and again I wondered why these people chose to begin every day faced with the remains of ruined lives.

'Reminds them to hate us,' Penda murmured, nodding at the debris, then he looked back to the round house. 'The door might be barred. It'll be no easy thing getting in. We'll make a noise like bloody thunder.'

'No, we make just enough noise, Penda, enough to wake them up but no more than that,' I said, staring at the place. No candlelight leaked out, nor could I see any smoke rising through the thatch. 'We'll wake them and when they come outside to check . . .' I shrugged.

Penda scratched his scar. 'Better than breaking down the door,' he admitted, and in a few heartbeats I found myself to the side of the round house, cradling a slimy piglet with Penda's hands clamped around its snout.

'It won't keep still!' I hissed, struggling to hold on to the muddy creature as it wriggled for its little life and kicked with sharp trotters. 'Do it now,' I said, 'before I drop it.' Penda jabbed his long, bone-handled knife into the piglet's arse and let go of its snout so that it gave an ear-piercing squeal. 'Freyja's tits!' I hissed. 'Kill the damn thing before it wakes the dead!'

'Hold it still then, whelp!' Penda growled. He was trying to slit the pig's throat, but the animal squirmed and squealed and squawked, and so instead of slicing across, he rammed the point of the blade into its neck by its forelegs and the squealing stopped.

I heard voices inside the house, then the scratch of flint and steel. I threw the flailing animal aside just as the door opened and Penda burst into the place, dropping a woman with a punch before she could scream, and I leapt inside, spun and slammed my knife's hilt into a man's face, sending him sprawling.

It was over in a breath. Penda kicked the man in the head for good measure and with him slung over my shoulder we made our way back to the waiting Wessexmen whose dark shapes now stood out in the landscape like timbers from King Offa's wall. I whispered my thanks to Loki the Trickster, the Sly One, who had seen fit to reward our mischief.

Then we fled north along the riverbank, through long grass and reeds, seeing by the starlight reflected off the fast-running water and hoping its murmur would smother our passing. I gave the limp Welshman to Coenred whose legs were thick as tree trunks and the Wessexman threw him over his shoulder like a sack of flour. I caught up with Penda who set the pace.

'We'll be lucky to get any sense out of him,' I said as we ran bent low across ground left marshy from the Wye's swollen months.

'He'll be fine, lad,' Penda replied. 'That's the thing about the Welsh. Hard buggers. Takes a lot to kill 'em.'

'Shouldn't we try to get him talking?' I asked, my

shield thumping my back, which was beginning to ache from running bent. I hoped Cynethryth's stitches would not tear open. 'Weohstan could be back in that village for all we know.'

'Lad's not there, Raven, I know that much,' Penda said, his loping run so smooth and natural that he looked like a predator. 'If he's still got breath in him, they'll have him in a bigger shit pit than that place. The boy's not a piece of meat like you and me. He's got a real price.' Just then a coot burst up from the reeds, making a sound like a hammer striking an anvil. 'And we're gonna bleed for it,' I heard Penda mutter.

We ran on in silence, each man aware of the danger we were in, for if Weohstan was being held in a Welsh fortress, how were thirty men going to free him? We mud-smeared few who loped like shadows along the riverbank were both hunters and hunted, perhaps closer to the afterlife than to our own homes. Certainly I was, and the thrill of it filled me, making my heart thump and my limbs tingle, and though Penda expected us to die with Welsh spears in our bellies, I believed the Norns had woven another fate for me.

The Wessexmen waited in the darkness on their haunches, catching their breath and looking out in all directions. Oswyn tilted his helmet, splashing water across the prisoner's face as he lay in the mud. When that had no effect, Oswyn kicked him in the balls, which seemed to work for the Welshman groaned and his eyes rolled as he came round. Oswyn kicked him again, hard, and the man cried out.

'Where's the Wessexman who was taken across the

331

wall?' I asked, holding up a hand to stay Oswyn's raised foot. 'Your people took a prisoner when the moon was lying down. Where is he now?' The man winced, holding his swollen face, then shouted and struggled and we had to hold him down and cover his mouth. Oswyn repeated my questions in the man's own language, but the Welshman spat and threw back his head, revealing the naked whiteness of his throat.

'He wants you to kill him,' Oswyn said, spitting in the man's face.

'He thinks we killed his wife, Penda,' I said with a grimace. 'He'll tell us nothing.'

'Shows what you know, whelp,' he growled at me. 'This piece of goat shit will tell us the last time he took a dump by the time I'm finished.' He removed his helmet and ran a hand through his short hair, raising it into spikes. 'He just needs a little persuasion.' Crouching, he drew his long knife and held the blade against the man's groin. The Welshman grimaced in defiance, his teeth white in the darkness. 'Keep him still,' Penda barked, cutting through the man's woollen breeches. The Welshman began struggling now. 'Hold him still if you want to keep your bloody fingers!' Penda hissed at Oswyn. Despite his bulk, Oswyn was struggling to keep the Welshman's legs on the ground. Then the man's prick was exposed and Penda grabbed it, putting the knife beneath it. The prisoner began babbling in his own tongue as a thin trickle of blood ran down Penda's blade. Penda raised an eyebrow at Oswyn who was grinning like a child, for it appeared that the Welshman wanted to help us after all.

'He says he heard of a raid into Mercia, but no men from his village were involved,' Oswyn translated. 'His village is war poor,' he said, sharing a look with fat Eafa, 'and its menfolk have no stomach for fighting the English.' The man prattled on wide awake and cooperative, though I doubted it would help him now. 'He does not know where they took the lad,' Oswyn said, looking at Penda. Penda shrugged his shoulders and bent back to his task, holding the blade against the man's shrinking penis. The Welshman yelped and Penda shook his head slowly, withdrawing the knife. The man looked pleadingly at Oswyn who dipped his head, encouraging him to speak for his own sake. 'He says if they took anyone important, any lucky bastards too valuable for the slave market, they would take them to Caer Dyffryn,' Oswyn said. 'It's a small fortress in a valley north of here.' Some of the Wessexmen murmured and cursed at the name.

'I know it,' Penda said. 'A lot of us do.'

'He swears he doesn't know more,' Oswyn said.

Penda scratched at the scar beneath his chin. Then he wrapped the Welshman's hair around his fist, yanked his head back and sawed through the gristle of his throat. The man's breath escaped with a soft gush.

'Óðin's teeth, Penda! He could have told us more!' I said, watching the Welshman die, his eyes bulging in panic. 'We could have asked how many men are at Caer Dyffryn. How long it will take to get there . . . anything!'

Penda wiped his knife on the man's tunic and stood. 'If we'd asked more, he would have begun lying to us, lad. Would have come up with a sack full of horseshit to dishearten us.' He gestured to the Wessexmen, who stood peering into the dark as though they expected arrows and spears to rain down on them at any moment. 'The lads don't need lies, Raven. It's bad enough as it is.' I stared at the Welshman, at the black blood bubbling through the tear in his throat. His body convulsed and his legs twitched pathetically. Then he was still.

I felt sick. There was no honour in what we had done and I feared what the gods would do to us. But then I remembered something Glum had said about us being too far from our own gods, and this chilled my blood even more, for if the Christian god ruled this land, where did that leave me? I shook my head, pushing the thought away. Penda punched my shoulder. 'Wake up, lad,' he said, 'we couldn't let him go, could we? Besides, the whoreson had nothing left to fear from us, so we couldn't rely on his prattle.' He pointed down to the man's groin and even in the gloom I saw that the man's trousers were dark and slick. 'Oswyn the clumsy ox didn't keep the bastard still enough,' Penda said grimly. 'I cut the vein. Poor turd would have bled to death.' Penda gestured for Oswyn and Coenred to throw the corpse into the river. 'He would have bled to death and he would have lied to us,' he said.

I guessed Penda was right in so much as the men did not need the Welshman feeding the fear that already gnawed like rats at their guts, because we were in enough danger as it was and fear can make a man weak.

The smooth stones we put in the man's clothes took

334

him down to the riverbed, and we were soon heading north again, much more quickly now without him. Oswyn led us away from the river, afraid that we might be seen by the light reflecting off the water, but we followed it from a distance, the going easier still now that we ran on solid ground. It seemed we had not been moving for long when a pink glow began to spread across the eastern sky. We wrapped our cloaks around us and slept for a couple of hours amongst soft green bracken. We woke at dawn and the birds were chattering so loudly that it seemed they were trying to warn everyone within earshot that we were there, and I feared the Welsh would hear them and come to kill us before we even set eyes on Caer Dyffryn.

That same morning, Eafa the fletcher killed a raven. The bird was sitting on the twisted limb of a blackened willow, watching us, when Eafa put an arrow through it with his yew bow.

'See how my arrows never miss?' he boasted to the others who slapped his back, impressed by his skill.

'You are a fool, Eafa,' I said, standing before him with my long spear. 'A fat, putrid, ignorant fool.'

The fletcher baulked at this, then smiled and looked to his friends. 'Ah, yes,' he said, 'I remember. You Norsemen believe the raven is a magical creature, don't you?' Some of the others laughed scornfully even as they made the sign of the cross. 'You believe they can see the future. If so, why did he not fly away as I drew my bow?' Penda looked on, saying nothing, and I did not know whether he hoped I would put my spear in Eafa or that Eafa would put his in me.

'You don't know anything, Eafa,' I said. 'You're a piece of pig shit. The raven has nothing to fear in this world because he is not of this world.' I touched the raven's wing that Cynethryth had plaited into my hair, and the fletcher's mouth twisted in disgust, but there was a flicker of doubt in his eyes. 'Fetch your arrow, pig shit,' I said. 'We'll see how skilful you are when the Welsh are coming to kill you.'

The Wessexmen were quiet then, because they knew they would soon have to fight. And they knew we were too few.

# CHAPTER SIXTEEN

WE DID NOT NEED ANY WELSHMAN TO TELL US WHEN WE
had come to Caer Dyffryn. Virgin meadows of yellow
rattle gave way to close-cropped pasture where the only
flowers remaining were tall clumps of white sneezewort
making a stand by the river's edge, besieged by finches
and tits.

'They know we're here,' Penda said, shielding his
eyes against the rising sun and scanning the higher
ground to the north and east.

'How can you tell, Penda?' a short, pockmarked
man named Saba asked. Saba worked in one of Ealdorman Ealdred's water mills. Now he found himself in
the land of his enemies and he was nervous. He carried
a short axe and had sheathed himself in toughened
leather, but he owned no helmet, instead wearing
a hard leather skullcap which made him look even
shorter.

'Look around you, Saba,' Penda said with a nod,
scratching the scar on his cheek. 'This morning, whilst
you were dreaming of grinding wheat, this meadow

337

was cloaked in flea-bitten Welsh sheep. They've moved 'em.' The Wessexmen, still with mud-blackened faces, looked around their feet. Sure enough, shiny droppings littered the short grass.

'God have mercy on us! That's it then!' a man called Eni exclaimed, his eyes wide and his beard trembling. 'It's over. We've got to go back. If the black-shields know we're here, we don't stand a nun's chance in a whores' hall.'

'Eni is right, Penda,' Saba said, trying to seem unafraid. 'We should go back. If they know we're here . . .' He left the words hanging, allowing the men to imagine their own fates. Some of them grunted in agreement or spoke up for heading back to Wessex, whilst others looked to Penda, waiting for him to speak.

'And what will you tell Lord Ealdred, Eni?' Penda asked eventually, when those advocating a return to Wessex had said their piece. 'Well, lad, let's hear it.' He was tightening the helmet strap beneath his scarred chin as he spoke. 'Er, sorry, lord,' he mimicked Eni, 'but we couldn't get your son and heir back from the bastard Welsh because . . . well . . . they saw us. So we said they could keep the lad and hared away from the horrible fucking heathens, like dry-cunnied virgins from a Norseman.' He turned to me. 'No offence, heathen,' he added.

'None taken,' I muttered. 'Penda's right,' I said, looking into the men's eyes and lingering on Saba's. There would be no convincing Eni, I knew that much, but if we could give the braver ones hope, that would be enough. Would have to be. 'We go on,' I said, 'and we take Weohstan back to Wessex. He'll be the ealdorman one day, lads, remember that. He won't forget those who crossed Offa's wall to bring him home.'

'And if he's dead?' Saba asked.

'Then he's dead.' I shrugged. 'But his father won't forget those who allowed him to put his son in the ground facing east.'

Oswyn slapped Saba's back. 'You never know, Saba,' he said. 'Ealdred might show his gratitude by giving you young Cynethryth to warm your bed.' The big man stuck out his fat tongue and waggled it. I clenched my jaw and saw that Penda was watching me, his lip curled in mirth. But in truth I was pleased, because Oswyn was the heart of the fighting men amongst them and where he went, they would follow.

We followed sheep tracks and by the afternoon found ourselves at the mouth of the Caer Dyffryn valley. Dark trees crowned the heights on both sides, disappearing to make way for pasture across the valley's slopes, and below us stood the fortress into which the Welsh had driven their livestock. In which they possibly held Weohstan. It was not a big place like King Coenwulf's fortress in Mercia, but it was too big for eleven warriors and twenty merchants and craftsmen to attack with any hope of success. Worse, we had yet to see a single Welshman, which suggested that they had been tracking our progress since we crossed King Offa's wall. If so, they would be ready for us. I rammed the butt of my ash spear into the ground and eyed the fortress. The defences comprised a ditch and mound set with a barricade of pointed timbers, the whole place built in a hollow with the river Wye on its eastern side and high pasture on its west rising to the north.

'Look there, Penda,' I said, pointing at a hilltop to the north-east which overlooked the fortress. 'Looks like a beacon. A watchtower maybe.'

'That red eye of yours sees well enough, lad,' Penda said, frowning as he tried to make out the squat structure on the distant hill. 'Whoresons are watching every move we make. We'll have to wait till dark before we try anything.'

'Dark?' Eni said, glancing anxiously at the sun which was still above us, though it had crossed the meridian.

'In the dark they won't know which direction we're coming at them from,' Penda said. 'We'll have that much, at least.' As he spoke one of the others noticed a faint line of black smoke curling up from the tor.

'They're calling for help,' Oswyn said, pointing his spear towards the rise. 'Won't be long before we're peeling the bastards off each other.'

'Don't get a hard-on, Oswyn,' Coenred blurted. 'Calling for help? They don't need any help, man. They're just spreading the good news about how they're about to dip their spears in Wessex blood.'

I thought Coenred was probably right. Behind their walls, the Welsh had little to fear from us. We were too few and had set ourselves up like the prize dish at a rich man's feast. But regardless of whether or not those in the fortress needed help, soon others would come to feed. For where there is fighting and death there are rich pickings and renown to be earned.

'We can't wait for dark now, Penda,' I said, watching the wisp of smoke make a dirty bloom against the blue sky, 'not if every blood-hungry Welshman for twenty miles is coming to repay Wessex kindness. We don't know the land like they do. In the dark we'll die cheaply.'

'The heathen's right. They'll put us down one by one,' Eafa agreed, wiping the sweat from his brow and gripping his yew bow as though it was the only thing standing between him and his fat ancestors.

Penda shrugged as though resigned to whatever was coming. 'We don't have too many choices right now, Norseman, but you're wrong if you think we won't make the black-shields pay dear. By Christ and his avenging saints, they'll know they came up against Wessexmen by tomorrow. Right, lads?' Some of the warriors nodded and murmured agreement, clasping each other's forearms in grim solidarity. Others stood ashen-faced, perhaps thinking of wives and lovers and children.

'There's another way,' I said, scanning the landscape. 'We'll make them come to us. Make them fight us on ground of our own choosing, Penda. If we go down into the valley, we'll be trapped between the walls and every bloody Welshman who comes to kill us.' I pointed to the black smoke, a dirty smear against the sky. 'We find a good bit of ground, high ground, and we dig in. They'll come to us eventually. Pride will make them.'

The men began to argue. Some suddenly thought it was our only chance, whilst others believed we should attack the fortress before reinforcements arrived.

341

I touched the Óðin amulet at my throat for luck. At least no one was talking about running back to Wessex now. If I have learned anything about the gods in my long life, it is that they love a stout heart and a strong sword arm, and they love a man who is not afraid to fight when the scales are tipped against him.

Eventually, Penda raised his hand and the men held their tongues. 'Raven,' he said, fixing me with cold, dark eyes, 'choose your ground.' He spat. 'Choose it well, lad,' he warned grimly, his hand resting on his sword's pommel. 'We've got guests coming.'

'There, Penda,' I said without hesitation, pointing to a place on our left where the ground rose gently at first, then more steeply until in five or six hundred paces it levelled off, home to a copse of pine and birch. Where the ground was steepest, rocks broke through the soil and I knew that any obstacle, no matter how small, would count in our favour if our enemies attacked up-hill in the dark. A man can break his ankle on a stone poking through the ground.

'It'll have to do,' Penda muttered. 'The trees up there might come in useful.' He turned to Oswyn. 'Take ten lads down to the river and look for fish traps. They moved their sheep out of our way, but they won't have taken the time to bring in their traps, and we'll be glad of a bite before we do some killing.' Oswyn turned to go, but Penda grabbed the big man's shoulder. 'And bring back as many stones as you can carry,' he said, clenching a fist, 'nice smooth 'uns that'll smash Welsh skulls when they come up our hill.' Oswyn grinned and set about his task.

I was watching the Welsh fortress when Penda banged his spear's butt against my helmet. 'You won't make it disappear by staring at it, lad,' he said. 'Better get up that slope and start laying roots.' We trudged up the slope with our heavy shields, spears and swords, looking up at the place from where we would give battle to our enemies. I watched fat Eafa with his unstrung bow stave across his shoulders and I hoped he was as good with the weapon as he said he was. I was glad I had not killed him.

We spent an uneasy night on the hill, made worse because we knew that with every passing hour more Welsh warriors might be coming, drawn by the orange glow of the beacon on the north-east hill, like moths to a candle flame. Oswyn had returned at dusk with four graylings, two large salmon, a trout and several small dace. We cooked and ate the fish with hard bread and cheese, filling our bellies and limbs with strength for the coming fight, and making the most of a good fire, as there was no longer any reason for trying to remain unseen.

'Build her up, lads,' Penda said, pointing at the fire. 'And sing a song. Sing a song and for the love of Christ sing it loud.' He sat in the grass, sharpening his long knife with its white bone handle. 'The happier we look to the Welsh, the more likely they'll be to run up here waving their spears to ruin our fun. With any luck they'll be so dog-tired that they'll fall on our spears.'

I smiled at the words. I do not think Penda knew the effect he had on the warriors around him. He was not a natural leader of men in the way that Jarl Sigurd was, nor did he fill their hearts with false hope. And yet, that night the warriors on that dark hill were glad to sing their song when he told them to. For Penda was a cold-blooded killer and that much was obvious to any man, and that was what they needed him to be.

That dawn, I stood facing east feeling the gentle warmth of the rising sun on my face, and I wondered if I would ever feel it again. Below, the valley still sat in cold shadow. I could make out small figures moving around between the houses, cattle certainly, but men and women too, and I knew they were making preparations to fight. *Let them come*, I thought. *We are ready*. Our water skins were replenished and our little hilltop was lined with piles of rounded river stones. There were fewer trees up there than I had thought, which was a good thing as they did not obstruct our view of the ground falling away on all sides up which the Welsh would have to climb to kill us. Also, there was room enough on the summit for the wall we would make with our round shields and our spears.

'I like it up here,' Penda said, breaking the spell. He came to stand beside me at the edge of the flat ground and together we looked down the slope. 'I might come back here and build a house. Just there,' he said, gesturing to a pile of stones. 'A small house, mind, nothing that five or six slaves can't look after well enough.' His scarred face was tight and I could not tell if he was joking. 'I'll come up here in the summers with that red-haired girl from back home. And I'll tell her about how there used to be a fortress down there.'

'Is she your woman?' I asked, though I was sure she was not, for she was beautiful and I could not imagine Penda showing tenderness.

'Not yet, Raven, but an itch has got to be scratched, lad.' I laughed as Penda absently stroked the scar on his cheek. 'I don't know what's so funny,' he muttered. 'If you can daydream about poking Ealdorman Ealdred's scrawny daughter, I can fancy a roll in the hay with the redhead.'

'I'll wager you wouldn't be the first,' I said.

'Wouldn't want to be, lad. You can keep the sweet young virgins, keep 'em all and good luck to you. They just lie there like planks of pine. Don't even seem to enjoy it, God bless their mothers. No, Raven, give me a woman who knows what gets her wet.' He bent, snatched up a pebble and cast it high into the air so that it landed halfway down the slope. 'Let's hope we both get the chance to dip our wicks,' he said, his face as hard as stone. Then I felt a sudden churning in the depths of my stomach. For the gate of the fortress, now bathed in dawn sunlight, had opened. The Welsh were coming.

'Here they come!' I yelled to the others, who were checking their war gear and sharpening their blades one last time. Many of them were mumbling prayers and crossing themselves. Even the experienced fighters amongst them hefted their round shields and inspected their long spears as though they had never fought with the things before, as though they wondered if wood and steel would hold when the killing began. The inexperienced men looked to the warriors, mimicking

345

their actions and asking advice, the pride they had worn previously abandoned now. The eight with bows strung the yew staves and chose the arrows they would shoot first, and those men knew they would be the safest of us all, at least in the beginning, for they would stand behind our skjaldborg, our shieldwall, pouring their wicked arrows into the advancing Welsh. But they would run out of arrows eventually and then they would take their places, filling the gaps in the wooden wall where men had fallen.

I gripped the thick ash spear. It was not Glum's any more, but mine, and its weight gave me confidence. I imagined the weapon as an extension of my body and believed I had gained some of the magic and strength of the tree from which it was fashioned. Whether there was any truth or magic in this, I could not say, but at least it helped to squash the fear that was gnawing at my bowels and tenderizing the insides beneath my sternum.

I watched the Welsh form their shieldwall with their backs to the fortress, and for some reason my mind turned to Griffin, the warrior from my village who had faced Sigurd with strength and bravery when he must have known there was no hope. Then there had been Olaf's son, white-haired Eric, who could not hide his fear as some men could, barely a warrior when he gave his life for his fellowship. Lastly, I thought of old Ealhstan, brave Ealhstan. He was feeble and mute and had had more courage than them all.

'Look how eager they are to come and die,' I shouted over my shoulder, grimacing at the tremor I heard in my own voice. Penda was building his own shieldwall so that every third man was a warrior, for then each levy man would have an experienced fighter beside him to give him heart and maintain the cohesion of the line.

'Keep your shields overlapping,' Penda barked. 'Half the width of the man's beside you. I'll gut any man who lets daylight through. And then you stand! You hear me? You bloody well stand!'

'We'll stand, Penda!' Oswyn shouted. 'Won't we, lads?' There was a chorus of yells and more than one man banged his spear against the back of his shield.

'You are oaks!' Penda yelled. 'You are no longer the bastard scum of Wessex, but great Wessex oaks that no pissing Welshman is going to move!'

The men knew the task facing them, knew what they must do to survive. Even the craftsmen and traders had been trained in the discipline of the shieldwall. But they listened to Penda, let his words sting them like wasps, the spit flying from his mouth. For the words gave them heart. For his part Penda knew he needed every one of them to fight with the strength of two. He knew that only if the wall remained solid could it become the foundation from which to stab and cut, to claw and bite. Then the shields might advance as one man, step by step, crushing the enemy underfoot and driving him from the field. 'No gaps! No openings! No weakness!' he screamed, for such will cleave the wall just as a man splits an oak along the grain. 'If we break we die!'

'We'll hold,' short Saba growled.

'No need to whisper now, lads!' Penda called. 'Look, the bastards are awake, so let them hear you!'

'Wessex!' Oswyn roared, hefting his spear above his head. 'Wessex!' Then every man took up the shout. 'Wessex! Wessex! Wessex!'

Penda caught my eye and nodded grimly. 'Welsh bastards will be wishing they'd stayed in their beds!' he shouted.

'Bollocks!' Oswyn roared. 'Have you seen the women round here?' He spat down the hill. 'They'd make any man jump from the straw to face a shieldwall.' The men laughed and Penda ordered Oswyn to tie Ealdorman Ealdred's banner to a long spear and plant it in the earth. There was no wind to speak of, but enough of a breeze to stir the dark green banner so that its leaping stag embroidered in golden thread could be glimpsed every now and again.

'Let them know where we are, lads! Wouldn't want them to miss us,' Penda called, his voice thick with pride. The men cheered and banged their swords and spears against the backs of their shields so that the Welsh might have believed there were sixty men on that hilltop, not thirty-one. 'Forward,' he yelled, and as one man the Wessex shieldwall advanced to where I stood at the top of the slope, and the noise grew when they saw their enemy at the foot of the hill. The clamour filled my head, making the hairs on my neck stand up and the skin of my arms prickle. My spit tasted bitter.

Then a thin horn sounded in the valley and Penda raised a hand to silence the Englishmen. The Welsh numbered perhaps one hundred and fifty warriors.

Beyond their battle line I saw women and children and white-haired old men come from the fortress to watch the fight. They had even brought their dogs. The horn sounded again.

'They want to talk before the blood-letting,' Oswyn said.

'Ah, they just want to tell us how they're going to stamp on our guts and throw our eyeballs to the crows,' Penda said. 'But I don't need their bedtime stories. I sleep well enough.' He stepped forward with his spear raised.

'Wait, Penda. We might learn something of Weohstan,' I said. He curled his top lip and nodded.

So Oswyn, Penda and I walked slowly down the slope until we were halfway between our two war bands, and our enemy's leaders came up the slope to meet us. There were two of them, both powerfully built men with long black beards and unkempt hair. One wore Norse mail and I recognized it as the brynja that had belonged to Glum's kinsman Thorleik. This man stepped forward and spat at my feet. Then the other warrior spoke with the same lilting voice as the man we had killed by the river days before.

'He says he looks forward to boiling your brains and feeding them to his children,' Oswyn said, allowing a smile to touch his thick lips.

'What did I tell you, Raven?' Penda said, gesturing to the Welshman. 'Bedtime bloody stories and it's still shy of midday.'

'Ask him if Weohstan of Wessex still lives,' I said to Oswyn who frowned, trying to find the words, though when he did the Welshman in leather armour smiled to reveal black teeth. Then he spat his reply as a serpent spits venom.

'He lives,' Oswyn said, wide-eyed. 'They had planned to ransom him, but now they have no need to.'

'Why not?' I asked, my heart pounding at the news that Weohstan lived. 'Why won't they ransom him?' I pointed my spear at the Welsh down the hill. 'This need not come to blood. There is still time.' Oswyn nodded and asked the question, but when the reply came the Wessexman tensed, the colour draining from his face.

'Well, you big bastard? Spit it out, man,' Penda said, frustrated at having to wait for every translation. He would rather the talking stopped and the killing began.

Oswyn cleared his throat. 'He says they no longer need to ransom Weohstan, because we have walked like a lame deer into a slaughter pit. Others are coming, kinsmen from across the hills, young men eager to prove themselves. He says that his people will soon be stripping our corpses as the eagle strips the hare's bones of flesh. Our arms, our swords and shields are the only riches they need.' Oswyn looked back to the Welshman. 'He says that their old folk, their grey-beards and their children and their women have not emptied their bowels yet today because they wait to shit on our eyes when we lie dead.'

'Enough jawing,' Penda said, stepping forward so that his face was a finger's length from the man with the black teeth. 'Piss off back to your women before I put those stinking teeth through the back of your head.' The Welshman spoke no English, yet he understood well enough, for he grimaced, turned his back on Penda and with his companion set off down the slope.

'He stank like a pig's innards,' Penda said, turning his back on the Welshmen and testing the balance of the spear he was holding. 'This thing's not worth a spit,' he mumbled. 'Damn thing couldn't kill a dead dog.' Suddenly, he twisted back and sprang forward, hurling the spear high into the blue sky. It dived like a hawk and pierced the black-toothed Welshman between his shoulders, dropping him to his knees. The other warrior jumped aside in shock, then screamed a curse at us before dragging his twitching friend down the hill, leaving the spear lodged where it was. Wessexmen cheered the first blood-letting of the day.

Penda made a surprised sound in the back of his throat as he stared after the dying Welshman whose head had slumped to his chest. Then he turned and we followed him back up the hill. 'I was wrong about that spear,' he said.

# CHAPTER SEVENTEEN

THE WELSH CAME AT US ON A WIDE FRONT, THEIR LEATHER-covered shields presenting a grim, black wall. Other than their shields it seemed they lacked for decent armour. Their helmets were of toughened leather, not iron and steel, and as far as I could tell only a handful of them had mail; not full brynjas, but rather strips of mail fastened over chests and throats.

'We'll tear these bastards apart, Oswyn,' I said, taking my place in the centre of the shieldwall.

'I'm slobbering like a dog, lad,' he replied, banging his spear against his shield. 'I look forward to seeing what you've got, Norseman,' he gave me a grim smile, 'so don't disappoint me.' Even though I was amongst Christians, I whispered a prayer to brave Týr who loves battle, and mighty Thór, and Óðin Spear-Shaker, that I would prove worthy and that my place in the wall would mean death to the Welsh. They were still two hundred paces away. I could see them clearly now, the hate in their snarling faces, the violence in their rhythmic, trudging step. I was afraid.

'Now's the time to send your arrows, Eafa!' I called. 'Don't need a bloody heathen to tell me when to shoot!' Eafa snarled. And I smiled. *That's it, Eafa,* I thought. *Hate is good. Hate will help you kill and go on killing when the lifeblood of the man beside you slaps your face and blinds your eyes.* Eafa's first arrow took to the sky in a low arc before embedding in a Welsh shield. It was a fine shot. But soon a man with half Eafa's skill would not miss, there were so many Welshmen coming up the hill. More Wessex arrows streaked like swifts over my head and the first Welshmen fell. When they were one hundred paces away we bent to the piles of stones and hurled them with curses. Most bounced off the black shields, doing nothing to slow their advance, but some broke noses or cut heads.

'Not long now, lads!' Penda called. 'Hold your line! Keep those shields up!' The Welsh were shooting their own arrows now, but they either dug into the slope below us or sailed harmlessly overhead. Men on both sides shouted and cursed as though they believed the noise might drown their own fear. Those who had been millers and farmers until now snarled and spat like wild beasts to sow terror in their foes' hearts, willing their own rage to consume them and turn them into killing creatures impervious to pain. Saba threw a stone which smashed into a Welshman's temple and the Wessexmen gave a great cheer as their enemies stepped round the fallen man.

'That's it, Saba!' Oswyn roared. 'Give them another like that!' But the next stone Saba hurled fell short and it was the Welsh's turn to jeer. In moments our shieldwalls would close and the killing would begin. Many times since that day I have taken my place in the shieldwall and felt my bowels turn to liquid and my belly turn sour. I have known fear and tasted bitter terror on my tongue. But that day the death calm fell upon me and I could not have been more thankful, because I believed that it was a sign from the Norns of fate that they were still weaving my life's pattern and if that was true then I could not die. I laugh now to think of the arrogance of youth. Young men believe they are immortal. They wear pride's son, conceit, like a mail brynja they believe will preserve them. Now, if I met myself as I was then, I would send me sprawling with the back of my hand to teach me humility. Yet in another way I am glad I was arrogant, that I knew the thrill of standing with other men on the edge of life, in the midst of death, together. For when I met the Welsh in battle that day, I believe Óðin All-Father was amused. He laughed at the red-eyed boy who shook his spear at the enemy and spilt their blood slickly across Welsh grass. It is good to amuse the gods.

With a great crash like breakers on flat rocks, our shields struck and men hacked and heaved and rammed their spears overarm into others' faces. The rancid stink of the enemy filled my nose. Deep roars liquefied to squeals as blades found unprotected flesh. Through my shield I felt the weight of the entire enemy shield-wall and I planted my right foot squarely behind me to anchor myself to the spot. The man I faced died easily enough. I jabbed my spear repeatedly but blindly over the top of my shield until it struck home, bringing a yell from the Welshman, who dropped his shield slightly so that I could see the gash where his eye had been, now a bloody black hole of torn flesh. I sank my spear's point home again, this time into his open mouth, twisting it to smash his teeth, then ramming it into his throat. His legs buckled and he fell, but the weight on our line was such that we were already being driven back up the rise. We formed a crescent, our bowmen moving to the flanks to pour their shafts into the Welsh who sought to come round the edges and get behind us. So far Eafa and the others were holding them back.

Penda worked with his long sword, battering shields and heads in a grim, remorseless rhythm, and Oswyn leant into the enemy wall, bracing himself against it as others around him did the killing. Oswyn knew we must not be pushed back too far or we would find ourselves retreating down the hill's far side with the Welsh taking the high ground. It would not last long then.

'Kill them!' Eni yelled. 'Send them back to Satan!' The little man fought like a demon, finding a talent for killing that he never knew he possessed. His sword arm worked deftly, the shorter blade finding its way under his shield to stab into his enemies before they even saw it.

'For Wessex!' shouted another man.

'For Ealdred!' called someone else as the fight settled into a terrible cadence. Blood flew in sheets, sliming the grass. Men grunted and screamed and pushed and died, and despite the fallen Welsh littering the ground we were still being forced backwards. Wessexmen whose names I had never known were down, broken

and lost behind the advancing tide, their souls hasten-
ing to the afterlife.

'To the left! The left!' Egric shouted. 'They're getting
round the back!' Ducking behind my shield I risked a
glance to the side where Eafa was now fighting desperately with sword and shield, having slung his bow. I
saw two Wessexmen cut down as the Welsh forced the
left wing to fold back on itself. In moments they would
be behind us and we would die.

'Raven! Can you hold?' Penda yelled, smashing
his sword across a man's face. He thrust his shield
forward into the space and the men around him roared
and took a step forward. Dread filled me for I knew
our shieldwall was growing ragged and gaps were
appearing. Still, Penda's surge gave us heart and other
Wessexmen struggled to push level with their friends.
'Can you hold?' Penda shouted again, for an instant
fixing me with blood-crazed eyes. His mouth was a
snarl.

I blinked through stinging sweat, and nodded. 'Push
them back to their bitches!' I yelled, giving another
great shove, and Penda left the shieldwall, dragging
another man with him to hold our left. In a heartbeat
he was killing men, a natural warrior, fast, strong and
skilled, but also a wild thing, a dealer of death. But
without Penda in the heart of the wall the Wessexmen
were dispirited. We lost more ground as we were forced
inexorably backwards. Blows rained down on me from
left and right, my fine mail and helmet marking me as
a worthy kill. A sword deflected off my helmet, striking
my shoulder as a spear blade came under the shields to

gouge my shin. I howled in pain and fury, pure rage surfacing again after having been anchored in the fight's rhythm.

We could do nothing for the Wessexmen who had fallen. They were dead men. All we could do was retreat in ragged order, keeping our shields locked and our heads down. We had been pushed back as far as Ealdorman Ealdred's leaping stag banner and I cursed as the green cloth was swallowed by the Welsh. Beside me, Egric heaved forward, stretching out an arm as though he believed the banner would fly to his hand.

'Leave it, Egric,' I growled, sinking my sword into a man's belly. I had long since lost my spear. Then hot blood sprayed my face as Egric's arm was severed, vanishing beneath trudging feet. The screaming Welshman then slammed his axe on to Egric's skull, and I heard it crunch above the din.

If you ask me now how to survive in a fight I will tell you it depends on your legs, on whether they can carry you far enough away from the carnage to enable you to screw your woman, raise fine children and live out your life in peace. But if you have to fight, if you love slaughter or if there is no choice, then I would say the best thing you can do is wear a helmet. Not a leather skullcap like the one that mixed with Egric's brains on that field long ago, but one of iron and steel.

The man at my right shoulder fell and my shield shuddered beneath a great blow that tore at the muscles in my left shoulder, shooting burning pain the length of my arm. It was all I could do to grip the shield as another blow rattled it, and another, and I dropped my sword and used two hands to hold the shield, which was splintering, all the while stepping backwards with the others. Týr Lord of Battle knows we were finished then. Our shieldwall was smashed and the real slaughter had begun. I put my shoulder against the shield and thrust the iron boss into my enemy, then screamed wildly and threw the shield at him, stooping to grab my sword. I would die with it in my hand so that the Valkyries might take me to Óðin's mead hall. But a Welshman slammed his war club into my face and I spun to the ground, bursts of white light blinding me.

'Get up, lad!' someone yelled. Through a blur I saw Penda standing above me, hacking wildly, taking down any man within reach. He had lost his helmet, his short hair stuck up in vicious spikes, and he was drenched in blood. 'On your feet, Raven! It's not over till I tell you! You hear me? You filthy bastard heathen son of a goat! Up you get.' The bloody grass around me was littered with Wessexmen, but others lived still, fighting with every searing breath, every screaming sinew – not for glory, not for Wessex, but because a man's life is all he has and he will not let another take it if he has the strength to fight. Penda hauled me to my feet. 'Fight, Norseman,' he snarled, 'or die here. Now. Fight, damn you!' Somehow, as though the All-Father, the Lord of Fury, had filled my lungs with his own breath, I was beside Penda, swinging my sword wildly, unable to see for blood and sweat and filth. 'That's it, lad!' Penda screamed. Unbelievably he was laughing. 'That's my boy! That's my blood-loving heathen son of thunder! Kill like the heathen bastard you are!' Blood hit my face. Screams filled my ears and the stink of shit filled my breath. Then another sound came to me and it was like a voice from another world, from the afterlife. It was a low sound, but clear and true, cutting beneath the battle's roar the way a spear bites a shin beneath the shield's rim.

The Welsh seemed to shudder as one man and their shrieks pierced the air. Suddenly there was empty space around me. My head pounded, still crammed with white sparks when I blinked, and I turned towards the familiar sound, gulping deep breaths as the Welsh re-formed their shieldwall. The ragged mass of black discs shuffled backwards over mangled corpses and writhing wounded, and I turned, shutting my eyes to the miraculous sight before me, believing it would be gone when I opened them. But it was not gone. It grew clearer and more real as I filled my belly with foul breath. A red banner showing a black wolf's head fluttered in the building breeze. Around it were shining warriors in mail and helmets, hefting round, painted shields, spears, swords and axes. It was a host to chill the blood, and the Welsh must have thought the gods of war themselves had come down from Asgard to make their slaughter. But these were not gods. They were Norsemen. I let out a roar of pain and triumph and fell to my knees. For Sigurd had come.

The Norsemen came from the east, perhaps forty of them, their shields overlapping to form a wall of wood and iron comprising not millers and merchants, but trained killers. It was a deadly wave. And it was perfect. With the sun behind them they swept across the hill, intercepting the retreating Welsh, and though the Welsh vastly outnumbered them still, they were all but helpless and must have seen their own deaths in the newcomers' cold blue eyes.

'Friends of yours, Raven?' Penda asked in a dry, cracked voice as he hacked into a fallen man's neck to finish him. He tried to spit but his mouth was too dry.

'Óðin's wolves,' I said, trying to blink away the pain and staring at the slaughter being done down the hill. The grey-beards and children come from Caer Dyffryn to watch us die were running back to the gate now.

'One Norseman within a stone's throw is enough for me, lad,' Penda said, watching the Norse shieldwall carve up the disorganized Welsh. 'Heathen swine know how to kill,' he acknowledged in a growl. 'So long as they don't turn on us. I'm tired as a whore's tits.'

Most of the Wessex fyrdsmen lay dead. Fat Eafa was dead. His white hands clutched the broken bow stave. Coenred's corpse lay close by, as did Alric's. Further down the slope more men of Wessex lay tangled with their enemies in death: Saba the miller, Eni, Huda, Ceolmund, Egric, and big Oswyn whom I had liked, but whose face was a bloody caved-in mess. In all, twenty-two of Ealdorman Ealdred's men had died. Of those that lived, five were experienced warriors and three were men of trades who stood stunned as though they had somehow clawed their way out of Hell back to the land of the living. Their eyes were vacant and their bodies trembled. Perhaps as many as fifty Welshmen littered the field, their bodies broken and their insides open to the sky and the flies, and the stink was awful.

Those dead would soon be joined by their kinsmen who fought on against the Wolfpack below.

'Well, Raven?' Penda said, nodding towards the carnage. 'Do I have to drag you down there by your pretty hair?' He turned. 'Come on, lads, are we going to let the heathens finish what we started?' The Wessexmen, stunned and blood-soaked and exhausted, took up their gore-slick arms without a word and trudged after Penda.

I climbed to my feet, stooping to grip a battered, discarded shield. 'Penda!' I called, wiping blood from my face with the back of my trembling hand. 'Wait for me.'

# CHAPTER EIGHTEEN

THOSE WELSHMEN WHO COULD SCRAMBLED TO SAFETY behind Caer Dyffryn's timber walls, leaving their kinsmen to be torn apart by the Wolfpack and the remaining Wessexmen. It did not last long and most of the men I killed then died with my blade in their backs. A few arrows fell amongst us, shot from the fortress walls, but they were released in panic by inexperienced men and did little damage. When we had broken the Welshmen's hearts and torn the life from all but a few, Sigurd bellowed an order to retreat. We raised our shields to the fortress and backed away out of bow range, Norseman and Wessexman, heathen and Christian, side by side, brothers in slaughter.

'Freyja's tits, Raven!' Sigurd exclaimed, turning his back on the Welsh fortress and embracing me in a great bear hug. Behind him I saw Svein the Red, Bjorn, Bjarni and the rest, all grinning at me through blood-splattered faces. 'I might have known you would be starting a war somewhere!' He gestured towards Caer Dyffryn. 'What did those savages do to upset you, hey?'

Bjarni stepped up, thumped my aching shoulder, then turned to his brother. 'Someone should have taught the lad the difference between rich pickings and a dung heap.' The Norsemen laughed.

Bjorn removed his helmet, wiping its bloody crown on a tuft of grass. 'We watched for a while,' he said, gesturing to the high ground to the east, 'just to make sure we were coming in on the right side.'

'It never hurts to watch the English die,' Bram growled in Norse.

I removed my own helmet, shook out my hair and wiped the sweat from my brow. 'My lord Sigurd . . .' I began, though my mouth was dry and my tongue swollen, 'how . . . where have you been?' He stepped up and touched the raven's wing still plaited into my hair, and he smiled, and I smiled too because my jarl had come for me. 'Glum took us, lord,' I said. 'That night in the forest . . .'

Sigurd raised a hand and with the other removed his own helmet, letting his sweat-matted golden hair fall to his shoulders. 'I know, Raven,' he said. 'I know that dog's treachery.' He spat in disgust, as though he could not say his old shipmaster's name, and then he snarled. 'And I confront Óðin Far-Wanderer in anger,' he said, pointing his spear at the blue sky, 'that I was not the one to open the coward's belly.'

'Careful, Sigurd,' old Asgot hissed, blood-smeared and terrifying and holding up a finger in warning. Sigurd seemed to accept the caution, though he rammed the butt of his spear into the ground.

'Bram is right, maybe I should be thanking these

363

Welsh, not killing them,' Sigurd said. 'That night, when you and the English brats were taken . . . well, that was not so important,' he smiled, his hand sweeping the air, 'but to lose the White Christ book . . .' He scratched his thick beard. 'I was a fool. I did not see that greed had blackened Glum's heart. I am a proud man, Raven. I did not believe my shipmaster could betray me. I hope the All-Father remembers Glum's worthier deeds and grants him a place at the mead bench.' He spat a wad of blood, his mouth twisting into a grimace. 'I will enjoy beheading his shade.'

Then I noticed that one of the Norsemen was missing.

'Where's Black Floki?' I asked, looking around me for his grim, flinty face.

'You'll know it all soon enough, lad,' Olaf assured me with a nod towards the Englishmen, which I took as reluctance to say too much in case one of them should understand Norse. Penda and the remaining Wessexmen were climbing the hill to strip the dead before the Norsemen could get to them, and I hoped for their sakes that they were quick about it. 'We saw riders in the forest, lord,' I said. 'King Coenwulf's men. We thought they must have ambushed you.' Though now, having the Wolfpack before me in all their viciousness, it seemed impossible that the Mercians could have routed them. 'Was there a fight?' I asked, scanning the Norsemen's faces in case there were others absent.

Sigurd smiled wryly. 'Black Floki caught their stink before they were a hundred paces from our fires,' he said. 'Gave us time to arrange a decent welcome.' He shrugged. 'But it was darker than Hel's cunny and some of them got away. We lay low as a snake after that.' He laughed. 'Seemed every whoreson in Mercia wanted to nail a Norseman's skin to his door.'

'Ah, there was no real slaughtering done, lad,' Olaf said, batting Sigurd's words away with a hand and glancing down at my brynja whose rings were filled with dark, congealed blood. 'You would have hated it,' he said.

'It is good to see you, Uncle,' I said, stepping up to embrace him.

He slapped my back hard. 'It is good to see you, too, Raven.'

'I've been spending too much time with the English,' I said.

'So, have they made a Christian of you?' Bjorn asked, slapping his hands together as if in prayer and looking at me with a solemn expression that reminded me of poor Father Egfrith, if Father Egfrith had been a bearded, gore-spattered killer.

'Not yet, Bjorn,' I said, laughing at his impression. 'But you would be surprised, my friend. They are not all prayer-hungry priest-lovers.' I looked up the hill at Penda who was stripping Welsh corpses of buckles, beads, knives, and any other small objects of value. 'Some of them are more savage than you.' His look was one of scepticism, then suddenly the fortress door gave a loud clunk and the Norsemen turned, thumping down their helmets in readiness for a Welsh sally. But the gate opened only wide enough for something to be dumped on to the hard, bare-trodden earth.

365

'Seems they've spat Ealdorman Ealdred's brat back out,' Bram said in his gruff voice, rolling his shoulders with a loud crack.

'Help me, Bjarni,' I said, then called to Penda. We ran to the gate, shields above our heads, but no stones or arrows fell. It seemed the Welsh had lost their appetite for death. Perhaps they hoped we would take the Englishman and be on our way. But Weohstan could not stand, so we dragged him out of bow range and stood around him as Penda knelt and tipped water into his mouth and across his bruised face. He was barely conscious, but he was alive, and the blood across Penda's face could not hide his smile, which I had not expected to see, because so many Wessexmen had died buying Weohstan's freedom.

'He's a good lad. Worth a lot of blood, this one,' Penda said, still grinning as Weohstan coughed and spluttered and spat a gobful of water back out. 'If the ealdorman had sent more men with us, we might have got the lad back without having to fight at all.' He shook his head. 'But they've had their fun with him, Raven. Boy's in no state to walk back to Wessex.' He looked up at me. The spikes of his hair were matted with gore and the whites of his eyes shone strangely against the filth. Even the Norsemen must have found Penda a terrible sight.

Sigurd looked Penda in the eyes. 'Then let the boy rest awhile, Englishman,' he said, for his blood was up and his eyes hungered for more slaughter. 'We'll have our fun with these savages before we go back to Wessex.' Penda looked up at the fortress and suddenly

I thought the timber walls did not look so sturdy. 'Tonight we sleep in Welsh beds!' Sigurd called, and the Wolfpack cheered, for there was more blood to be spilled in honour of their gods.

The afternoon brought a stirring, westerly breeze to cleanse the air of the stink of faeces and death, and the sun was warm on my skin as we made preparations to drive the Welsh from their homes. Sigurd had ordered the warriors of Wessex to gather as much dry wood as they could before dusk. They had not liked being told what to do, especially Penda, but Sigurd seemed so confident in his scheme that they obeyed him anyway. What choice did they have? Some of the Norsemen joined the Wessexmen, whilst the others stood before the fortress gate, ready with sword and shield in case the Welsh should attack.

'Come with me, Raven,' Sigurd said, heading off round the eastern side of the fortress. I gathered all my war gear and followed him, wondering what he planned to do with the wood, for we would never get close enough to the walls to set a fire beneath them. Not without suffering a rain of rocks, arrows and Welsh piss. 'Do you think there is a little Welshman still sitting in that tower up there?' he asked, gesturing to the stone structure up on the hill from where smoke had risen the previous day.

I shook my head. 'He'll be long gone. I would if I'd watched what happened down here.' Sigurd nodded.

As we climbed the tor, Sigurd explained how he had led the Wolfpack back into Wessex after evading King Coenwulf's Mercians. The Norsemen had stopped for food and rest, as he put it, at a small village. I did not ask what happened there.

'I had no thirst to return to Ealdred without the White Christ book, Raven, but there was no other way. This is not our land.' He grimaced. 'Hoped to catch up with Glum there, as I knew he would take the book to Ealdred. That dog would have filled his journey chest with my silver.'

'Glum's was a good death, lord,' I said, wincing as pain from aches and cuts flooded my body. 'Too good for the likes of him.'

Sigurd nodded, though I believe some part of him was pleased that the man had died as a Norseman should. 'The Englishman wouldn't give me my ships,' he said, grunting as he hauled himself over a rocky outcrop, 'but he coughed up half the silver he owes me.' A smile touched his lips. 'It's a fair hoard too!' He laughed. 'I've never seen its like, and that's only half of it.'

'And Floki?' I asked.

'What would you do with an Englishman's hoard, Raven?' he asked, kicking into the soft ground to gain purchase. 'Imagine you're surrounded by enemies and about to head out after a murderous, blood-eyed boy who can't keep his sword in its scabbard.' He shot me a knowing look which I ignored because I knew he was teasing me about Cynethryth. 'Well, lad, what would you do with enough silver to raise an army?'

I thought for a moment. 'Bury it,' I said.

Sigurd smiled again and nodded. 'When I knew the English were in their beds I buried Ealdred's silver.

Buried it deep near the beach. I left Floki to watch over it. He's happier on his own anyway.'

I must have betrayed my misgivings then, because Sigurd stopped to catch his breath and looked me in the eyes. 'Floki is not Glum,' he said. 'I know he can be a foul-tempered doom peddler, but you don't have to worry about his loyalty, Raven. Not Floki. He'll be at my side when the dark maidens come. The Norns have woven this. It is destined.'

'I have heard him say as much, lord,' I said.

Sigurd nodded, then continued climbing. 'Ealdred told me that Weohstan was his son.' His eyebrows arched. 'Didn't see that coin in the well. He said that you had set out with fifty men to steal him back from the Welsh.'

'Fifty?' I blurted. 'Mean bastard gave me thirty and only ten were warriors. But they fought well.' I thought of Eafa and Saba and Eni and the rest. 'But he keeps your ships, lord?' I asked. 'I gave him the book. Put it in his hands. You should have been free to take *Serpent* and *Fjord-Elk* across the sea.'

'And leave you here in the White Christ's land?' he said. I shrugged. 'I've told you, Raven. Just as Floki's life thread is woven into mine, mine is woven into yours.' He stopped again and this time his brow furrowed and his jaw clenched beneath the golden beard. 'I will always come for you,' he said, 'so long as my blood still streams through my body.' Then his face softened. 'You've done well, lad. By Óðin, you've done well. The men were worried about you, you know.' He smiled. 'Even old Asgot, I think.'

'And Aslak?' I asked.

'You broke his nose, Raven. Norsemen can be as vain as women.' He frowned. 'But I think he has forgiven you.'

'He should,' I said. 'Asgot set the bone straight for him. Mine's crooked now. Like a warped strake.' I turned, showing Sigurd my profile.

He laughed. 'So it is, Raven. So it is.' He stepped towards me, concentration suddenly etched on his face. 'Want me to have a go at straightening it?' he asked, studying my nose. 'I'm sure I can do it.'

I leapt back, my hand clutching my sword's hilt. 'With respect, lord, I'd rather fight you here and now,' I said. Sigurd laughed even more.

We found the watchtower abandoned. Inside, chicken and fish bones littered the ground and a heap of white ash sat smouldering in a ring of stones. Birch and green bracken had been piled against the wall so that it could be burned to dirty the sky with yellow smoke, and a plump ale skin leant against a log, though we did not drink from it in case it had been poisoned and left for us.

'The skinny brat was there,' Sigurd said, standing at the edge of the bluff, looking down on the fortress and the figures beyond its southern gate. 'The ealdorman's girl.'

'Cynethryth?' I said, my stomach churning.

'Aye, Ealdred's flat-chested daughter. Don't think she cares much for me.' He chuckled and for a moment he did not look like a killer at all.

'You can hardly blame her, after everything.'

Sigurd pursed his lips and shrugged. 'I don't see why she's so sour. You returned her to her father, didn't you?' He gestured to Caer Dyffryn. 'And we persuaded those filth-smeared whoresons to spit out her brother. The girl ought to show her appreciation, lad.' He winked mischievously. 'I've seen more meat on a flea-comb, but I'm sure she can't be as frail as she looks.' I scowled and Sigurd held up his hands. 'I'm teasing, Raven,' he said. 'You're a serious one, aren't you? The girl spoke to me. Must have burned her tongue, me being a savage heathen, but she seemed keen that I should come and find you before you got yourself into too much trouble.'

I leant my shield against the stone wall, unplugged the ale skin and sniffed the contents. 'I'm honoured that you came for me, lord,' I said.

'I want my ships back,' Sigurd said, 'and I want the rest of the silver that's owed me. The Englishman gave his word,' he spat, 'for what it's worth. I'd get what's due if I crossed this King Offa's wall and helped you get his precious son back.' He looked down into Caer Dyffryn. 'I've half a mind to ransom the lad. I'd sooner trust a dog not to chase a hare than trust the ealdorman. What kind of man sends thirty farmers and a crew of outlanders to fight for his son's life?'

'Some of them are good fighters, lord,' I said again, gesturing to the Wessexmen below.

Sigurd huffed. 'Ealdred is a snake.'

Regretfully, I tipped out the ale, watching as the foam sank into the hard ground. Sigurd bent and snatched up a handful of grass, which he dropped over the edge and watched as the breeze carried it away. I grinned, forgetting the cuts and bruises that nagged my body. 'You have more schemes than Loki himself,' I said, shaking my head. For I suddenly understood what Sigurd had in mind for the Welsh.

It was dusk when I blew into the bundle of dry grass and twigs, nurturing the embers that glowed delicately within. I was thinking I would have to strike the flint again when a burst of flame licked out, followed by a puff of yellow smoke that made me cough.

'Put it in here, Raven, before you burn off your first beard,' Svein the Red said, bending by the huge pile of wood at the edge of the bluff near the watch-tower. It had taken us a long time to carry the timber up the hill and I was bone tired when I thrust the kindling into the grass-filled cavity. Svein and I stood back as the fire slowly took hold, whilst the other men waited in battle order in the valley below, their helmets and spear tips reflecting the last weak light of the day.

'Only Sigurd could have come up with this plan,' Svein said, picking up the ale skin I had discarded earlier. He looked miserable when he discovered it was empty, and threw it aside, reaching down the neck of his brynja to produce a stale crust from inside his tunic. He began to chew absently.

'Do you think it will work?' I asked, watching the big man's jaw bulging and contracting beneath his thick red beard.

'It'll work, lad,' Svein mumbled. 'Might also bring

every whoreson ever weaned on a Welsh tit.' He screwed up his face. 'We'll see.'

Luckily, the wind still came from the east and it was not long before the fire spat the first bright red cinders up into the air to be carried over the bluff's edge. They looked like fireflies taking wing for the first time, and when the sun began its descent in the western sky the fire was roaring and crackling noisily and throwing off so much heat that we had to toss new branches on from a distance, even then shielding our faces with our forearms. Svein had removed his mail and tunic, and his heavily muscled chest and arms, criss-crossed with scars and old wounds, glistened in the firelight. His great red beard and hair resembled the flames that challenged the gathering dusk. To me he was the very embodiment of the god he favoured, mighty Thór, slayer of giants.

'It's working!' I yelled, pointing to a house down in the fortress below. Its thatch sprouted a small, hungry flame.

Svein looked up. The sky was full of flying cinders and ash. 'Looks like black snow,' he said, hands on hips, his eyes following thousands of cinders as they drifted over the bluff. Most would be spent and harmless by the time they reached the dry thatch of the houses below, but some would be still glowing, full of the promise of the fire that had spawned them. It was these embers that now began to do their work, smouldering awhile before bursting into flame. The Welsh were running around frantically, flinging water on to roofs and wattle frames, but their livestock hampered their

373

efforts. Fearful of the falling cinders, sheep and cows ran in all directions making a din that carried up to us as we stood above looking upon Sigurd's mischief.

'Of course it's working,' Svein the Red said eventually, throwing the last of the branches into the angry flames. Embers were landing on his bare shoulders but he did not seem to notice. 'Well, lad, let's get down there and join the fun.' He bent to gather his gambeson and brynja. 'There's nothing more we can do up here and I don't intend to miss out on the bitches that come running out with their braids burning.'

'Maybe we should stay up here for a while, Svein?' I said, scanning the darkening hills. 'Our fire could bring men from every village this side of Offa's wall. They'll think Caer Dyffryn is in trouble.'

'It is.' He grinned.

'We're not staying to keep watch?'

'We're not,' Svein said, wriggling into his massive brynja. His red hair appeared first, followed by his broad face and bushy beard. 'If they come, we'll kill them,' he said simply. And with that we left the seething flames and climbed back down the tor to join the others facing the southern gate.

The fire had taken a hold on their homes, so the Welsh had no choice but to come out and face us, which they did bravely, old and young taking their places behind their warriors in the shieldwall. But it was butchery. For the second time that day the dry grass was made wet with the blood of the slaughtered. Their chief, the man who had met Penda and me between our two war bands at the beginning, was taken bloodied but alive.

As the sun set, old Asgot performed the Blood Eagle on him and sent his soul screaming to the afterlife. There were other screams too, those of women whom the Wolfpack used for their own enjoyment. My hands were still shaking, my muscles still shivering with the battle clamour, when Svein brought me a girl, small and black-haired and no older than sixteen with terror in her eyes. I was covered in dark, stinking gore and must have looked like some hellish creature as I stood in the darkness which was stirred by the glow of burning timbers.

'Here, Raven. The lads were slobbering over this one,' Svein said, 'but I told them she was your pillow for the night.' He laughed. 'You look like a sack of horseshit. Have some fun, lad. Celebrate the happiness of still breathing and still having all your bits where they belong. Come and find me when you're done. We'll drink till we can't remember our own names. It's been some day, eh?' He pushed the girl to me and I took her arm without a word. Svein nodded and flashed his teeth, then turned and walked off into the shadows, back towards the cauldron of noise amongst the ruins of Caer Dyffryn.

There was a small thatched shelter by the fortress's main gate, in which guards must have been stationed, and I took the girl into that dark hut. At first she fought. She did not cry out – not once – but she scratched my face and even bit my cheek. I was slathered in the blood of her people and she must have tasted that blood in her mouth. I felt filthy to the soul, far worse than the lowest beast. And yet the self-disgust, the shame that burned

375

in my heart, did not make me stop. If anything, it urged me on, blinding me to the tears that must have soaked the girl's face. When I had finished, I rolled on to the filthy earth and let the emptiness claim me. Exhaustion and loathing pulled at my deepest being, dragged me down like some malevolent shadow spirit from Satan's pit, and I let it take me.

When I woke, the girl was still there, shivering beside me whilst other women's screams pierced the night. We sat in the darkness and after a while I took her hand and, perhaps because she was afraid and feared I would hurt her, her fingers curled round mine. I thought of Alwunn from Abbotsend, whom I had lain with once. But now I could not remember Alwunn's face, though I could remember Cynethryth's.

When the noise inside the fortress died down I gave the black-haired girl some smoked ham and cheese and led her through the darkness away from Caer Dyffryn. Once out of sight, I told her to go but she could not understand me, or perhaps she had nowhere to go. So I took three silver coins I had taken from a dead Welsh-man and put them in her hand. I turned my back on her and I did not hear her go, but when I eventually looked behind me there was no sign of her.

Finally, when his men had finished with them, Sigurd let the women run off into the night and I wondered how many Norsemen had planted their seed in Welsh bellies. I wondered if I had planted my own seed in the black-haired girl and I felt sick at the thought of what I had done. Added to this, the wound in my shin now stung like fire, though it was not enough to make me forget about the girl. Asgot smeared the cut with a poultice of herbs, then bound it tight with rough linen from a dress and when he was finished I sat alone in the darkness watching out for torches in the Welsh hills. And I was afraid because I did not know who I had become.

We burned the bodies of three Norsemen and two Wessexmen killed by the Welsh in their last struggle, and then we, along with the six remaining English, carried Weohstan into the fortress whose palisade stood mostly untouched by fire. Inside, we searched for food and ale by the light of the fires still burning and found plenty of both. We gorged on pork and beef too and it was not long before we dropped beside collapsed fires, our beards wet with ale and our ears full of song.

'Pagan or Christian, a man is never happier than when he has emptied his balls and drunk his fill,' Penda shouted, his words sliding into each other and his eyelids heavy. For a few hours at least, the Englishman would forget the friends who had died beside him.

Sigurd must have ordered men to stand watch that night, but if he did I was not aware of it. We saw no sign of the Welsh and I don't believe any of us thought they would come whilst the fires yet burned in the fortress of Caer Dyffryn. As for the Welsh dead, if their souls still clung to the place, deaf to the call of the next life, they would have thought their killers dead too, such was the stupor that lay over us. We were exhausted and drunk and relieved to be behind stout wooden walls for once, protected in a hostile land.

By dawn, Weohstan was conscious enough to eat the

warm but dried out pottage Penda had found above a Welshman's hearth, and though the young man had suffered, he was safe now and would shortly be reunited with his father. As for us, we would soon be aboard our ships. I imagined *Serpent* and *Fjord-Elk* sitting low in the water, their bellies heavy with English silver as the wind filled their great sails and carried us across the sea.

It was strange to see Norsemen and Englishmen sharing the spoils of a beaten enemy and that night I learned that violence and slaughter can sometimes bind men, forging unseen chains. In blood and fear and chaos, these men had forgotten their differences, laid aside the shackles of faith and come together. Hah! Perhaps I am speaking words that were nowhere near my tongue or even in my mind at the time. I was young then and arrogant and blinded by blood. But is it not often the case that the old, having the advantage of experience, cast the spear of acquired truth into the heart of their memories? Am I alone in wishing I knew back then what I know now?

# CHAPTER NINETEEN

WE WOKE AMONG THE SMOULDERING REMAINS OF THE
fortress village of Caer Dyffryn, holding our aching
heads and rubbing our smoke-reddened eyes.

'How is your leg, Raven?' Sigurd asked. Even he
looked weary, the creases around his eyes lined with
black soot.

'It will be fine in a day or two,' I said, coughing and
spitting sooty phlegm and pulling up my breeches after
a lengthy morning piss.

Sigurd ran a hand through his hair and tilted his face
to feel the new sun's warmth upon his closed eyelids. 'It
always troubles me, you know,' he said, suddenly opening his eyes at the crack of a smouldering beam, 'how
the world just goes on as though nothing has changed.'
I looked at him questioningly, not wanting to interrupt
as he gathered his thoughts. 'How many men did we
send into the afterlife yesterday?' he asked.

'I don't know, lord. Many,' I said.

He nodded. 'Look around you, Raven. The birds still
sing and the dogs still piss up trees. Even the women

we took last night will wet their faces and pin on their brooches. They'll begin the new day and forget the last. If they can.'

I thought of the black-haired girl, of what I had done that night. The memory sent a shiver down my spine and I hoped Sigurd could not see my shame. 'The world is stronger than any of us, my lord. It goes on,' I said, remembering that Ealhstan had conveyed as much to me once in his own way. 'It has always been so.'

'Yes, it has,' Sigurd said, turning to face me. 'And that is why we must do great things. I don't just mean killing. By all the gods, there must be greater things than sowing death amongst your enemies. No, we must achieve things that are beyond most men. Only by doing what seems impossible will we ensure men remember our names and sing of them around their fires when we are long gone.' He put a hand on my shoulder. 'I see something in you. I cannot explain it yet but I know I am bound to you.'

'Bound, lord?'

He nodded solemnly. 'The gods have marked you and my sword will honour their favour.' Something caught his eye, a shiny black beetle crawling from a pile of smoking, white ash. 'The world goes on,' he said, 'despite the chaos we make. May Óðin grant us the time to carve our names in the earth, Raven, so that others must watch where they tread.'

I touched the carving of the All-Father hanging round my neck and whispered a prayer that it be so.

After a breakfast of cold meats we prepared to set off back to Wessex. The men were in good spirits, if a little sore-headed. For the Wessexmen, though, the new day brought with it the harsh reality that they had lost many friends and neighbours whose wives and children they would soon have to face. Sons and apprentices would become millers and smiths and fletchers and farmers before their time. Perhaps some women would have to take on their dead husband's work to survive.

Weohstan was weak and pale as death, but refused the pony Penda offered him, saying he would walk out of Wales so as to remember the ground beneath his feet for when he returned with men and swords. He spoke little, saving his strength for the journey, but he did thank me for coming for him, and asked after Cynethryth. 'I will never forget what you have done for me, Raven,' he said, choosing the words carefully, his tone hard and unyielding. He showed little sign of the pain he was surely in and seemed a different man from the one who had walked into Coenwulf's church. It was as though his very soul had hardened like ice.

'Have you forgotten I'm a filthy heathen savage?' I asked, gripping his forearm to seal our friendship. 'Did the whoresons beat you round the head with iron bars?'

'I know what you are,' he said with a grimace, 'and I'm alive because of it.'

My muscles were raw with pain and my head was aching terribly from the ale, so I did not notice the rider when we came to King Offa's wall. Bjorn pointed out the figure standing motionless on the far bank of the river Wye, his cloak and the horse's brown coat concealing both against the dark wood of the palisade behind them.

'Could be one of the ealdorman's men come to see if we have the boy,' a grizzled Wessex warrior said, raising an arm in greeting.

'Could be a Welshman come to spit in our eye,' Penda warned. But the rider seemed to be alone, the treeless flat ground on this side of the wall affording few hiding places for anyone with bloody intent. We approached the river and the earthen bank with caution but without fear, and it was Weohstan who recognized the horse and the small, hooded figure on its back.

'Cynethryth!' he called, smiling so that his face looked hideous for the missing teeth and swollen eyes. 'It's Cynethryth!' The mare lowered her head to the ground, pulling Cynethryth forward and giving a screeching neigh, then the beast began to circle until Cynethryth pulled her sharply round with the reins.

Weohstan fell. 'Steady, lad,' Penda warned, putting his shoulder beneath the man's arm. 'We're nearly there. You'll be with your sister soon enough.'

The skins we had used to float across the river lay discarded further along the bank and Cynethryth must have seen them and hoped we would re-cross the river at the same point. But we did not need the skins now, because Olaf had a coiled rope over his shoulder and he threw one end across a narrow point to Cynethryth on the other side. She tied it to the half-buried roots of a fallen willow and one by one we slid into the Wye and pulled ourselves along the rope until we stood dripping on the far bank. Offa's wall was deserted. With luck we would cross the southern border of Mercia into Wessex without running into a Mercian levy. The Norsemen had begun to talk of their longships again, eager to put to sea after so long. But we would soon be made to forget about the blue sea and Rán's wind-stirred, white-haired daughters, and the silver promised us by Ealdred of Wessex.

Cynethryth wrapped her arms round Weohstan, the water from his clothes soaking her own as she clung to him. Tears rolled down her cheeks.

'What are you doing here, Cynethryth?' Weohstan demanded, holding her at arm's length. 'Are you mad? It's not safe.'

Cynethryth turned to look at me properly for the first time since we had found her, or rather since she had found us. I thought of the black-haired Welsh girl I had raped and my chest hammered with guilt. Cynethryth's face was tight, her eyes full of indecision, and I could tell she was struggling to find the words. 'My father means to betray you, Raven. All of you.' She looked at Penda. 'He has taken the gospel book of Saint Jerome and means to cross the sea a few days from now.'

'And the remaining hoard he owes me?' Sigurd boomed, water from the Wye dripping from his golden beard. Cynethryth ignored him, searching her brother's face. 'Well, girl?' Sigurd said. 'Has the ealdorman left me what he owes?'

'Are your ears full of duckweed, heathen?' Cynethryth snapped. 'He means to cheat you. He has the book and he will sell it. Without it there *is* no money. Certainly not what he promised to pay you,

383

anyway.' Sigurd cursed and Cynethryth turned back to Weohstan. 'The book has blinded him, brother. It has stolen his judgement. He believes it will make him richer than any king in England.'

'These men saved my life,' Weohstan said, but his face betrayed that he was all too aware why Ealdred would not want to leave vengeance-thirsty Norsemen in the heart of Wessex.

'We kept our word, Cynethryth,' I said. 'Many men died for it.' The Norsemen began cursing and shouting as Olaf roughly translated Cynethryth's words, whilst the Wessexmen glanced around nervously, their hands finding their sword grips as though they expected to be cut down where they stood for their lord's betrayal.

'I rode through the night to warn you,' Cynethryth said to me. Her face was pale and drawn and her eyes were full of the pain of a daughter betraying her father. 'You don't have much time.'

'The ealdorman won't get far,' I said, my blood simmering as the truth sank in.

'I'll have his head,' Sigurd growled in Norse and his men declared their own murderous intentions regarding Ealdred.

'Listen to me, Raven,' Cynethryth pleaded, shaking her head, and I saw fresh tears moisten her eyes. 'He has sent men to kill you. I came as soon as I learned of it. Why do you think he gave Sigurd half the silver? Because he knows he will have it back soon enough. They're coming, Raven. You have to get away. They're coming now!'

'But we have Weohstan,' I said. Sigurd was frowning

at the girl as though wondering what else she would say to ruin his day. 'And what about these men?' I asked, pointing at Penda and the last remaining Wessexmen.

She shrugged wearily. 'I don't think my father ever believed you would succeed, Raven.' She paused for a moment, then took her brother's hands in her own. 'Or even that Weohstan was alive. Consider the men he sent with you.' She glanced at Penda, though for shame of her father could not hold his eye. 'Only a few were his household men.' Penda spat at this, though he must have recognized the truth when he heard it. Ealdred had not wanted to waste his best warriors on a fool's mission. *Apprentices, sons, and women becoming millers, smiths and fletchers*, I thought to myself. 'Others are on their way to make sure Sigurd never returns to Wessex,' Cynethryth went on. 'The priests assured our father that this was God's will. They said the land must be cleansed of the filth of the heathens.'

Sigurd grimaced. 'The dogs still piss up trees and life goes on, Raven,' he said. Then he shook his great ash spear. 'And we go to earn our reputation.'

'Kill the Englishmen, Sigurd!' Asgot shrieked in Norse, jabbing his spear towards one of them. The Wessexmen stepped away from the Norsemen and Penda glared at Sigurd, the challenge clear in his fierce eyes.

'These men have been honourable, Asgot,' I said, fixing him with my blood-eye. 'Would you kill everything that breathed that was not a Norseman?'

'You know I would, Raven,' the old godi snarled, revealing black teeth.

'We go to Wessex,' Sigurd said, looking first to Olaf, then to *Serpent*'s steersman Knut. Both men nodded. 'We go to Wessex and we get to our ships before the English dog burns them.'

'He won't burn the ships, lord,' I said in English, gripping the sword's hilt at my waist and glancing at Weohstan. 'He'll take them. What better vessels does he have to cross the sea?'

'Raven's right,' Weohstan said, looking at Cynethryth as he spoke. 'My father has a couple of broad trading ships, but nothing to be proud of. Nothing that would turn the head of a high lord or king.'

So, full of flaming fury, we used our axes to cut through King Offa's wall, for Cynethryth had forded the Wye down-river where there was no wall and she would not now leave her mare behind. Then we turned south into the Hwicce forest and whatever trap the treacherous ealdorman of Wessex had set for us.

'They're close,' Bjarni warned some time later. He turned to Asgot who had his ear pressed against the trunk of a storm-cleaved oak.

'He's right, Sigurd,' the godi muttered. 'It won't be long now.' Sigurd nodded grimly and kissed the iron rim of his round war shield. He had put the last six Wessexmen within the belly of the Wolfpack so that his men could take them down if necessary. Asgot and Olaf had pleaded with Sigurd to disarm the English, but Sigurd had said no. Nor had he allowed Penda to unfurl Ealdorman Ealdred's leaping stag banner. His own red wolf's head banner hung limply on Hakon's spear.

'These English may yet have a part to play in this,' Sigurd muttered to Olaf, gripping the older man's shoulder reassuringly. 'We'll let them keep their swords within reach for now.'

We marched quietly, brynjas and helmets secure and spears and shields ready, each of us lost within our own preparations for battle. Because we did not know the land and because Sigurd did not trust the English enough to seek their advice, we sprang the trap. A volley of arrows poured out from a copse of elder and sweet-briar and Hakon went down, a shaft jutting from his face. Because he had held Sigurd's banner at the war band's heart, those around him were hit worst. Wessexmen were filled with Wessex arrows as the Wolfpack formed a circle, presenting their painted war shields to an unseen enemy. Arrows whipped through the trees, snapping against bright leaves to thud into limewood and glance off mail. Penda's men must have wanted to yell to their countrymen, but they knew the warriors beside them would cut them down if they did. As for Penda himself, blood was in the air and the fight was on and that was all that mattered.

Men grunted as arrows struck them, yet the forest was strangely calm. An arrow skimmed off my shield's rim and I cursed under my breath. It was not so long ago that I spent whole days in just such a place, choosing and felling trees with old Ealhstan's axe. Now the tool in my hand was for felling men. Now my stomach was ice cold with the fear of mutilation.

'Keep those shields up, lads,' I heard myself say, but who was I to give advice to these warriors? They knew their work and endured the assault patiently, waiting for the chance to face their enemies. Even the Wessexmen cursed behind their shields, seething under the deadly rain, and I wondered if they would take their swords to their countrymen if they got the chance. It was possible if their blood was up, and perhaps that was what Sigurd had meant when he said they still had a part to play. The arrows came sporadically for a while, then stopped altogether.

'We'd be downing mead with the All-Father now if it weren't for this mail,' Bjarni said, pulling a broken arrow from the rings of his brynja. Even so, several Norsemen and all but three of the Wessexmen were down, shafts jutting from their bodies. Then the forest came alive with shouts, animalistic shrieks that cut through the foliage to disorientate and inspire terror, and I tensed, glancing at the men around me. On my left was Bjarni, on my right Penda. Then the English came, bursting through the trees. They threw their spears and ran at us, hitting the shieldwall from every side with axes and swords and shield bosses. Penda rammed his sword through a man's neck, his choice made. It was fight or die now.

A woman's scream cut through the din like an eagle's cry and I risked a glance behind to see Cynethryth standing over Weohstan, who was down. She was covered in bright blood. I screamed a curse at the

English and battered a man's shield, my sword splitting it down the middle. I struck it again and again, then Bjarni rammed his spear into the man's cheek so that it tore out through the other side. Someone yanked the dead man back and another Englishman took his place. I began the shoving match that would end with one of us being torn apart. It is strange how even in the midst of a fight warriors will talk. Sometimes there is only the silence of individual struggles, but not always. Penda and I leant into our shields, trying to force the English back so that we could use our swords on them.

'See the bastard back there . . . amongst the bushes?' he asked through teeth gritted in effort. The veins in his neck bulged like cords beneath the skin.

'Can't look right now, Penda,' I growled, tucking my head into my chest as a spear blade came over my shield's rim.

'It's Mauger,' he spat. 'Ealdred's pet. You know him, don't you?'

'I know him,' I said, 'and I'm going to kill the bastard if I get out of this.'

'He's mine, lad,' Penda snarled.

I heard Sigurd encouraging those around him and hurling insults at the English. He called for the Wolfpack to make their enemies pay a great blood-price for their treachery and when we were even harder pressed he called the names of men's wives and women back home in Norway, rousing them to great feats for their sakes. The Norsemen fought like demons and their jarl would have expected nothing less, for they were no ordinary war band. These were the best warriors ever to cross the angry grey sea, each one chosen by Sigurd for his skill and bravery and love of bloody glory.

The man to Bjarni's left fell back, blood spurting from the vein in his neck. I stamped on a spear jabbing at my shins, and snapped off the blade.

'Urchin! Urchin!' Sigurd roared and several men stepped back from the wall, the others closing the gaps before the enemy could exploit them. The Urchin contracted the circle, allowing spearmen to form an inner defensive ring, thrusting their spears over their comrades' shoulders into English faces. Sigurd's voice boomed out and his men made their slaughter.

'He knows how to fight,' Penda growled as a spear ripped into the man he was heaving against. The air was thick with sweat and men's breath and the first stench of bowels opening in death came to my nose. My own guts had turned to liquid and I tasted fear on my tongue. Somewhere behind me was Cynethryth, whilst in front were men fighting for their lives because she had warned us of their treachery. It was not hard to imagine what they would do to the girl if we lost.

A war horn sounded above the clash of arms and shouts, and in good order the English trudged backwards, their shields overlapping as they retreated into elder and sweet-briar, the foliage half swallowing them. There they waited, a spear's throw away, hurling insults and threats, and I gasped for breath, dragging warm air into stinging lungs. My heart thumped in my chest like a sword on a shield. I feared it would burst.

'How old are you, Raven?' Penda asked, wiping sweat from his eyes.

'I don't know,' I replied. 'Sixteen, seventeen maybe.'

'You're a natural bloody killer, lad,' he said with a malicious grin. Sweat dripped from the scar on his hairless chin. 'Whoever named you saw corpses in that red eye of yours.'

'I got the name from Sigurd,' I said, checking my sword for damage. There was a deep notch a finger's length from the iron guard and I whispered a prayer to Völund god of the forge that the blade would not break before the fight was decided.

'It's a good name,' Penda said, kicking a body at his feet to see if the man was alive. He was not.

I looked around. Incredibly, old Asgot stood breathless but unharmed, and I wondered what spirits protected the old godi when younger, stronger men lay dead. Hakon, who had carried Sigurd's banner, was dead, his lifeblood congealing around the arrows in his face and neck. Thormod and young Thorolf were dead. Kon, who was always complaining, lay writhing as Olaf knelt beside him, trying to push the man's slippery guts back through the gash above his crotch. The man's mail had been useless against the axe, and Olaf must have known his efforts were in vain, but he tried anyway. Five of the Wessexmen lay dead or dying, leaving only Penda who cursed the English now for killing their own people. He hurled insults at them, calling them shit-eaters and sons of whores, and challenged Mauger to step into the open to look upon the Wessexmen he had had killed. But when Mauger did step forward, his huge frame covered in dark mail

391

and his hand gripping a great war spear, it was not to mourn dead Englishmen.

'Sigurd!' he yelled, and Sigurd stepped forward from the shieldwall threateningly. His helmet was blood-smeared and his golden beard was plaited, giving his face a lean, vicious, wolf-like look.

'What do you want, Mauger?' he asked. 'I am here. Come and fight me.' He threw his arms wide in invitation. 'What are you waiting for, snake? Come, you lump of rancid snot.'

Mauger laughed, ignoring the Wessexmen who lay mutilated before the Norse shieldwall. 'Why would I deny my men the pleasure of sending Norsemen to minister for Satan?' he asked, and the English growled, banging their swords and shields. 'Look around you, Sigurd the Lucky. This is where your adventure ends. Not what you had in mind, is it?' Mauger looked up at the forest canopy and casually scratched his black beard. 'But then, you should not have killed Lord Ealdred's son.' Sigurd did not dignify the lie with an answer. Every man beneath that forest canopy knew the truth. We were still heavily outnumbered. Only half of the remaining English wore any mail, though nearly all had iron helmets, leather armour, and wicked blades. I knew we could not win.

'You do a coward's bidding, Mauger,' Sigurd said, 'and that makes you a man without honour.'

'And you have led your men to their deaths, Sigurd,' Mauger answered, shrugging his broad shoulders. 'God knows none of us is perfect.' He planted the butt of his huge spear into the forest litter. 'Throw down your weapons and I swear I will kill you and your men quickly. I will do it myself.'

'You know us better than that, Englishman!' Olaf called.

'Yes, Uncle, I know you,' Mauger said, using Olaf's nickname with a smile that did not reach his eyes. Then he turned his back on us and pushed past his men.

Sigurd called out to us in Norse as we braced ourselves and mumbled prayers to Týr god of the brave, Thór the mighty, and Óðin god of war.

'What does your heathen lord have in mind?' Penda asked. He looked exhausted.

'We're going to charge them,' I said, making sure my helmet was pushed firmly down. 'If you want to join your people, Penda, now is the time.'

'They can suck the Devil's prick,' he said, shrugging some life back into his shield arm.

A hand gripped my shoulder and I turned to face Bjorn. 'Raven, Sigurd says you must take the English girl and get out,' he said sternly. Blood was spilling into his fair beard from a cut below his eye. 'Get away from this place.'

'No, brother, I stay here,' I said. I caught Sigurd's eye and he nodded firmly, confirming his wishes. The English took up their chanting again, this time repeating the word 'out, out, out', thumping swords against shields. I left the shieldwall, pushed past Bjorn and strode towards Sigurd, catching Cynethryth's eye as she knelt with Weohstan's head on her lap. 'I am staying with you, lord,' I said, glimpsing Svein the Red who was snarling like a beast, so that even the numerous English could not have relished the thought of fighting him. 'We can win this fight,' I said, though I knew we could not.

Sigurd smiled then, his eyes that held the blue ocean shining brightly below the helmet's rim. 'You have been loyal to me, Raven,' he said, 'and I do not expect you to change now. Do as I tell you.' I clenched my jaw. 'Or are you still an Englishman after all? Like them?' he asked, gesturing towards the shouting warriors who were preparing to come again.

'I am a Norseman, lord!' I said angrily. 'I am a wolf and if I must die here, I am ready.'

'Then who will tell of these brave men,' he asked, 'and how they spent their last moments in this world? You *will* be a great warrior, Raven, but these men *are* great warriors. Look at them.' I glanced at Svein the Red, immovable like a great rock. Bram, growling like a hungry bear. There was old Asgot, still and menacing, and the brothers Bjorn and Bjarni, both light-hearted men, yet efficient killers. Even the Englishman Penda. Sigurd was right. They were all great warriors and I was arrogant to believe I belonged amongst them. Sigurd's face softened. 'Get to Floki. He is with the ships. You must go so that you can tell others how they fought,' he said. 'How they cut the English down as a man cuts wheat. They must not be denied their story because of a boy's pride.' Those words stung me and the chanting was deafening now and the Norsemen took up their own chant of 'Óðin! Óðin! Óðin!'

'Think of the girl, Raven,' Sigurd said above the noise. He nodded towards Cynethryth. 'There is another way

394

to gain immortality, lad. Take the girl! Put your seed in her belly. Raise children who will grow up around you. Live, Raven.' He held my eye for a heartbeat and then turned and gave a roar that somehow drowned out every other voice. Sigurd charged and the Wolfpack with him. And I ran towards Cynethryth.

# CHAPTER TWENTY

I SLASHED MY SWORD ACROSS A BEARDED NECK AND then we were clear, briars tearing at our hands and faces, conspiring to trip and bind us as I savagely pulled Cynethryth on. Sigurd's charge surprised the English and the bloody chaos covered our escape, but a horseman at their rear saw us and cantered south through the trees to cut us off. Luckily, though, the stallion had not seen us. It reared in shock as we burst from a clump of elder, and I let go of Cynethryth and slammed my shielded shoulder into its belly. It shrieked and fell sideways, crushing the rider, and we ran on, hoping every other Wessexman was too busy fighting for his life to care about us. For the second time, Cynethryth and I found ourselves fugitives in the Wessex forest.

The battle's noise receded, smothered by countless ancient trees, and we stopped for breath by an old oak. I vomited, unable to hold the burning shame in my belly. 'I should be with them!' I yelled, spitting out the bitterness. 'What am I doing?'

'Shhh, Raven,' Cynethryth hissed. She was bent over, heaving for breath. 'My father's men will hear you.' She was drenched in her brother's blood and looked like a wild creature.

'I am of the Fellowship, Cynethryth! I should be with them, not running like a hunted animal. Like a coward.'

She strode forward and slammed her fists against my chest. 'And what should I do? Should I fight them, too? Am I a warrior?' She stepped away. 'How brave you must be, fighting like some starved beast!' She wiped her face, smearing Weohstan's blood across her cheek. 'What about me? Look at my fine brynja. My sword,' she clutched a fistful of her blood-soaked linen dress, 'my helmet and gambeson. Look, Raven! Should I go back there and fight the men I betrayed today? Then stop them from raping me?'

'Óðin will think me a coward, Cynethryth,' I said. I was weeping. 'I have nothing without them.' The noise of battle was faint now, but every now and again a louder scream or the ring of iron carried to us on the breeze.

'Then I should never have betrayed my father,' Cynethryth said, turning her back on me.

Why are we men such fools? Freyja knows we can make sheep look quick-witted. This beautiful woman had risked everything for me. Alone, she had ridden many miles, crossing the fast-flowing Wye to warn me of her father's treachery. Now her brother, whom she adored, was dead and she was wet with his blood, and I talked of honour. We men know how to kill and believe

397

this makes us great. But women possess innate knowledge of the pain of *giving* life. Perhaps this is why they feel its loss more keenly. Women bury their men and go on living, and they are much braver than us.

I stepped up to Cynethryth, removing my helmet as she turned to me. 'I am sorry, Cynethryth,' I said, 'and so long as I breathe and even in the life after I will remember what you did for me. For us.' My throat tightened further. 'By the All-Father, I swear I'm bound to you, Cynethryth. I would slit my own throat and be denied Valhöll if you asked it of me.'

'Must it always be about death, Raven?' she asked, a tear rolling down her cheek. 'What about life?'

I had no answer to that. 'Come,' I said, putting on my helmet and taking her hand to lead her south. 'We must reach the ealdorman before he sets off across the sea.' Because she needed answers too, or because she had nowhere else to go, Cynethryth went with me.

That night we slept amongst a stand of straight birches. Their rough, white bark looked dry, but the trunk's cracks and crevices still held a previous rain. Old Asgot had taught me that such trees are imbued with feminine purity, a kind of seidr, he said, which can protect a man against witches.

'So long as they hide us from the English, old man,' I muttered, as we made a bower with bracken and hornbeam whilst the night forest came alive with foraging creatures. We slept lightly and set off before dawn with empty stomachs and aching feet. The forest was damp and quiet and I winced at the noise my war gear made, though it could not be helped. Cynethryth was clear-eyed but wild-looking, her fine features reminding me of a peregrine, and though Weohstan was dead and his blood still on her, she pushed on, and with my war gear weighing me down it was all I could do to keep up.

'What will you do, Raven, when we catch up with the ealdorman?' Cynethryth asked. She had not said her father. A cold rain began to fall amongst the canopy above, fat drops bending the leaves before tapping on to branches, exposed roots and my helmet. It freshened the air and I was relieved to no longer smell blood and death.

'Well?' She grabbed my hand and stopped me. 'What will you do? I want the truth.'

A lie came to my tongue, but died there, because something in Cynethryth's green eyes, in the strong line of her lips, said she knew what was in my mind. 'I will kill him,' I said.

A cumbersome silence swelled between us. Then, after a while, she looked at me. 'He will have his household men with him. You wouldn't get within a spear's throw of him.'

'You have not seen me throw,' I said petulantly. 'I'll think of something.'

'Raven,' she said, pushing her golden hair behind her ears. Beneath the gore she looked fragile though I knew she was not. 'I hate the ealdorman now. Because of his greed, my brother is dead. He cares nothing for me, because I am a woman. Because I am not my mother,' she added, a deep sadness touching her face. 'I cannot inherit his power. Even Weohstan was a sacrifice he was willing to make.'

'Sacrifice?'

'Weohstan's death gives the ealdorman a tenable reason for war with Mercia. My brother was under Coenwulf's protection, wasn't he?'

'You don't believe he meant to let his son die,' I said, thinking of the millers and farmers Ealdred had sent with me to bring Weohstan back.

She hesitated. 'I don't know.' Then she shook her head. 'I cannot watch you kill him. Even if you got the chance.' It was hard to imagine this was the same girl who had come giggling into King Coenwulf's church when I had climbed out of a coffin. She was beautiful still, yet somehow immeasurable, like a deep gorge, and I did not know what to say to her.

'Ealdred must pay for his treachery, Cynethryth. There is no other way. He must die, or there is no honour.'

Cynethryth blinked rain from her eyes, the drops resting on her lashes and running down her cheeks. 'There is another way,' she said, her mouth tight. 'We could take his silver and go. Ealdred is blinded by the gospel book. He won't find us. We'll take his money and that will be your revenge and we will be safe. Safe, Raven,' she repeated and I admit the word sounded sweet as honey. I remembered Sigurd's last words to me before he had raised his sword and charged at the English. I *could* run away with Cynethryth. Perhaps she would grow to love me and perhaps I could put my seed in her belly and raise children whose eyes were green like hers and not red. Maybe we would grow old and those we brought into the world would remember us long after.

But I was a Norseman. And my eye *was* red.

'I will kill Ealdred,' I said, pushing on, 'and I will throw the White Christ book into the sea as an offering to Njörd.' My war shield thumped against my shoulder and the iron rings of my brynja chinked. My enemy's daughter walked on in silence, her wet face towards the new dawn.

As we neared Ealdorman Ealdred's lands, we tried to make ourselves inconspicuous. We stopped at a mill on the banks of a fast-flowing stream and I paid the miller two small silver coins for an empty flour sack into which I put my war gear, except for the shield which I kept slung across my back. Cynethryth washed off her brother's blood and then raised her hood so that it partly hid her face, and in her simple dress of undyed linen – though it was now stained brown in places – no one would know her for the ealdorman's daughter. Even so, the sight of my battered war shield was enough to make folk wary of us as we moved along the well-worn paths leading to Ealdred's hall. The locals had seen plenty of warriors come and go over the last weeks and they must have caught a whiff of blood in the warming summer air, for they gave us a wide berth and eyed me suspiciously.

Next morning, we arrived before the timber walls of Ealdorman Ealdred's small fortress, having travelled through the night. I hated watching Cynethryth walk through the gates alone, for I feared what Mauger might do, if he still lived, to prevent her from telling Ealdred the truth about Weohstan's death. But she assured me that even if Mauger had made it back to his lord after the fight in the forest, he would not dare harm her here, despite her having ridden to warn me of the Wessexmen's ambush. Nor could Cynethryth believe that her father would hurt her. I promised to wait until she returned with news of how things stood within the walls, and though she was probably right, I whispered a prayer to Loki the maker of mischief that she would be back soon and unharmed. I did not pray to Óðin, because I was unsure how I stood in the Far-Wanderer's eyes for having fled from the Wolfpack when all was against them. With the prayer barely past my lips, I put my rolled-up cloak beneath my head and fell asleep in a ditch beside a thick hedgerow of hawthorn and hazel.

'Wake up, Raven.' Cynethryth's voice was low and urgent. She was back before my dreams had taken shape. 'Wake up. Ealdred is at the coast already. He waits for a good wind to take him across the sea. And he has his silver with him.' She was holding a linen sack.

'My jarl's silver,' I said groggily. She nodded, coming into focus as I knuckled my eyes. 'Ealdred's a fool, taking his fortune on to a boat. A boat he has never sailed before. Rán's white-haired daughters will smell the silver and spill it into the sea and him with it.' I rubbed my aching neck.

'The Lord God will turn your tongue black for saying such things and it will fall out one day and you will be left mute,' she chided, frowning. 'Food,' she added, following my eyes to the sack in her hand. I nodded, my belly rumbling. 'Godgifu the cook said Ealdred intends to sell the gospel book of Saint Jerome to the great Emperor Charlemagne.'

'Charlemagne? Are you sure?'

'We have to hurry, Raven!' She pulled at my brynja.

'So Ealdred was never going to give the book to King Egbert?' I asked. Egbert was king of Wessex back then, after Beorhtric, though he had yet to become Bretwalda, ruler of all Britain.

'I don't know. I don't think the king knows anything about it,' Cynethryth replied, handing me my shield.

'That makes sense,' I said, slinging the shield across my back and picking up my helmet. 'King Egbert would not have had Sigurd's Norsemen roaming his land. Of course he wouldn't. How would it look to his people? To his churchmen?'

'And our people went along with it because Ealdred told them it was their king's wish,' Cynethryth said, putting the puzzle together. 'They had no choice.'

'Ealdred plays a dangerous game,' I said. 'He's a scheming bastard, I'll say that for him.'

Charlemagne was a legendary warrior by then, the most powerful Christian alive, but for the Pope. Though some said even Pope Leo bent the knee to Charlemagne. If God wouldn't listen, you prayed to Charlemagne. That's what the Christians said. Still do and the man's been dust for years.

'I hope the wind blows his piss back into his face,' I said, meaning Ealdred and feeling the breeze across my eyes and wondering if even that would side with the ealdorman to carry him out of my reach. Cynethryth handed me a hunk of bread and cheese and some salted meat and we set off, bypassing Ealdred's fortress to get to him before the wind changed.

Also in Cynethryth's sack were peas, leeks, turnips and two small onions, and this food kept our strength up on the two-day journey to the southern Wessex coast. But it was a different kind of hunger that stirred in my guts when I eventually smelled the sea, long before its wild sound filled my ears or its grey vastness crammed my eyes.

'You miss it, don't you?' Cynethryth asked as I stopped to test the wind's direction by throwing a handful of grass into the air. I nodded, inhaling the salty air. The wind still blew from the south and this was good because it meant Ealdred could not have sailed yet. Sigurd could have taken *Serpent* against the wind, but Ealdred was not Sigurd, and I hoped he would not dare risk the ship's being thrown back against the coast. Of course, he could have rowed her instead. It would be backbreaking work against the waves, but it would take him away. But then, Ealdred did not know he had anything to fear, and so we had to believe he would wait for a good wind.

'I have come to love the sea,' I said, thinking of the Fellowship, of Sigurd and Svein and Olaf. 'The sea can tell you much about yourself, but the knowledge does not come easily. First you must trust your life to her.' I grimaced. 'Being out there in a storm is terrifying, Cynethryth,' I said.

404

She frowned. 'My mother used to fear the sea. She said it was hungry for men's souls and that's why so many drown trying to master her.' She gave a humourless smile. 'Sounds like something a heathen would say, doesn't it?'

I nodded. 'But your mother gave birth to you, Cynethryth, and you are as brave as anyone I have known.' She dragged her teeth across her bottom lip and the ache to kiss her was so strong that I looked away. 'I think fear can kill you in its own way,' I said quietly. I removed my helmet to mop my brow. 'Fear keeps a man by his hearth and sees him grow old before his time. Fear makes a man betray his friends when it seems the gods have abandoned him,' I said, thinking of Glum. 'Did you ever look into Jarl Sigurd's eyes? Right into the dark holes at their centre? Or Bjorn's or Bjarni's or Olaf's?' She shrugged. 'The sea lives within them, Cynethryth. They are wild as the sea is wild, but they are free. No man commands the waves.'

'My mother would not have liked you, Raven,' Cynethryth said. 'She would not have let me walk with you to the market, let alone this.'

'Your father will like me even less,' I said with a grin. But Cynethryth was not smiling.

'I no longer recognize my life,' she said. 'Everything has changed. I am alone.'

'No, Cynethryth, you are not alone.' I felt my cheeks fill with warmth and for a few moments there was just the low roar of the sea and the decaying screech of far off gulls. We watched a great black cormorant head out to sea, its wingbeats strong and even.

'The wind has dropped,' Cynethryth said suddenly, and she was right. 'We must hurry.' I looked out to sea and saw a distant island of grey rock and knew that the longships sat further to the east, where we had moored them those many weeks ago. I knew also that our luck had run out. The wind had suddenly changed, coming from the west now and whipping the scent of yellow horned poppies off the far hills towards us. We stuck to the higher ground, tracking eastwards in the hope of rounding the bluff to see *Serpent* and *Fjord-Elk* rocking below us on the rising tide. What would we do then? What patterns were the Norns of fate weaving for us?

I took my war gear from the flour sack and put on the mail brynja, helmet and sword, re-clothing myself as a warrior of renown. Perhaps I was the last of the Wolfpack. Perhaps Sigurd and the others were already feasting at Óðin's table in Valhöll, waiting for me to join them in preparation for Ragnarök, the final battle of the gods. I shivered at the touch of the cool iron, finding its weight comforting though thinking it strange what courage forged iron and steel can give a man, even when in his heart he knows it will not be enough.

'Horses! Listen, Raven!' Cynethryth said above the noise of the surf. 'Hide! Quickly!' With my helmet on I heard nothing, but looked around, thinking there must be a ledge out of sight below the chalk cliff edge. But it was too late. Riders galloped over the rise before us, trampling the thick grass.

'Your father's men?' I asked, then recognized the banner tied to a rider's spear. A leaping stag on a green cloth. 'You don't need to answer that,' I murmured, gripping my sword's hilt and resisting the urge to unsling the round shield.

'Leave it to me. Don't kill them,' she warned, and I was flattered, because there were twelve of them.

The horsemen reined in before us, yanking back on their mounts' necks to stop them, and I noticed that the animals were still fresh, meaning that Ealdred was probably close.

'Lady Cynethryth?' one of the warriors asked, leaning across his saddle to get a better look at the girl. They all wore leather armour, but all had swords at their waists.

'Where is my father, Hunwald?' Cynethryth demanded, throwing back her hood.

'The ealdorman is putting out to sea in the Norseman's ship, my lady,' he said, thumbing behind him. 'What in God's name are you doing here?'

'I must speak with Ealdred,' she said. 'Take me to him.'

Hunwald looked at me, taking in my arms and my blood-eye. 'You are the heathen,' he said, drawing his sword. The other men bristled, then kicked their mounts to surround me.

'You will not touch him!' Cynethryth yelled as they dismounted and drew their swords or levelled their spears at me.

'Stay back, Lady Cynethryth. We have orders to kill any Norsemen we find in Wessex,' the warrior said flatly. He was a young man with a sand-coloured beard, but he was powerfully built.

'Don't be a fool, Hunwald,' Cynethryth snapped. 'This man has helped me. He saved me from those bastard Norsemen.' Hunwald was taken aback by her tone, though a couple of the others were smirking. 'Now, take me to my father before it's too late.'

Hunwald shook his head. 'He must be disarmed,' he said, planting his feet ready for my attack. Cynethryth turned to me and nodded and I reluctantly handed my sword and long knife over to one of the warriors. Then, having no other choice, we mounted, each behind a Wessexman, and rode down to the beach.

My heart sank as I saw *Fjord-Elk* under sail heading out of the bay, her benches manned by Englishmen and her dragon-headed prow gone, replaced by a wooden cross which rose on the waves to greet the southern sky. We rode down a worn path to the shingle beach where the breaking foam bubbled before sinking among the stones, and there we dismounted. There was no sign of Black Floki and for a moment I wondered if he had made a bargain with Ealdred and was even now at *Fjord-Elk*'s bow, looking out to sea, his journey chest brimming with silver.

Hunwald raised his hands to his mouth and called out to the vessel. *Serpent*, Sigurd's favourite ship, sat forlornly at anchor, watching her sister ship sail away while she remained fettered and bound to the land of her enemies. Hunwald called again and from that distance I recognized Ealdorman Ealdred when he came to the stern and stood there gripping the top strake and looking back to the beach. Beside him was the hulking figure of Mauger. If Ealdred caught Hunwald's words

408

in the wind, or recognized his daughter, he made no sign of it as he stood swaying with the ship's rise and dip.

'It's no use,' Hunwald said, shaking his head. 'They cannot hear us and we cannot hear them.'

'We don't need to hear them,' one of the other warriors said. 'Look at Mauger.'

Ealdred had turned his back and was now lost amongst the shapes of other men, but Mauger still stood at the slender, curving stern. At first it was hard to be sure what sign he was making over and over again, but then it became clear. One arm was raised, the hand pointing at us. In his other hand he gripped something. A knife. He was drawing the blade across his throat.

# CHAPTER TWENTY-ONE

'WE'LL KILL THE NORSE SCUM, BUT NOT THE GIRL. THAT'S the end of it,' Hunwald said, raising a hand to quiet another warrior. The Wessexmen stood amongst several ox-hide shelters on the grassy salt marsh beyond the high tide line, and they were arguing about what Mauger had been telling them to do. Cynethryth and I sat back to back on the weed-strewn shingle, our hands and legs bound, and I cursed myself for handing over my sword. The Wessexmen had overpowered me without breaking a sweat, though one was nursing a split lip.

'I agree with Cearl,' another warrior said. 'Mauger meant both of them.' He mimicked Mauger's throat-slitting gesture. 'That's why Ealdred turned his back, see? He wants done with it. The Lord rain a pot of piss on me if I'm wrong.'

'If you're so sure, Hereric, then you put your sword in Cynethryth,' another man said, waving his arm wildly. 'I'm not having my balls cut off and rammed down my throat for murdering the ealdorman's daughter.'

'Listen to him, Hereric,' Hunwald said. 'If you're wrong . . .' he paused, letting the thought sink in, 'it will be the last mistake you ever make.' He turned to the others. 'Look, we're safe enough cutting the Norseman's throat. No harm can come of that. But no one touches Cynethryth. Christ, lads! She's the ealdorman's daughter!' The others grunted and nodded, then turned to watch the distant longship once more, as though hoping for some last sign from their lord.

I noticed a fire pit beyond the shelters, a circle of soot-blackened rocks, and it confirmed what I had thought. These men had been left behind to guard *Serpent*. I guessed that Ealdred lacked the seamen to take both ships across the sea and he had chosen *Fjord-Elk*, perhaps because it was the less fire-damaged of the two longships, and now he was gone. I cursed those bitches the Norns. If not for these Englishmen, I would have somehow put together a crew and taken *Serpent* after Ealdred and caught him upon the grey sea. There he would have died, and I would have thrown his body to the fish. But I could do none of this now, because Hunwald and three grim-faced men were striding towards us and their swords were in their hands.

'Lady Cynethryth, we have our orders. The Norseman cannot live,' Hunwald said, kneeling to cut Cynethryth free so that the others could deal with me.

'It's not your fault, Hunwald,' Cynethryth said, standing and rubbing her red wrists. 'Though it is no wonder my father left you behind. He needs men with him who can think for themselves. Not worms who fear their own shadows.'

411

Hunwald ignored the insult though it was obvious it stung his pride. 'Go back to your father's hall, girl,' he said disrespectfully, 'and be grateful that I will send one of my men to escort you. Go now. Or, if you prefer,' he said, turning to me, 'you may stay to watch us open this dog's belly.' He grinned with a malice that did not suit his face. I struggled against the rope binding my wrists, ice-cold fear squeezing my heart because I was about to die a dishonourable death, unarmed and unnoticed by Óðin's dark maidens. I was more afraid than I had ever been, and I tried to hide my fear by shouting insults at those who gathered to kill me.

'You are sons of Welsh whores! You're pig snot! Dogs and bastards!' Just as I was about to die Cynethryth screamed and threw her arms round Hunwald's neck and he did not throw her off because he felt the blade of her eating-knife at his windpipe.

'Get away from him!' she screamed at the Wessex-men. 'I'll rip Hunwald's throat out! Stay back!' The others stopped dead.

'Careful, Cynethryth!' I said. There was blood at Hunwald's throat. 'Don't kill him before I get free.'

'Get away!' she screamed again and this time the others backed off, holding their hands up. 'Hunwald, throw your knife to Raven.'

'You mad bitch,' Hunwald squeaked under his breath. 'You're a dead whore now.'

'Give him your knife! I won't say it again!' she shouted. Hunwald drew his long knife and threw it to the shingle. I shuffled over and cut through the ropes, then exchanged places with Cynethryth and held the knife at Hunwald's throat, my other arm round his chest. I could feel him trembling through his leather armour.

'Take his sword, Cynethryth,' I said, which she did, forcing it into my empty scabbard because it did not fit well. Then she fetched two spears and my own sword from a rock by the shelters and stood beside me, gripping the weapons with white knuckles.

'You going to stand there till judgement day, Norseman?' Hereric sneered. He was pockmarked and ugly and I hoped I would be able to kill him. 'Because I'd like to see that, I would. You'll get tired, and then we'll spill your guts across the beach for the gulls. Yours too, bitch,' he said to Cynethryth.

'Not before we've fucked the life from you,' another warrior shouted with a childish grin. He was the youngest, by the look of him, and his eyes sought the other men's approval. But they ignored him.

'Throw down your blades,' I said, forcing Hunwald's chin up with the knife.

'Don't do it, lads,' Hunwald muttered through clenched teeth, trying to regain his courage, for the others had seen the terror in his face.

'You want me to cut your throat, Englishman?' I hissed.

'You won't do that,' Hereric answered for him, shaking his bald head. 'You know what they'll do to the bitch. Or do you think you can take all twelve of us?'

Some of the men laughed. Others threatened me. All itched to hack me to death.

413

So we waited, the Wessexmen not attacking for fear I would kill Hunwald, but knowing that it was a simple matter of time before they got what they wanted. Some of them would get more than they wanted, I promised myself. Some would die.

The sun had burned the sky red and orange and gilded the rolling waves out at sea when the Wessexmen began to grow restless. My arm burned from holding the knife at Hunwald's throat, but I did not know what else to do, and now I could see in some of the men's faces that they were building up to come for me even though it would mean Hunwald's death. I had heard Bjarni say that boredom can kill a man and I smiled grimly at the memory, because boredom was about to kill Hunwald.

Cynethryth had stuck my sword in the sand so that she could grab it easily and she still clutched the spears, watching, still sharp. *My peregrine,* I thought. Not once did she seek their favour or pity. She had planted her banner and proved as steadfast as any warrior I have ever known. But it was getting dark, the western sun throwing our shadows like thin, misshapen giants across the salt marsh. Like all hunters the Wessexmen saw in the approaching night their ally. Soon then they would come at us from all sides and in my heart I knew I would be lucky to kill a single one other than Hunwald. But Hunwald would die. Whatever the Norns had woven, they could not unpick that thread.

A horse whinnied. I looked across at the Wessexmen's mounts which were tethered to stakes driven into the sand at the top of the beach where they could feed on sea lavender and viper's bugloss. But the beasts were not eating now. They flared their nostrils and dragged their forelegs across the shingle, rattling the stones. Another whinny, the noise shrill against the low breath of the surf. The Wessexmen looked around nervously.

'Go and see what's spooking them,' Hereric said to the man beside him who nodded and walked off towards the horses. 'Wybert, go with him.'

Hunwald suddenly jerked forward but I yanked my arm even tighter round his neck and he gasped.

'Don't test me again, Hunwald,' I hissed. The muscle in my arm was trembling and cramping but Hunwald must have known he had missed his last chance to break free.

'Where in Saint Aidan's beard did they get to?' Hereric said suddenly, watching me with baleful eyes. I had forgotten about the two men who had gone to the horses some time before. Darkness had fallen across the salt marsh and only the shingle by the sea was touched by the stars' light. The horses were quiet now.

A warrior gestured back towards the horses, seeking Hereric's permission, and when the ugly man nodded a knot of Wessexmen gathered their shields and ran up the beach. The others remained facing us, waiting for either Hunwald or Hereric to tell them what to do.

'Jarl Sigurd?' Cynethryth said. But I did not answer her because I was concentrating on keeping the blade at Hunwald's throat and my arm across his chest.

'They're not here, Hereric!' a man called from the top of the marsh.

'What are you saying, man?' Hereric shouted, the edge of fear in his voice.

A stone clacked near the Wessexmen and when they turned to the sound a spear thudded into Hereric's back. He screamed, fell to his knees and then collapsed on to his belly, still screaming. The English crouched low because they were not holding shields. They called out in alarm to each other and to Hereric too who lay on the stones yelling in agony. They were fools because in their panic they had not thought to make the shieldwall. They squatted anxiously on the shingle, their weapons quivering in their hands. Then another man cried out in the darkness. Frightened faces looked to Hunwald, but they would get no advice from him because I was squeezing his windpipe so that he could barely breathe.

'Come on, Hrothgar,' one of the crouching men snarled and he and the other stood and stepped towards me and I knew they meant to finish it. Then Hrothgar spun and fell clutching his face, pulling at the bone hilt of the knife that jutted from his cheek. He gurgled and bawled and the other man bent, stepping back into the shadows.

'Who's doing this, Raven?' Cynethryth muttered. She gripped her spear and stepped towards the screaming Wessexman.

'Leave him,' I said because the man's wailing along with Hereric's was terrifying these English and as long as their heads were filled with fear they would not be filled with sense. They should have been afraid, for death was stalking them in the salt marsh and that death was silent and cruel.

But the men who had gone to the horses were marching back down the beach towards us now and their shields were overlapping. The three crouching on the shingle saw the small shieldwall and slowly stood, looking to each other for courage.

'We've got to move, Cynethryth,' I said, stepping backwards, pulling Hunwald with me. She nodded. Then I saw a shadow fly across a Wessexman and he went down without a sound.

'Floki,' I whispered and I could not help but smile even as the English shieldwall strode towards us.

'Ready to kneel before your god, Hunwald?' I spat. Then I ripped the knife through his neck and threw his corpse to the shingle and stood before Cynethryth, sword raised. 'A spear, Cynethryth,' I called and she threw me one. I hurled it at a man but he turned and the spear flew wide.

Then Black Floki appeared beside me, shieldless and blood-spattered. His feet were bare which must have been how he had moved silent as the breeze amongst the English, cutting them down.

'Sigurd?' he asked, staring fiercely at the approaching Wessexmen.

'There was a fight. I don't know,' I said. He looked at me, his cheeks and jaw sharp lines beneath his black beard. 'Thank you, Floki,' I said. He tilted his head. 'You could have stayed a spirit and guarded Sigurd's silver.'

'And watch these bastards cut down one of the Fellowship?' he asked, his teeth flashing in the reflected starlight.

I grimaced and took Cynethryth's hand. 'Any ideas, brother?'

He spat towards the Wessexmen who were emboldened now that they could see their attacker. 'Ask the girl if she can swim,' he said.

I turned and looked at the sea and Cynethryth must have understood for she squeezed my hand. 'I am ready,' she said. The Wessexmen were twenty paces away.

'Now!' I yelled and we turned and ran into the breaking surf, pushing out until the cold water was up to our chests and still further until my feet began to flail for the sandy bed. Any deeper and our mail would drag us under and we would drown. I tried to say as much to Floki but salt water poured into my mouth and I choked.

A spear splashed nearby and Floki yanked my hair and pointed to a low tooth of rock that broke through the water.

'Cynethryth, can you make that?' I asked, not knowing if I could get there myself. She nodded, her hair slick against her skull and the whites of her eyes gleaming.

'Let's hope Rán is asleep,' I gurgled. Cynethryth was helping me more than I was helping her, but the tiny island was getting closer. Slowly.

We hauled ourselves up through slippery kelp on to the rock and lay there exhausted as the surf beat and sucked at the island. I saw blood mixing with water on Cynethryth's legs and arms where barnacles had ripped her skin, then I looked back to the shore, a white jagged line of breaking surf. The beach itself was cloaked in darkness.

418

'At least they can't see us,' I said, taking Cynethryth's hand again. The Wessexmen's shouts carried to us across the water but got no louder, which meant they were staying put.

'If those swine row out here with bows we'll have to think of something else,' Floki said. He had left his helmet on the beach and now he was casually loosening his braids and squeezing water from his black hair whilst Cynethryth and I shivered in the dark.

'After what you did to them, Floki, they won't be too quick to follow us,' I said, hoping it was true.

'I was good, wasn't I?' he said with a boyish smile. It was the first time I had seen that smile.

'You made them piss in their breeches.' I slapped the wet mail at his shoulder. Cynethryth was shaking now. 'You're cold,' I said, putting a hand on her back. 'Can I?' She nodded and so I rubbed her back roughly and then her arms, trying to put some warmth back into her limbs.

'We need to get back to dry land,' Floki said, 'before sunrise.' He was right, because with the dawn the Wessexmen would see us and then they would come in boats. Besides which, it was quite likely that come high tide our little island would sink beneath the sea and we would be carried off or drowned.

So we gathered our strength. When we were ready we slid off the tooth of rock back into the cold sea. We half swam, half waded a little way towards the shore and then, keeping the sound of the breaking surf on our right, followed the silhouetted coastline until we had rounded a small bluff and could no longer hear the Wessexmen or see their torches. Then we dragged ourselves through the foam and on to the shingle and headed up the salt marsh to the higher ground where we hoped to find shelter.

'There?' Cynethryth asked, pointing to a dune covered with marram grass which reminded me of Penda's spiky hair.

'Good enough,' Floki said. We climbed the dune and found its most sheltered side where, with shivering hands, we dug a hollow. There was still a breeze but we were happy for it because it would dry out our clothes and there we waited in the dark, cold and wet and hungry and wretched, but alive.

'He's drying out, too,' Floki said, nodding at a cormorant a spear's length from our hiding place. The huge black bird sat watching us from amongst the marram and I had not even seen it. 'We'll stay here and get some sleep. Then we'll see what tomorrow brings.' Then Floki stood and drew his sword so that the sea air would dry it. 'I'll wake you in a few hours, Raven,' he said, stealing off.

'Where are you going?' I hissed, drawing my own sword and laying it in the grass beside me.

'I'm going to keep an eye on those English turds,' he said.

And on Sigurd's hoard, I thought.

When the sun rose I was still wet, for I had slept in my mail in case the English found us. Cynethryth lay with her head on my thigh and I was glad when she stirred

420

awake, because the muscle in my leg felt as dead as a rock.

'Where's your friend?' she asked, sitting up and checking the scabs on her legs.

'I don't know,' I said, standing. Black Floki had not woken me for my watch in the night. I climbed to the top of the dune to look east towards the Wessexmen's camp. But another group of low mounds obscured the salt marsh beach and so I ran back down and grabbed my sword and Cynethryth's hand. 'Come on,' I said, pulling her across the dune.

There was no sign of the English. Their tents were still there but their horses were not. The dead were gone too. *Serpent* still lay at her mooring.

'Thank Óðin they didn't burn her,' I said, breathing deeply and drinking in the sight of Sigurd's dragon lolling on the calm sea.

'But that likely means they'll be back,' Cynethryth said. 'They will have gone back to Ealdred's hall to raise a levy.' She was right. The English knew two men could not handle a ship like *Serpent* and they would come with spears to finish us.

'Raven!' a voice called up to me. 'It's a beautiful morning, isn't it?' I looked down to see Floki dragging an iron-bound chest across the shingle towards *Serpent*. 'Are you going to help me or not?'

'Jarl Sigurd's silver?' I called, already moving towards him. 'But we can't take *Serpent* out alone.'

'Look to the west, red-eye!' he yelled, standing and placing his hand on his hips.

I looked west but could see nothing and so I ran to

higher ground and looked out again. And then I saw them. Warriors. Helmeted and shield-bearing, and one held aloft a red banner which sagged against a spear shaft.

'It's Sigurd!' I shouted. 'Floki, you cunning bastard, it's Sigurd!'

'Of course it's Sigurd!' he yelled up to me, the smile on his face clear even from that distance. 'Freyja's tits, who else would it be, lad?'

I ran to Cynethryth then and took her into my arms and swung her round, yelling with joy. Because my jarl had come.

'I told you to go and raise children!' Sigurd boomed, coming down the grassy dune on to the salt marsh. With him came his Sword-Norse, their eyes shining as they hungrily breathed in the sea air.

'Leave off the lad, Sigurd,' Olaf said, a great smile breaking his bushy beard. 'There'll be plenty of time for that after we've made ourselves rich.' Olaf grabbed my head and pulled me against him, planting a great kiss on my head. 'Good of you to look after *Serpent* for us, Raven,' he said, kneading my skull with his knuckles.

'You've Black Floki to thank for that, Uncle. I've had my hands full looking after myself.' I laughed.

'Laughter, the balm for the soul,' said a voice from within the knot of warriors.

'Father Egfrith?' I said, but I knew it could not be Egfrith because the monk was dead. But then the Norsemen parted, as men would from a wet dog that is about to shake, and there he was, leaning on a broken spear shaft, his head bound in bloodstained linen. 'I saw Glum kill you,' I said, astonished. Some of the men touched amulets and sword hilts to ward off evil. Cynethryth ran and threw her arms round the little man and he winced at her touch.

'There there, my girl,' he said, sniffing loudly. He looked at me. 'The good Lord has preserved me, Raven, in spite of that bast—' he made the sign of the cross, 'in spite of that animal Glum's attentions.' He pushed Cynethryth away. 'There there, child,' he said again, 'it's all right. God is with us and all will be well.'

'You saw him dead?' Bjarni asked me, staring at the monk and scratching his blond head.

I shrugged. 'He looked dead,' I said. 'There was a lot of blood.'

Bjarni batted those words away as though blood had nothing to do with it, and I knew what he was thinking, what they were all thinking, and that was that the monk must have some power. Or else his god did.

'Dead or not, here he is,' Bjorn said, 'with a head like a mashed swede.'

Egfrith seemed to be enjoying the attention. He made the sign of the cross over Cynethryth's chest, then closed his eyes and began to mumble in prayer.

'Glum must have cut half his brain out,' Arnvid said, pointing his spear at the monk. 'Little bastard's madder than old Asgot.'

'Watch your tongue, Arnvid, or I'll cut it out while you're next asleep and feed it to the snails!' Asgot called, crossing the shingle towards *Serpent*.

423

'You should be dead, monk,' I said, still staring in disbelief, for I had seen Glum's sword crack his head.

Egfrith suddenly stopped his mumbling and turned to me.

'Should I? You think so?' he said, gingerly touching the bloodstained linen and staring at me. 'Then could it be any clearer that the Lord on high has chosen me to do His work? I will teach these heathens the mysteries of the true faith.' His little eyes were darting like tadpoles. 'I had not thought such a thing possible, but there it is. Perhaps there *is* hope for you creatures after all.' He shrugged. 'Perhaps I needed the sorest of tests to learn it.' I felt myself grimace. 'Did you know all of Wessex is celebrating?' he said. 'Even now men and women give thanks to God and light beacons on the high ground. *The heathens have gone,* they told me, *back to the sea. Back to the depths of Hell to minister for the Dark One.* But I knew different, Raven. I knew you had not gone yet.' He wagged a finger at me. 'I knew I would find you here on the shore. I felt the Lord's breath on my face and I knew I would not be too late.'

Unable to understand his words, the Norsemen suddenly seemed bored of the monk and disbanded to continue their preparations for leaving. Cynethryth touched Egfrith's shoulder affectionately, then turned and walked down to the sea.

'Is he working his magic on you, Raven?' Sigurd said, coming to stand beside me and planting his spear's butt in the shingle. A slight grin touched his lips, but beneath his breeze-stirred golden hair his eyes were slits of suspicion as they probed the monk.

'If he tries anything slippery I'll finish what Glum started,' I said in English for Egfrith's benefit.

'I am thinking you would,' Sigurd said, showing his teeth.

'I shall baptize you, Jarl Sigurd, and you will become one with the true faith,' Egfrith said firmly. He pointed a finger at me. 'And you will be next, Raven.'

'You mean to stay with us, Father?' I asked, glancing at Sigurd.

'My lord Ealdred has lost his mind, God have mercy on his soul,' Egfrith said. 'His wits have addled.' He looked up at me and pointed again, this time accusingly. 'The gospel book of Saint Jerome belongs here in an English house of prayer,' he spat angrily. 'It is no bauble! Such a thing is not for barter like a swine at market. Not even if the buyer *is* Charlemagne, God praise his hatred of heathens.' He raised his palms, closed his eyes and crossed himself, and I think he knew he had said too much, for if he intended to retrieve the Christ book, the last thing he ought to do was let us heathens know its value in silver. 'I will show Sigurd the most holy light, Raven. It will warm his ice-encrusted, maggot-ridden soul.' His eyes flicked to Sigurd, but the jarl appeared to take no offence. 'We shall all know the rewards of Paradise if the good Lord wills it. Perhaps even you, Raven,' he said as though he were offering me the world.

I shook my head. 'Not me, monk, but I'll be there when you baptize old Asgot.' I turned to see the godi wading out to *Serpent*, his arms raised to the blue sky. 'I wouldn't miss that for Svein's weight in coin.' Sigurd

425

seemed amused by it all. 'Are you letting him ride *Serpent* with us?' I asked. I could not believe the jarl would take a useless Christ slave aboard his longship. I was horrified. 'Lord?'

Sigurd pursed his lips, then nodded. I bit my lip. Egfrith shot me a triumphant look and I shook my head and looked towards the shore. Cynethryth was staring out to sea, twining her hair into one thick braid, and the sight of her twisted a knot of pain in my chest, for I realized I would soon be gone, crossing the grey sea with the Fellowship. I would not see her again.

Later, Sigurd told me of the fight in the forest against Ealdred's men. His charge, as ferocious as a winter storm at sea, had surprised and shattered the English. It had cleaved them as a man drives a maul into an oak timber to split it along the grain.

'That whoreson Mauger didn't stay to the end. He does not know how to lead men.' Sigurd spat the words as though they were poison. 'Bjarni saw him mount up and ride as though his arse was on fire. The English fought bravely but they had no war leader and we cut them down, Raven, until their corpses lay thick as litter across the forest floor. The rest fled into the trees. It was a great victory.' He gripped the sword hilt at his hip. 'The gods were watching. I could feel them.'

The Wolfpack emerged ragged and bloodied but victorious. In all, seven Norsemen and all but one of the Wessexmen who had stood with them died that day and many others suffered grievous wounds which old Asgot was hard pressed to treat.

'Many good men now sit at the All-Father's mead

bench, Raven,' Sigurd said, his fierce blue eyes threatening to fill with tears.

'They will shake the dust from the rafters, lord. Óðin will be proud to have them.' I did not know what else to say.

The Fellowship was one again; thirty-seven Sword-Norse oathsworn to Jarl Sigurd. The morning was clear and bright and the Norsemen busied themselves checking *Serpent*'s hull, sail and oars. 'I'm happy that your friend chose to come with us,' Sigurd said, smiling and pointing at Penda who stood a little way off, running a whetstone along his sword's battered edge. 'I think he likes silver as much as he likes slaughter.' The jarl shook his head. 'A strange Englishman, that one. Fights like a demon. Perhaps his father was a Norseman, hey?'

'He's a vicious bastard, lord,' I said with a smile.

'Aren't we all?' Sigurd ran a hand through his golden hair. Then his eyebrows arched mischievously and he batted one of my dark plaits, the one with the raven's wing still entwined in it. 'Freyja's tits, lad! You look like Black Floki, but even meaner,' he said.

I glanced at Floki who was goading Svein the Red. 'No one looks as mean as Floki,' I said, loosening my aching neck and shoulders. 'I'm sorry I did not cut Ealdred's head from his neck, lord.' I looked out to sea and the glittering lip of the world. 'He has the Christ book and it will make him rich.'

'And he has *Fjord-Elk*,' Sigurd growled. Then he gripped my shoulder and watched as Svein the Red walked up *Serpent*'s boarding plank with a sack of food over each shoulder. We had found several such sacks amongst the shelters on the beach. I considered telling Sigurd about the cross Ealdred had put at *Fjord-Elk*'s prow, but thought better of it.

'It's time we rode Rán's daughters again, Raven,' he said, his eyes blazing hungrily. 'Will you bring the girl?' I had not dared to hope Sigurd would take a woman aboard *Serpent*, but then again, he was taking a monk. What did I know?

'Yes, lord,' I said, my stomach rolling over with hope. 'If she will come.' Cynethryth was sitting on a rock a stone's throw from *Serpent*, looking at the glittering sea as she had been for hours. It was as though she expected to find something there.

A gust blew Sigurd's golden hair across his face and he gave a dour grin. 'She'll come, lad,' he said.

I stood there for a long time, staring south across the sea as a wind blew down from the north, whipping the white hair off Rán's daughters and promising to fill *Serpent*'s great square sail.

The Norns of fate were weaving still.

# EPILOGUE

WILL SOMEONE PUT SOME MORE BEECH ON THE FIRE? MY
old bones don't keep out the cold like they used to.
Ah, that's better. There is something magical about a
good fire. A man can read a fire if his heart is open and
his eyes are clear. Even old Asgot's magic was new in
the world against the mysteries of dancing flames. So,
where was I? The Wolfpack took to the grey sea once
more and *Serpent*'s dragon-headed prow, Jörmungand,
with his faded red eyes, dipped and fell as a kind wind
carried us away from the land of the English. For a
while, we would breathe the salty air licked cool by
Rán's leaping daughters, and leave the reek of blood
far behind in the soil on which many brave warriors
had fallen.

My tale does not end there. But I see that some of
you are tired. Young men today. No stamina. Is it
morning already? Is that daylight creeping beneath
the stout door? Perhaps I will say no more this night.
All good tellers of tales know they must leave their
listeners hungry for more. Are you listening still, Óðin?

And you, Thór? Are these things of which I speak still as fresh to you as they are ancient to me? No, I will say no more this time. Come again tomorrow night and I shall continue. Brave Týr, you know the rest as well as any in Valhöll. You know that I speak the truth. That I, Raven, sailed with Sigurd the mightiest jarl and the fiercest wolf of them all. And though the fresh, whipping wind cleansed me of the stink of blood, there would be more. Because I was a Norseman.

# HISTORICAL NOTE

*Raven: Blood Eye* is of course a work of fiction. Nevertheless, it was largely inspired by real events such as the raid on the monastery of Lindisfarne in 793, which was reported as the first such raid by the heathens on the islands of Britain. The event sent shock waves of alarm rolling through Europe, and is thought to have marked the dawn of the Viking Age. Yet it seems to me unlikely that the Christians of the British Isles had not come into contact with pagans from what we now term modern Scandinavia (Denmark, Norway and Sweden) prior to the Lindisfarne raid. And some of those meetings must have been, at least initially, peaceful. Given favourable conditions, a seaworthy vessel could cross the North Sea in twenty-four hours, and though such a journey would have been fraught with risk, there must have been ambitious merchants who were willing to undertake it in order to sell their wares beyond the normal sphere of their competitors.

Still, the society of the time was largely illiterate, with the clergy being the only exponents of the written word. It was in the Church's interests to sensationalize encounters between Christians and pagans. In his wonderful book *The Vikings*, the late Magnus Magnusson tells us that the Northumbrian scholar Alcuin used the Lindisfarne raid as the basis for a sermon, not against the Vikings, but rather against the English. Alcuin claimed that the attack was a visitation of divine wrath against the English for their sins, which included fornication, adultery, incest, avarice, robbery, violent judgements, luxuriousness, long hair and flashy clothing, to name but a few. The Church was the all-powerful institution of the day and its motives were many and varied. In short, when looking into the past it is always worth lifting the grubby hem of politics to glimpse what lies beneath – just as it remains so today.

Yet this is not to say that the Vikings were peaceful peddlers of home-made handicrafts. They were not. Most were violent men shaped by violent times, and their indifference towards the Christian faith and members of the clergy undoubtedly inspired fear and loathing among those constrained by religious laws and accepted practice. I do not think I have neglected this in *Raven: Blood-Eye*. In fact, it was my intention to show how a Fellowship of warriors could bond through adversity and violence. There is no doubt they could be horribly cruel, but we can admire their courage, determination and daring, perhaps exemplified best by their willingness to cross the North Sea, and even the Atlantic Ocean, in their open, shallow-draught boats.

King Coenwulf and King Egbert both existed and the wars between the kingdoms of Wessex, Mercia and Northumbria were constantly redefining the map of Britain. The Welsh were a thorn in the sides of all three kingdoms, though I feel I have given them a bit of a raw deal in my book. Looking back, it would seem that everyone was as violent and opportunistic as each other, and there was very little moral high ground to be found.

I have deliberately avoided the word 'Viking' in this book. Its origin is still disputed to this day. Some scholars believe it derives from the Old Norse word *vik*, meaning 'bay' or 'creek', suggesting that a Viking was someone who kept his boat in such a place. Others believe the word comes from the Old English word *wic*, borrowed from the Latin *vicus*, meaning a camp or trading place – so a Viking might describe someone who trades. Whatever the word's etymology, I feel that it has become too loaded. When some people think of Vikings they picture brutish, ignorant warriors with horned helmets. It is perhaps obvious then why I have steered clear of the word, especially given my own heritage (my mother is Norwegian). Instead of 'Viking' I have used 'Norseman', a word whose meaning is unmistakable.

In reality, the Norsemen who raided Britain's east and south coasts were more likely to be Swedes or Danes than Norwegians. The latter tended to visit Scotland, Britain's west coast and Ireland. But I see no reason why a dragon ship could not have crossed the North Sea from Norway and hugged the eastern coast of Britain, if only because such vessels were largely at the mercy of winds and tides. Still, my own roots are undoubtedly responsible for my choosing a band of Norwegian adventurers as the protagonists in the story. They are my Norsemen and I am proud of them. *Raven: Blood-Eye* commemorates these pioneers whose wanderlust took them wherever boats could go. Men such as these were the first. But they would not be the last.

# Giles Kristian writes about the ideas that inspired his *Raven* trilogy.

Q: *Raven: Blood Eye* is your first novel, and the first of a planned trilogy. How did the idea for the story first come to you? Did you start with a character and work from there, or did the story or setting come first?

A: I am half Norwegian and have always spent a lot of time there, mostly at our family cottage in the fjords outside Bergen. Every morning I wake up looking out across the deep, cold water. In clear weather you can see the magnificent Folgefonn Glacier in the south. Having carved into the mountain for an age, the old ice floe sits congealed in its ravine, tinged blue after absorbing the very essence of the sky for millennia. And that is part of the magic for me; to live and immerse myself in a landscape that has barely altered and would have appeared to my ancestors' eyes as it now appears to mine. In our inconstant, technology-driven world I can still place a hand on a cool rock and connect with the past, imagining a Viking touching that same rock a thousand years ago. No exhaust fumes poison the air and no traffic noise clutters your ears. For me there is just the past, lapping against the rocks and echoed in a gull's cry. As a writer I could not hope for a more inspirational backdrop, and ever since I was a young boy I have imagined fellowships of adventurers climbing aboard clinker-built boats to set off into the fjord, beginning along what the saga writers called the Whale Road.

*Raven: Blood-Eye* has been weaving itself in my imagination ever since my first breath of Norwegian air. I'm not sure which came first, the story or the character, but I think they are probably the same thing. Being a half-blood myself, the thread of identity and belonging was always going to entwine itself within the story. Also, having been a pop singer with all that that entails, I thought it would be interesting to explore the nature of fame and suggest that the thirst for it is nothing new. If anything, my characters' fame-thirst outstrips even today's *Pop Idol* wannabes. In a time when life could be nasty, brutish and short, a man's reputation might be all that he had, making him utterly determined that the name he left behind would endure through saga-tales and hearth-side stories. For warriors such as Raven and the Fellowship, renown is the ultimate prize, the path to immortality.

When you are writing I believe you will invariably include elements of yourself in your hero, especially in a first-person narrative like *Raven*. Nevertheless, I was conscious that I did not want Raven to be me. I have been lucky enough to be blessed with a loving and supportive family and so I wanted Raven to be my opposite in this much at least. I wanted him to be an outcast, a lost soul. On a summer's day in 2004 I scribbled in my notebook, 'I do not know where I was born. When I was young, I would sometimes dream of great rock walls rising from the sea so high that the sun's warmth never hit the cold, black water . . . I know nothing of my childhood, of my parents, or if I had brothers and sisters. I do not even know my birth name.' I knew I had my beginning.

Q: What kind of research did you do for the book? There can't be many first-hand accounts about Viking raiders available to you.

A: The only accounts we have of Viking raiders were written by Christian monks and are therefore not what you might call objective. Other than these biased accounts we have the sagas, but most of these were written down between 1190 and 1320, long after the end of the Viking Age. Their distance from the accounts they describe make the sagas fairly unreliable as historical sources, though many of them are great reads. So, when researching for a book like *Raven: Blood-Eye* you must turn to history scholars and archaeologists. Over the years I have collected many history books, mostly concerning the medieval period, with some forty on the Viking Age alone. Some of these books sit gathering dust, but others are constant companions, such as Magnus Magnusson's rich and wonderful book *The Vikings*, and Paddy Griffith's *The Viking Art of War*.

In terms of research it's hard to say how much I did. Having been a keen student of Viking history since childhood, much of my knowledge of the subject was already at my elbow, so to speak, before I began to write the book. Nevertheless, before I started *Blood-Eye* I completed a Medieval History diploma at the University of London, which helped me brush up on my research. Inevitably for historical fiction there is a considerable amount of groundwork that must be done before you can begin to write, and with that comes a certain moral obligation. I believe as an author you have a responsibility to get things right to the best of your knowledge. These days we tend to learn much of the world's history through historical novels and so it is important that we writers do our homework. Having said that, we must be forgiven a few excesses, a little embellishment here and there – the gilding of the tale. After all, we're writing novels, not history books. I have been very conscious of not encumbering my readers with all the facts I have learned along the way. The story must come first, with the historical context serving to enrich it, not to overpower it. I have read historical novels in which the author seems determined to let you know how much hard research he has done, and whilst this is admirable in some ways, it can make for a boring, cumbersome novel.

Q: When you sat down to write the first book, did you already have the entire trilogy mapped out in your mind? Did it change as you started to write, or did you stick fairly rigidly to the plan in your head?

A: I must be honest here even at the risk of frightening my editor. I don't plan. Ever. Every day when I sit down to begin writing I have to decide where the story is going. Sometimes this can cause me a massive headache (I'm indecisive by nature), but mostly I absolutely love working this way. I never really enjoyed school and the thought of planning my books reminds me of homework and gives me the fear. When I write I want to be excited. I want to take the same journey that my readers will take, which means never quite knowing what the destination is until you arrive. I suppose I have a very basic geographical plan, in as much as I knew book one would be set in England, book two in Frankia and book three in Byzantium. But that's about as far as it goes. I tried writing a one-page plan for book two and when I finished the book I looked at that plan and realized that it was very different to the story in front of me. The story was much better! The fact that I might end up writing five or six books in the Raven 'trilogy' I think sums up my feelings about plans.

Q: Raven is a great hero. How did you create him? What sort of characteristics did you want him to have? Is he based on anyone you have encountered, either in life or in books?

A: Raven is a bit of a misfit. I suppose we all are in some way. I certainly always have been. If I ever applied for a normal job (heaven forbid) and had to write a CV, it would say somewhere on it, in contrast to every other CV in the pile, 'I am *not* a team player.' I like working alone, doing my own thing, and I always have. I would rather strain a muscle carrying a table from A to B than ask someone to help me lift it. I like to have tasks to get on with on my own and in my own way. In my music career I was always the lead singer, and before that I played semi-professional football as a goalkeeper – both are individual positions, different from the others. I've fenced, kickboxed and swum competitively, all individual sports. I've modelled, written advertising slogans, and now I write books, each of these being solo activities.

Raven is an outcast, a boy unsure about where he fits into the world, but he finds purpose and ambition among a band of brothers. He becomes a warrior like them and lives as they do, and yet he always remains to some extent apart, as though he is searching for something else, reaching for something more. I don't think I have consciously based Raven on anyone real or fictional, perhaps because he is so young and still has to develop and grow as a person. It will be interesting to see if he finds his own way.

Q: This was a fascinating period of British history. You have mentioned that King Coenwulf and King Egbert were real historical figures. Did you base any of the other characters on real people? Would each county have had an Ealdorman, for instance?

A: I chose Britain of the ninth century for the setting of *Raven: Blood-Eye* because that is when it saw the first Norse raiders come ashore with the fire of plunder in their eyes. Britain was not yet a country but rather a seething land of competing kingdoms in which power fluctuated between the most powerful kings. With the kingdoms of Northumbria, Mercia and Wessex at each other's throats, the land provided ripe pickings for sea-borne raiders, and not until late in the ninth century would the kingdom of Wessex rise to dominance under the reign of Alfred the Great. In *Blood-Eye* Britain is ill-prepared for the arrival of Fellowships of warriors such as Sigurd's Wolfpack. It is still a sparsely populated land in which the great armies of Alfred's time are as yet unknown.

Coenwulf became King of Mercia in 796, the same year that King Offa died. He crushed a revolt in Kent, fought to regain control of the kingdom of East Anglia, led several campaigns against the Welsh and fought the Kingdom of Northumbria. He must have also had his work cut out keeping the Kingdom of Wessex in line. Egbert became King of Wessex in 802 and it is thought that he spent much of the first twenty years of his reign maintaining Wessex's independence from Mercia. However, he would go on to consolidate Wessex power and even achieve the title of Bretwalda 'Ruler of Britain,' though this dominance was short-lived. These must have been hard men in hard times but

441

I find the chaos of those times appealing – and so did the Norsemen!

An ealdorman (literally 'elder man') was a high-ranking royal official and magistrate, from about the ninth century to the time of King Cnut. It is likely that he would have commanded the fyrd (militia army) of the shire and districts under his control on behalf of his king. Every shire would have had an ealdorman. In *Blood-Eye* Ealdorman Ealdred is a slippery character, who I actually quite like because he is a survivor.

Other than the kings Coenwulf, Egbert and Eardwulf, none of the characters we meet in *Blood-Eye* really existed, nor are any of them based on real people. Having said that, I'm sure elements of people I know creep into my characters. In the next book, *Sons of Thunder*, Raven meets two real historical figures: Alcuin of York, who was a scholar, ecclesiastic and teacher who became an influential figure of the Carolingian court, and Karolus (or Charles), Emperor of the Franks, an extraordinary man who would be known to posterity as Charlemagne.

Q: You've said that you're a huge fan of many best-selling historical novelists, particularly Bernard Cornwell and Conn Iggulden. Could you recommend any other titles or authors who might be less well known, which have had a particular influence on you?

A: One of my favourite Viking novels is *The Sea Road* by Margaret Elphinstone. It is not full of battles

442

and pillaging (my usual cup of tea) but is instead a beautiful and compelling book. It tells the story of the exploration of the North Atlantic from the viewpoint of an extraordinary woman, Gudrid of Iceland. There is an honesty about this book, and yet the prose is at times haunting and lyrical. Another historical author who I greatly admire is Robert Low. *The Oathsworn* series shows Low's ability to take our language by the scruff of the neck and use it masterfully to place you amongst his band of brothers. It is great stuff and so you can imagine how thrilled I was with Robert's praise for *Raven: Blood-Eye*. Another favourite historical novel of mine is *Pride of Carthage* by David Anthony Durham. A beautifully crafted book, it tells the epic, sweeping story of the legendary Carthaginian military leader Hannibal and his assault on the Roman Empire. It is a sprawling tale with a cast of compelling characters and enough battles to keep me happy, written in fluid, confident prose. This book really seems to divide opinion, but I loved it.


Q: Tell us a little bit about what we might expect from the sequel, *Raven: Sons of Thunder.*


A: Raven and the Fellowship seek revenge for their betrayal by Ealdorman Ealdred, who has taken Sigurd's second ship, *Fjord-Elk*, and is sailing to Frankia to sell the Gospel book of Saint Jerome to the Emperor Karolus. In contrast to Britain, which is a divided land of warring kingdoms, Frankia is a formidable empire ruled by the most powerful man in Christendom, and the Fellowship must tread carefully if they are to survive. Now fully immersed in the Norsemen's ways, Raven continues to demonstrate the low cunning that marks him as a favourite of Óðin. But that favour comes at a price, for wherever Raven goes, the blood that marks his eye follows, and the Fellowship's fame-thirst may be its undoing.

If you have questions of your own for Giles Kristian, you can contact him through his website: www.gileskristian.com

The story of Raven and the Fellowship
continues in

# SONS OF THUNDER

*Here, as a taster, are the prologue
and first chapter . . .*

# PROLOGUE

HAVE YOU EVER SAILED IN A LONGSHIP? NOT A STUBBY, robust knörr laden with trade goods and wallowing like a packhorse across the sea, but a sleek, deathly quick, terror-stirring thing – a dragon ship. Have you ever stood at the bow with the salt wind whipping your hair as Rán's white-haired daughters cream beneath the beast's strong, curving chest? Have you travelled the whale road with wind-burned warriors whose rare skill with axe and sword is a gift from mighty Óðin, Lord of War? Men whose death work feeds the wolf and the eagle and the raven? I have done all this. It has been my life and though it would make those skirt-wearing White Christ followers sick with disgust (and fear, I shouldn't wonder) I have been happy with my lot. For some men are born closer to the gods than others. By the well of Urd, beneath one of the roots of the great life tree Yggdrasil, the Norns, those sisters of fate, of present and future, take the threads of men's lives and weave them into patterns full of pain and suffering, glory and riches, and death. And their

447

ancient fingers must have tired at the spinning of my life. Ah, but wait. The ale has greased my tongue and it slides ahead of itself. Come in, Arnor! Come flatten some straw, Gunnkel, we have all night ahead of us and very far to go. That is if my old head has not leaked memories like a rotten pail. Last night you heard just the beginning, slurped merely the froth from the mead horn. Now, together, we shall drink more. That's it, Hallfred, stir some life back into the embers. Make the flames dance. Make them leap like the fires of Völund's own forge. Yes, yes, there you go. Ingvar, give that threadbare hound of yours something to eat, for the love of Thór! He's been chewing some poor clod's shoe for the last hour! Is young Runa not here? That is a shame. There's nothing like a plump pair of tits to make an old man add a little more gilt to his tale. I'm no skald, I admit. My only song has been the sword song, the whisper of the great bearded axe as I made it dance before my enemy's shieldwall. But skalds venture so far up their own arseholes that a man cannot smell the flowers amongst the farts. In their tales they paint Sigurd as one of the Aesir, the gods of Asgard, his sword the slayer of mountain giants. Their Raven is a red-eyed monster, an ugly death-sowing beast. Pah! What do they know? Did they ride the whale road with Sigurd the Lucky? Whoresons. Sigurd was a man. His sword was like any other sword, a thing forged of iron and steel by another man who knew his business. As for myself, am I a monster? I was handsome . . . after a fashion. I was young, anyway, and that is good enough. I had grown from carpenter's apprentice, from

448

a boy skulking on the toe end of his village, to a wolf amongst a pack of wolves. I was part of a fellowship of warriors. I had become a rider of the waves and a killer of men.

So, haul up the anchor. Raise the old battered sail. Tomorrow's labour is far away and the night stretches before us like the starlit ocean on a spring night. So . . . we are away . . .

# CHAPTER ONE

YOU DO NOT BETRAY A FELLOWSHIP AND LIVE TO SEE YOUR hair turn white. For a fellowship is an honour – and oath-forged thing, as strong as a bear, as fast as a dragon ship, and as vengeful as the sea. If you betray a fellowship you are a dead man, and Ealdorman Ealdred of Wessex had betrayed us.

With the sail up and the spruce oars stowed the men looked to their gear. They took whetstones to sword edges, patiently working out the notches carved in battle, and the rhythmic scraping was to me a soothing sound above their murmured conversations and the wet whisper of *Serpent*'s bow through the sea. Men laid mail brynjas across their knees, checking for damaged rings which they replaced with ones taken from brynjas stripped from the dead. Two of the Norsemen were throwing a heavy-looking sack back and forth, grunting with the effort. The sack was filled with coarse sand and if you put your mail in it and threw it around the sand would clean the rust from the mail and make it as new again. Other men were smearing their brynjas with sheep grease, winding new leather and fine copper wire around sword grips, mending shield straps and stretching new hides across the limewood planks. Dents were hammered out of helmets, spear blades were honed to wicked points slender enough to skewer a snail from its shell, and axe heads were checked to make sure they would not fly off at the first swing. Silver was weighed, furs were examined and men argued or grumbled or boasted about the booty they had piled in their journey chests. We combed fleas from our beards and hair, relived fights, exaggerating our deeds and prowess, played tafl, checked *Serpent*'s caulking, laid leather strips in boots to fix holes. We nursed wounds, exchanged stories about friends now sitting at Óðin's mead bench in Valhöll, watched gulls soaring high above, and revelled in the creak of the ship and the low thrum of the rigging. And all the while we believed Njörd, god of the sea, who is kind to those who honour him, filled our sail and that we would soon spy our quarry, *Fjord-Elk*, as a speck on the sunlit horizon.

For we were blessed with a lusty following wind and were making good progress so that the land of the West Saxons was soon little more than a green ribbon on the horizon to the north. If Njörd's favour held, Sigurd would sail *Serpent* through the night to try to shorten the distance between us and *Fjord-Elk*, and when we came across her and the treacherous men who sailed her, our swords and our axes would run red.

Asgot the godi produced a hare from an oiled sack. It was a mangy thing that must have been kicking and

452

scratching furiously ever since we set off, for its fur was sweat-soaked, its mouth was bloodied and its eyes were wild with fear. The godi took its head in one old fist, drew his wicked knife and jabbed it into the animal's chest. Its long feet ran hopelessly in the air. Then Asgot dragged the blade along the hare's belly. Some of its guts fell across *Serpent*'s sheer strake and still it kicked as though it hoped to dash across a summer meadow. Then he wiped the bloody knife on the hare's fur, sheathed it, and ripped out the rest of the guts, the throbbing heart and the dark twine of the creature's intestines, and threw them into the sea, followed by the carcass itself. We watched for a while as the waves bore the tiny offering away, and then *Serpent* carried us on and the hare was lost amongst Rán's daughters. All the while Asgot spoke to the gods, asking them to bless us with fair seas and good weather. Father Egfrith made the sign of the cross to ward off Asgot's old magic and I believed he was muttering counter-spells, though I stayed away, not wanting those Christ words to maggot into my ears.

It would be a blood-drenched fight, this one. A real gut-ripper. For Ealdorman Ealdred of Wessex and his champion Mauger were feckless, snot-swilling whoresons who had betrayed us all. Ealdred had the holy gospel book of Saint Jerome, which we had stolen from the king of Mercia, and the toad's arsehole raced now to sell that Christian treasure to the emperor of the Franks, Charlemagne, or King Karolus as some called him then. The worm would become as rich as a king, having betrayed us and left us for dead. But

Ealdred's god and that god's peace-loving son were not strong enough to make all this happen. They could not save him from us who held to the true gods, the old gods who still shake the sky with thunder and curse the ocean with waves as high as cliffs. And I believed that we would catch the half-cocked maggot the next day or the day after that, because the English did not know *Fjord-Elk*, did not know her ways. For ships are like women – you cannot touch one in the same places as another and hope to get the same ride. But Sigurd knew every inch of *Serpent*, and his steersman Knut knew every grain of salt in every rolling wave. We would catch the English and then we would kill them.

'These Christians know how to puke, Raven!' Bjorn called, the sunlight gleaming across his teeth. 'The fish will eat well today, I think.'

'And we shall eat the fish and therefore be eating Christian puke,' I said in Norse so that Cynethryth would not understand.

She and Penda leant side by side over the sheer strake, emptying their guts into a sea so calm that Bjorn's brother Bjarni was bailing *Serpent*'s bilge with all the urgency of a cow on its way to the slaughter. I had seen *Serpent* flex and writhe like a supple sea creature, so that water continuously seeped in through the seams of her clinkered hull. But not that day. On that day the sea was calm as a breeze-stirred lake, yet it was enough to curdle the Saxons' stomachs. The Norsemen were grinning and laughing at the two new crewmen and whilst I pitied Cynethryth I was happy it was not me

454

they were laughing at this time, because I had done my share of puking in the early days.

As for Penda, the Wessexman was as vicious a man as I have ever known, and I had seen him slaughter the Welsh outside Caer Dyffryn so that the green pasture turned blood-slick. But Penda did not look vicious now, with his spew splashing on to the glass-like surface of the sea.

'It's not fucking natural to float across the sea on a piece of kindling,' Penda said, turning from the ship's side and dragging the back of his hand across his mouth. 'It's not civilized,' he growled, and I smiled because Penda was as civilized as a pail full of thunder.

Sigurd grinned knowingly at me because he knew I had stood in Penda's shoes not so long ago, but though this was true I would never have referred to *Serpent* as 'kindling'. I had always appreciated her workmanship, because I had been apprenticed to old Ealhstan the carpenter and so I knew woodcraft when I saw it. *Serpent* was a beauty. Seventy-six feet in length, seventeen feet in the beam and made from more than two hundred oak trees, she could originally accommodate sixteen oarsmen on either side, but Sigurd had built raised fighting platforms at bow and stern, meaning now there was only space for thirteen rowers on each side. With a crew of thirty-two men and one woman now it was to my mind a little cramped, but not uncomfortable. Olaf told me that on one of Sigurd's expeditions, when *Serpent* was newly built and before he had *Fjord-Elk*, she had carried a double crew of seventy warriors, one crew resting whilst the other rowed. This must surely have been a useful thing when it came to a fight, but I could not imagine sharing sleeping space with so many fart-stinking men. The ship had a small open hold for trade goods and supplies and a sturdy mast step and keel. She was fourteen strakes high, had a great square sail of wool which had been dyed red, and at her bow stood the head of Jörmungand, the Midgard-Serpent that encircles the earth. That beast's faded red eyes stared out across the grey sea, into our futures. Every Norseman aboard, every warrior sitting on the sea chest containing his possessions, respected *Serpent* as they respected their mothers, loved her as they loved their wives, and relished her as they relished their whores.

Cynethryth turned round, palming sweat from her forehead, and I swear her face was as green as a new fern. She caught my eye and seemed embarrassed so I looked away, pointing out to Black Floki a length of tarred rope caulking which was working itself free of two of the strakes beside him. The Norseman grunted and with a gnarled thumb began to press the thin rope back in. Once I had thought Floki hated me, but we had since grown close, as sword-brothers do. Today though it seemed he was back to his miserable, brooding self.

Father Egfrith, as far as I could tell, suffered no ill-effects from *Serpent*'s motion and maybe that had something to do with Glum's having cracked open his head with a sword blow. Somehow, the little monk had survived. Worse than that, he had chosen to come aboard – an odd path for a monk to board a ship full of heathens – and maybe that had something to do with the sword blow too. He was a sniffling little mörd, a weasel, but in a strange way I admired him because he must have known that any of us could squash him like a louse if he gave us reason, or merely for want of something to do. Truly, the Christ slave believed he would turn *Serpent* into a ship full of Christians, just as he boasted his god had turned water into wine. Though if you ask me, turning Norsemen into Christians would be more like changing wine into piss. Perhaps he even hoped to change *Serpent*'s name to *Holy Spirit* or *The Jerusalem* or *Christ's Hairy Left Ball* or who knows what? Egfrith was a fool.

By the time the day's heat had been chased away by a cold breeze whipping off the sea and the gold disc of the sun had rolled into the west, we had yet to set eyes on *Fjord-Elk*. At *Serpent*'s prow Jörmungand nodded gently, its faded red eyes staring seaward, tirelessly searching for his sister ship. I almost believed the snarling figurehead would give a roar of triumph if *Fjord-Elk* came into sight.

'I am thinking that the crawling piece of pig's dung might have set a more easterly course than our own,' Olaf said, dipping a cup into the rain barrel and slurping. He stood by Knut, who gripped the tiller with the familiarity of a man holding his wife's hand. Sigurd was behind and above them, standing on the fighting platform, looking out as the sun which plunged towards the world's rim washed his long fair hair with golden light.

'You think he's that shrewd?' Knut asked, hawking

and spitting a gob of phlegm over *Serpent*'s side. Olaf shrugged.

'I think he's got the sense,' Sigurd said, 'to take the shortest crossing and then head south within spitting distance of the coast rather than crossing the open sea as we have done. Then he will enter the mouth of the Sicauna, that great river that eats into the heart of Frankia.' Olaf raised one bushy eyebrow sceptically, but I thought Sigurd was probably right. As a Christian lord, Ealdorman Ealdred would have less to fear from Frankish ships patrolling the coast than we as pagans would. He would also have more to fear from open water than us, for even though the sailing conditions were perfect now, a sudden change in the weather or an irreparable leak could make a man wish he had stayed in sight of land. And Ealdred did not know *Fjord-Elk*.

A quizzical look nestled itself amongst Olaf's bushy beard, like a dog settling in a pile of straw. 'So, that English arse leaf is sucking the coast like it's his mother's tit,' he said, 'and that's why we've not had so much as a sniff of him.'

Sigurd pursed his lips, scratched his own golden beard, but did not reply. He looked up at the square sail, studying the way the wind moved across it, rippling the cloth. He watched the dance of the thick sheet ropes and the direction of the waves and then he looked towards the sun. It was low, so gave him a reliable east–west bearing. His thick lips curled like a wolf's just before the teeth are bared, because if Sigurd was right and Ealdred had crossed the shortest stretch of sea, putting him further north along the Frankish

458

coastline, then all we had to do when we came to the coast was choose a mooring with a good view of the open channel. And wait.

With dusk came land. Frankia. I knew nothing of Frankia then, but even so the word was a heavy one. It was a word that meant power, a word that carried with it, at least to pagan ears, the threat of sharpened steel and hateful warriors and the new, ravenously hungry magic – the magic of the White Christ. For the king of the Franks was Karolus, lord of Christendom. Emperor they called him, as the Romans had named their kings who ruled lands as far and wide as the skies above. And despite his fealty to the nailed god, men said this Emperor Karolus was the greatest warrior in the entire world.

'Can you smell that?' Father Egfrith called. He was standing at *Serpent*'s prow, being careful not to touch the carved beast-head of Jörmungand. Perhaps he feared it had a taste for Christians. 'You can smell the piety!' he called, sniffing eagerly, crinkling his weasel-like face in pleasure. The coast loomed ahead, a low, green line broken by grey rock. 'The Franks are a God-fearing people and their king is a light in the darkness. He is the cleansing fire that guides men from iniquity, like a beacon, a great, wind-whipped flame which saves ships from splintering against the rocks,' he said, taking altogether too much pleasure in the comparison. 'If we are lucky, Raven, we will meet the great king and because God loves him, and because Karolus is said to be a generous and gracious king, maybe you will be given the chance to wash your black soul. Scrape the sin from it like fat from a calf's skin. Christ the almighty will drag Satan out of your blood-filled eye by his gnarly ankle.' The mörd was grinning and I wondered what it would feel like to put that grin through the back of his head. But then I smiled, because although Egfrith thought I was the spawn of Satan, worthless as snail slime, there was something about him that I had come to like. No, not like. Rather the little man amused me.

'Your god had better have strong arms, monk,' I said, encompassing *Serpent*'s Norse crew with a sweep of my own arm, 'if he is to yank the devil from us all. Perhaps he will find Satan hiding in Bram's armpit, or skulking up Svein's arse.'

'Sin has no refuge, young man,' Egfrith chided, as *Serpent* reared a rogue wave, causing him to unbalance and stumble, though he somehow kept his feet without reaching for Jörmungand. 'For the wages of sin is death; but the gift of God is eternal life through Jesus Christ our Lord!'

'What's the little man creaking on about, Raven?' Svein the Red asked, turning to me, his massive head cocked to one side. He was tugging a new ivory comb though his thick red hair and I guessed he had already forgotten about his old one with the missing teeth. Svein was the biggest man I had ever seen, a fearsome warrior of few words, and he was watching Father Egfrith the way a battle-scarred hound watches a playful pup.

'He says his god wants to look for Satan up your arse,' I said in Norse. 'I told him you might enjoy that.'

The others laughed but Svein frowned, his hairy red brows meeting above his bulbous nose.

'Tell him that he and his god are welcome to anything that comes out of my arse,' he said, rousing more 'hey's. Then he lifted his right buttock and farted and Rán must have heard it at the bottom of the sea. 'There you go, Christ slave,' he said, 'come and get it while it's warm.'

The smile was still on my face when I caught Cynethryth's eye. I clenched my teeth and cursed myself for an insensitive fool. Cynethryth's eyes, the colour of ivy, were distant and heavy, as though she saw in mine the terrible events that had ripped her life apart. Her soul was singed by those memories like silk left too near a flame. Her face was pale and drawn from the seasickness and yet she was still beautiful. She blinked slowly, as though in nothingness there was freedom, then she turned away to watch the distant shore as *Serpent* slithered through the water. The girl, thin as a birch sapling, had all but carried me away from a fight with the Welsh when I was too weak to carry myself. Together we had hidden in a hollow oak and she had stitched my shoulder and fed me berries from the forest and kept watch for our enemies. But her father had betrayed us and now, with the Frankish coast looming, Cynethryth must have known it would not be long until we faced Ealdred. She knew also that we had nothing for that treacherous worm but cold, ripping steel. Every man aboard was a better warrior than I, except for Father Egfrith I dare say, and so now, despite what I had hoped earlier, it seemed unlikely that

I would be the one to kill Ealdred. Yet for his betrayal of my jarl and for the hurt he had caused Cynethryth, but most of all because I was young and ruled by pride, I wished Ealdred to die by my blade. Maybe with the ealdorman dead and cold Cynethryth would gain some peace. But maybe she would hate me.

# SONS OF THUNDER

## The Second RAVEN Adventure

*If you betray a Fellowship you are a dead man, and Ealdorman Ealdred of Wessex had betrayed us...*

With revenge on their minds, Raven and the Wolfpack plough the sea road in pursuit of the traitor Ealdred. Having left the Fellowship for dead, the ealdorman sails in search of the Frankish Emperor Charlemagne to sell the holy book of St Jerome for riches beyond his imagining. There will be a reckoning, but in following Ealdred, Raven and his sword-brothers find themselves in the heart of a Christian empire that would wipe their kind from the face of the earth...

A mysterious young man with no memory and a blood-tainted eye, Raven has found friendship and purpose amongst this fierce brotherhood. He has proven himself in battle and is certain now that Viking blood flows in his veins, but to survive, his cunning must be as sharp as his blade.

A thrilling new chapter in the Raven saga, *Sons of Thunder* confirms that, in Giles Kristian, action-packed historical fiction has a new master.